HE WAS CHARGED WITH A MISSION
THAT COULD COST HIM HIS LIFE. . . .

Hamilton folded his hands over his waistcoat. "Arrange passage for yourself on the first merchantman sailing for France. Go to Paris and see the marquis de Lafayette. He's one of the best friends this country has ever had, and he's fully aware of all the details of my plan. He'll give you all necessary instructions."

Jeremy was astonished. "You're telling me nothing more?"

"Only that your mission will take you to France, then on to the Ottoman Empire. Be good enough to mention nothing of this meeting to anyone. It would suit my purpose perfectly if you seemed to vanish from the face of the earth without a trace. And Morgan"—Hamilton cleared his throat—"this time it would be unwise of you to deviate from the path of duty. If you succeed, no reward will be too great. But if you fail . . . don't come back."

YANKEE

Dana Fuller Ross

**Author of *Nevada!* and the
Wagons West series**

A DELL BOOK

 Created by the producers of
The Australians, Wagons West, and
The Kent Family Chronicles Series.
Executive Producer: Lyle Kenyon Engel

Published by
Dell Publishing Co., Inc.
1 Dag Hammarskjold Plaza
New York, New York 10017

Produced by Book Creations, Inc.
Lyle Kenyon Engel, Executive Producer

Dell ® TM 681510, Dell Publishing Co., Inc.

ISBN: 0-440-19841-0

Printed in the United States of America

First printing—April 1982

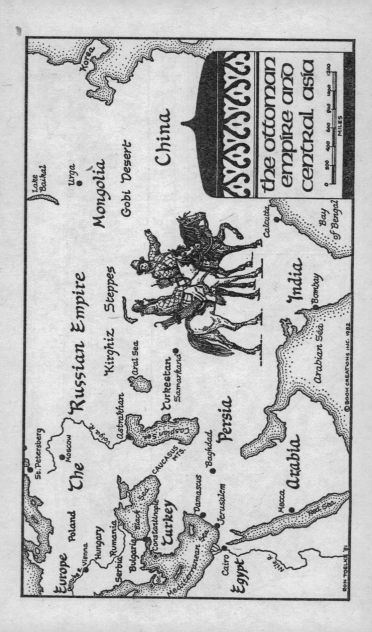

the ottoman empire and central asia

MILES
0   200   400   600   800   1000 1200

RON TOELKE '81

© BOOK CREATIONS INC. 1982

Europe
St. Petersberg
Moscow
Poland
Danube R.
Vienna
Hungary
Serbia
Rumania
Bulgaria
Constantinople
Turkey
Black Sea
Greece
Mediterranean Sea
Damascus
Jerusalem
Dead Sea
Mecca
Cairo
Egypt
Nile R.
Arabia
Red Sea
Baghdad
Persia
CAUCASUS MTS.
Volga R.
Astrakhan
Caspian Sea
Aral Sea
Turkestan
Samarkand
Kirghiz Steppes
The Russian Empire
Mongolia
Urga
Lake Baikal
Korea
Gobi Desert
China
Calcutta
Bombay
India
Arabian Sea
Bay of Bengal

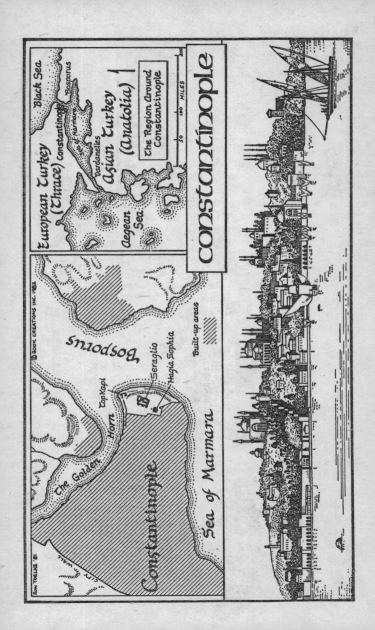

Constantinople

The Region Around Constantinople

European Turkey (Thrace)
Constantinople
Asian Turkey (Anatolia)

Black Sea
Bosporus
Dardanelles
Sea of Marmara
Aegean Sea

0   50   100   200 MILES

FROM TOLLAGE '81

The Golden Horn
Bosporus
Topkapi
Seraglio
Hagia Sophia
Built-up areas
LAND WALL
Constantinople
Sea of Marmara

© BOOK CREATIONS INC. 1982

I

~~~~~~~~~~

At twenty-six Jeremy Morgan was first mate of the only merchantman from the United States ever to sail to Turkey. He stood on the quarterdeck as the pilot guided the brig through the waters of the Bosporus, and he stared ahead in excitement at the impressive, totally alien skyline of Constantinople. Six long, hard years had passed since the War of Independence had come to an end, and now, in 1789, it seemed that his luck finally had turned.

He had been hardly more than a boy when he had served with distinction in the American Navy under John Paul Jones during the war. And when the newly organized United States had established the Revenue Service—later to be called the Coast Guard—Jeremy was elevated to the rank of gunnery officer. The tall and handsome twenty-year-old ensign had served his country admirably, on the alert for foreign merchant ships trying to avoid the payment of tariffs imposed on them for bringing the manufactured goods of Britain and Europe to the New World.

Then an incident had occurred that caused a precipitous decline in the young man's fortune. Out of youthful indignation he had incited the crew members of his ship to mutiny against the captain, whom Jeremy deemed senile and incompetent. Jeremy Morgan had been convinced that the old captain was endangering his frigate and his crew—and was failing to collect needed revenues for the United States—by refusing to give the command to apprehend foreign merchant vessels attempting to leave New York harbor without paying tariffs. A complaint was lodged against Ensign Jeremy Morgan, and court-martial proceedings were scheduled to take place, but the captain died while on a voyage to the West Indies and was therefore unable to testify against his rebellious young officer. The case was dropped, and no charges were lodged against Jeremy, although the young American refused to serve any longer in the Revenue Service, out of both hurt pride and embarrassment.

For some time his luck did not improve. He and Selim, his gunner's mate and principal assistant from the Revenue Service, had decided to cast their lot together and had fought the Cherokee in the Cumberland Valley, had traded with the Iroquois in New York State, and had done some cattle driving in North Carolina. Selim, perhaps the only Turk to have been in the service of the United States, enjoyed the change from sea life, but Jeremy was downcast because he still had not acquired the wealth and renown he craved. Certainly wherever he went, women found the brown-haired, hazel-eyed young man very attractive— and indeed Jeremy had his share of amorous adventures —but he still felt as if he were going nowhere. Then, just when he was sure the stars were against him, Jeremy and Selim were engaged by Captain Ned Raynor, master of a brig that was carrying a wealth of New World furs to the marts of Constantinople.

Jeremy's knowledge of the principal language of the Ottomans, which Selim had taught him during their years together at sea, combined with his wartime experience, had made him a logical choice as first mate. He was further bolstered by the presence of Selim, who had signed on as the ship's boatswain. According to rumor, there were fortunes to be made in the Grand Bazaar, and Captain Raynor had obtained the services of the only two men in the New World who knew the tongue of the natives and understood local customs. He had promised them a large share of the profits, and Jeremy and Selim were ecstatic.

Jeremy stood gazing in silence as the skyline of Constantinople loomed larger, and Selim understood his friend well enough to know what he was thinking.

"You are hoping that somewhere in that city lies fame and fortune," the dark-eyed Selim said in Turkish.

"You're a mind reader, Selim," Jeremy said. "Yes, that's what I'm hoping. After everything that's happened in the past four years, I could use a stroke of good luck."

"If that is your kismet," Selim said, "it will come to pass."

"I don't believe in that kind of fate," Jeremy said quickly, "that whatever you get in life is inevitable. I believe a man's got to make his own destiny. That's why I came to Constantinople; this is where I believe I'll make my fortune. I suppose I could have stayed in America and gone out to the Ohio Valley wilderness, where a lot of land claims are now being made. I was born and bred on the frontier, but I'm not eager to go back there. I want to have fame, recognition, not to flounder in the wilderness. I was recognized as a superior gunnery officer—"

"There was none better," the Turk solemnly assured him.

"—but what good would it have done me in peacetime? Even if there were still a need for gunnery officers, there was still the little matter of my near court-martial."

"I'm sure that matter has been completely forgotten, and you should forget it, too. You should instead rejoice, my friend, because you have contributed so much to your nation's victorious fight for freedom."

"That doesn't pay for the silk tailcoat with pewter buttons I crave. Or buy me the best meal that the White Hart in Boston has to offer. Or buy me a mansion like Alexander Hamilton's in New York!"

"There is an old Ottoman saying that you would do well to ponder," the Turk declared. "The peasant from the hills of Anatolia should not try to eat the food served to the pashas at the court of the sultan. Such meals will give him indigestion."

"I'm no peasant," Jeremy said ferociously. "I'm as good as anybody else in the United States!"

Selim was unmoved. "That well may be," he said, "but as one who comes from a land where the great nobles are all-powerful and the slaves have nothing, I find it hard to agree with your countrymen who say that all men are created equal. There will always be those who rule and those who obey; those who have and those who have not. Surely you will admit that the fire of ambition burns deep within you?"

"That it does," Jeremy conceded. "And it may be that sometimes I am too ambitious."

"And too lacking in patience as well, my friend. At your age you already want to own the world."

"Jefferson and Hamilton have made names for themselves while they're still young."

"They are more than twenty-six years of age."

"The Frenchman, Lafayette, was a major general at twenty-one, with command of his own division!" Jeremy retorted.

Selim could only sigh, shrug, and fall silent. It was useless to discuss the inequities and injustices of the world with an American, who thought his birthright entitled him to inherit the earth. As one who had been born and bred in Constantinople, the ancient capital of the Ottoman Empire, as a seaman who had come to the New World on a French merchantman and had been stranded there by the war, Selim counted his blessings and was grateful for them. Now he was returning to his native land, but with this difference: He was a free man who now had his own means. He could come and go as he chose.

Glad that his friend was no longer lecturing him, Jeremy grinned at him and was transformed by the smile. "You may be as mean and deadly as any gunner afloat, laddie," John Paul Jones had told him, "but your charm is more potent than all the cannon ye can fire. Forget it at your peril."

Certainly Jeremy knew better than to bear a grudge

against Selim, his one true friend, the man who had enthralled him with tales of life under the sultans of the Ottoman Empire, so different from New World existence that they sounded like products of an overly fertile imagination. And now that they were actually approaching Constantinople itself, Jeremy felt contrite. "I do have a tendency to rant on occasion," the young American said, and at that moment they were joined on the quarterdeck by the white-bearded Captain Raynor.

As the brig made her way past Ottoman galleys and disreputable Greek barques, Selim pointed out the sights. "There on the heights," he said, "is Topkapi, the principal palace of my namesake, Selim III. The tallest of the minarets on the European shore is that of the mosque built by Suleiman the Magnificent. The huge dome—you cannot see it clearly because of the minarets that block the view—is that of the great Hagia Sophia."

He was speaking in Turkish, and Captain Raynor, standing beside his mate, bristled. Jeremy promptly reassured him by translating Selim's remarks into English, and the ship's master was mollified. The sights of Constantinople meant nothing to him, but he lived in dread of being cheated.

As they entered the waters of the inner harbor, the silent pilot grinned cynically as Selim explained, "We have two choices. Either we can anchor in the harbor, where we will pay the sultan's tax collectors for the privilege, or we can rent dock space for a few extra dollars."

Jeremy translated, and Captain Raynor demanded, "Why pay extra?"

The reasons were so obvious that Jeremy did not wait for Selim to reply. "We can't unload our cargo until we've made a deal with a trader in the suq—the Grand Bazaar. It will be worth the additional expenditure for the sake of convenience. We may have as many as a dozen traders coming to the waterfront to inspect our furs."

"Also," Selim added in English, "it would cost more in the long run to anchor in the harbor. We would depend on the local boats to take us back and forth to the land, and the boat owners would demand baksheesh when they learn our cargo is valuable."

"Baksheesh?" Ned Raynor was puzzled.

"Bribes," Jeremy told him.

"I'll be damned if I'll pay out a penny in bribes!" Raynor exclaimed indignantly.

"You will, sir, or you won't do any business here." Jeremy spoke patiently but forcefully. "Bribery is a way of life in the Ottoman realm."

"As an American I resent—"

"Look here, sir," Jeremy interrupted urgently. "Have you seen the attention our flag is getting from the ships we pass?"

"Well, no," Raynor admitted. "To be honest, I hadn't noticed."

"First they stare at it because it happens to be new to them. They don't recognize it, which is only natural, because they've seen so few American ships here, if any. And then they immediately lose interest in us. We're foreigners, and that satisfies them. The Ottoman Empire is a world unto itself, Captain."

Selim nodded sagely. "You speak true words, Effendi," he said in Turkish. "No matter how important and rich one may be in his own land, in Constantinople he is nothing."

Captain Raynor looked at Jeremy, awaiting a translation.

"He urges you to rent dock space, Captain," Jeremy told the penny-pinching ship's master. "He says it will be well worth your while in making a deal here."

The master's sigh was lugubrious, but he capitulated. "Instruct the pilot to take us to a vacant wharf," he said.

A quarter of an hour later the brig was tied up at a dock, and a new complication developed. "Now we must pay baksheesh to the janissary officer who commands the troops that patrol the waterfront," Selim said.

Captain Raynor protested vehemently, and Jeremy thought his stubborn ignorance of local ways was annoying beyond measure. "Our furs are very valuable," he said. "Would you have us overrun by thieves while the troop commander looks the other way? Bribe him well, Captain, or we'll have no cargo to sell or trade."

"You take care of it, then," Raynor muttered.

The battalion commander-of-five-hundred soon appeared in person, and Jeremy, discovering he had a flair for such things, slipped him ten dollars in silver.

The janissary was unfamiliar with the currency but bit a silver dollar minted in Rhode Island, weighed the coin in his hand, then grinned broadly. "Your property," he said, "will be as safe as the virginity of my own daughter."

"Guard us well," Jeremy replied, surprising him by speaking in his own tongue, "and you shall receive another, equal amount before we sail."

The waterfront district, aside from the foreign quarter, where the legations of nations accredited to the Ottoman Empire were located, was unique. It was the only part of the city in which aliens were free to wander as they pleased, the only place in all the realm where alcoholic beverages could be purchased by the drink or the jug. There were innumerable houses of pleasure, too, boasting inmates of every color and many nationalities; in some, which catered to North Africans, the inmates were boys who wore female clothes and makeup. The quarter also catered to other vices: There were establishments where one could purchase a gummy substance that, when chewed, produced an effect similar to that of intoxication. And there were other places that, taking a cue from India and China, allowed their customers to smoke pipes filled with opium.

The open licentiousness of the district fascinated many of the foreign seamen who came to Constantinople, and Ned Raynor quickly fell under its spell. "You two mosey around and find us some potential trading partners," he said. "I'll sample some of the waterfront wares."

Jeremy and Selim decided to waste no time. The first obstacle they confronted was a gate manned by janissaries whose scimitars discouraged foreigners from straying beyond bounds. But Selim gave the leader-of-fifty a handful of coppers, and the officer stared off into the distance while the pair slipped through the gate. "He who thrives in the Ottoman Empire," Selim said, "is the man who remembers that every law exists to be broken—for the right price."

They soon encountered an open carriage for hire, pulled by an elderly horse, and Selim stood aside purposely to allow Jeremy to haggle with the turbaned driver.

"We wish to be taken to the suq," Jeremy said politely, "and we will gladly pay for the privilege."

"Fortune smiled upon you when you were led to me," the driver declared grandly. "I will deliver you with the speed of the wind and in comfort known only to caliphs."

"What is your fee?" Jeremy wanted to know.

The stranger spoke accentless Turkish, but nevertheless both men were easily identified as foreigners by their attire. "Five piasters of silver." The driver sounded as though he were doing them a favor.

"I'll pay you a half piaster to deliver both of us to the suq," Jeremy replied.

"Hauling two such large men will give my horse an even larger appetite than he already possesses, and the cost of hay is dear. Four piasters."

Jeremy discovered he was enjoying himself. "Our legs are cramped after our long sea voyage. Surely it would be cheaper to walk. Besides, we will enjoy the exercise."

"You take lamb and lentils from the pot in which my wife cooks food to feed our young ones," the driver protested. "Three piasters."

They continued to bicker until they compromised on a mutually satisfactory price of one and one-half piasters, and the driver was willing to accept two silver ten-cent pieces minted in New Jersey.

"You have the knack of a native, Effendi," Selim said as they climbed into the carriage. "The knowledge of how to strike the right bargain is a rare gift. One would think you had been born and reared in Constantinople."

Jeremy was forced to admit he had conducted the nego-
tiations with appropriate cunning.

"I will act as your guide in the suq," Selim told him,
"but your voice alone will be raised in the trading of our
cargo. I lack your skills." He could have paid the young
American no greater compliment.

Jeremy was startled by the sights, sounds, and smells in
the cobbled streets after they crossed a rickety bridge built
on pontoons and drove through the portion of Constantinople located on the other side of the Golden Horn. Never
had he seen such gaunt, ragged creatures as the wretches
who begged for a living, and nowhere had he set eyes
on such magnificent, silver-trimmed saddles as those of the
janissary officers and expensively clad civilians who rode at
a reckless canter, forcing pedestrians and pushcart owners
to flee for their lives. Veiled women concealed beneath
voluminous black yashmaks carried shockingly heavy burdens as they plodded on the cobblestones, and the American
was stunned when he saw a white-haired man bent double
as he staggered beneath the crushing weight of an ornate
chest of drawers.

To think that he had mistakenly regarded the capital of
the Ottoman Empire as a sophisticated, cultured metropolis!
"I gather," he said dryly, "that the principal beasts of
burden here are humans."

Selim shrugged. "They eat less than horses or donkeys,"
he replied.

Every town in the empire had its own suq, or market,
but the Grand Bazaar was extraordinary. Some of the
shops with stone walls dated back to early Byzantium,
and the imitation of Roman architecture marked others as
having been built under Constantine the Great and his
Christian successors. The Grand Bazaar was a sprawling
mass that extended for miles in every direction, with some
of its streets cobbled and others only hard-packed dirt. What
made it unique was the haphazard roofing that had been
built over the centuries to cover every street. Roofs rose
and fell like waves in the sea, but shoppers in the streets

below them remained dry during the seasons when rain or snow fell.

Everything imaginable was sold in the Grand Bazaar. Jeremy and Selim made their way up a street featuring cooked foods that ranged from bits of lamb on skewers broiling over open charcoal pits to flat Arab bread and freshly roasted pistachio nuts. There were long rows of shops devoted to the sale of men's and women's clothing, as well as attire for children. Firewood could be purchased, as could lumber or bricks for the construction of entire buildings, and the section devoted to furniture and bric-a-brac seemed endless.

On one street slaves were bought and sold, and Jeremy was startled to see black Africans, yellow Orientals, and white Europeans, all of them in chains, regardless of whether they were men, women, or children. All were stark naked, and hard-eyed potential buyers examined them carefully, prodding them and prying open their mouths to examine the soundness of their teeth.

During his travels he had seen slave markets in Virginia and South Carolina, but never had he encountered such callous disregard for the feelings of people. "This is disgusting," he muttered.

Again Selim shrugged. "In the Ottoman Empire," he said, "life is cheap." He was grateful that he lived now in the new United States.

They wandered past shops devoted to the selling of Ottoman, Indian, and Chinese rugs, then increased their pace when they passed shops that sold precious gems. "It is too easy to be cheated here," Selim explained. "Only the imperial jeweler at the court of my namesake would be able to tell the real from the false. In some of these places colored stones are offered, and the sellers swear on the lives of their mothers that they are genuine, but they are only glass. One must know where to shop."

Jeremy was already dazed by the experience, but he recovered his wits quickly when they came to the street of goldsmiths and approached an establishment that displayed no wares in its windows. "This is the shop of the imperial goldsmith," Selim said. "He would lose both his license and his head if he dealt in anything but gold of the finest quality."

The proprietor, who introduced himself as Ibn Ali, bowed them into the shop, and his turban of pure dark silk bobbed up and down as Jeremy described the furs available for barter in glowing terms. Selim had been right; the young American had the temperament of a bazaar merchant, and his description of the furs was so dramatic it was irresistible.

Ibn Ali decided to examine the cargo at once, taking with him a cousin who knew furs. It was agreed that Selim would escort the pair to the brig, but Jeremy was urged to wait in the goldsmith's shop in order to have ample time to study the gold works of art, admire them, and covet them. Food and coffee, a beverage he had never before tasted, were ordered for him, and Ibn Ali was solicitous.

"I will arrange for musicians to amuse you while you wait for us," he said. "Or perhaps you would prefer a girl to entertain you. The daughter of my cousin is very beautiful, and I will gladly make her available to you."

Jeremy's mind was on business, and he didn't want to be distracted, much less indebted, to a trading partner, so he refused the offer. The trio left for the ship, and Ibn Ali's son brought a dish of kebab, roasted lamb with peppers and onions. While the visitor ate the meal, the son produced a succession of gold jewelry pieces, each of them lovelier than that which preceded it. The craftsmanship was superb, even the smallest earrings and necklaces were fashioned of heavy gold, and Jeremy knew he was looking at products well worth the furs.

After he had waited a long time, Ibn Ali returned, flanked by his cousin and Selim. The goldsmith's eyes glowed, and Selim confirmed his excitement with a surreptitious wink.

"The furs I have seen are beautiful beyond compare," Ibn Ali declared.

"The gold I have examined also is exquisite," Jeremy replied.

"Very well. Let us bargain."

They sat on padded stools, facing each other, and a pretty dark-haired girl who wore neither a veil nor a yashmak brought them cups of strong Turkish coffee, so thick that the silver spoons used to stir it could almost stand by themselves in the brew.

Ibn Ali was a shrewd bargainer, and Jeremy, enjoying the game, proved to be his match. They argued and haggled for hour after hour, trading a bale of fox pelts for a heavy gold necklace, a pile of beaver pelts for a bracelet of wrought gold.

Jeremy understood precisely what he was doing. The animal skins were so common in the new United States they had little value there, and the same was true of the gold in the Ottoman Empire. His product and Ibn Ali's had value to each other.

At length the bargaining was completed, and both parties were satisfied. Selim's grin told Jeremy he had done well, that in return for his pelts he would be going to America with handcrafted gold that would be worth a fortune to the jewelers of New York, Philadelphia, and Boston. Certainly Ned Raynor would be delighted. While he had roistered, his mate had made him a wealthy man, and Jeremy's mind reeled when he thought what his share would earn. His luck truly had turned, and he would be able to live in comfort and style for years on his percentage of the profits.

George Dankins, managing director of the Royal Theater in the Haymarket, shifted his bulk in his seat in the virtually empty auditorium and exchanged glances with the subordinates who surrounded him. All of them loathed these auditions for new talent, which were almost invariably boring exercises in futility, but once in a blue moon a rare gem emerged, and Dankins curbed his mounting sense of excitement.

Staring up at the girl who stood alone on the bare stage,

he examined her critically in the light of the single, large oil lamp whose reflector illuminated the stage. Her dress was voluminous, its style and cut identifying her as a lady of means and concealing her figure, but as nearly as he could determine she was as shapely as she was tall. Nothing could conceal her chiseled features, her long red hair, or the deep green of her luminous eyes, although she had no idea how to use cosmetics to advantage.

The girl waited patiently, her manner calm.

"Miss Ellis," George Dankins called, "are you familiar with Judge Fielding's play, *Tom Thumb*?"

She took a step toward the apron of the stage, shielding her eyes from the glare of the oil lamp. "I've seen a performance, Mr. Dankins, but I can't truly say I'm familiar with it."

"So much the better," he replied. "Anthony, give Miss Ellis the comedy speech from the first act to read."

An assistant bounded up to the stage and handed the young woman the script of Fielding's play.

Mary Ellis quickly scanned the lines, then began to read:

"Lo, when two dogs are fighting in the streets,
With a third dog one of the two dogs meets,
With angry teeth he bites him to the bone,
And this dog smarts for what that dog has done."

As she continued to read, Dankins found himself grinning broadly, and his associates, in spite of their familiarity with the material, were laughing aloud. His judgment of this aspiring actress had been accurate: She had a natural wit, a sense of the droll that enabled her to make the most of the lines.

"Thank you, Miss Ellis," he called when she was finished, and sent yet another script up to her.

The mood of Portia's famous speech from *The Merchant of Venice* was far from comic, and Mary Ellis's voice had a soaring, majestic quality, her manner impassioned yet reflecting great inner strength as she recited Shakespeare's immortal words:

> "The quality of mercy is not strain'd,
> It droppeth as the gentle rain from heaven
> Upon the place beneath. It is twice bless'd;
> It blesseth him that gives and him that takes,
> 'Tis mightiest in the mightiest; it becomes
> The throned monarch better than his crown;
> His sceptre shows the force of temporal power,
> The attribute to awe and majesty . . ."

As she continued to read, George Dankins felt a chill run up his spine, and he rubbed his arms vigorously, then looked at his assistants. They were completely under the spell of this slender girl. "That's enough, Miss Ellis," he called. "Will you join me out front, please?"

Mary Ellis's walk was regal as she approached him and, at his bidding, sat beside him.

"You've had no previous acting experience, I take it."

She shook her head, and her red curls danced. "Only in amateur theatricals, Mr. Dankins."

"Miss Ellis," he said ponderously, "you have the rarest of rare attributes, a natural talent for the stage. How old are you?"

"Eighteen, Mr. Dankins."

"Do I judge correctly from your attire that you come from a family of substance?"

"My father is Sir John Ellis, formerly our envoy to France and the Kingdom of the Two Sicilies. He is presently a deputy to the foreign secretary."

Dankins peered hard at her. "And what does the estimable Sir John think of the dishonor that awaits his daughter when she joins that most disreputable of professions and becomes an actress?"

Mary's green eyes flashed. "I trust you're joking, Mr. Dankins. I resent the automatic assumption that every actress is a woman of questionable morals! Surely a woman can devote her talents to the stage without lowering her personal standards."

"Bravo!" The managing director of the Haymarket Theater applauded her. "Well said, my dear, and long may you prosper. Forgive the impertinence of my question, but the prejudice against actresses is so common that I wanted to make certain of your situation before making you an offer."

"I see." The girl's brow clouded. "To be honest with you, Mr. Dankins, I anticipate a problem with my father, but I intend to prevail. As he well knows, ever since I saw Sarah Siddons play at Drury Lane when I was a small child, my one ambition in life has been to go on the stage and become as great an actress as she. I shall allow nothing to stand between me and that goal."

He was impressed by her earnestness. "You're willing to work hard?"

"As many hours in a day, a week, and a month as is necessary to learn my craft, sir," she replied.

"Very well. You're hired as an apprentice. For the next year you shall work at least sixteen hours a day, perhaps twenty when a new play is being added to our repertory. You'll be paid only a pittance for your labor, but I can promise you that your diligence and your talents will pay you handsome dividends. At the end of the year you shall become a permanent member of my company, and after two years you'll be playing leading roles."

Mary clasped her hands and became starry-eyed. "I swear that you won't regret hiring me, Mr. Dankins. I shall repay you in the only way I can—by developing a following that will fill every seat in the Haymarket every performance!"

After agreeing to be at the theater at nine the following morning, the ecstatic young woman rushed out to the street where her carriage and driver were waiting for her. As she rode to her father's house in the fashionable northwest section of the city, she began to rehearse a new speech—the one she would perform for her father at the dinner table that evening, when she would explain to him what she intended to do.

Sir John Ellis was a stately, dignified widower of means, and his house reflected his personality and stature. The heavy silverware that graced his dinner table gleamed on a white linen cloth, the exquisite hand-blown glasses were rainbow-hued in the light from the cheerful fire in the coal grate, and even the handsome bone china dishes gleamed. Sir John's passion was his work, to which he devoted himself with single-minded zeal, and he was unaware of the machinations of the widows who set their caps for him. Similarly, he relegated his daughter to the background.

Mary sat silently through the soup course, nodding agreement when her father discussed the complications of dealing with the Ottoman Empire, but her mind was elsewhere.

"The confounded Turks cannot be ignored. They control too much of the world for that," Sir John said. "And now that they've added Mongolia to their realm, Sultan Selim has become one of the most powerful monarchs the world has ever seen. But he's a barbarian, and so is every last minister at his court! It's disconcerting, to say the least. I'm afraid that one of these years we shall be obliged to teach the beggar a lesson."

"Yes, Papa," Mary said dutifully as she absently spooned her soup.

Sir John glanced at her obliquely. "You aren't listening to me, Mary," he said mildly.

The girl looked at her father, suddenly laughed aloud, and then launched into the story of her audition at the Royal Theater in the Haymarket that very afternoon. She was still so filled with the wonder of her experience and its fantastic results that the words poured out.

Sir John ate his soup in silence as he listened, his trained diplomat's face revealing no emotions.

"I know you disapprove, Papa, but that can't be helped. I've seen wives of our class cheat on their husbands, and I've watched young ladies attain great popularity by following the path of least resistance. I can only assure you that I have no intention of becoming a trollop just because I'm going on the stage!"

To her astonishment her father nodded complacently. "Your objectives have been plain to me for some time, so I've had a study made of the theater," he said. "I've been assured that Eva Maria Garrick was faithful to her husband through the many years of their happy marriage, and that Mistress Cibber was equally devoted to her husband. I've taken pains to discuss the subject of theatrical morality with Sheridan, the playwright, and before he died some years ago, with Dr. Samuel Johnson. I'm satisfied that the theater does not erode the personal standards of those who have a high sense of morality. As you have."

"Then you'll agree to my apprenticeship at the Haymarket?" Mary asked eagerly.

"Not so fast, my dear," he replied, chiding her gently. "My approval is conditional."

"What are your conditions, Papa?" She responded to the challenge unhesitatingly.

"As you know—or should know—my position at the Foreign Office gives me access to information not available to the general public. I'm frankly apprehensive about your career, but at the same time I don't want to thwart your ambitions. So you're free to become an actress, provided you understand that I'm equally free to keep watch over you. And if any hint of scandal attaches itself to your name, your career will end that same day."

"I agree without reservation, Papa," Mary said calmly. "I thank you for your faith and trust in me, and I can promise that you'll be proud of my accomplishments."

Like Rome, Constantinople was built on seven hills, but there the resemblance ended, even though the capital of the Ottoman Empire used Roman viaducts to bring water to the inhabitants, and the ruins of the Circus that had been so popular during the long reign of the Christian emperors were reminiscent of similar structures in Rome. Of all the world's great cities Constantinople was unique, with one part situated in Europe and the other in Asia, on opposite banks of the Bosporus.

Always huge, always bustling, Constantinople was the true crossroads of the world and had been since earliest antiquity, when it had been known as Byzantium. Constantine the Great had renamed it for himself in the fourth century, and his successors had kept Christianity alive there when Rome had fallen to barbarians. Now, since the fifteenth century, the city had been the capital of the Ottoman Empire, the largest single domain on earth. The sultan's subrulers held sway in Bulgaria and parts of Greece, and the feared corps of janissaries—the Turkish army—had penetrated through Serbia and Hungary to the gates of Vienna. The sultan was acknowledged as omnipotent in Samarkand and the wastelands of central Asia, on the North African shores of the Mediterranean Sea, and far into the continent of Africa. All of Asia Minor was part of the empire, and so were portions of what had been Russia, which the sultans had wrested from the tsars.

In theory, if not in practice, all of the great religions of the world were equal under the law. The Jews of Constantinople lived in their own quarter and worshiped in their synagogues, and the Eastern-rite Christians did the same in their churches. There were temples built to Buddha, temples in honor of Zoroaster, and temples for the B'hai faith of the Persians. But the sultans were Mohammedans, and the predominance of Islam was everywhere evident. Just as the minarets of the mosque of Suleiman the Magnificent and the Blue Mosque dominated the skyline, so the Hagia Sophia, once the largest and most beautiful church in all of Christendom, now was a mosque. Other religions were practiced with discretion, but daily the muezzins called the faithful to prayer in scores of mosques.

The priests of Islam insured that the law was obeyed by all. The janissaries kept the peace on land, their endless corps of infantry, cavalry, and artillery omnipresent, and at sea the great galleys, many of them rowed by luckless slaves who lived and died chained to their oars, ruled the Mediterranean and adjacent seas.

High on the cliffs of the European shore of the Bosporus stood the heart of the empire, surrounded by a high double wall and guarded by elite regiments of janissaries. Here were the dwellings of the grand vizier, the ministers of state, the generals and admirals who were known as pashas of three horsetails. Here, too, stood the imperial treasury and the harem where the wives and concubines of the reigning monarch had lived in strictly regulated comfort, although Sultan Selim had abolished the harem of his predecessors, and his two wives lived with him in the palace.

Indeed, the largest and most ornate structure on the heights was Topkapi Palace, the offices and living quarters of His Magnificence, Selim III, king of kings and monarch of monarchs. As the citizens of Constantinople well knew, Selim was an enlightened, intelligent man—for a sultan. He owed his good fortune to an accident of fate because, unlike his predecessors, he had not been forced to spend years of his life in a cage. This practice was followed by his predecessors, who had caged their heirs to prevent plots and possible insurrections. Selim had been fifth in line for the throne but had been catapulted to the top when all four of those ahead of him had died of poison. No one knew who had administered the lethal doses, and the wise did not inquire.

So many kings and other subrulers came to Constantinople to pay homage to the sultan of sultans that the court of the Imperial Ottoman Empire had become blasé, and scant attention was paid to the arrivals and departures of these monarchs. Today, however, there was a sense of suppressed excitement in the air, and the reason was obvious.

The khana Tule Yasmin, sister of the great khagan of Mongolia and cousin of the sultan, had arrived in the city the previous night and this morning would make her official obeisances to the sultan.

Everyone at court had heard stories about Tule Yasmin

and repeated them with relish. The grand eunuch himself was the authority for saying that the khana had indignantly refused the accommodations provided for her in the harem and had been given a house of her own in the seraglio so she could keep her male bodyguards nearby at all times. The second wife of the pasha of three horsetails, who was the commander of the janissaries, had paid a courtesy call on the khana and had been astonished to discover that, like the Ottomans themselves, her heritage was European rather than Asian. Her hair was brown, with blond streaks on the top that had been bleached by the sun of the Mongolian deserts, and her eyes were actually green-flecked rather than brown. The commander-of-one-thousand, who had been in charge of her cavalry escort of honor for the past two weeks, swore that she was the most vile-tempered, imperious female he had ever encountered on earth. His deputy was equally insistent that she was the most beautiful woman he had ever seen, for Tule Yasmin scorned the use of the veil that women—other than slaves—were required to wear. And the harried minister of the interior, who had been responsible for her security ever since she had reached Samarkand on her long journey to Constantinople, insisted that her jewels rivaled those of the sultan himself in size, quantity, and quality.

So the great audience chamber of the Topkapi seraglio was filled with curious notables a half hour before the audience was scheduled to begin. No one was surprised to see that the sultan had elected to receive his cousin while seated on the throne of thrones, which had been moved into the audience chamber for the purpose. Obviously Selim III had heard the stories about the khana's collection of gems and intended to dazzle her. Certainly the throne was unique—and priceless. Fashioned of pure gold, its back, arms, and sides were encrusted with diamonds and emeralds, rubies and sapphires and black pearls, each of them worth a king's ransom. The minister of the imperial treasury once had been heard to comment that the throne of thrones was worth more than all the wealth accumulated in the vaults of Stamboul, Constantinople's banking district.

Precisely three minutes before the appointed hour a company of tall, strapping janissaries, each armed with a razor-sharp, double-edged scimitar and, for good measure, a pistol in his belt, marched solemnly into the chamber and formed a hollow square around the throne of thrones. They were followed by a balding, somewhat overweight man whose sense of humor had impelled him to wear the clothes of the West, a drab tailcoat, waistcoat, and breeches of dark wool, with unornamented shoes and stockings of cotton. He was bareheaded, too, and the only symbol of his exalted rank was the blood-red star ruby, the size of a hen's egg, that graced the index finger of his left hand.

As he came into the audience chamber, the greatest and most powerful men in all the empire lowered themselves to the floor and touched the mosaic marble tiles with their foreheads.

"The weather is a trifle chilly today, so that marble will be uncomfortably cold," Sultan Selim III remarked in a conversational tone to no one in particular. "Please rise, gentlemen. I appreciate your devotion to our person, but I'm susceptible to your head colds."

No one dared smile as the officials and nobles struggled to their feet. A sultan who was endowed with a dry sense of humor was still quite new to them, having served until just recently under Selim's unremarkable predecessor.

At precisely the appointed hour the imperial chamberlain announced, "Her Imperial Highness, the khana Tule Yasmin of Mongolia!" The double doors at the far end of the audience chamber were opened, then a trumpet fanfare added to the drama of the occasion.

Tule Yasmin advanced slowly across the priceless rugs that covered the approach to the throne of thrones and did not disappoint the astonished officials and nobles who gaped at her. She had elected to make her initial appearance before Selim III in the attire of a dancing slave girl—a tiny breastband above a bare midriff and a skirt that enveloped her supple figure tightly—but both the breastband and skirt were made of cloth-of-gold. She was barefooted, and on her long, tapering fingers flashed a variety of gorgeous gems. Her shoulder-length hair indeed was brown, with the outer layer a wheat-colored blond, and her green-flecked eyes were rimmed with kohl, just as her full lips were scarlet. She had dared to use cosmetics like a dancer, too.

Her hips swayed suggestively as she walked, a provocative half smile was on her lips, and the long strands of diamonds dangling from her ears moved in tempo to the beat of her insolent walk. Her self-confidence was overpowering, and it was obvious that she was enjoying the sensation she was creating. Her eyes widened for an instant in surprise as she saw the plainly dressed sultan, who watched her impassively, but she recovered quickly, and her obeisance was executed with style as she lowered herself to the rug.

Selim III, who always knew what he was doing, allowed her to remain stretched out on the rug at his feet before bidding her to rise.

Either Tule Yasmin was ignorant of Ottoman court protocol or she chose to ignore it, and those who came to know her best in the months ahead suspected that she deliberately elected the latter course. For whatever her reasons, she sprang to her feet in a single, graceful bound before the sultan ordered her to rise. Again paying no attention to custom, she also spoke first. "Your Magnificence," she said, "I am overwhelmed to be in your presence at last!"

Selim always was impressed by courage, and he was curious as well, so he did not rebuke her. "Do I assume correctly that the veil is not worn by women at the court of our cousin the khan?" he asked.

Those in the assemblage who had been rebuked by him in the past heard the hidden menace in his voice and shivered. But Tule Yasmin smiled. "Efforts were made by the officials and the priests sent to Mongolia as administrators after the kingdom was joined to the Ottoman Empire," she said, "but I have chosen to abide by the custom set by Selena, third wife of the sultan Suleiman the First, and have elected, as a member of the imperial family, to dispense with the wearing of a veil. My brother," she added in a confidential undertone, "is convinced I'm too vain."

The sultan couldn't help chuckling at her audacity, and the tension was eased. "You may sit beside us, Cousin," he said.

Needing no second invitation, Tule Yasmin looked cat-like as she lowered herself to the throne of thrones, one hand caressing a pure cloth-of-gold covered cushion.

"Your journey was uneventful?" Selim asked politely.

Her bare shoulders rose and fell in a disdainful shrug. "It was dull," she said. "I tried to enliven it by challenging your horsemen to race me, but they refused."

The commander-of-one-thousand, who had been in charge of her cavalry escort, reddened and called out, "The horse janissaries play no games when they are on duty. But now that Your Highness has reached Constantinople safely, I will personally accept your challenge to a race."

A buzz of excitement swept through the audience chamber. Anyone who rose to the rank of a leader of one thousand crack horsemen was necessarily a superb rider.

"Done!" Tule Yasmin's eyes gleamed.

"We shall arrange the details and watch the race ourself," the sultan declared and decided to place a wager on this extraordinary young woman. If he knew character, and he was proud of his judgments, Tule Yasmin would defeat the colonel.

"Have I the permission of Your Magnificence to offer you some trifling gifts?" the khana asked, swiftly changing the subject.

Selim III nodded. The receipt of rare and expensive gifts made ceremonies somewhat easier to tolerate.

The girl clapped her hands together twice, and a procession of women, all of them heavily veiled, all of them concealed beneath voluminous yashmaks, made the long march down the carpets to the throne of thrones, where they lowered themselves to the floor.

"You may rise," the sultan said impatiently.

The women approached one by one, and as they did, Tule Yasmin took an object from each. "My brother, the khagan, sends you this red stone as a token of his esteem." She handed Selim a gem larger than the ruby he was wearing.

"Is it a ruby?" he demanded, moistening his lips.

"I suppose so," Tule Yasmin answered carelessly. "Here is a scepter of diamonds, and this is an uncut sapphire of untold worth."

Selim III had a weakness he had inherited from the ancestors who had sat on the throne of thrones before him. Although his collection of precious gems was unmatched on earth, his greed for jewels was limitless, and he inspected stone after stone with a care that would have done credit to his curator of gems. He nodded in approval as Tule Yasmin presented him with one dazzling gift after another. Most of the officials were dazed by the presentation, but the members of his court who knew him best sensed that he was dissatisfied.

Indeed, the sultan looked hurt, and after Tule Yasmin had presented him with the last of the gifts, he asked her in an aggrieved tone, "Is that all?"

She was so taken aback she could only nod, and for the first time her confidence appeared shaken.

"Aside from the joy of greeting a blood relative," Selim III said slowly, "I was looking forward to your visit for a special reason. I had reason to hope that you and the khagan would present me with the Great Mongol Emerald."

She drew in her breath sharply and held it for a long moment. "The Great Mongol Emerald has been in my family for generations," she replied. "It is the heart and soul of the crown jewels of Mongolia."

"All the more reason I should own it," he replied, his manner cheerful but firm. Tule Yasmin remained silent, defying him with a long, hard look.

The sultan's rule was absolute, which meant he had the power of life or death over all of his subjects, and the courtiers stared at the slender young woman in wonder. Even the fact that she was the blood relative of Selim III would not save her if she continued to refuse his demand.

But the sultan remained unruffled, and he continued, "Aside from its worth—which I am told is inestimable—I have been reliably informed that the Great Mongol Emerald possesses special properties. Are my informants correct?"

The beautiful young woman knew it was useless to dissemble. The imperial espionage service was noted for its awesome efficiency, for its ability to unearth precise information from the most remote portions of the far-flung Ottoman domain. "According to legend," she replied reluctantly, "he who wears the emerald is assured of long life, good health, and success in all of his ventures. It is only a legend, of course," she added hastily.

"Your great-grandfather wore the Great Mongol Emerald and lived to a ripe old age while extending the borders of his realm. Your grandfather enjoyed the same experience. Your father did not believe in the legend, and evil befell him when he did not wear the emerald. It was during his reign that our janissaries succeeded in the conquest of Mongolia. No, dear cousin, the legend happens to be true. So I must have that stone! My enemies are everywhere, and I must wear it to protect myself from them!" The sultan paused a moment, his gaze unwavering. Then he said, "I have been informed by my most trusted advisers— who have their special sources of information—that the emerald is on your person this very moment. They have learned that you wore it on your journey because you believe it will protect you when you travel. Though," the sultan added as he leaned back in his chair, an ironic smile on his lips, "its special properties are, as you say, only a legend, of course."

Tule Yasmin realized she was helpless in the face of the sultan's determination to possess the precious heirloom.

Long accustomed to imposing her will on others, she had to give way to the one man in the Ottoman Empire whom she could not influence.

Slowly she twisted several rings off her fingers, then removed an iridescent green stone from her middle finger and dropped it into the sultan's outstretched hand.

Selim III seized it eagerly, slipped the ring onto his pudgy little finger, then held up his hand to the light that poured in through the high windows.

Only now could the court appreciate the remarkable beauty of the Great Mongol Emerald. It was flawless, and in the bright sunlight it sparkled with a clear purity that was breathtaking. It was small wonder that the khana had concealed it in the welter of lesser precious stones that covered her fingers.

"At last I am invincible!" the sultan declared triumphantly. "The assassination plots of my enemies will fail. I shall remain sound of limb and sound of mind until I am very old. And the empire I rule will become larger, greater, and more powerful than ever before in Ottoman history!"

The attention of the court was riveted on the ring as he spoke, and Tule Yasmin was momentarily forgotten. Had anyone bothered to look at her while the sultan gloated, he would have seen that her green eyes had become as hard and unyielding as the Great Mongol Emerald itself.

Upon the completion of their trading deal with Ibn Ali, Jeremy and Selim agreed to spend the night at the house of the shopkeeper. "It is an act of good faith," Selim told his friend. "Ibn Ali would lose face if he did not entertain us after we concluded our bargaining." Thus an enormous fifteen-course banquet was served, and the bowing and toasting and protestations of friendship lasted well into the night.

The following morning Ibn Ali arranged to deliver the gold to the brig and to pick up the cargo of furs at noon. Further bowing and protestations of friendship were exchanged before Jeremy and Selim could take their leave.

As they strolled slowly toward the Grand Bazaar's exit, Jeremy told Selim, "A bo's'n ordinarily gets only a tiny share of a cargo's profits. But if you hadn't known where to go, we'd never have made such a great deal."

"It was your bargaining that was responsible," Selim replied. "But I shall not argue the matter with you. I will be happy to receive a larger share."

They were interrupted by loud shouts and screams of terror behind them, and they turned to see a number of janissary officers riding with reckless abandon down the covered, cobbled street.

"Make way for the khana, cousin of His Magnificence!" the officer in the lead shouted, waving a scimitar over his head to emphasize his words.

Fruit carts were overturned, melons were trampled under the horses' hooves, and the merchants raised their hands over their heads as they chanted, "*Allah akbar Allah! There is no God but Allah.*"

Never had Jeremy seen such ruthless recklessness, and he was rooted to the spot. Selim was so startled he could not fling himself to the side of the road either.

Before Jeremy quite realized what was happening, the officers swept past him, their great stallions brushing him as they rode. Bringing up the rear was a woman with brown hair streaked with blond, mounted on a spirited mare and dressed in man's clothing. Jeremy caught only a brief glimpse of her face, and even as it occurred to him that she was relishing her dangerous sport, Selim crashed to the cobblestones after being struck and trampled by her mount.

By the time Jeremy knelt beside his crushed friend, the woman and her entourage had disappeared in the labyrinths of the Grand Bazaar.

It was obvious at a glance that Selim had been badly injured. "All these years I thought that being a namesake of the sultan would bring me good fortune, but I was mistaken," he murmured. "At least I shall sleep in the land of my ancestors. May Mohammed watch over me. I commend my soul to Allah." He lay still, his labored breathing stopped, and his sightless eyes stared up at the patchwork roof of the Grand Bazaar.

Life in the Ottoman Empire was cheap indeed, Jeremy thought bitterly. The wanton killer of his friend had escaped unharmed, and he knew better than to imagine that he could bring her or the janissary officers who comprised her escort to justice. Such aristocrats were above the law.

Thanks to the arrangements that Jeremy made, Selim was buried a few hours later in a quiet graveyard overlooking the Golden Horn. Jeremy was the only mourner, and the mullah, or priest, who conducted the ceremony spoke so rapidly in a strange dialect that the American could not understand a word he said.

He paid the mullah, then shivered as he started back to the waterfront. His only consolation, he thought as he looked up at the minarets that dominated the skyline, was that Selim truly had been laid to rest in the land of his fathers.

Ibn Ali appeared at the brig at noon, expressing his condolences over the death of Selim and confirming that nothing could be done to bring the reckless riders to justice. "The janissaries have their own laws, and no civilian judge would dare put them on trial. As for the woman, I have heard that she has just arrived in our city and enjoys the protection of the sultan himself. It is best that you put your friend's tragedy out of your mind."

He and his helpers departed with the furs, and Ned Raynor, as Jeremy had anticipated, was delighted with the gold that the merchant left in place of the cargo. Chortling gleefully, he took the pieces to his cabin and locked them in his safe. Then he announced that the brig would sail on the afternoon tide, and Jeremy became frantically busy taking on supplies of food and water.

The brig sailed on schedule, and Jeremy took his regular watches as she went from the Bosporus into the Sea of

Marmara, through the Dardanelles into the Aegean, and then into the Mediterranean Sea. He grieved for the loss of his friend, but at the same time he consoled himself with the prospect of the wealth he would enjoy.

Not until the third day out of Constantinople was he summoned to the master's cabin. "You sent for me, Captain?"

"That I did," Ned Raynor replied. "I'm thinking of altering course and putting in to Venice to see what may be available in the way of cargo. It's a waste to return home with an empty hull."

"That makes sense, sir," Jeremy replied.

"Well, you'll stand to earn a few dollars extra. Remember, you'll get one percent of the profits from the cargo, just as you'll get one percent of what I make out of the gold I picked up in Constantinople."

"One percent?" Jeremy was so shocked he thought his hearing was playing tricks on him.

Raynor looked at him steadily, his deep-set eyes unwavering. "I get fifty percent as the brig's owner and another twenty-five percent as her master. I've also decided to award myself another fifteen percent as a finder's fee for locating the goldsmith who sold me the gold in return for our cargo of furs."

Jeremy was so stunned he could not reply.

"Who is to say me nay?" Raynor demanded in a soft voice. "Selim is dead, Constantinople lies three days' sail behind us, and the crew was so busy in the waterfront fleshpots that they know nothing of any transactions."

"You—you're cheating me!" Jeremy shouted.

Captain Raynor remained calm. "Let's say, instead, that I'm taking advantage of the opportunity of a lifetime."

Jeremy instinctively reached for the hilt of the long knife he carried in his belt, but Raynor smiled coldly. "I wouldn't if I were you, Morgan. It's your word against mine, and I can think of no court in any American state that would rule in favor of a mate who defies the sworn word of a ship's owner and master. What's more, if you attack me, I swear I'll have you hanged from the yardarm for mutiny. You've gambled—and you've lost. So accept your defeat like a gentleman, there's a good lad."

Afraid he might murder the man in his blind rage, Jeremy hurled himself out of the cabin and stomped up to the deck. There he leaned against the aft rail, staring out at the blue waters of the Mediterranean. The stiff sea breeze gradually cooled him, restoring his reason.

It was all too true, he realized, that Ned Raynor held all the cards in a showdown. Jeremy would be unable to produce as much as a scrap of paper to show that he was responsible for the deal with Ibn Ali, that he had negotiated the acquisition of the handcrafted gold jewelry. His one witness, Selim, was dead. No living member of the crew could substantiate his word.

All he could produce in his favor was his ability to speak the language of the Turks, and he knew enough of the law to realize that no court in any of the thirteen states would regard that as substantial evidence in his favor. There had been talk, before he had sailed from Boston, to the effect that delegates to what was being called the Constitutional Convention intended to establish a new national judiciary, but that day was still far distant. Besides, he had no hope that a national court would listen to a man who was nearly court-martialed any more sympathetically than would a state court.

He wanted to drive his knife into Ned Raynor again and again, until the man confessed his crime and begged for mercy. But such thoughts were childish, and he knew he would cause himself great harm if he didn't abandon such temptations.

Facing the issue squarely, Jeremy knew he had been cheated. Selim had found the goldsmith, and he himself had negotiated with Ibn Ali, but the furs he had bartered had not been his property, and neither had the ship that carried them. He was serving as an officer, to be sure, but that made him no more and no less than a hired hand.

No matter how hard and how bitter the pill was to swallow, he had to take Raynor's advice and accept the fact that he had been cheated out of a large sum of money. Once again, it seemed, the stars were against him.

II

The new Constitution of the United States had been duly ratified by all of the original thirteen states except North Carolina and Rhode Island, which were forced to accept the inevitable, and a new federal government had been organized and elections were held. In April 1789, President George Washington had taken the oath of office as President, and the two houses of Congress, the Senate and the House of Representatives, formed quorums and began to initiate legislation.

One of the first acts of the new government was the official opening of the Ohio territory, where illegal settlers had been defying the British ban on settlements. The soil was rich, the land was covered with uncounted millions of trees, and pioneers eagerly set out from Virginia, Connecticut, and New York for what they called the promised land.

The first town established in Ohio was Marietta, but Cincinnati soon outshone it in both size and importance. The taming of the Ohio wilderness, which had been going on intermittently for decades, was no easy matter and was complicated by the fierce opposition of the Indian tribes of the territory. It was known that the Indians were being encouraged by the British, who secretly supplied them with arms and ammunition. Great Britain still coveted the region, even though it had been awarded to the United States in the Treaty of 1783.

This posed a problem for the infant nation, and President Washington took steps to solve it. First he appointed the Scottish-born Major General Arthur St. Clair as the first governor of Ohio, and then, the standing army being too small to be effective, St. Clair built an effective militia by offering large tracts of land to veterans of the Revolution who settled in the territory.

One of the first to accept the challenge was Jeremy Morgan, who had returned to the United States after his misfortunes on the voyage to Constantinople. Although he had once thought that the Ohio territory held no promise for him, he was now aware that a great opportunity was presenting itself and that his luck might finally change. Accepting a choice plot of 480 acres on the Ohio River near Cincinnati, he was appointed a major in the territorial militia, and when General St. Clair borrowed some cannon from Secretary of War Henry Knox, who had no other use for the guns, Jeremy was assigned to train crews of gunners.

Jeremy's efforts kept him in Cincinnati for many months and prevented him from clearing and developing his own land, building a house there, and planting crops, but he was relatively content with his lot. "Cutting down trees and uprooting the stumps is mighty hard work," he said. "I have a knack for gunnery, so my own property can wait."

General St. Clair was a blunt, imperious man who quarreled with the territorial legislature and made many enemies, but the old soldier was impressed by Jeremy's knowledge of cannon and his knack for teaching gunnery, as well as by his ability to live and flourish in the wilderness. So it appeared now in the winter of 1790–91 that Jeremy, almost twenty-eight years of age, at long last had found an influential mentor and that his luck had finally changed.

His day-to-day existence, certainly, was more satisfactory than it had been in years. He made his home in the so-called officers' quarters of the militia, a complex of log cabins that resembled virtually all of the buildings situated behind the stockade that surrounded Cincinnati on all sides, including the riverfront.

He drilled his gun crews daily, and the results were remarkable. They used scarce gunpowder sparingly, then employed tinderbox and flint to light the length of loosely-woven rope that served as a fuse on the cannon, and whenever Jeremy gave the order to fire, there was a roar, followed by the appearance of a thick cloud of black smoke. The wind off the river was usually strong, quickly dispelling the smoke, and Jeremy and his gun crew would watch eagerly as the iron ball soared high in the air, then dropped into the river so close to one of the rafts that it nearly capsized. They were almost on target, and Jeremy showed the men how to make minor adjustments in the trajectory. Then, even as he gave the order to fire, he was supervising the reloading of another of the cannon on the riverbank.

The more experienced members of the gun crew needed virtually no instruction as they swabbed out a cannon, packed another charge of powder into it, and dropped in an iron ball. The guns roared, and they created havoc with the rafts. One ball made a direct hit and utterly destroyed its target, and another shot landed inches away from a raft and capsized it.

General St. Clair began to take Jeremy's superior gunnery and instruction for granted and watched complacently as his cannon methodically cut the rafts to ribbons. There was no question in his mind and in the minds of the members of the gun crew that Jeremy Morgan was superior. The general—who was not one to pay compliments lightly—could not help remarking, "Seeing you use so little ammunition and powder, Morgan, I'm amazed at the effectiveness of your crews."

Most evenings Jeremy dined at the "Governor's House," which was a large log cabin located near the riverfront. Arthur St. Clair was noted for his quick, violent temper, but he was fond of Jeremy, who had the good sense to listen to the governor's interminable stories about his experiences in the Revolution. The hero of all of his tales inevitably was Arthur St. Clair.

The general's niece and ward, Aileen, kept house for

him, so Jeremy saw a great deal of her, too. She was a rawboned, awkward girl who lived in awe of her uncle and was so shy that she dressed plainly in linsey-woolsey, and pulled back her dark brown hair, which she fixed in a bun at the nape of her neck. She would have been shocked had anyone suggested that cosmetics might enhance her appearance.

Jeremy treated the girl with gallant courtesy, partly because it was his nature to deal politely with ladies, and in part, too, because he realized her uncle was fond of her.

Jeremy's flair for the dramatic fascinated Aileen St. Clair, and in the spring of 1791 it occurred to him that she was showing signs of having fallen in love with him. She flushed whenever he looked at her or spoke to her, she studied him constantly, even when her uncle was speaking, and she listened avidly when he mentioned his own exploits in the war or talked about the bitter disappointment he had suffered on his voyage to Constantinople.

The girl's partiality to Jeremy created a problem for him. By no stretch of his fertile imagination was he in love with her, although he was willing to admit that she had a fair enough figure, which appropriate clothes could show off to better advantage, and that a more flattering hairstyle and the use of makeup would make her more attractive.

The fact that she was in love with him neither surprised nor dismayed him. Women always were drawn to him, and consequently he accepted her admiration calmly. What to do about it was the question that vexed him.

The better part of his youth was behind him, and in a short time he would be thirty, with little to show for his efforts. True, he was a major in the territorial militia, but he still did not own the grand house and fine clothes he dreamed of. And though he owned a sizable piece of property in the Ohio country, Jeremy well knew that anyone who came here could establish a similar claim. If he tried to sell his land, he would be fortunate to find a buyer willing to pay a few pennies per acre.

Reluctantly, little by little, he was forced to conclude

that it was logical to think of a marriage to Aileen St. Clair as the solution to his problems. Certainly she would be a devoted wife, but that was of little consequence. What mattered was that her uncle and guardian was the first citizen of the Ohio territory, that he enjoyed the confidence and support of President Washington, and, having been a major general of the Continental Army during the War of Independence, he was acquainted with virtually all of the new nation's leading citizens. Certainly he would be helpful in obtaining a lucrative, important position for the husband of his niece.

Jeremy gradually found himself playing up to Aileen more and more. "Ah, the lovely Mistress St. Clair!" was his customary greeting whenever he came to the house, and he always swept the ground with his tricorn hat, then took her hand and kissed it. He was careful, too, to hold her chair for her when she sat down at the supper table, and he insisted, much to General St. Clair's amusement, on helping her to clear the table and dry the dishes.

"Morgan," the general said frequently, "you're the most domesticated fighting man I've ever seen."

Jeremy hated himself for taking advantage of Aileen, yet he continued to treat her with conspicuous gallantry. You've sunk so low you've become a damned fortune hunter, he told himself savagely, yet he did nothing to cool his relationship with her.

One night after supper, while she washed dishes in a tub of soapy water, then rinsed them in another of clear water, their hands touched accidentally when he took a dinner plate from her. Aileen reacted as though she had touched the top of the iron wood-burning stove, and Jeremy couldn't resist the temptation to brush against her a second time, then a third.

The girl took the initiative suddenly and hurled herself into his arms, pressing close to him as she raised her face to his. He reacted instinctively and kissed her. She returned his kiss fervently, then nestled in his embrace. "I knew it," she murmured. "I've been sure you feel as I do."

He knew he was swimming in a dangerous current and made no reply.

"We've got to speak to Uncle Arthur," she said and, grasping his hand, led him toward the parlor, where General St. Clair sat before the hearth, reading and signing documents.

There was no escape, Jeremy realized, and he was obliged to make the best of a miserable situation. So he allowed himself to be dragged unwillingly behind her.

"Uncle Arthur, we want a word with you," Aileen said shyly.

The governor of the Ohio territory looked up from the papers he was holding and stared at the young couple who stood before him, their hands intertwined. "What's this?"

"Jeremy has something to say to you," Aileen prompted.

Somehow Jeremy found his voice and the courage to use it. A decision had been made for him, and it was impossible for him to avoid the fate that awaited him. "Sir," he said, "I—I'd like your permission to court Aileen."

"So?" Arthur St. Clair's pale eyes failed to reveal his thoughts. "Sit down!" he commanded, and gestured toward a small couch that faced him. Aileen pushed aside a stack of documents, and seated herself close to Jeremy.

The general cleared his throat and spoke as he always did, as though addressing a division of troops assembled on a parade ground before him. "Morgan," he said sharply, "you're the best gunnery officer I've ever encountered, and although I've yet to see you in actual combat, the reports of your gunnery in our recent war with Great Britain are very enthusiastic. Indeed, based on my observations, you're superior to any of the officers who served in Henry Knox's artillery corps in the war. But that doesn't make you a good husband. Judging by the expression on Aileen's face, you've already courted her, with or without my permission, so it requires little imagination to see that she'll accept a proposal of marriage from you."

"Yes, sir," was the best Jeremy could manage.

"How do you plan to support a wife?" General St. Clair asked in a rasping voice.

Jeremy did the best he could with the material at hand. "As you know, sir, I own four hundred and eighty acres near the river—"

"Four hundred and eighty acres of tree-choked, uncultivated land. It will take two years of hard labor to clear that property, build a house on it, and start earning a living from the crops you grow."

"I—I was thinking of hunting and trapping in the meantime, sir," the younger man said, a note of desperation creeping into his voice.

"The hunters and trappers I know are a shiftless, lazy, drunken lot, totally lacking in a sense of responsibility."

Aileen caught her breath, and her uncle glared at her. "I merely call your attention to facts, Aileen," he said. "Major Morgan earns no pay from the militia, which gives him his quarters and provides him with food. He's in no position to pay court to you—or to anyone else."

The girl began to weep, but the sight of her tears only enraged her uncle. "It's better you cry now than later." He was losing his temper, and he was working himself into a fury. "I know your sort, Morgan. You're an adventurer, a soldier of fortune who has played on the sympathies of a young, inexperienced girl in the hope of taking advantage of me!"

There was a grain of truth in the accusation, but events were moving more rapidly by far than Jeremy had anticipated, and he became angry, too. "Now, see here, General!"

"You listen to me!" Arthur St. Clair was on his feet now, his voice raised in a shout, his emotions out of control. "I tell you plain, Morgan, that I've had high hopes for Aileen. She'll find a husband far more suitable than you to look after her!"

Color drained from Jeremy's face as he rose to his feet, too. He could make short work of the general in a fight but realized it would ruin him if he attacked the governor of the Ohio territory.

"I'll gladly accept your resignation from the militia, Morgan!" the general barked.

"You have it, sir," Jeremy replied recklessly.

"You mistook my kindness to you as license, and I assure you, Morgan, that you've made the mistake of your life. Get out of this house at once, and don't come back. If I set eyes on you again I'll take a horsewhip to you!"

St. Clair was beyond reason, so it was senseless to prolong the conversation. Jeremy felt sorry for the stricken Aileen, but their relationship had been so shallow he knew she would recover quickly. He bowed to her, turned on his heel, and stalked out of the house.

Not until the cool night air struck him did he realize he had nowhere to go. As he started toward his cabin to collect his belongings, the thought occurred to him that he might be hunting and trapping for furs far sooner than he had anticipated. Once again he was being forced to start from the bottom and claw his way up the slippery ladder in search of the success that had eluded him for so long.

The audience at the Royal Theater in the Haymarket applauded steadily, and as the members of *The School for Scandal* company came on stage to take their bows, there were cries of "Lady Teazle!" in the audience.

Then Mary Ellis, who had portrayed the leading role in Sheridan's masterpiece, came onto the stage, and the audience went wild, standing, stamping their feet, and shouting, "Bravo!"

Mary sank to the stage in a deep curtsy. She had grown accustomed to applause in the two years she had worked in the theater, but never had she heard such an ovation. As she rose to her feet again, an usher hurried down the aisle and handed her a huge bouquet of flowers. The audience applauded even more loudly. Mary glanced at the card, then looked up at the royal box and curtsied again.

The pudgy young man sitting at the front of the box tugged at the velvet lapels of his tailcoat. The prince regent, the future King George IV, who had assumed the burdens of the crown because of the so-called temporary mental incapacity of his father, was fond of the theater, which he attended regularly. And as even the least informed of his future subjects knew, he was even fonder of pretty and talented actresses.

The prince regent turned to the equerry who sat beside him and murmured, "Be good enough to go backstage and inform Mistress Ellis I would like to extend my congratulations on her splendid performance to her in person."

"Yes, sir." The equerry rose, then vanished behind the drapes.

Five minutes later the entire cast was gathered in the Green Room, where actors and actresses were encouraged to entertain. Mary, still wearing her costume and powdered wig, made certain her beauty patch was still in place on one cheek, then sank to the floor in another graceful curtsy as the prince regent came into the room. All of the men of the company bowed low, and the women curtsied.

"Please carry on, ladies and gentlemen," he said. "You've earned your triumph this evening, and I don't want to spoil your fun."

Everyone relaxed or pretended to be at ease, and George Dankins made his way through the throng and offered His Royal Highness a glass of chilled French champagne. The prince regent was pleased to accept and emptied half the contents of the glass in a single gulp.

Mary concealed her nervousness behind a fixed smile as His Royal Highness approached her. She looked very sure of herself, older than her twenty years, and none of those who were watching her covertly would have guessed she was apprehensive.

"If I may express an opinion, madam, your performance was remarkable. Dickie Sheridan happens to be a close friend, so I've seen no fewer than a half-dozen companies play *The School for Scandal,* and your Lady Teazle is by far the most memorable. All theatergoers are in your debt."

She accepted the lavish praise with becoming modesty, even though she knew he was right. No other actress played the part with her flair for high comedy.

"What other roles are you undertaking this season?" he asked, and his interest seemed genuine.

"Mr. Dankins and I have been discussing my playing Lady Macbeth, Your Royal Highness."

Astonishment registered on the prince regent's puffy face. "Lady Macbeth, eh? You possess a most extraordinary range, Mistress Ellis."

"Nothing is settled as yet," Mary murmured.

"I say, Dankins!" Prince George called. "Be sure to hold my box for me when Mistress Ellis plays Lady Macbeth. I wouldn't miss that evening for all the gems in my father's collection of gewgaws."

"It will be an honor to have you in the audience, sir," Dankins replied as he bowed.

A beaming prince regent turned back to the girl. "As you can see, Mistress Ellis, I have become your devoted follower."

"I'm flattered, sir." She guessed what was coming next and braced herself for it.

"I would very much like to become better acquainted with you, my dear." He lowered his voice so eavesdroppers would not hear him. "Perhaps you'd care to accompany me to supper at the Cork and Bottle? They serve a tasty steak and kidney pudding there, and they've put in a special wine cellar for me, so I can promise you the food and drink will be better than passable." His easy manner indicated his assumption that her acceptance would be automatic.

Mary knew they would occupy a private room at the Cork and Bottle and that he would waste no time making advances to her. Steeling herself, she smiled and shook her head. "I'm so sorry, Your Royal Highness," she said, "but I already have a supper engagement this evening."

Dankins, who hovered nearby, looked at her in horror.

An invitation from the prince regent was tantamount to a royal command, and no one in her right mind ever insulted him by rejecting an opportunity to spend time in private with him.

The future George IV was stunned by the rebuff but recovered quickly. "I regret your engagement, too," he said suavely. "Another time, perhaps?"

"Another time," she replied vaguely, making it plain that she was avoiding him deliberately.

He bowed stiffly, then turned and left the Green Room, followed by his entourage.

Dankins immediately approached Mary, his glare baleful. "You must be mad to insult the prince regent!"

She faced him defiantly. "He's a man, like any other, and he made it abundantly clear that he was interested in me as a woman, not as an actress. If I'm to be pawed, it will be by a man whom I find attractive and in whom I've developed a romantic interest. I can assure you, Mr. Dankins, that I have no intention of spending several hours being chased around a private room at the Cork and Bottle by a fat, ugly man whose only attraction is his rank!" Not waiting for his reply, she gathered her full skirt and swept off to her dressing suite.

Three people awaited her in her sitting room. Her father, soberly dressed as usual, was escorting her cousins, Robert and Rosalind Tate, twins who were about two years her junior. Both were short and dark, and the athletic Robert was wiry, while Rosalind, who looked like a miniature version of the stately Mary, had a trim figure that she owed to incessant horseback riding and hiking. All three rose at once.

"You were wonderful!" Rosalind exclaimed as she embraced her cousin. "Even more wonderful than when you played Cleopatra."

"You've taken the town by storm again," Robert said. "You have all the family talent. I couldn't playact if my life depended on it!"

"You do have a tendency to express your feelings in

such a way that will make it difficult for me to enroll you in the diplomatic corps," Sir John said with a grin, and turned to his daughter. "Congratulations on another sparkling performance," he said as he kissed her.

"Thank you, Papa." Mary disappeared through the curtains that separated the sitting and dressing areas. "I'll be ready soon, and I'm sorry to have kept you waiting, but the prince regent came to the Green Room, so I was obliged to be there."

Sir John glanced at the prince regent's flowers, which had been transferred to a vase. He frowned but made no comment.

"Did you speak to him?" Rosalind wanted to know.

"Oh, I did much more than that. I turned down a supper invitation from him, and I made it as plain as his long, bulbous nose that I have no personal interest whatsoever in him."

"You didn't!" Rosalind was shocked.

"Now who is the blunt one in this family?" Robert wanted to know.

Sir John remained silent but smiled in relief. Mary had kept her promise to him, and no whisper of scandal had been attached to her name in the two years she had been on the stage.

"How could you reject a supper invitation from the prince regent?" Rosalind's dark eyes were wide.

Mary had changed into a deceptively simple silk gown that showed off her now-renowned figure, so she opened the curtains, then returned to the dressing table, where she removed her stage makeup. "It was very simple. I told him I had another supper engagement, which happened to be true."

"We'd have understood if you'd canceled your engagement with us," Robert said.

"I wouldn't dream of it," Mary replied, stripping off her beauty patch and wiping cosmetics from her eyelids. "After all, little country cousins, you don't come up to London all that often."

"But why did you turn him down?" Rosalind was still perplexed.

Mary turned away from her mirror and looked directly at the younger girl. "The prince regent," she said succinctly, "is a lecherous billy goat who beds every attractive woman who happens to catch his fancy. And most do. I would be neither honored nor flattered by an affair with George IV, thank you very much."

Rosalind gasped, and Robert clenched his fists. "Just because he's the heir to the throne doesn't give him the right to seduce chaste ladies!" he declared fiercely.

"Precisely so, dear Rob," Mary replied calmly, and rose from her dressing table.

Her father held her cloak for her and patted her shoulders. "You've passed the ultimate test," he said. "I'm proud of you."

"I thought you would be, Papa," she replied complacently. "I hope I caused you no professional problems."

"Good heavens, no!" Sir John said with a chuckle. "This is England, where the Crown is a symbol of authority. We don't live in the Ottoman Empire, where all officials are creatures of the sovereign and lose their heads if they flout his will!"

"Well, that's good, because what I want to propose at dinner tonight requires your approval, as well as the king's." The beautiful young woman said no more as she draped her cloak over her shoulders and led her bewildered father and cousins to the waiting carriage. A crowd had noted her coach and carriage outside the theater, and when Mary Ellis emerged they surged forward. Her mysterious proposal to her father was forgotten, and he stood in the background watching his daughter patiently signing her name on the papers her adoring admirers thrust on her.

In fact, not until they were comfortably seated in the fashionable West End restaurant and had placed their orders did Mary finally tell the others what was on her mind. Timing was of paramount importance offstage as well as on, and as always her sense of timing was perfect.

"I want to go on a voyage," the young actress said as she demurely sipped from her cut-glass wine goblet, which the steward had just filled.

"Well, that's fine, Mary," Sir John said, relieved that his daughter's proposal was, after all, just a simple matter. "Your theater season is about over, and you'll have a ten-week holiday. I'm sure a relaxing voyage would be enjoyable, but you hardly need to consult me about that."

"I do if I intend to travel through the Ottoman Empire."

Sir John's long training as a diplomat didn't help him conceal his alarm and dismay, and he gasped. "As I tell you repeatedly, Mary, the Ottomans are a hostile, barbaric people who don't take kindly to the presence of Westerners in their lands—"

Before Sir John could finish, however, Rosalind spoke up in a burst of enthusiasm. "Oh, Mary! I think it's exciting! How romantic!"

"I'm not going for the romance or adventure," the young actress replied flatly, looking directly at her father. "I'm going for the benefit of my career."

"What could a trip to the Ottoman Empire possibly have to do with your career?" the matter-of-fact Rob put in as he fingered his silverware, impatiently awaiting the arrival of their dinner.

"Well, dear cousins—and Father," Mary said, a beguiling smile coming to her lips, "if you'll give me a moment to explain." The young woman, drawing from her experience as an actress, allowed for a long pause, then continued. "I've already spoken to George Dankins. He has agreed—after some persuasion on my part, to be sure—to include Sophocles's *Antigone* in the repertory next season. I, of course, will play the title role."

"Oh, Mary," the excited and spirited young Rosalind couldn't help interrupting again, "all the critics say that's the most difficult role an actress can play!"

"And well I know it. The critics will sharpen their knives for me. The part is so long, and there are so many difficult monologues that the audience can become restless.

But it's a great challenge, and as I told George Dankins, I adore challenges. What it boils down to is that if I don't continue to grow as an actress, I'll stultify. I've got to keep adding new parts to my repertoire."

Sir John finally spoke up, and it was clear to see where his daughter learned her acting ability. Sir John allowed a long pause to ensue as he looked at each of the young people at the table, then said, "It's all very well, my dear, to talk of ambition and challenges. You've already more than proved to me that you could become a fine actress. But what in the name of the good Lord does your role in *Antigone* have to do with a voyage to the Ottoman Empire?"

Mary was not to be outdone by her father's sense of the dramatic. Lowering her eyes coyly and speaking in a quiet voice, she said, "I was coming to that, Papa."

"Well, go on." Sir John Ellis drummed his fingers on the fine linen tablecloth on the table.

"If I'm to persuade an audience to believe I'm really a Greek woman like Antigone, I must learn about Greece and the Greeks. I plan to take a ten-week voyage through the Aegean Sea—which, I know, is part of the Ottoman Empire—and study the Greek people and Greek culture. I will become so imbued with things Greek that I will actually *become* Antigone!" The passionate Mary Ellis was no longer acting a part but fervently believed every word she was saying. "I've already got George Dankins's support, and now I need yours, Papa. Surely someone in your position can pull enough strings to gain permission from the Ottomans for me to take a harmless voyage through the Aegean. I don't plan to subvert the Greeks, after all, and persuade them to rebel against the rule of the Turks."

"I doubt if a mere woman could do that," Rob said absently, his hunger growing by the minute.

"Antigone did," Rosalind quickly said.

"What do you know about it?" Rob asked, scarcely interested in anything but the arrival of their dinner.

"I've read the play many times," the girl said. "Antigone rebelled against the rulers of the land in order to do what she believed was right."

Sir John was still impressed by his daughter's talent, as well as her fame, and he had to admit that contrary to his fears, she had achieved theatrical stardom without compromising the qualities of decency and goodness he had always tried to instill in her. So he addressed his daughter discreetly, even somewhat lightly. "A voyage through the Aegean isn't quite the same as making a trip to Paris, you know."

"Surely the sultan of the Ottoman Empire hasn't forbidden Westerners from sailing in the Aegean!" Mary said.

"Not exactly, my dear. But there are so many problems involved. You don't need me to tell you that you're an exceptionally handsome woman. You'd be asking for problems and complications if you sailed the Aegean without a chaperon."

"I've already considered that aspect. Rosalind, Rob, what would you say to being my chaperons?"

Rosalind beamed, and Rob forgot his hunger. "I'd love to go with you!" the young man exclaimed. "What a great adventure it would be!"

"Oh, do you mean it, Mary?" Rosalind clasped her hands. "Could we really go with you?"

"Of course. I know you have a great sense of adventure, Rosalind, and I'm sure Rob won't allow any Greeks or Turks to come near us." The young actress, her green eyes glowing, looked at Sir John. "What do you say, Papa?"

Sir John had to admit the idea made sense. "The three of you traveling together," he said, "would make quite a lot of difference. Do I assume, Mary, that you'd be paying for the twins' transportation and other expenses?"

"Of course, Papa. I have so much money coming in that I don't know what to do with it other than to buy more clothes, and my wardrobe is already overflowing."

He nodded and was lost in thought as Mary and her cousins looked at him expectantly. He was wondering if perhaps Mary was going too far, if perhaps her ambition was going to create problems for her. "I can obtain visas for you and the twins to travel on an English ship," he began hesitantly, "but that doesn't necessarily mean they'll be honored in the Ottoman Empire. But that isn't my biggest concern. I'm more worried that there might be an unpleasant incident—an attack on your ship, for instance."

"We'd be traveling on an English ship," the now-animated Rob said emphatically. "Let those Ottomans just try to attack us. We'll show them a thing or two. The English can whip anybody." The young man was so enthusiastic that he forgot his appetite completely and paid no attention as a livery-coated servant put their dinner on the table.

Rob had touched a sensitive chord in his uncle. Sir John would never admit that his country could ever be forced to submit to a group of barbarians. "All right," the elderly statesman finally said as he put his napkin on his lap and prepared to eat his meal. "I'll arrange for your visas in the morning. It will take a while to process them, but by the time they're ready your season will be over and you will be ready to sail."

"And ready to learn about the most challenging role in my career!" Mary added, her face beaming.

In the private apartments of the sultan in Topkapi Palace was a special room with a double ceiling and walls, thick rugs on the floor, and several small divans clustered close together. Tapestries covered the walls, and heavy drapes could be drawn over the high windows that overlooked the imperial gardens. The chamber was as soundproof as a succession of rulers over the centuries could make it, and here the reigning monarchs held their most private discussions with key subordinates.

Mahmoud ben Ibrahim, the grand vizier, was a white-haired, spidery man who had served the sultan's father before him and enjoyed the complete confidence of Selim III. No protocol or custom erected barriers between them, and in the privacy of the so-called silent room, Mahmoud ben Ibrahim felt free to express his mind with candor. He poured himself a cup of thick, black, extra-sweet Turkish coffee, to which he added a heaping spoonful of sugar. Stirring the brew, he sighed as he waited patiently for the bitter grounds to settle at the bottom of the cup.

The sultan knew his principal adviser well. "Whenever you use too much sugar in your coffee, Mahmoud," he observed, "I know you're fortifying yourself for the bad news you feel obliged to tell me."

"Fortunately I'm not forced to give you bad news often, Selim, or I'd become as fat as an old eunuch."

The sultan twisted the Great Mongol Emerald on his finger, then leaned closer to the grand vizier. "Well?" he demanded.

"It's that woman again."

Selim groaned. "I've twice written to her brother, suggesting politely that he call her home to Mongolia. After all, she has been visiting with us for over two years now—though it seems like an eternity. But the khagan ignores my hints. Not that I can blame him. Tule Yasmin is the most spoiled, imperious, and unpredictable woman on earth, and her brother is well rid of her. Allah's mind was on something else when he made her a female rather than a male, and a voluptuous female at that. What has she done now?"

"What hasn't she done! She's been nothing but a nuisance ever since she arrived here and ran down and killed that unlucky devil in the Grand Bazaar. She offered a prize of twenty talents in gold to any janissary-of-horse who could beat her in a horse race. She bought two new slaves in the market and had them whipped to death for her pleasure, even though I pointed out to her that we have laws that specify when slaves may or may not be killed. And now she's taken the court jeweler as her lover!"

The sultan raised an eyebrow. "He's too valuable to me to die of the poison she usually administers to her lovers when she tires of them. I think I shall have to intervene."

"I have already done so. I called him to my office this morning, and I described—rather graphically, if I do say so—the unspeakable death agonies suffered by his pre-decessors. He became badly frightened, and I doubt whether Tule Yasmin, with all of her wiles, will be able to entice him to her house in the seraglio again."

The sultan leaned back, took a nut-stuffed date from a gold platter, and popped it into his mouth. "You did well, Mahmoud. I should have known I could rely on you."

The grand vizier's gaze was unrelenting.

"Now what?" Selim demanded.

"Consider. The court jeweler is a fair enough specimen of a man, but he is approaching his fortieth year, he can-not wield a scimitar or shoot a pistol, and I doubt if he could keep his seat on a spirited mount. Why does Tule Yasmin find him attractive?"

"An interesting riddle. I wonder."

"Wonder no more, Selim," Mahmoud ben Ibrahim said grimly. "I had my suspicions, so I questioned the poor fool closely, and he admitted far more than he realized. He was being used."

"In what way?" The sultan was perplexed.

The grand vizier leaned toward him and plucked the Great Mongol Emerald from his finger, then waved it beneath the imperial nose. "Your memory does you little credit. You recently remarked at dinner that you wanted this stone reset so it would stop slipping on your finger."

"So I did," Selim muttered, and looked blank.

"It was immediately after you made that innocent com-ment that Tule Yasmin suddenly developed an interest in the court jeweler!"

"Aha!" A light began to dawn.

"Aha, indeed. You will recall, I'm sure, her reluctance to present you with the gem when she first came to Topkapi. She wore it, having brought it with her from Mongolia. Just to be on the safe side. But surely you don't need me to remind you that you had to force her to present it to you."

The sultan's silver-slippered feet thudded softly on the

rug. "Do you mean she was plotting to use the jeweler in some way to obtain possession of the emerald again?"

"Precisely, and what she had in mind is no mystery. First, she would have persuaded the jeweler to make a duplicate of the stone. In glass, or whatever the substance. Then, at some convenient time during their affair, she would have exchanged the real and the counterfeit. You would have worn the imitation, and you wouldn't have known the difference. She would have regained the Great Mongol Emerald and would have hidden it."

"She deserves decapitation!" the sultan said indignantly.

"Granted. But please keep in mind that she's of royal blood. You'd have to convene an Ottoman Council in order to convict her, and that would mean bringing your brothers and cousins back to Constantinople from the far reaches of the empire, where we have scattered them so effectively. I doubt if her execution, as satisfying as it would be, would be worth the risk of bringing your relatives together. You know full well that in no time they'd be plotting your removal from the throne of thrones. We're trying, in France and elsewhere in Europe, to create the impression that we've become a civilized nation. How they'd laugh if you were forced to have your brothers and cousins put to death!"

Selim gnawed his lower lip. "Then you advise me not to punish Tule Yasmin?"

"I strongly urge you to give her no indication that you're knowledgeable about her schemes and her greed."

"Then we must send her home to her brother at once!"

"As you just said, the khagan of Mongolia is not eager for his sister's return, and if we forced her to go back, he would be grievously upset. We cannot risk the displeasure of the khagan, not after working so hard to come to peaceful terms with the people in the far-flung reaches of our empire."

"Then what would you have us do?" The sultan was almost beside himself with worry.

"Ah, Selim, employ the cunning you've inherited from

your distinguished ancestors. Use the wiles that have made the Ottomans great and strong."

The sultan blinked at him. "Do you have something specific in mind, Mahmoud?"

The grand vizier smiled confidently. "There are other places we can send Tule Yasmin besides Mongolia."

"Where? Her visit to one of our subordinate kingdoms might cause untold problems for the viceroy there."

"I suggest that we send her abroad, on a state visit. I have already talked with her about it, and she admits she has grown bored and restless here. She would not be averse to traveling abroad."

"What country would have her?" the sultan replied, raising an eyebrow.

"France, for one. The French are losing their allies, due to the unrest there, and they would welcome closer ties with the Ottoman Empire."

"The French are engaged in a full-scale revolution," the sultan replied severely. "Radical elements there are actually demanding the lives of King Louis and Queen Marie Antoinette! Do you truly think a state visit would be advisable in a time of major unrest and upheaval?"

Mahmoud ben Ibrahim concealed his impatience. "If harm should come to Tule Yasmin on her travels in France—and I believe it would be best if she travel extensively there, rather than confine herself to a visit to the palace at Versailles—you would be obliged to rebuke the government of France severely."

The sultan smiled, and ultimately he laughed aloud. "If something untoward should take the life of the khana, I would issue a proclamation declaring a three-day state of official mourning." Suddenly his manner changed. "We will do it!" he said briskly. "We will send for the French minister and make all of the necessary arrangements. We must make certain that the khana and her entourage are not bottled up at Versailles with Louis XVI and his Austrian queen. We will see to it that she spends time in Paris, in Normandy, in Lyons, and in Marseilles. We will make certain she travels extensively—and at length. I suggest a visit to France of no less than six months' duration. And the sooner she leaves Constantinople, the sooner our lives will return to normal!"

Jeremy Morgan was desperate.

On the top of an inexpensive pine chest of drawers was a small pile of newly minted silver and a few dollar bills bearing the guarantee of Secretary of the Treasury Alexander Hamilton that they were redeemable in cash. When the week ended and Jeremy paid for his food and lodging at the little inn, he would be lucky if he could jingle a few pennies in his pocket. Certainly there wouldn't be enough left to pay for his transportation by public coach out of New York, much less buy himself a horse. Worst of all, he had no idea where he would go should he be forced to leave. He smiled wryly and told himself to face facts. At the age of twenty-eight he was a complete failure, and it was small consolation to realize that his case was not unique. Like so many other veterans who had helped to win America's independence from England, he had rejoiced when the Confederation had died and had been supplanted by a stronger and more stable United States, which governed itself under the new Constitution. But it seemed as though there was no position of importance in the America of 1791 for a man whose principal attributes were his audacity and a supreme disdain for his own safety.

He had come to New York several months ago, leaving behind Aileen St. Clair and a large tract of uncultivated land in the Ohio territory. He had heard that appointments to posts of importance in the new federal government were being made daily, and although he had not been acquainted with anyone in a position to help him, he had been confident of his ability to win influential friends. Now facing his situation squarely, he had to admit to himself that he had been unable to secure a single interview with a cabinet member or a senator. He had been introduced to a number of highly placed gentlemen at social occasions, where they had been affable enough, but they had become decidedly chilly when he had suggested that he was seeking employment.

His only success so far had been with the ladies, and that was no novelty to him. Women had always found him irresistible, and remarkably few of them had ever rejected his advances. Occasionally, of course, his ability to fascinate members of the opposite sex had led to unforeseen difficulties, such as the incident with Aileen St. Clair and her uncle, who had threatened to horsewhip him. But now, at least, his charms were keeping him circulating, for scarcely a day passed when he failed to receive an invitation to one of the late afternoon receptions that so many of the government leaders attended. If he had done nothing else, he had at least charmed the right hostesses and had been asked to the right parties.

Time was working against him, Jeremy knew. With his funds running out, he would not be able to continue the siege for more than a few days, so he now had less than a week in which to achieve his goal. Risks were unavoidable if he were to overcome a desperate situation, and he promised himself to do whatever was necessary. Scruples rarely bothered him, and now, of all times, he had no intention of allowing conscience to interfere. His whole future was at stake, and he could not permit himself to forget it for a moment.

Shaking off his unaccustomed lethargy, he dressed with care for the reception at the home of the Fitzroy Eatons, who were said to be good friends of the secretary of war and of Vice-President and Mrs. Adams. He combed his crisp brown hair and put his velvet-edged tricorn hat firmly on his head. Let others wear powdered wigs if they chose; he always attracted more attention by shunning such artifices. He glanced again at his reflection in the mirror, and his spirits lifted. His clear hazel eyes, his firm lips, and his strong jaw were undoubtedly those of a man of courage, a natural leader, and someone in a position of authority was sure to recognize his qualities. He slipped into his one good broadcloth coat, with a row of silver buttons down each side, and then dropped his watch into a waistcoat pocket, letting the fob dangle elegantly. The watch was the only thing he owned that had belonged to his father, and he always felt better when he wore it.

He buckled on his light sword, then took his gloves from the chest and sauntered out into the chilly November air. He was too early for the reception, but it was best to allow enough time, since he could not afford to hire a carriage and would have to walk. The day would come, he told himself, shivering slightly, when he would wear a greatcoat lined with fur. His steps took him past the imposing house on Broad Street where President and Mrs. Washington were living, and a few minutes later he glanced enviously at Federal Hall, where the Congress was meeting.

Perhaps, he thought, he had been impatient and unwise in leaving Ohio so hastily. Eventually the region would achieve statehood, and had he been content to live there in anonymity and bide his time, eventually he might have won election to Congress. But a man who had spent so much of his life at war could not afford to wait; a new generation was already growing up, and Jeremy felt that unless he hurried he would miss his opportunity. In a raw, bustling country that was expanding rapidly, a man had to be bold, to recognize his chances, and to seize them ruthlessly, or he would be lost in the faceless crowd.

The reception was in full swing by the time Jeremy arrived, and after flattering his hostess so outrageously that her husband scowled, he accepted a small cup of rum and brandy punch and began to wander through the rooms where the guests were congregated. The drink was strong, and he sipped it cautiously; he did not care for strong spirits, as he preferred to be in absolute control of himself at all times. Much to his disappointment the vice-president was not in attendance, and the only men he saw were minor government functionaries whose influence was limited. He began to think that he had wasted one of his few precious days, and he was growing annoyed with the Eatons and with himself, when he noticed a guest in the far corner of the drawing room. Mrs. Penelope Fielding was the wife of a minor official who had no special standing in the government.

Certainly he was not of sufficient importance to make his wife a center of interest, but she was nevertheless surrounded by half a dozen men, all of them trying hard to impress her. Jeremy smiled to himself and shook his head. It was common gossip that Mrs. Fielding was the newest favorite of Secretary of the Treasury Hamilton, whose reputation as a gallant was almost as great as the brilliant name he had made for himself as a statesman, administrator, and political philosopher. Inspecting the young matron carefully, Jeremy had to admit that Hamilton had excellent taste. Her blond and wavy hair hung in ringlets down her back, her blue eyes sparkled, and her cosmetics, which she had applied with a practiced hand, enhanced her natural prettiness. She wore a gown of flattering hunter's green silk, with a bodice obviously intended to show off her full but graceful figure. A white gauze ruffle known as a Medici collar edged the deep square neckline of the bodice, which fitted smoothly down to her hips and was finished by a band of unexpectedly demure white ribbon. A spray of artificial daisies was tucked into one side of the neckline, providing a touch that Jeremy immediately recognized as being provocative while pretending to be modest.

It occurred to him that if he could persuade Mrs. Fielding to put in a word for him with Secretary Hamilton his fortune would be made. The very way she held herself was an indication to his experienced eye that she would not object to the type of approach at which he excelled, and he decided to get rid of the fops who crowded around her. Taking a cup of the rum and brandy punch from a tray carried by a passing liveried servant, he walked straight to her, shouldering her admirers aside.

"Mrs. Fielding, your servant, ma'am." Jeremy bowed

politely but grinned impudently at the young woman. "It appeared to me as though you were in dire need of refreshment."

There was a shrewd intelligence behind her bland, wide-eyed expression. "How thoughtful of you, Mr. Morgan."

"You remember me, then," he said, pretending surprise.

"Of course. We met two weeks ago at that big reception given by Colonel and Mrs. Bates." She accepted the cup of punch, and for a moment their fingers touched.

Jeremy noted that she was in no hurry to withdraw her hand. Encouraged, he grasped her elbow and skillfully piloted her toward a small unoccupied divan. The men to whom she had been speaking protested, but he did not seem to hear them. "Your memory is almost as good as mine," he said, waiting until she made herself comfortable on a pair of silk pillows before sitting beside her. "If you'd like, I can tell you precisely what you wore that day."

"Really?" Mrs. Fielding sipped her punch and glanced at him archly over the rim of her cup. "I thought Mrs. Bates was taking up all of your time."

A disdainful shrug quickly disposed of Mrs. Bates. "No man could ever fail to be aware of your presence," he declared, staring at her boldly, and to prove his truthfulness he described the costume she had worn when they had met. The details came to him easily, for he had long ago trained himself to be observant of women's clothes; he needed to expend little effort, and they were invariably pleased.

Mrs. Fielding made it plain that she was aware he was insincere, yet she could not help responding to his attention. He had the knack of making her feel that she was the only woman present, and so, after they had chatted for the better part of an hour, she gladly accepted his invitation to escort her to her home. A few eyebrows were raised when they left the reception together, but Jeremy was indifferent to the opinions of the other guests. He was making excellent progress, and if all continued to go as he planned, the views of unimportant people would never again matter to him. Recklessly squandering his meager reserves, he hailed a public carriage, and after carefully handing Mrs. Fielding in, he took his seat very close to her. She was a little giddy from the punch, and she leaned against him, whether by accident or design he could not tell.

"If you have no other engagement," she said softly, "perhaps you'll have supper with me."

"You're very kind," Jeremy replied cautiously, "but Mr. Fielding might not be in the mood to entertain a guest."

"Mr. Fielding," she said distinctly, "is in Pennsylvania on business."

Jeremy relaxed and slipped an arm around her. "In that case, I shall be delighted to accept. We'll endeavor to entertain each other." He cupped his free hand under her chin and raised her face to his. She pressed against him, and his kiss lingered on her soft, amenable lips.

When the carriage jolted to a halt in front of her small house, neither of them bothered with the usual preliminaries, and by unspoken consent they walked straight up the stairs to the bedroom on the second floor without first wasting time in flirtatious fencing in the parlor.

As soon as the door was closed behind them, Jeremy took the luscious young woman into his arms. He kissed her hard on the mouth, and she responded fully, pressing herself against his body and holding him tightly.

Then wasting no time, she took him by the hand and led him to the bed. There he began by unfastening the clasps of her gown, lowering her bodice and cupping her breasts in his hands. Filled with desire, she began to take off his clothes, too, first removing his coat, then unbuttoning his shirt, and finally unbuckling his pants. Soon they were both nude, and they climbed into the four-poster bed to begin making love in earnest. She was as fully aroused as he, and she moaned with pleasure as he slid on top of her and entered her. She had never had such a strong, confident lover, and she reached climax after climax as he thrust deeply into her.

Jeremy was enjoying his simple, direct conquest, and he, too, moaned aloud as his release finally came. They rested in each other's arms for a time, catching their breath, until desire overtook them once more and they began to make love a second time.

Afterward they donned their clothes, and Penelope went to her vanity to reapply her makeup. Occasionally she glanced in Jeremy's direction and smiled slyly, and he was tempted to bring up the real point of his visit at the first opportunity. But the stakes for which he was playing were too high, and the cost of failure would be too great, so he restrained himself and waited until they sat down together to a meal in the tiny dining room.

A slattern in dirty cotton, the only servant in the house, placed a steaming dish before them and withdrew. Jeremy waited until Mrs. Fielding had served the venison pie, and then, after complimenting her on it, he took a deep breath. "I wonder if you'd do something for me, Penelope."

"Anything I can, my dear," she replied warmly, her cheeks flushed with the memory of his lovemaking.

"I've been trying for some time to find a responsible place for myself in the government," he began.

"Oh?" Her voice was guarded, and she seemed to grow tense.

Jeremy laughed, hoping to disarm her. "You know very little of my background, but I can assure you I have a great deal to offer to the right department."

"I can imagine," she murmured.

"My problem is that I have so few connections with the right people. Everyone is too busy to see me, apparently." He was looking straight at her, and for an instant he thought he saw a strange expression in her eyes. He could not identify it, and he felt a twinge of uneasiness, but the moment passed, and her eyes were once more round and smiling. "I'm hoping there might be someone to whom you could give me an introduction. The right word in the right place always opens the right doors."

Mrs. Fielding toyed daintily with the food on her plate.

"As you know, my husband is in government service," she said, then added scornfully, "I can't pretend that he's important to anyone, however. It just so happens, though, that I am slightly acquainted with a few people of rather high rank."

"Is that so?" Jeremy tried to sound and look politely surprised.

"And I heard very recently of an opening that's caused considerable difficulty. They can't seem to find the right man to fill it."

"That's interesting." It was time to end the sham. "In what department is it?"

"I couldn't say." That same odd look came into her blue eyes again, and her soft lips tightened. "I've been told very little about the position. If you'd like to learn more, I suggest that you present yourself at the office of the secretary of the treasury at ten o'clock tomorrow morning."

Jeremy was so startled that he could only stare at her. She made it sound as though an appointment had already been arranged for him, yet common sense told him that was impossible. All the same he could not help feeling that Penelope Fielding had in reality seduced *him* and that he was no longer in control of his destiny. And he could not resist asking, "How do I know I won't be turned away?"

Mrs. Fielding ended the subject. "The secretary will see you," she said firmly.

Promptly at ten o'clock the following morning Jeremy sat in a small anteroom of the crowded house on Independence Street that was the headquarters of the Department of the Treasury. It was obvious that he was expected, for an aide nodded brightly and hurried off when he gave his name, and it was clear that the secretary would see him. Jeremy wondered, as he had through most of the night, whether Penelope Fielding had been requested by Hamilton to seek him out and to urge him to come here this morning. Her reaction had certainly indicated as much, although he was sure that Hamilton would be outraged if he knew his mistress was also enjoying an affair with an impecunious position-seeker.

What Jeremy could not understand was why the secretary would have chosen such a roundabout method of establishing contact with him. It would have been far simpler, if there was indeed a post that Jeremy could fill, for Hamilton to have sent a letter or even a messenger to him at his inn, instructing him to appear here this morning. The man who, along with Secretary of State Jefferson, ranked next to the President himself in prestige and power could have no need to use a woman of less-than-immaculate virtue as a go-between with a man who was desperately seeking employment. It was probable, Jeremy reflected, that he was allowing his imagination to play tricks on him, but in spite of his attempts to reassure himself, he could not shake off the feeling that he was being manipulated.

After a wait of more than half an hour, during which time the anteroom became filled with other visitors, he was finally led down a corridor to what had once been the drawing room of the house. There he was ushered into the private office of the secretary of the treasury, and the rumors he had heard about it were accurate. It was furnished opulently, and the secretary did not try to hide his love of elegance and comfort. A thick Persian rug covered the floor, the walls were filled with paintings and tapestries, all in excellent taste, and thick silk drapes of dark green were hung at either side of the bay windows. The chairs were of carved, polished oak, and a fire of hickory logs burned brightly in a tiled Dutch hearth. At the far end of the chamber was a large desk of hand-tooled leather, and behind it, looking out over the top of several mounds of neatly stacked papers, was the secretary.

Alexander Hamilton was no longer the fresh-faced youth who had made his mark during the war as Washington's aide. Authority and responsibility had aged him, but he still looked remarkably young for one in so high a position. His face was square, and although he was fleshy, there was power in his body as well as in his features. He wore his

own hair, brushed back and tied in a queue, but his clothes
reflected his appetite for good things. His shirt and stock
were of the finest "lingerie silk," his waistcoat was brocaded, and the revers of his silk-lined coat were of maroon
velvet. Jeremy had heard that he was so conscious of his
short stature that he never rose to greet a guest; whether
the story was true was impossible to determine, but he did
not stand now.

"Sit down, Morgan," he said brusquely, and continued
to study a sheaf of papers. He scribbled a few notes in the
margin with a quill pen, then rang a small ivory-handled
bell on his desk and tapped his fingers impatiently until an
aide came into the room. "Dispatch these at once," he
directed, and only when the assistant had gone did he finally look at Jeremy. "Well, Morgan," he said.

Jeremy knew that he must be civil at all costs, but he
resented Hamilton's attitude. "Mr. Secretary," he replied
in the same curt tone.

Hamilton's penetrating eyes studied him for a long moment. "Why are you seeking a position with the government?" he asked unexpectedly.

"I'm sure you know the answer to that, Mr. Secretary."
Jeremy realized he was being incautious, even rude, but
he could not bow or scrape to any man, particularly one
who seemed to be making a deliberate attempt to antagonize him. "You're in government service yourself, though
you surely earned a better living when you were in private
life. What I want is recognition." He didn't mention that
he also wouldn't mind wearing a fine linen shirt and brocaded waistcoat like Hamilton's.

"Fair enough." Hamilton was amused by his impudence
and grinned. "You have private means, then?"

"I do not. Aside from a few questionable dollars that
you've recently run off your printing presses, I don't have
a penny in the world."

"Fame means more to you than money, then?"

"I could use a bit of both," Jeremy said, laughing.

The secretary continued to regard him intently. "You

spent some time in the wilderness. What made you decide
not to remain there permanently?"

So Hamilton had already taken the trouble to look into
his background, Jeremy thought. Encouraged, he decided
this was a moment when frankness would not hurt. "I've
seen too many men struggling to establish themselves out
there. They work to clear the land, they work to raise
crops, they fight off the Indians, and after years of the
hardest kind of labor they're lucky if they haven't gone so
badly into debt that they've lost their property."

If the secretary found his bald cynicism shocking, there
was no sign of it. "You've dabbled in many fields, from
what I gather. Why did you give up the sea?"

Jeremy wondered exactly how much Hamilton knew
about his past. He decided to be evasive, and he said, "I
grew tired of the sea. It's the most boring existence I know.
However," Jeremy added, and for the first time there was
a note of pride in his voice, "I was a good gunnery officer.
There was none better."

Those who claimed that Alexander Hamilton was a hard
man who felt none of the emotions that moved other people had often seen him as he was now, with his face
resembling a stiff mask. He seemed lost in thought for a
long moment, then he asked abruptly, "How were you
treated in Turkey?"

The question surprised Jeremy, and he replied slowly,
"Well enough, I reckon. They've never been friendly to
people from Christian nations, but I had no trouble with
them. I confined my relations to the trade deal I was making and saw only a few Europeans in Constantinople. They
told me things are going to be different under the new
sultan, Selim III." He had no idea why the secretary was
interested in his opinion of the Turks, but he decided to
make it plain that he was familiar with many elements of
Turkish life. "I know that the sultan has taken several steps
in the right direction. He has made peace with the empress of Russia, and he's now secure from attack. He's
reorganizing his corps of janissaries—his army, that is—

and he's been weeding corrupt officials out of his government."

"In your view, what makes the new sultan different from his predecessors?"

From the very way the question was asked Jeremy realized that Hamilton already knew the answer and was testing him. "He's the first ruler of the Ottoman Empire in the past one hundred and fifty years who has been in his right mind. All the others had to live in cages until they came to the throne. That was how the reigning sultan protected himself from assassination by his ambitious heirs. But nobody ever expected Selim to become sultan. From all I heard about him, he's quite a man. Naturally I didn't meet him, or even see him. No foreigners are allowed at the court, especially people who speak English. He hates the English—which is proof enough of his good sense."

"Why does he hate them?" the secretary persisted.

"Because Turkey and England are the two strongest naval powers in the world, naturally." Jeremy wished Hamilton would stop trying to bait him with the obvious.

A faint smile touched the corners of the secretary's mouth, but his eyes remained cold. "I gather that you hate the English, then."

"Certainly. Who doesn't?" Jeremy demanded impudently.

"My idealistic colleague in the Department of State, Mr. Jefferson, for one," Hamilton said, and for the first time he seemed stirred. "There's much I admire about England and her system of government, but I'm a realist, and that's more than can be said for Tom. He can't see that England is still our enemy and that London is still badly upset by our independence, even though the war ended more than seven years ago. There are forces both in and out of the king's government that would do anything to reduce us to a colonial status again."

"If you're looking for somebody to fight them, I'm your man," Jeremy said promptly.

The secretary did not seem to hear the offer. "We've been safe until very recently because a delicate balance of power has kept the English from our throats. France has been our best friend and would have gone to war on our side at once. Unfortunately, the French have their own troubles these days. King Louis is virtually a prisoner, and reckless, lawless elements have been usurping the power of Mirabeau, the chief minister. Jefferson is delighted, of course," he added contemptuously. "He says they're following our example and claims they're liberalizing their form of government."

Everyone in New York knew of the feud between Secretaries Hamilton and Jefferson, and Jeremy decided that this was the moment to keep his mouth prudently shut.

"Tom is so filled with lofty ideas about the natural dignity of man that he can't see we need strong allies to prevent England from destroying us. That's why, as usual, I've had to step in, and that's why I wanted to see you, Morgan."

So Hamilton had actually arranged this meeting after all, using Penelope Fielding as a go-between. Jeremy tried to hide his recognition of the fact, but the secretary was watching him too closely.

"I can't allow myself to be charged with interfering in the functions of the Department of State," Hamilton said. "I shudder to think of the unpleasantness that would enliven the next cabinet meeting. I have too many enemies to take unnecessary chances." He scowled and then, in a quick change of mood, looked pleased with himself. "Now you see why I elected to use an unorthodox means of getting in touch with you. I was happy to learn that you were interested in hearing more about my proposal."

Jeremy, thinking quickly, realized that Penelope Fielding had merely reported to Hamilton that she had followed his orders. Clearly she had not said that Jeremy himself had sought such a meeting, and obviously she had in no way indicated that she had allowed him to make love to her. A feeling that he had outsmarted the brilliant secretary of the treasury swept over Jeremy, and he sat back in his chair, grinning. "Just what is your offer?" he asked airily.

Most men would have taken offense at his tone, but Hamilton, who was, as a rule, highly sensitive to the least slight, remained unperturbed. "I intend to send you out of the country on a mission of extraordinary delicacy."

"As a representative of the Treasury?"

"I had hoped to find you more alert," Hamilton said reprovingly. "At best your mission will be semiofficial. Your wages will be paid out of secret funds which the President has allotted to me on the approval of Congress. Fortunately, I may do what I please with such money, and no one may ask questions. Particularly no one in the Department of State." He paused, and when he spoke again his voice was icy. "If you should fail in the mission, your status will not even be semiofficial. I'll be forced to deny any connection with you."

Jeremy flushed and felt a surge of wild anger; Hamilton's proposal was so unfair that he managed to control himself only by exerting enormous effort. "You'd claim that I wasn't working for you?" he asked, almost choking on the words.

"More than that," was the calm reply. "I'd insist I didn't know you and that I'd never heard of you." The secretary's smile was chilly, correct, and impersonal. "On the other hand, if you should succeed you'll be given full official recognition. You'll achieve renown far beyond your dreams."

"I see." Jeremy's voice was as cold as Hamilton's. "It's plain to me that you require a man of special attributes for the task you have in mind, whatever it may be."

"True."

"Then I'm sure you're willing to pay a substantial wage accordingly, as an inducement."

"You'll receive forty dollars each month."

The sum was far more than Jeremy had expected. Few men earned that much money, and under less unusual circumstances he would have accepted a fraction of that amount without question. But the conditions Hamilton had outlined convinced him that he possessed attributes that made his services particularly desirable. He did not know what they were, but ignorance did not make him reticent. "I couldn't consider any position that paid less than sixty dollars," he said.

"You'll get forty." Hamilton's tone was flat and uncompromising.

"Suppose I were to accept. What then?"

The secretary cocked his head to one side and studied his visitor. "I am not a merchant in one of the bazaars of Constantinople. You can't haggle with me, you can't change the terms, and you can't win a better bargain. Either you'll accept now, on the conditions I've already outlined, or this interview is at an end. I'm offering you opportunity, glory, and a generous amount of money. I refuse to cajole you. And I have no intention of threatening you. You're a free citizen of the United States, and you have a free choice. But be good enough to make up your mind, as I don't have all day to spend with you. I'm scheduled to appear before a committee of the House of Representatives in thirty minutes, and I've got to finish a report to the President before that time."

Jeremy knew the secretary was goading him, forcing his hand before he could examine the matter fully. At the moment he knew virtually nothing about the mission, as Hamilton certainly realized. On the other hand, he believed what he had already been told, that the assignment was one in which he could distinguish himself. And the wages were not only more than enough to cover all of his needs; the offer was so generous that he was sure the task he would be required to perform was important. He hated to admit to himself that anyone could master him, for he prized his independence of spirit above all else. But his alternatives were either starvation or a return to the precarious existence he could eke out for himself on the frontier, and apparently Hamilton was aware of his situation, too.

"All right," he said. "I accept."

The secretary seemed to relax and smiled benignly. "I won't pretend that I like you, Morgan. I don't. But my own judgment confirms the reports I've received on you. And the very traits that make you personally obnoxious to me should enable you to carry out the task. You're over-bearing, rude, and insufferably insolent. You have far more confidence in yourself than your record warrants; you're an opportunist, and you're a gambler. In short, you're just the man I've been seeking. You may now consider yourself in my employ. Congratulations."

"Thanks," Jeremy said dryly.

Again the secretary seemed to be unaware of his impertinence. "First, one or two questions. You aren't married, I've been told. Is that correct?"

"It is." Jeremy wondered if Hamilton was about to bring up his affair with Penelope Fielding. He would refuse to answer any questions on the subject merely to satisfy the suspicions of a man who was concerned over his own vanity.

"You're not betrothed?"

"I am not."

"And you have no living relatives?"

"My grandfather died shortly after the war started. I have no family."

"Better and better." The secretary nodded approvingly. "Very well." He opened a drawer of his desk, took out a small deerskin purse, and handed it to the younger man. "This will take care of your expenses."

Jeremy weighed the leather bag in his hand and was pleased to find that it was heavy, far heavier than its small size indicated. Apparently it was filled with gold coins. "What do you want me to do?"

"Arrange passage for yourself on the first merchantman sailing for France. Go to Paris and see the marquis de Lafayette, who is now head of the National Guard there. He's one of the best friends this country has ever had, and he's fully aware of all the details of my plan. He'll give you all the necessary instructions."

Jeremy was astonished. "You're telling me nothing more?"

"Only that your mission will take you to France, then on to the Ottoman Empire. I can tell you nothing more." Hamilton folded his hands over his waistcoat. "You can afford risks. I can't, and neither can the United States of America. If I haven't already made this clear to you, be good enough to mention nothing about this meeting to anyone. Our conversation today has never taken place. Tell no one you're going to France, and when you sail, leave as unobtrusively as possible. It would suit my purposes perfectly if you seemed to vanish from the face of the earth without a trace."

Never had anyone accepted a position under more absurdly mysterious circumstances, Jeremy thought. But they were provocative and therefore challenging. So in spite of himself, he felt a kindling of a sense of excitement. "You can depend on me," he said, standing and drawing on his gloves.

"I hope so, for your sake as well as for mine." There was no mistaking Hamilton's heavy, threatening tone.

Jeremy bristled and glared at him. "Just what is that supposed to mean?"

The secretary remained unruffled. "Among my duties as head of the Treasury is that of supervising the Coast Guard, formerly the Revenue Service. As a matter of fact, I've long been interested in the Coast Guard, even when I served as a colonel in the army. When your name was first proposed to me several weeks ago, I was sure that I remembered you. Then my investigation showed that you spent several years in the Coast Guard, and so I found I was right."

"I was a gunnery officer for several years," Jeremy said, raising his voice.

"Indeed. And at one point, toward the end of your career, you were a lieutenant on board the Revenue cutter, *Yankee Girl*."

"So I was," Jeremy said defiantly, hiding his dismay over what he felt sure was coming next.

"You led a mutiny against the captain of the ship."

"He was a fool," Jeremy replied bitterly, aroused by the memories he had hoped were dead. "He endangered his frigate and his crew. He—"

"You were to be court-martialed," Hamilton interrupted. "But your trial never took place, partly because the Coast Guard was short of trained officers, and in part because the captain conveniently died of a heart attack during a hurricane in the West Indian Ocean and therefore couldn't press charges against you."

"It would seem, Mr. Secretary, that you've gone to a great deal of trouble to pick up every scrap of my background that you could find."

"It was no trouble at all, I assure you. When dealing with someone of your sort, Morgan, I always think it best to have at my disposal every available weapon to make certain that I'll be able to maintain complete control."

Jeremy wondered how long a prison term he would be forced to serve if he punched the distinguished secretary of the treasury in the face.

"As I don't enjoy this any more than you do," Hamilton continued imperturbably, "let's confine ourselves to facts. Your trial never took place. On the other hand, it was never removed from the active file. If it so suited my purposes, I could order a court-martial board to convene within twenty-four hours."

The one incident over which Jeremy felt a deep and abiding sense of shame rose up out of his past and seemed to choke him. He had been right in opposing the commands of a stupid captain whose wits had been further addled by illness. But he had been wrong to incite the other officers and the men to mutiny; as he had subsequently learned, there was no excuse for insubordination and rebellion, and it was at best a flabby justification to tell himself he had

been young then and knew better now. But he allowed none
of his emotions to show and stood with his shoulders
squared and his face rigid as he looked stonily at the secretary.

"I'm merely reminding you, Morgan, that this time it
would be unwise of you to deviate from the path of duty.
If you succeed, no reward will be too great for you, and I
give you my unconditional guarantee that your desires will
be fulfilled. But if you fail—well, don't bother to return
to the United States. The climate here won't be beneficial."

III

~~~~~~~~~~~~~~~

Paris was in a state of increasing ferment, and the hint of violence was ever present in the air. The very atmosphere encouraged fanatics who had never before been able to attract attention, and rabble-rousers sprang up from nowhere, eager to incite the mobs and to win power for themselves. All work had stopped, and no one seemed to bother with the essentials of earning a living. Shops were closed, artisans did not report to their jobs, and only food purveyors continued to function. Had they refused, their places of business would have been wrecked, and so they wearily bought produce from the farmers and sold it to the public at cost. They baked bread and offered milk and butter for sale, and if their merchandise was sometimes stale or rancid, no one was in a position to protest.

The courts had ceased to function, the nobility was powerless to exercise its ancient authority, and even the clergy no longer had a restraining influence on Parisians who were rapidly discarding all of the standards that had guided their forefathers for generations. Many voices were heard, but they contradicted each other, and the people, confused and downtrodden after generations of abuse, listened to no one. The nobles either engaged in intricate, futile plots to recover the privileges that were being stripped from them, or else they retired to the comparative tranquillity of their country estates and sulked. The new rulers of Paris were the poor, who swaggered through the streets and tried, almost overnight, to compensate for centuries of injustice and oppression.

Louis XVI still sat on his throne, but no monarch had ever been in a more precarious position. Had he handled the situation firmly and with equity, he might have been a stabilizing influence, but the mobs terrified him, and he did not know how to deal with them. So he and his pretty, vapid wife remained in the Louvre, where they were virtually the prisoners of the people. They continued to hold court daily, to receive foreign envoys, and to maintain a semblance of the pomp and dignity that had so long been associated with the Bourbon family, but the fiction that the king still reigned was becoming threadbare.

Jeremy, arriving at the city of Brest after an uneventful voyage on a small, cramped brig, hired a horse and rode straight for Paris. It took the better part of the day to find an inn that was open and would accept travelers, and after he at last secured lodgings, the problem of locating a tavern that still served food confronted him. The new clothes he had bought for himself caused the crowds in the streets to view him with suspicion, and several times, when he was accosted, only his American accent prevented a serious fight. He quickly discovered that the Parisians admired the United States extravagantly, and his irritation over the personal inconveniences he was forced to suffer was more than alleviated by the cheers that greeted him when the throngs discovered his nationality.

He was anxious to learn his assignment and to begin work at once, but the necessities of life came first, and by the time he found a place that would serve him an inferior cut of beef, a soggy boiled potato, and a watery lamb stew it was too late to go anywhere except his room, where he fell asleep on a hard, lumpy mattress. In the morning he paid the innkeeper an outrageous price for a slab of bread, a slice of cheese, and some sour wine, on which he breakfasted, and then he set out for the headquarters of the National Guard near the Tuileries. When he arrived there he discovered that the soldiers of the guard were smartly uniformed and managed to display a sense of quiet and disciplined strength that was unique in the city. Only a general of extraordinary talents could have inspired such loyalty and devotion, and when Jeremy saw the faces of the men who entered and left the suite of the marquis de Lafayette, he knew that here was the one sane force in a community that had become hysterical.

After a brief wait Jeremy was admitted to the austere inner office and found the marquis awaiting him with a smile. Lafayette, slight and slender, looked remarkably boyish in his dark blue uniform, but in spite of his small stature he wore it with an air that many of his admirers had tried without success to copy. As he stood, Jeremy noticed that prominent among the medals he wore on his chest was the one that the new United States Congress had voted him as one of its first official acts.

"Welcome to Paris," the marquis said. "I regret you have come here at a time when our hospitality is limited by unfortunate circumstances." His English was perfect, and he spoke with only a trace of an accent.

"I'm glad to be here, all the same, General." Jeremy took the seat to which Lafayette waved him, and there was a sudden silence as the marquis studied him intently.

"I believe you'll be suitable, Morgan," he said abruptly. "Forgive me for my failure to observe the usual social amenities, but time is very important these days, and I have been waiting for you with something less than the patience of Job. Colonel Hamilton's description of you in the letter I received from him only a few days ago made me believe that at last we had found someone who would be of service to both the United States and France, and I'm inclined to think he was right." He leaned forward and stared hard at his visitor. "You are familiar with the uses of a pistol, I trust?"

"There's no better shot anywhere," Jeremy replied quietly, and meant it.

"And your sword is not merely a decoration?"

"I've fought my fair share of duels" was the laconic response.

"You may need both weapons in the days ahead. But our first task is to find out what the lady thinks of you."

"Lady?" Jeremy was surprised.

"We can do nothing until she has given her approval. Present yourself at the town palace of the duc d'Orléans on the rue du Roi at twelve o'clock. She will be expecting you and will conduct her own interview. When it is finished, come back to me."

Jeremy made an effort to remain polite. "You'll forgive me, General, if I find this air of mystery rather irritating."

"Of course." Lafayette nodded sympathetically, and there was a hint of humor in his eyes. "But when a woman is concerned, one must proceed with caution. Everything depends on whether or not she likes you, and I assure you it will be best for everyone concerned if I don't burden you with too many details before we learn her reaction to you. The whims of the female are unpredictable, and it could be that you will have made your journey here in vain. In that case you will enjoy the voyage back to America without cares."

Remembering Hamilton's warning not to return home unless he succeeded, Jeremy thrust his jaw forward. "Who is this lady?"

"The khana Tule Yasmin. The name means nothing to you? I thought not. She is a princess of royal blood from the East and has recently arrived as the state guest of France. She is the cousin of her overlord, Selim the Magnificent, the Ottoman emperor, and she is the sister of the khagan who is the ruler of the land of the Mongols. She is, I believe, the direct descendant of Genghis Khan and Kublai Khan. It is vital to your country and to mine, as I hope to be able to explain to you later, that the khana approve of you. Let me prepare you for the interview by telling you that I have rarely encountered anyone so difficult." The marquis passed a slender hand across his face.

"Could you be more explicit, General?" Jeremy had yet to meet the woman he could not charm and began to feel more at ease.

"You are an American, so you have been spared acquaintance with royalty. All who have royal blood in their veins are imperious, and Easterners, if the khana is a fair example, are the worst. Although she has been here for just a short time, she behaves as haughtily as if she were in Constantinople or Urga."

"Urga?"

"Her brother's capital. Remember when you see her that in the East a potentate has the power of life and death over his subjects. Her Sublimity cannot seem to realize that we view people in a somewhat different light." He smiled wearily. "Whatever you do, Morgan, please don't try to convert her to the American belief that all men are created equal. The very notion would be shocking to her."

A lieutenant came into the room to report that a riot had broken out in one of the workingmen's districts across the Seine, and the meeting came to an end. Jeremy returned to his inn, and after spending the remainder of the morning fruitlessly wondering what possible interest the United States could have in a princess from the distant land of Mongolia, he saddled his horse and rode to the small town palace of the duc d'Orléans.

The homes of most members of the higher nobility were surrounded day and night by jeering, insulting mobs, but the Orléans family was still popular because it was in favor of sweeping reforms. Hence the rue du Roi was virtually empty, and the sound of the horse's hooves echoed on the cobblestones. A servant in silk livery admitted Jeremy to the building and led him to a small drawing room furnished in simple but elegant cream and gold. The duc d'Orléans and his immediate ancestors had never succumbed to the ornate, rococo fashions that had become popular under the Bourbons.

The American was asked to wait, and after sitting on a low settee for the better part of an hour, he became annoyed as well as impatient. His knowledge of etiquette when dealing with royalty was nonexistent, but he felt an urge to send another servant to remind the princess that he was here. Several times he went to the door, but the corridor outside the room was empty, and so he had no choice but to continue to wait until such time as the imperious lady deigned to receive him. Her treatment humiliated him, and the longer he sat, the angrier he became.

At last he heard soft footsteps, and when he looked up he saw a young woman standing in the frame. His irritation promptly vanished, and he was so startled that he could only stare at her. From Lafayette's description he had expected the khana to be elderly and homely, and he was totally unprepared for a meeting with one of the loveliest young women he had ever seen.

Had Jeremy been unaware of her nationality he would have mistaken Tule Yasmin for a European. Her hair was piled high on her head in the latest French mode, and her skin was fair. Her eyes of deep, smoky green were of the West, and only the faint lift at the corners hinted at her Eastern ancestry. Obviously many of her forebears had been Circassians. The overall impression she created was contradictory and therefore confusing. She was tall, even by the standards of an American who had seen many pioneer women. But her bones were fine, and in spite of her height she seemed to be rather delicate. She held herself regally erect, but her hauteur embellished rather than detracted from the attractiveness of her beautifully sculptured face and lithe, slender body.

Her lips, rounded and full, when in repose formed in a shape that slightly resembled a pout. In some women the expression would have appeared sulky, but it added to the khana's appeal. Her eyes indicated an imperious reserve, but Jeremy was aware of a smoldering fire behind the look that instantly challenged him. He reacted to her immediately, and he felt an almost overwhelming urge to conquer her, but he reminded himself that he had to be circumspect, so he bowed to her and hoped she could not read the desire in his eyes.

Jeremy had imagined that the khana would be dressed in the Turkish style, with her figure hidden beneath layers

of billowing veils, but he was mistaken. Her gown was in
the latest French vogue, and by the circumspect standards
of the New World it was extremely daring. A bodice of
canary-yellow silk fitted low over her firm, high breasts,
and exposed the cleavage between them. Close-fitting
sleeves that began at the points of her shoulders were orna-
mented with tiny lavender bows, and a double row of
similar bows emphasized her tiny, supple waist. The dress
had two skirts, and the outer one of lavender was looped
high above the underskirt of canary satin.

Only a few deft touches were reminiscent of the East.
Miniature incense baskets of beaten silver, dangling from
fine silver chains, hung from her ears, and a necklace of
gem-studded, beaten silver half-moons with fringed edges
clung to her neck and rested in the hollow of her throat.
The shoes that showed beneath her gown could only have
come from the Orient, too; made of canary-yellow satin
and encrusted with silver discs, they had pointed, curled-
up toes, which were embroidered with silver braid.

The silence in the little drawing room grated on Jeremy,
and when he stood erect again he saw that the khana was
examining him carefully but impersonally. "Good morning,
Your Highness," he said.

Tule Yasmin seemed to stiffen. "We are called 'Your
Sublimity,' not 'Your Highness.' And you may address us
only when we grant you permission." She spoke in French,
as he had done.

A slow flush crept up Jeremy's neck and face, and he
had to remind himself forcibly that his future depended
on his ability to win the good will of this overbearing and
arrogant young woman. He bit back the quick retort that
came to his lips, but he discovered he was trembling with
impotent rage.

If the khana realized that he was obeying her command
only by exercising enormous self-control, she gave no sign
of it. Walking slowly into the room, she made a circle
around him, and something in her attitude reminded him
of the expressions of buyers at cattle and horse sales. At

last she drifted to the settee and sat; as she smoothed and arranged her skirts, Jeremy could not help thinking that in spite of her lordly manner she was unable to hide her femininity.

"We have been informed that you speak the tongue of the Ottomans. You have leave to address us in that language," she said, her voice incongruously high and sweet.

"The information given to Your Sublimity was correct," he replied in Turkish.

He spoke fluently, easily, and without a trace of accent, thanks to the long, intense instructions he had received from his late friend, Selim. The khana seemed surprised, and for a moment she dropped the barrier she had been at such pains to erect. "We were told you were once a man of the sea. You learned the tongue of the Prophet when you served in the galleys of our cousin the sultan after being captured by brigands in the Mediterranean, perhaps?"

The suggestion that he had ever been a slave made Jeremy indignant, and he forgot his pose of careful, balanced restraint. "Certainly not!" he said.

Apparently Tule Yasmin was amused, for she smiled condescendingly. "You were a janissary, then," she suggested. "Many Christians have fought under the banner of Selim the Magnificent."

"I have fought only for my own country, in the war that made us independent," he replied fiercely. "And I learned your language from a good friend, who was a Turk and who was killed in his native country when he was trampled by a horse belonging to a member of the aristocracy." Had Jeremy known that the rider of that horse was standing in front of him at this very moment, he would have been even more vehement.

Tule Yasmin ignored his ardor and looked him up and down speculatively. "You have the appearance of a fighting man," she said, and made the simple statement sound like a grudging admission.

Again Jeremy had the feeling that she was inspecting livestock. "My enemies know I have taken part in many battles." If she expected him to boast of his exploits, after the manner of the Moslems, she would be disappointed.

The khana seemed more interested in the substance of what he was saying than in his lack of graciousness. "You ride?"

"Of course," he said, and then added belatedly, "Your Sublimity."

"But you have never ridden a Mongolian pony?" she persisted.

"No, I—"

"Then it cannot truly be said that you have ever ridden a horse," she said smugly, her tone indicating that the subject was closed.

Never had Jeremy encountered such an irritating female, and had she been anyone but a princess whose good opinion of him was a vital necessity, he would have taken her across his knees and spanked her. Under the circumstances, however, he could only shrug.

"You may approach closer to our person," she said, and stood.

He walked toward her slowly, warily. For an instant he had the absurd feeling that she was going to reach out and pinch the muscles in his arms. But she remained motionless and gazed at him calmly for such a long time that he began to grow tense. Although he was more than six feet tall, she could look at him without raising her head, and their eyes met, then held. Jeremy felt that a battle of wills was in progress, and when the khana did not turn away he continued to look at her steadily.

"Well?" he demanded at last.

Perhaps she was unaccustomed to such blunt speech, and she seemed inclined to lose sight of the fact that she had not given him permission to address her. Suddenly and unexpectedly she laughed, and for a moment she looked like a carefree young girl rather than a self-consciously imperious member of a powerful royal house. "Impudence is unpardonable," she said, "but in this instance it pleases us. We have use only for a man of spirit."

Before he could probe the meaning of her cryptic comment, she extended her hand to him to kiss. It was the first time in his life he had performed such a gesture, and as he bent over her long, slender fingers he felt gauche and a little foolish. "You have leave to withdraw," she told him. "You may inform the marquis de Lafayette that we find you satisfactory and that we will consequently tolerate no further delays."

He walked out of the door before he remembered that it was improper to turn one's back on royalty, but by then it was too late. However, it did not matter, Jeremy told himself. In their future dealings—and it was clear that they were to see each other again—she would learn that he was neither a galley slave nor a craven servant who would jump when she snapped her fingers. An American bent his back to no one, as she would discover.

On the ride to the headquarters of the National Guard he tried without success to dispel the air of mystery that had enveloped his mission from the beginning. Any number of ideas, none of them logical or reasonable, came to his mind, but he rejected them one by one. He would know the answers soon enough now, he thought.

The usual mobs were in the streets, and several groups attempted to halt him, but he was concentrating so hard that he was barely conscious of them. He unconsciously urged his horse forward, and once, when the mob refused to give ground, he absently reached for his sword. Perhaps the Parisians realized that he was a man who would tolerate no nonsense, for crowds, like individuals, could sometimes sense a man's strength. In any event he completed his ride without incident and hurried to the suite of the commander-in-chief of the guard.

The marquis de Lafayette was in conference with his staff, and Jeremy had to cool his heels for more than half an hour before he was finally admitted to the general's presence. But this time he was more eager than ever to learn his assignment, for he had been thinking incessantly about the khana while he had been waiting, and he had to admit to himself that although she annoyed him beyond measure, she fascinated him, too. Lafayette looked tired and depressed, but when he heard Tule Yasmin's message he brightened at once.

"At last!" he said, and sighed deeply in relief. "So she wants no delay, eh? Perfect! She cannot be more anxious than I am."

Jeremy sat without waiting to be invited. "Do you suppose," he asked with a wry smile, "that it would be too much to tell me the nature of my mission now?"

The marquis shook off his weariness, rose, and walked to the window, from which he could see the magnificently landscaped gardens of the Tuileries. "Her Sublimity," he said, "has been a source of embarrassment and potential danger to France, not to mention that she has also been a sharp thorn in my side when I have been trying to devote myself to the cause of keeping the peace here. Thanks either to ignorance or indifference, she chose the worst of all possible times for a visit to France. The sultan of Turkey sent her here as his personal emissary, so it was necessary to receive her with full honors, of course. But royalty has been increasingly unpopular in the city, as you have probably gathered. Parisians do not care if they spill the blood of Bourbons or of Ottomans. Although she has recently arrived, it has been necessary for me to restrict her movements and forbid her to leave the house which the duc d'Orléans so kindly lent her."

Jeremy nodded and tried to control his impatience. He could not see how the problems of the Mongol princess concerned the United States.

"I have been badly frightened, I can tell you, and so has First Minister Mirabeau," Lafayette continued. "If any harm should befall Her Sublimity, our relations with the Turks would suffer. France cannot afford bad relations with our foreign allies when we are weakened at home, as I am sure you will understand."

Jeremy was about to reply, but the marquis, turning away from the window, held up a hand and silenced him.

"From the start it has been our wish to send her back to Constantinople, and as social life here has been sharply curtailed, she has wished to leave without delay. I'm sure she has been bored, although that is beside the point. I suggested to her that she might be able to depart without calling attention to herself if she dressed inconspicuously and traveled modestly, without her retinue. Certain risks would be involved, of course, and I myself have been loath to allow her to chance them. The possibility has always existed that even if the princess should travel in disguise, someone would recognize her. The people of Paris would like nothing better than to crack the head of a woman who is called 'Her Sublimity,' and even in the provinces she would not be safe. Now, you will ask, why do I not send her out of the country with an escort of a company or two of guardsmen?"

"I must admit I was wondering just that," Jeremy said.

"I will be frank with you, Morgan. In the first place I cannot spare the men. And in the second place I'm not certain that I could depend on my troops once they were not under my immediate supervision. Such problems are irrelevant, however, as the khana flatly refuses to do anything that would reduce her stature or cause her to be accused of cowardice. She feels that she would suffer what the Easterners call loss of face, and although I cannot truly appreciate the position she has taken, I certainly sympathize with it."

Jeremy knew from experience that everyone in the Ottoman Empire was constantly concerned over the almost indefinable subtleties of "face," which were incomprehensible to Westerners. He could understand why Tule Yasmin felt as she did, even though he would not have been able to explain her stand. Only someone who had lived with the Turks would know why she was being so stubborn.

"Let us now examine the predicament of the United States for a moment," Lafayette said. "America is my second home, and I feel as strongly for her as I do for

France. Your country is in grave difficulties, Morgan. France helped you win your independence, but if England were to attack you now, there is nothing we could do to save you, nothing. America needs friends."

"So Secretary Hamilton told me."

"Colonel Hamilton is a wise and farseeing man. And while I have great respect for Secretary Jefferson, I must admit that he deals better with principles than with the vagaries of human behavior. A treaty—even diplomatic recognition of the United States by Turkey—would hold the English fleet at bay. For the past ten months Jefferson has tried to establish diplomatic relations with the sultan. He has sent three ambassadors to Constantinople, one after another, but Selim has refused to admit any of them into his presence."

"That doesn't surprise me," Jeremy murmured thoughtfully.

"Nor did it surprise Colonel Hamilton. We correspond regularly, and when he learned of my predicament with the khana, he concocted one of those superb schemes that come so easily to his fertile mind. He proposed that an American should act as the princess's unofficial escort to Constantinople. Obviously he would need to be a man who would be ready and able to fight for her, should it be necessary, in order to enable her to leave France." Lafayette smiled at his guest. "Judging by your expression, you already see the rest of the plan."

"Yes, I do." Jeremy jumped to his feet and began to pace up and down the office. "Hamilton believes that the khana will be grateful if she's delivered safely to Selim's palace. As well she should be. Then I'm to ask for something in return. The privilege of an audience with the sultan. It will be my task to convince him that it will be to his advantage to exchange ambassadors with the United States."

"You're as quick-witted as Hamilton led me to believe."

"I can see a great deal now," Jeremy went on, pacing even more rapidly. "I couldn't understand the need for so much secrecy. It's obvious why I had to come here in an unofficial capacity, and why, when I escort the khana, it will be as a private citizen. In that way the United States won't be embarrassed in any way if I should fail."

Lafayette was about to interrupt but decided to wait.

"There's another reason for all the stealth." Jeremy halted for a moment and laughed. "Naturally the Department of State knows nothing about the scheme, and Mr. Jefferson would resent Hamilton's interference if he learned about it. If I succeed, the whole story can be brought out into the open, and Jefferson will be in no position to object. If I don't, Hamilton will have lost nothing, and what Jefferson doesn't know won't hurt him—or the United States." Nothing less than complete and unqualified success would be meaningful, Jeremy realized. If he failed, he would remain a nonentity who would be unable to return home.

The easiest part of his assignment, he thought, would be to escort Tule Yasmin to Constantinople, and he dismissed that portion of the task from his mind. It would be far more difficult to persuade the sultan to welcome an American ambassador at his court and to send an envoy to the United States in return. Even the most enlightened Turks hated all Christian nations, so he would have to struggle against great odds to win the trust of a man who was deeply, if falsely, prejudiced against his nation. It would be to his advantage to win the friendship and confidence of the khana on the journey and to learn all he could from her about the habits and tastes, likes and dislikes of Selim.

He came back to the immediate present when he realized that Lafayette was speaking. "I have reason to believe," the marquis said, "that certain obstacles will be placed in your path after you reach the Turkish capital. The English, as I hope you know, are not stupid, and they undoubtedly realize that Turkish recognition of the United States would not serve their best interests. Our envoy in Constantinople has told us repeatedly that there are English agents operating in secret there. We don't know who they are, nor have we any information as to whether they are

English or Turks in the employ of London. But you may be sure that if they learn of your mission, they'll do everything in their power to hamper you."

Jeremy's eyes became dark, as they always did when trouble threatened. "They won't stop me," he said.

"For your sake as well as that of the United States, I hope not," Lafayette replied. "Unfortunately our envoy will not be able to help you, as we need to maintain friendly relations with England these days. Our official interest will end when the khana reaches Constantinople. But you will not find us lacking in gratitude for your help to us, and when you return here on your way back to New York, we will make you a gift of one hundred dollars in your own currency. I wish it could be more, but our funds are limited. If you wish, you may consider our payment as something of a dowry."

"A dowry?" Jeremy glanced across the room and saw that the marquis's expression was enigmatic.

"The princess insists on traveling in a style befitting her rank, as I've already tried to explain to you. There are thousands of my compatriots who have lost all respect for royalty and who would enjoy nothing more than to destroy her possessions and do her personal injury." Lafayette hesitated and took a deep breath. "I have saved the core of Colonel Hamilton's scheme for the last. It certainly demonstrates his brilliance, although I am not certain you'll agree. You are to marry the khana Tule Yasmin before you leave Paris."

Jeremy was too stunned to reply.

"As your wife, she will travel not as an Ottoman princess but as Mistress Jeremy Morgan. You will carry the documents that will prove she is the legitimate wife of an American citizen. In that way, but only in that way, will it be possible to escort her out of France in safety. My countrymen have an enormous admiration and respect for the United States, and under this plan we will trade heavily on that love. Otherwise it would have been easy enough to secure the services of a Dane or a citizen of one of the

German states. But I am convinced, just as Colonel Hamilton is, that the whole scheme will succeed only because the khana will be married to an American."

A violent protest would be useless, Jeremy knew. He was trapped. Through the years he had made love to many women but had never seriously considered marriage to any of them. He had always clung to the thought that someday he would meet a girl he would truly love and would settle down with her in marriage, and the realization that he was being forced now to give his name to a woman for the sake of political convenience infuriated him. It was a moment before he could control his rage sufficiently to speak rationally.

"Such an arrangement is satisfactory to the khana?" It was absurd even to think of having a wife who insisted on being addressed as "Your Sublimity."

"Naturally it will be a marriage in name only," Lafayette said distinctly. "And the union, such as it is, will be terminated after your arrival in Constantinople. Divorce is never difficult under Moslem law and will be particularly simple for a member of the royal family. In the meantime you might think of the advantages you'll enjoy, even temporarily, as a cousin by marriage to the sultan Selim."

Jeremy knew the marquis was right and tried to concentrate on the practical aspects of the matter. But he was distracted by memories of the close inspection to which the khana had subjected him. It was possible, he conjectured, that in spite of the temporary nature of the alliance, Tule Yasmin might not be thinking in terms of as formal and impersonal a marriage as Lafayette imagined.

"The ceremony will take place tomorrow morning, immediately prior to your departure from Paris," the marquis said. "Be ready to leave as soon as it is finished. It will be performed by a Swedish minister who happens to be in Paris and who has kindly consented to officiate. I chose him partly because it's preferable that no French cleric subjects himself and my nation to a possible charge of conspiracy, and in part because I felt sure you would prefer a Protestant clergyman."

"That's very kind of you," Jeremy said dryly.

The irony was not lost on Lafayette, but he chose to ignore it. He walked back to his desk, then sat down and searched for a moment through a pile of papers. "I have a message from Colonel Hamilton for you. He asked me to read it to you after all the other arrangements were concluded."

"Oh?"

"I don't understand his meaning, but I presume that you will. Here it is." The marquis found several folded sheets of paper inscribed in Hamilton's characteristically bold hand. "He wishes you well, and he expresses the hope that you will be more successful than the husband of Penelope Fielding."

Alexander Hamilton knew, then, of Jeremy's betrayal with Penelope and was quietly enjoying the last laugh.

A freezing rain began to fall shortly before dawn, and a few hours later it changed to snow. The skies were leaden, but Jeremy's spirits improved when an orderly arrived from the headquarters of the National Guard, bringing him a brief note and a gift from the marquis de Lafayette. The general regretted his inability to attend the wedding in person, but he assured the American that the coachmen who would drive the khana's party would lend him every possible assistance in case of need. They were guardsmen who would travel in disguise, and they were the most reliable and trustworthy members of the organization their commander in chief could find. The gift was even more welcome, for it proved to be a lively sorrel gelding from Lafayette's own stables, and Jeremy vastly preferred the mount to the tired horse he had rented.

He wrapped his cloak around him as he rode through the streets to the little town palace of the duc d'Orléans, with his spare clothing and his few other worldly possessions in a saddlebag. His sword was at his side, and his pistol, which he had oiled and loaded, was in his belt. The day was similar to many Jeremy had known during winter storms at sea and in the Ohio Valley, and he thought it ironic that in those times he had always looked forward to possible excitement and adventure. But at this moment he felt nothing and could only conclude that the situation in which he found himself was so strange, so bizarre that it robbed him of all feeling.

When he arrived at the palace, however, his sense of anticlimax began to evaporate. As he left his horse with a groom, he saw that three carriages were standing in the courtyard, and he wondered if any of them could have brought guests to the wedding. A solemn majordomo led him through a maze of rooms and corridors to a small chapel at the rear of the ground floor. There he discovered that the only "guests" were several members of the household staff, who looked at him with expressionless faces. The chapel was lighted by a score of long, smokeless tapers, and their reflection played softly on the multicolored panes of the high stained-glass windows. The air was fragrant and sweet, and Jeremy saw that incense was burning in two small brass pots before a simple altar of carved oak.

A moment after he arrived the minister entered, severe in an untrimmed black robe. He introduced himself as the Reverend Mr. Arneldson, but he was a taciturn man, and after giving Jeremy several papers to sign, he fell silent. For the next quarter of an hour or more Jeremy stood, shifting his weight from one foot to the other and wondering if what was happening was real or whether he was dreaming the whole incident. He began to think his imagination had indeed played tricks on him; then he heard a stir at the rear of the chapel, and when he turned he knew better.

The khana Tule Yasmin walked slowly down the short aisle, unaccompanied, and although she did not look like any bride Jeremy had ever seen, she was nevertheless ravishingly beautiful. Her hair had been freshly dressed for the occasion in a series of waves that swept to a peak at the crown of her head, and from her ears hung a pair of miniature gold scimitars suspended from strands of perfectly matched, deep red rubies. Her lips were rouged, and a shining black cream had been dabbed on her eyelashes, but in the candlelight her face looked pale. Jeremy bowed to her and thought that the lack of color in her cheeks enhanced her loveliness.

Only a woman of great wealth could have afforded the dress she had chosen, and no one but a princess who set her own standards would have dared to wear it. A double rope of pearls and rubies edged the wide, shockingly low neck of the pearl satin gown, then crossed between her breasts and was bound and fastened at her waist. Her sweeping skirt was embroidered in gold, pearls, and rubies, and several bracelets glittered on her bare arms. Jeremy stared at her and thought incongruously of the American frontier, where a ten-pound sack of milled flour and a side of bear bacon were often considered luxuries.

The khana inclined her head slightly in greeting the minister, but she did not acknowledge Jeremy's presence in any way as she took her place at his side before the altar. Before the wedding could begin there were a number of papers that she, too, had to sign, and she seemed to be impatient as she went through the routines. Then the Reverend Mr. Arneldson was ready to begin, and he intoned the brief service rapidly, pausing only when it was necessary for one or the other of the principals to reply to a question. Jeremy gave his responses in a loud, clear voice, which sounded rather surly and resentful in his own ears. Tule Yasmin spoke quietly, and he thought there was a trace of amusement in her tone.

It suddenly occurred to him that he had made no provision for a wedding ring, but the majordomo came to his rescue at the right moment and handed him a wide band of gold set with rubies. As he slipped it onto the khana's finger, it crossed his mind that she had obviously seen it previously and had either dressed accordingly or had selected a band that would match her clothes.

Suddenly the ceremony was over. The minister looked first at Jeremy, then at the khana. Neither moved, and the Reverend Mr. Arneldson frowned at them. "It is customary at this time," he said in an annoyed voice, "for the groom to kiss the bride."

Jeremy needed no urging, and as he turned to Tule Yasmin he saw that she was startled. Either she did not know of the practice or else had thought it unnecessary; in either event she was too surprised to object. And Jeremy gave her no chance. Placing his arms around her, he drew her quickly to him and kissed her. She seemed to yield to him for a moment, and his hold on her became tighter. Then she slid a hand to the back of his head as though to caress him, and when he felt the gesture he was elated. But his joy faded when she surreptitiously dug her long, lacquered fingernails into his neck. He kissed her still harder, and she clawed at him more viciously, until he felt sharp pains shooting up his scalp.

He released her then, and the khana, completely in control of herself, smiled at him tranquilly and impersonally. Jeremy knew there were undoubtedly deep scratches on his neck, but she had been so deft that not one of the witnesses realized it. The minister was smiling jovially, and he handed the principals still more papers to sign, along with the official register, and then the members of the household staff had to put their names on the documents, too. Apparently they had been chosen to see the ceremony because they knew how to write, and Jeremy realized that nothing connected with his wedding had been left to chance.

The Reverend Mr. Arneldson shook hands with everyone present and departed, and the servants, bowing low, left hastily. Jeremy was alone with the khana, and it suddenly occurred to him that they had not yet spoken a single word to each other. Tule Yasmin gave him no chance to address her now. "You will see that our trunks and cases are in place and that all is made ready for our immediate departure," she said, speaking in Turkish. "We will change

into more suitable attire for traveling, and as we will not
be gone long, see to it that you do not tarry." She swept
out of the chapel, leaving her bridegroom alone under the
flickering tapers.

Rousing himself, Jeremy rubbed the back of his neck
gingerly as he picked up his cloak and his hat. Then he
hurried to the courtyard, and when he arrived there he
halted in dismay. All three of the carriages, it was plain,
were going to be used to transport the khana and her entourage. Palace servants were lashing mounds of leather
boxes to the tops of each of the vehicles, and a number
of veiled women in the long, shapeless dresses of Turkish
servants were milling around, chattering anxiously. There
were eight of them, he realized, after carefully checking
his count.

He began to understand that the trip through France
might not be as easy to accomplish as he had so blithely
supposed. The three carriages, the servingwomen, and the
mountains of luggage would make them conspicuous everywhere, and there were sure to be problems no matter where
they went. His expression apparently mirrored his feelings,
for a man in the livery of a coachman came up to him
and smiled ruefully.

"It won't be an easy time for any of us, monsieur," he
said.

"We'll be lucky if we get half these things out of the
country," Jeremy replied bitterly.

"What you mean, monsieur, is that we'll be lucky if
we're alive by the time we cross the border into Italy. But
it's like I told the general when he asked me to take this
job: You can rely on me, monsieur. Sergeant Devereaux
has never failed in his duty to France, and the general
has explained to me how important it is that the lady be
preserved from harm. The others will do their part, too,"
he added, nodding in the direction of two similarly dressed
men who were conversing with each other in low tones at
the opposite side of the courtyard. "They're only corporals,

of course," he said self-importantly, "but they're good fellows."

Jeremy shook hands with Sergeant Devereaux and then took pains to make himself agreeable to the others as well. Unless he missed his guess, all four of them would see more action than any of them would find pleasant in the days to come. Shivering in the wet snow, Jeremy caught a glimpse of his own reflection in one of the windows of a carriage, and he smiled wryly. He had often been told he was an opportunist, and he had always agreed with the designation. To some it had meant that he was an unsavory person, but he had always been proud to consider himself as a practical man, a realist who would do anything to advance himself in the world provided that he would not suffer. Yet here he stood, damp and cold in the biting wind, waiting for the woman who was now his "wife" and whom he would have to lead out of a country on the brink of revolution. Glancing again at the Turkish servingwomen, he told himself he must be mad.

At last all of the boxes were made secure, and the khana's servants climbed into the second and third carriages; they would have drawn the blinds, but Jeremy hurried to them and ordered them to leave the glass uncovered at all times. They would surely be halted every five minutes if they tried to conceal themselves and thus arouse the curiosity of the French. The eyes of the women above their veils revealed their fright, but they obeyed with alacrity: It was enough for them to hear a man giving commands to them in their own tongue.

The first carriage, which was being held for the khana, was far more ornate and spacious than any conveyance Jeremy had ever seen in the United States, and as he examined it, he wondered angrily whether there was anything else the princess could possibly do to call attention to herself. The padded seats were of thick maroon velvet, the ceiling was gilded, and ornately carved little chests of drawers were set into the woodwork on either side for the convenience of passengers who might want to unpack some of their personal belongings and have them close at hand on a long journey. The rear seat was wide enough to accommodate four persons, and a woman would not be cramped if she chose to lie down on it. A thick fur robe was neatly folded in one corner, and a hamper containing various food delicacies sat on the floor.

It was warm and dry in the coach, and Jeremy decided to wait in it until the khana made her appearance. She was certainly taking her time in spite of her admonition that she would be ready very shortly, and Jeremy thought that the longer they delayed, the closer they would still be to Paris at nightfall. She was doing everything in her power to complicate his task. However, he had long ago learned that it was a waste of time to harbor resentment over anything he could not control, and he began to study the map of the route they would take. The journey to Venice, where a Turkish galley would meet them, could not be made via Switzerland at this time of year, as the mountain passes were uncertain. That meant they would have to travel south across the face of the better part of France to the Mediterranean, and not until they left Nice behind them and crossed into northern Italy would they be truly safe.

Jeremy was so engrossed in the map that he failed to hear a commotion outside, and he did not know that Tule Yasmin had finally made her appearance until she opened the door and stood at the entrance to the carriage, glaring at him. She was wrapped in a long coat and hood of rich, almost black sable, which she wore in obvious total disregard of the feelings the French people were demonstrating against any show of ostentation or wealth. She looked very feminine and very sweet; however, her voice was anything but lovely as she tapped a royal foot on the courtyard cobblestones. "You will leave our carriage at once! We will not tolerate such familiarity again!"

Jeremy wanted to ask just how she proposed to keep him at a distance when she would be in his charge for many days to come. It would serve no useful purpose to antagonize her unnecessarily, however, and he knew that at best he would have no easy task to win her gratitude sufficiently to enable him to accomplish his mission. He climbed slowly out of the carriage and silently handed her into it. All of the others in the courtyard were watching them, and he was glad that neither the National Guardsmen nor the French servants understood Turkish. His position was sufficiently humiliating without being forced to undergo additional embarrassment.

He mounted his horse, the guardsmen climbed onto the boxes of the carriages, and he gave the signal to depart. The little caravan rolled out into the rue du Roi, and Jeremy took his place to the left of the khana's coach, near to the window at which she sat. She was gazing out, and she seemed to look through him and beyond him, as though he did not exist. It was probable, he thought, that she resented his proximity and would prefer to have him ride elsewhere, but he had no intention of changing his position in the cavalcade, no matter how unpleasant she might become. Her safety was his direct, immediate responsibility, and he intended to remain close to her at all times, no matter how violently she might protest.

The weather, Jeremy told himself, was in their favor, for comparatively few people were abroad, and those whom the party encountered seemed intent on their own affairs. However, Sergeant Devereaux was taking no chances: He avoided the streets where riots had taken place in the past, and he stayed as far as possible from the avenues that the nobility normally used when they crossed the city. Nevertheless he had to drive down thoroughfares broad enough to permit passage space for the carriages, and when he directed his team of horses onto one of these, the Street of Stonemasons, trouble promptly developed.

Jeremy was the first to see that a blockade had been erected a short distance down the street, but by the time he called out a warning the second coach had followed the first, and it was too late to turn back. A group of men in rough clothing was ignoring the snow and was keeping warm by drinking what appeared to be either wine or cheap brandy out of earthenware jugs. When they saw the first carriage, they raced toward it, gesturing and shouting. They swarmed all over the street, so Sergeant Devereaux had no choice but to bring his vehicle to a halt, and the other guardsmen behind him were forced to do the same.

The noise seemed to arouse the neighborhood, and people began to appear from houses on both sides of the street, hurriedly donning coats and cloaks. Jeremy exchanged a significant glance with the sergeant, and both of them sat very still, avoiding any sign or gesture that the crowd might consider hostile. The khana continued to sit at her window, her expression one of bored indifference. Either she was utterly fearless, Jeremy thought, or she failed to realize the extent of the danger that threatened.

One of the workers, a burly red-faced man, pushed through the throng and brandished a jug over his head. "Drink!" he shouted, his unsteady gait and thick speech indicating that he had been following his own advice. "All who want to get through this street must drink to the death of kings!"

Wild cheers greeted his words, and someone else roared above the din, "Drink to the people! Long may they prosper!"

Tule Yasmin sat erect in her carriage, and Jeremy saw she had grown so pale that her face looked as though it had been chiseled out of marble. She would never drink any such toast, he knew, but if the mob discovered her attitude there would surely be bloodshed. This was the worst of all possible predicaments, and it had developed so rapidly that he did not know how to handle it.

The Parisians pressed closer. The self-appointed leader peered inside the coach, and after squeezing between it and Jeremy's gelding, he tried to open the door, only to discover that it was locked from the inside. "Who is that?" he demanded, pointing a thick, grimy finger at the princess. "Take those damned furs away from her and I'll tell you who she is—nobody. She'll be no better than the rest of us then!"

When the shouts of approval began to die down, Jeremy smiled affably, and anyone who did not know him would have imagined that he was actually enjoying himself. "She happens to be my wife, lads!" he called.

The leader pressed his nose against the glass of the window. "She's a foreigner!" he announced.

An old woman in a tattered coat and stocking cap shook her fist. "Marie Antoinette is a foreigner, too," she screamed shrilly. "Kill all the foreign bitches who think they're better than us!"

Jeremy half stood in his saddle and cupped his hands. "We're no better than you, and no worse, either," he shouted, doing his best to sound jovial. "It so happens that I'm a citizen of a nation that owes its very existence to France. If it weren't for you—and you—and you," he continued, jabbing a finger in the direction of several of the most belligerent, "my country would still be a land of colonials instead of a race of free and independent men. I'm an American!"

His announcement caused a sharp change in the climate, for the French were well aware of the contribution their volunteers had made to the cause of American freedom, and virtually every curbstone orator in Paris paid lip service to the American ideals of equality and liberty. Jeremy realized he had not yet won over the mob, but he had created a distraction, and for the moment attention had been diverted from the khana. "Why shouldn't she wear furs?" he asked. "Why shouldn't every last one of you wear furs?"

The questions weren't logical, but the women in the crowd began to smile and nod, and the men seemed less angry. The burly leader, however, was apparently annoyed at the idea that he might be cheated out of his prey. "How do we know you're what you say?" he demanded. "How do we know this woman is your wife?"

"You want to see my papers. Fair enough." Jeremy started to reach into his pocket.

But the heavyset man was not interested in proof. "Papers

mean nothing. Papers can be forged. You're a damned royalist pig, and so is the woman!"

Jeremy leaned down and handed the documents to a middle-aged man with alert, intelligent eyes, who seemed to be sober. "Examine these and you'll discover I'm telling the truth," he said, and turned back to the burly leader. "All this talk makes me thirsty." He snatched the jug and held it aloft. "Death to all royalists!" He tilted the mouth to his lips and almost choked on the raw liquor. It burned his throat, but he continued to grin.

The man was not satisfied. "What about them?" he cried, pointing at the Turkish servingwomen in the other two carriages. "I suppose you're going to tell me they're Americans, too!"

The crowd became ominously quiet; the drunken leader had, with unerring instinct, touched a vitally sensitive spot. Jeremy realized that almost no explanation he might give would be accepted. The Parisians were in a mood that would be satisfied only when they had seen violence done, and he had to give them what they wanted.

He surveyed the situation rapidly, while continuing to smile. Sergeant Devereaux, he was pleased to see, was sitting quietly on the box of the coach and was making no attempt to reach for the pistol under his short cape. The other two guardsmen were pretending to be placid, too, so it was still possible to prevent an explosion, provided that no one tried to question the khana. Tule Yasmin, Jeremy knew, would not demean herself by lying or trying in any way to placate the mob, and if the people became aware of her attitude she would be badly mauled. It would be equally dangerous to allow any of her servingwomen to be dragged out into the open; if one of them should become hysterical, the display of emotion might inflame the crowd.

In fact, the mere suggestion that the eight women were servants could start a riot, and Jeremy knew he had to act decisively and quickly. Pretending to be angry, he tossed the jug to someone in the crowd and jumped to the ground. His mind always functioned coolly in a moment of crisis, and although he seemed to be in a towering rage, he had never been in more complete command of himself. He took his precious documents from the man to whom he had given them and handed them up to Sergeant Devereaux, along with his sword and pistol, which he removed with exaggerated flourishes. Then, after tossing his reins to an elderly man with ink-stained fingers, he turned to the bully.

"I don't like your questions!" Jeremy said loudly. "And I'm damned if I'm going to answer them." That, he thought, was the best possible way to avoid saying anything about the servingwomen. "You like to prattle about equality, don't you? Well, here's your chance. An American is going to teach you the real meaning of the word!"

He was delighted to see that his challenge suited the temper of the people, and he knew he had judged them correctly. Excited by the promise of sport, they began to surge forward until someone cried, "Give them room, give them room!"

Jeremy stood still for a moment, until he could be sure that most of the onlookers had a clear view of what was happening. Then, flexing his hands, he moved toward the burly man, who was standing with his head lowered and his shoulders hunched, looking like an animal about to spring. "Now, then!" Jeremy said, and his right fist lashed out.

His blow caught the Parisian on the lower lip; blood spurted out, and the throng howled in glee. But the workman was not seriously hurt. The freely flowing cut merely enraged him, and he lunged at his antagonist. Jeremy sidestepped neatly, almost contemptuously, but a wild swing of the other's left caught him just above the eye and caused him to lose his balance on the slippery cobbles. He dropped to one knee, and before he could recover, the Frenchman landed on top of him, sending him sprawling. They grappled and, pounding each other unmercifully, rolled over and over. Fights of this sort were common in Paris, and the workman had learned the art as a child in the gutters of the city, but Jeremy was a graduate of an even sterner school. Rough-and-tumble, as it was practiced on the American frontier, was a deadly pastime, and a bout in the wilderness country rarely ended until one of the participants was either dead or unconscious. No holds were barred, gouging and biting and kneeing were common, and no one ever gave or requested quarter.

Jeremy knew every trick that a man needed to win a free-for-all, but he was reluctant to use tactics that might seriously maim his opponent. His sole purpose in this fight was to satisfy the bloodlust of the crowd and to insure a safe and speedy exit from Paris for the khana, and he bore no real grudge against the workman. But he quickly discovered that he had underrated his opponent: The Frenchman was powerful and had consumed just enough brandy to make him reckless. His thick legs held Jeremy in a vise, his left arm curled around the American's neck, and his right fist smashed repeatedly into Jeremy's face and body.

Jeremy had to respond in kind or be overwhelmed, and when a particularly solid punch on the side of his head made him groggy, he summoned his reserves of energy and struck back furiously. The Seneca Indians, the fiercest of the Iroquois nations, never bothered to defend themselves in a fight but relied completely on the vehemence of their attack to achieve victory, and Jeremy knew how to use their techniques. Ignoring the blows that bruised and jarred him, he jabbed repeatedly at the fleshy face of his foe, striking the same spots again and again. Gradually the workingman's left eye began to swell, and eventually it closed. His lip was bleeding again, too, this time profusely.

The crowd was screaming wildly now, but neither man was aware of the commotion, and when the Frenchman uttered a shriek of pain and frustration, only Jeremy heard him. Suddenly the nature of the fight changed, and the people fell silent when they saw their compatriot raise a bone-handled butcher's knife into the air. He slashed blindly, frenziedly, and Jeremy escaped death by inches. His instinct rather than his reason saved him, for his opponent had drawn the knife so quickly that he was unprepared for the vicious assault. As the blade descended, Jeremy jerked to one side involuntarily, and the steel, which otherwise would have cut deep into his chest, merely ripped through the fabric of his sleeve. The shock numbed him for an instant, and in that moment he knew he was engaged in a fight to the death.

He had to equalize the odds again at all costs, and he fought desperately for possession of the knife. The fingers of his left hand closed around the workingman's thick wrist, and he hung on desperately in spite of the other's mad efforts to wrench free. Once more they rolled over and over on the cobbles, struggling viciously for the knife. Jeremy's fingers ached, and he was dizzy, but he knew that if he lost his grip he would surely be killed. With a supreme effort he shook off his sense of panic and forced himself to think clearly.

Common sense told him that the Frenchman, who was huskier and heavier, held the natural advantage, and the knife was still in his possession, too. Therefore Jeremy knew that he could win only if he utilized his superior intelligence. He searched for an idea, and when one occurred to him he did not hesitate, even though he knew he was taking a frightful risk. Pretending that a punch had finished him, he fell back onto the street in what appeared to be a stupor, and in doing so he released his foe's wrist. The Frenchman, gasping for breath but still strong, snarled triumphantly and raised the knife for the kill. Then, at the precise instant that he was about to strike, Jeremy came to life.

The American's knee drove hard into the heavier man's fleshy paunch, and he brought the top of his head up sharply under the other's broad jaw. The impact could be heard by all of the stunned spectators, and as they watched, Jeremy pressed his advantage and lashed out with a hard, short left to his opponent's pain-drawn face. The knife thrust had gone wild, of course, but the dazed Frenchman was not ready to give up, and he lifted his arm to try again. But this time his movements were slow and feeble, and

Jeremy ended the fight with a devastating punch, full in the face, which he delivered with every ounce of his remaining energy.

The burly Frenchman moaned and fell back onto the street, and as he lost consciousness the butcher's knife slid from his hand and clattered onto the cobbles. Jeremy picked it up, stood, and swayed unsteadily until he caught his breath. After a moment or two his strength flowed back into him, and brushing himself off, he jammed the knife into his belt. The crowd was watching him nervously, uncertain of his mood, and he forced himself to smile broadly.

"Does anyone else dispute my nationality? My documents prove I'm an American, and so does the way I fight. But if there's someone who doesn't believe it, I'll be glad to convince him."

The crowd laughed, and he knew he had won the sympathy of the people even before he saw the relief on Sergeant Devereaux's face. No nobleman would have behaved as he had, and he knew that his generosity to his fallen opponent had won the appreciation of the throng, too. The man had tried to kill him, but the vengeance he had exacted had been mild, and he sensed that the Parisians were inclined to be magnanimous to him in return. But he had to act quickly, before an unthinking word from someone transformed them into an ugly mob again.

"I thank you for the afternoon's entertainment," he said, and snatched a jug from one of the men standing nearest to him. Pretending he liked the brandy, he swallowed a small amount of the stuff and then moved toward the khana's carriage. "I'm sure my wife is thirsty, too, after the day's sport," he declared, and placed a hand on the latch.

Jeremy realized that he was dealing with an unknown quantity in Tule Yasmin, and that if she kept the door locked they would again be in grave danger. To his infinite relief she raised the latch, and he quickly jerked the door open. Her face was wooden as she looked at him, but he felt the cold hostility in her eyes, and he was afraid the crowd would see it, too. "Come out," he said softly, and when she did not respond instantly, he reached in, caught hold of her wrist, and pulled her into the street.

She stood beside him, erect and unmoving, facing the throng proudly, ignoring the murmur that went up as the mob admired her beauty. Jeremy held out the jug to her, hoping she would have the sense to take it from him and to satisfy the crowd with a token sip. But she remained motionless, and Jeremy did not hesitate. Slipping an arm around her waist, he drew her close to him and prayed that the crowd would interpret his act as a gesture of playful affection.

"Drink some of this," he whispered to her fiercely, raising the jug to her lips. "Drink, or I swear to you in the name of Allah that I'll pour it down your throat."

Because he gave her no choice, the khana was forced to swallow a little brandy. Jeremy was sure she had never before tasted such raw spirits, and although he could feel her shudder slightly, not a single flicker indicating her revulsion crossed her face. By her standards, he thought, it would be a sign of weakness to let commoners see her feelings, and for once her pride served them well. The crowd cheered her, and Jeremy quickly turned her around and shoved her toward the coach. She started to climb into it, her dignity intact, and suddenly Jeremy knew what would convince the mob beyond all doubt that they were not dealing with members of the nobility. Reaching out roguishly, he slapped the khana hard on the backside.

Tule Yasmin slammed the door behind her, but the Parisians were laughing too hard to be aware of her icy indignation. Jeremy took full advantage of their good humor, and handing the jug to the nearest spectator, he retrieved his weapons from Sergeant Devereaux and mounted his horse. He did not dare glance at the khana, and he felt positive she would hate him for humiliating her and subjecting her to public ridicule, but regardless of her reaction, he had assured her safety.

"Come with us to the gates!" he shouted, as though the entire experience was a lark.

He was overjoyed when he saw several men remove the barricades, and he knew beyond all doubt that he had won. The crowd, now in a holiday mood, formed a procession behind the carriages, and Sergeant Devereaux, starting off at once, wisely maintained a slow pace. The Parisians started to sing a ribald ditty as they escorted the American and his charges to the old gates of the city, and no one bothered to glance back at the unconscious man lying on the cobblestones of the Street of Stonemasons.

Jeremy did not relax until the crowd had bidden him and his companions a rowdy farewell. Then, when he saw the open countryside stretching out ahead, he felt a sense of anticlimax. A cut he had sustained over his left eye throbbed, his whole body ached, and he felt unutterably weary. The snow turned to sleet, compounding his misery, and as he hunched under his upturned collar, he wondered whether his mission was worth all the effort. Tule Yasmin, her serenity and dignity restored, sat warm and dry in the carriage, blithely unaware of his existence. She did not bother to thank him for having saved her from the mob, and nothing in her attitude suggested that she felt even a spark of gratitude. Jeremy cursed Alexander Hamilton and his scheme and reflected bitterly that it would have been preferable to send him alone to the court of Sultan Selim III.

Sir John Ellis stood alone on the Blackwall dock as the four-hundred-ton merchant ship slowly left her berth on the Thames River. His daughter, niece, and nephew were on board, and he was hoping to get a parting look at the trio as they set sail for the Aegean Sea.

Their ship would travel down the Thames, through the Strait of Dover and the English Channel, out into the open Atlantic. She would follow the coast of Spain and, after passing through the Strait of Gibraltar, would sail over the Mediterranean and into the Aegean. Along with her crew and passengers, the merchant ship was carrying a cargo of manufactured goods to trade. Sir John had figured that by traveling on such a vessel, Mary, Rosalind, and Robert would be less likely to come to any harm, since the Turks were still eager for British goods. But as an added precaution Sir John had used his government connections to arrange for an unobtrusive escort of a forty-two gun navy frigate.

Just then he caught a glimpse of red hair glinting in the sunlight, and he saw his daughter coming around the deck rail of the ship, followed by the Tate twins. Even from this distance he could see Mary's exuberance as she strolled rapidly down the deck and blew kisses to her father on shore. Rosalind and Rob bounded after her, and they were waving their arms and shouting.

It was a pretty picture, Sir John thought, as the ship slowly made its way down the Thames and the shipboard figures became smaller. He understood his daughter and her cousins well enough to know that they thrived on challenges and adventure, and he just prayed that the trio would come to no harm.

IV

In spite of the sleet, snow, and cold the party did not halt for the night until it reached the inn designated on the marquis de Lafayette's itinerary for that evening's stop. It had been dark for more than an hour by the time that Sergeant Devereaux pulled his tired team to a halt before the main entrance to the hostelry, which was located more than twenty miles south of Paris. The yellow lights winking in the windows were warm and cheerful, and Jeremy, who was chilled to the bone, looked forward to a hot supper and a comfortable bed. But first he had to contend with the innkeeper, who was, according to Lafayette's notes, violently antiroyalist.

There were few travelers on the roads these days, due to the unsettled conditions of the times, and the innkeeper was pleased to entertain such a large party, but he nevertheless carefully scrutinized the identification papers that Jeremy handed to him, and not until he had satisfied himself that this was not a noble entourage did he agree to provide accommodations. Then he assigned a suite comprising a small drawing room and a very large bedchamber to Tule Yasmin and Jeremy. The servingwomen were given three small rooms at the opposite end of the second floor in which to distribute themselves, and the National Guardsmen were taken to an outbuilding where quarters were available to coachmen.

The khana retired at once to her bedchamber, and several of her women appeared to minister to her wants. She demanded large quantities of hot water for a bath, and when these were brought, Jeremy commandeered one tub for himself. He washed in the little drawing room, changed into clothing more presentable than the battered coat and breeches he had worn during the fight, and waited for Tule Yasmin to reappear. He had assumed that she would maintain the fiction that they were a happily married couple by dining with him, but she sent word to him through one of the women that she wished to be served in the suite and that she intended to eat all of her meals alone. Telling himself that he should have realized she was incapable of cooperating with him and that she would make any given situation as difficult as possible, he went off alone to the taproom on the ground floor. The khana, he thought, could do what she pleased; he was ravenous, and he intended to enjoy his meal.

There were only three other guests in the large taproom as Jeremy entered and sat down at a small table near the blazing hearth. One was a priest, eating alone, and the other two, presumably merchants, were just finishing their meal. A barmaid brought Jeremy a succession of savory dishes, and he thought that he had never tasted better grilled fish, more succulent duckling, and more tender roast lamb. With his meal he drank a small bottle of light wine, and by the time the girl brought him a cherry tart, juicy on the inside and baked a golden brown on the top, his good spirits had been restored.

Yawning, he looked into the fire and then smiled as he recalled the fantastic events of the day. Tule Yasmin was without doubt the most unpleasant woman he had ever known, as disagreeable as she was beautiful, but he was fulfilling his end of the bargain, and before the journey ended he felt confident he would win her regard. Pouring himself another glass of wine, he toyed with the idea of making love to her at some time during the trip. After all, he told himself, she was his legal wife, and if he chose to disregard the conditions that Lafayette had outlined to him, she had no legitimate cause for complaint, at least in the eyes of the law. She was a woman, and so caresses might accomplish far more than the loyal performance of duty to influence her in his favor.

It would certainly be no hardship to make love to her. Jeremy had to admit to himself that he found her allure irresistible and that her seeming indifference piqued him. He had never yet encountered the woman he could not master, and he felt sure that the khana was merely feigning a lack of interest in him. In any event, he realized that her coolness was a direct challenge to his masculinity, and although he did not lose sight of his mission, he knew he would not be satisfied until he conquered her.

The merchants and the priest had gone, but he continued to sit before the fire, sipping his wine and musing, and he was so relaxed that he did not realize the innkeeper had entered the taproom until the man came to him and dropped onto the bench opposite him. Jeremy smiled, but the host was looking at him so carefully that his sense of well-being vanished and he became instantly alert again. However, he gave no sign of his feelings and continued to smile lazily.

"Join me in a glass of wine, monsieur?"

"I finished my supper long ago," the innkeeper said, waving the bottle aside. "I ate with my wife," he added pointedly.

Jeremy nodded pleasantly. "That's customary."

"Exactly so, monsieur." The innkeeper eyed him suspiciously. "I am surprised that you do not follow the custom. It is unusual, is it not, for a man to dine alone when his wife is beautiful?" He paused, then went on with increased emphasis. "It is very strange indeed for a bridegroom to spend his wedding night alone."

So the man had noted the date on the certificate of marriage. He was plainly no fool, and something had to be done quickly to disarm him. Jeremy laughed loudly, swallowed a large quantity of wine, and winked broadly. "Women," he said, "are strange little creatures. We are agreed?"

"So far, monsieur."

Jeremy realized he was getting nowhere and decided to change his tactics. "It is not customary for the owner of a public lodging house to question his guests or their habits," he said boldly. "May I ask your reasons for prying into what I consider to be strictly my private business and that of my wife?"

"To be sure." The innkeeper was neither embarrassed nor abashed. "Many members of the nobility who have been guilty of offenses against the people of France are afraid the day is soon approaching when they will be called to account for their misdeeds. And so they are trying to flee from the country. Only two weeks ago the comte le Brun and that harlot wife of his came to this very inn after leaving Paris in disguise. Le Brun, believe it or not, actually made an attempt to fool me into believing he was a silk merchant from Lyons. Imagine—me!"

"I see." Jeremy began to see a great deal.

"Naturally I penetrated his foolish disguise at once. My sons and several of our neighbors escorted them back to the city to await the justice that will surely be meted out to them."

"Excellent!" Jeremy said enthusiastically, beginning to perspire.

"Now you, monsieur, your papers are in order, and your accent is that of a foreigner. Your wife is obviously a foreigner, too, but I heard her talking to one of the women who is accompanying you, and they were not speaking in English, which is your tongue, and which I happen to understand. Many English guests have patronized this inn. It is natural that I wonder about you. And it is essential to the security of France and the cause of justice that you tell me why you and your bride have dined separately and why you linger in a public room on your wedding night."

"Your point is well taken, so I do not resent your interference," Jeremy said slowly. "My wife was fatigued by the excitement of the wedding and the long ride out of Paris. So it was only natural that she wanted a little time to herself. She wished to rest, so naturally I obliged her."

The innkeeper nodded, partly convinced, but some doubts remained in his mind. "If she merely wanted rest, why has she locked the door to the suite you occupy together? Answer me that, monsieur!"

Jeremy tried to conceal his surprise. "You say she has locked the door?"

"I tried it myself only a quarter of an hour ago."

"I should have expected it." Jeremy winked at the host again, hoping desperately that a slightly ribald approach would establish a bond of sympathy between them. "My bride is a very shy young woman, as I'm sure a man of your experience has guessed. This is a most important night in her life, and although she has been looking forward to it for some time, she has been afraid of it, too."

"Ah." The innkeeper grinned and looked wise. The mystery was no mystery at all, and he had no desire to appear unworldly.

"Some women give themselves easily," Jeremy continued, embroidering on this theme. "Others, like my wife, want to surrender but must first satisfy what they think is their honor by making a show of resistance. It's just as I told you, monsieur. She is extremely shy."

"You'll have a night you won't forget for a long time." The man licked his thick lips, his eyes envious.

"It would seem," Jeremy replied with a grin, "that it will be memorable only if you will lend me your assistance." He was acting the part of the eager bridegroom so convincingly that he almost believed the role was real.

"Anything, monsieur! I am at your service!"

"You have a spare key to the suite that you will allow me to use, then? I can't begin my campaign until I've gained admission to the fortress."

The innkeeper chuckled and took a large ring of keys from a loop attached to his belt. He studied them one by one, and then he chuckled. "Both of the keys to the drawing room are in your bride's possession. She summoned me an hour ago and questioned me. When I admitted to her that there was an extra key to the drawing room, she demanded that I give it to her at once. It was her attitude that started me thinking. I should have known from the start that she was merely bashful."

"She has raised the drawbridge, then." Jeremy thought angrily that the khana certainly left nothing to chance.

"The moat may still be crossed, monsieur." The innkeeper removed an iron key from the ring and handed it triumphantly across the table. Then he stood and slapped Jeremy on the shoulder. "This is a key to the bedchamber, which is all you need. You have no interest in the drawing room tonight, eh?"

"None," Jeremy assured him, and this time the laugh that bubbled up in him was genuine. "You have no idea how much I'm obliged to you, monsieur." He tossed the key into the air, caught it when it descended, then jumped to his feet.

"Not at all, not at all," the man said, falling into step beside him. "Hospitality is my business, and I'm here to make sure my guests are satisfied under my roof." He dug an elbow slyly into the American's ribs. "There's no need to worry about you tonight, though, eh, monsieur?"

"Don't give me—or my wife—another thought," Jeremy declared emphatically, and meant it.

"Ah, but I will. I'll think about you for the rest of the night."

"That's very kind of you." Jeremy increased his pace, afraid that the man would accompany him to the bedchamber door. He had no specific idea how the khana would react when he let himself into the room, but he knew she would not be pleased, and he didn't want the innkeeper, whose suspicions he had finally lulled, to be a witness to a violent scene.

"Kindness, you say? It's my pleasure." They arrived at the top of the stairs, and the host linked his arm companionably through Jeremy's. "You didn't see my wife, I suppose? The fat pig of a woman out in the kitchen?" He sighed lugubriously and shook his head. "You're lucky, monsieur, very lucky."

The bedchamber door stood only a few feet down the corridor, and Jeremy decided there was but one way to be rid of the man. Halting, he held out his right hand. "I'll bid you good night," he said firmly.

The innkeeper wrung his hand and remained in the hall, chuckling, as Jeremy walked the remainder of the distance to the door. There was no possible way to send the fellow packing, so Jeremy had to make the best of a situation that was already extremely delicate. Removing the key from his pocket, he inserted it into the lock as quietly as he could, then quickly turned it. Raising the latch silently, he stepped inside and closed the door behind him, carefully bolting it in the same motion.

The drapes were drawn, and four tapers that burned in double holders on either side of a dressing table at the far side of the room, beyond a large canopied bed, provided the only light. Tule Yasmin was seated at a mirror before the table, combing her long hair, and when Jeremy saw her his blood raced. She had no right, he told himself, to look so lovely. She was wearing a nightdress, the bosom and tiny sleeves of which were made of ivory lace and the long, clinging skirt of apricot-colored, heavy silk. Over the gown was a flowing dressing robe with long, full sleeves; the robe was a matching apricot color but was made of a fine, almost transparent silk. Her backless, high-heeled slippers were of ivory satin, and when she saw Jeremy's reflection in the mirror, she jumped to her feet so suddenly that one of the slippers almost fell off.

She turned, and by the time she faced him she had gained complete control of herself. "Leave at once," she said coldly.

"I didn't come by choice," Jeremy replied glibly. "I had no choice in the matter, madam."

The khana's eyes flashed dangerously. "You were instructed to address us as 'Your Sublimity.' And you have no right to be here merely because it suited our temporary convenience to indulge in an otherwise meaningless ceremonial rite with you."

He smiled but made no move. "I assume that you're an intelligent person, so I beg you to use that intelligence. It doesn't really matter what I call you. In the eyes of the French, including the owner of this establishment, you and I are husband and wife. He noticed the date of our marriage on our papers, and he became suspicious when you asked him for the extra key to the drawing room. You blundered, and both of us must now pay the penalty for that error."

Her mouth became hard, and for an instant she looked anything but beautiful. "In my land not even a prince has a right to condemn or criticize the khagan or a member of his family. If we were there now, I would have you whipped to death!"

Jeremy realized that she had finally referred to herself in the first person but did not comment on the fact. Instead he grinned impudently and leaned against the wall. "Then I'm fortunate, perhaps. But it so happens we're in France, so both of us are in danger of losing our heads, and you've made a mistake that I've had to rectify. I've spent the last half hour with the innkeeper, who hates blue bloods, and I finally convinced him that you locked me out because you were incurably shy. In case you've forgotten it, madam, this happens to be our wedding night."

"You bring the subject rather forcibly to my attention." Tule Yasmin smiled humorlessly and took a single step forward. "Your story of the suspicious innkeeper is excellent," she said, her hands on her hips. "I congratulate you on your ingenuity, and I applaud your imagination. It is too bad—for you—that they will avail you nothing."

A scent had been sprayed on her hair, and when Jeremy inhaled it he found it difficult to concentrate on conversation. But he managed to shrug indolently. "I have no reason to tell you anything but the truth. Why else would I have come here?" That, he told himself, would shock her; she was so accustomed to adulation that she undoubtedly had never dreamed it might be possible for a man to be indifferent to her charms. The actual fact that he felt powerfully drawn to her was, of course, irrelevant.

The khana shook back her hair, which was hanging loose at her shoulders, and stared at him. "You lie," she said at last.

"See for yourself." Jeremy gestured toward the door. "He's probably out there right now. I've never seen anyone so anxious to share in the joys of a nuptial night."

Tule Yasmin did not believe him, but she finally started toward the door, motivated either by curiosity, which was unlikely, or by a desire to prove him wrong, which was more probable. As she passed Jeremy, she brushed against him, and her proximity aroused him. He restrained himself with an effort, forced himself to maintain his lazy pose, and when she slid back the bolt he smiled ironically. She opened the door a few inches, then promptly slammed it again and pushed the bolt back into place.

"Very clever of you, I'm sure," she cried, her composure shaken for the first time since he had known her.

"Clever?" He continued to feign amusement, while telling himself that she was obviously capable of achieving great depths of emotion.

"You paid him to wait out there, just to substantiate your story."

Jeremy laughed aloud. "I probably would have done it at that. If I'd thought of it. And if the circumstances had been slightly different. Allow me to remind you that I almost lost my life for your sake in the streets of Paris today. I'm very fond of my life, and I have every intention of preserving it. What's more, I've agreed to deliver you to Constantinople, and that's exactly what I'm going to do, whether you give me your help or not. I'm not going to let some overly zealous farmers return us to Paris, either, and that's final. So I'm staying right here."

The khana appeared to give consideration to his statement and managed to look extraordinarily appealing in the process. She could not doubt that he meant what he said, and common sense seemed to tell her that he was right.

"Very well," she said imperiously. "Your petition is granted. You may remain."

He did not take his eyes from her as he began to unbuckle his sword belt.

"You will sleep in there," she said firmly, pointing toward the drawing room.

Jeremy made no reply, and after dropping his sword onto the foot of the bed, he carelessly tossed his pistol and the bone-handled knife after them. There was no mistaking his intent, but Tule Yasmin surprised him by neither making a scene nor objecting. She stood very still, her hands at her sides and her expression inscrutable. He felt encouraged and started to walk slowly toward the spot where she stood, close to the side of the bed.

"As long as we're both in here," he murmured, "I'm sure we'll find this chamber far more comfortable."

He put his arms around her, and Tule Yasmin did not draw away from him. Further emboldened, he kissed her, and she remained passive; then he began to caress her, and when she allowed him to take whatever liberties pleased him, he pressed her back onto the bed. Then, as he was about to begin his lovemaking in earnest, he felt a sharp metal point prick his throat, and opening his eyes, he saw the khana groping for his pistol with her free hand.

"Don't move," she said, and her voice was soft and warm.

The pressure of the metal point increased, and Jeremy watched helplessly as she took hold of the pistol, cocked it expertly, and pointed it at him. "Now you will stand," she commanded.

Deeply chagrined, he stumbled to his feet and saw that in her right hand she held a tiny, double-edged dagger, no longer than her thumb. Apparently it had been concealed somewhere either in her robe or in her nightdress, but she gave him no time to wonder about the matter. "You will sleep in there," she repeated, and then she laughed pleasantly. "Your weapons will be returned to you in the morning, so you will be better able to protect me against anyone who might try to harm me."

Jeremy retreated into the drawing room, and Tule Yasmin closed and bolted the bedchamber door. He was alone, and after a time he ruefully looked around for a place to sleep. There was no divan in the room, so he had no choice but to arrange a makeshift couch by placing a hard bench and two delicate chairs together. He removed his coat, stretched out, and tried unsuccessfully to make himself comfortable. The innkeeper, he told himself bitterly, had been right about one thing: This was a night he would not forget for a long time to come.

The pattern of day-to-day living on the road was established at the inn outside Paris, and thereafter the khana consistently maintained an attitude toward Jeremy that was remote, impersonal, and barely civil. Every evening she dined alone in her bedchamber, and each morning her women served her breakfast there; during the day, when the party was on the road, she addressed Jeremy only when necessary. He tried to atone for his error by making unceasing attempts to exert his charms on her, but his gallantry made no impression on her, and nothing he said or did melted her icy reserve. He began to despair of ever establishing a relationship of any sort with her, and he wondered if he was dealing with a woman who was incapable of feeling anything.

She never complained, no matter how many hours they spent on the road each day, and she made no objections when they were served inferior food or when the living accommodations were cramped and uncomfortable. Roving bands of peasants or artisans halted the little cavalcade several times each day, but Tule Yasmin was always calm and unafraid, and Jeremy gleaned what little satisfaction he could from the knowledge that on such occasions, at least, she seemed to deem him competent. She invariably left the handling of these situations to him, and took care not to interfere. On the other hand, she seemed to assume that he would extricate them from any unpleasantness that might arise; that was his job, and she did not bother to acknowledge his services with as much as a smile or a compliment.

Jeremy was so discouraged that at times he toyed with the idea of abandoning the whole project, leaving the khana to her own devices, and enlisting in one or another of Europe's mercenary armies. Once or twice he even thought of proceeding to Constantinople alone and trying his luck at the sultan's court on his own, but he knew he was too deeply committed to indulge in any such rash action. He could not abandon his mission now, for there was too much to gain if he succeeded and too much to lose if he failed. He had a bear by the tail, as people on the American frontier often said, and no matter what the provocation, he had to hang on.

The weather became warmer when the party crossed the Maritime Alps and drew near to the Mediterranean, and Jeremy's sense of restless futility increased. Sergeant Devereaux headed back into the mountains to make a detour around Nice, where feelings against the nobility were running particularly high. Then shortly before noon the carriages rolled across the French border into Italy, and the task of the National Guardsmen was finished. They turned the party over to local professional coachmen, and as they were anxious to return to Paris, they bade Jeremy a hasty good-bye. As they were about to ride off on their hired horses, the khana called them back and much to their surprise handed each of them a small bag of gold coins as a sign of appreciation. Jeremy, watching the ceremony, told himself bitterly that she would probably dismiss him in the same way when they reached Constantinople.

Now that France was behind them and there was no longer any danger, Jeremy relaxed in his saddle as the carriages started off again through the mountains to the town of San Remo, where the first night on the soil of Italy would be spent. The rest of the journey promised to be dull, he thought; until today, in spite of the khana's attitude toward him, he had felt that his presence as her escort had meant something. But from now until they reached the

Turkish galley that would be waiting at Venice, he would be even less useful than the servingwomen.

Glancing surreptitiously at Tule Yasmin as he rode beside her carriage, he knew that one of the principal reasons he was so disgruntled was because she had injured his vanity. No woman so disinterested in love had any right to be so attractive. Due to the warmer weather her sables had been packed away, and she was dressed in a long black velvet coat, worn open down the front, and held close to her slender waist by a wide belt and a jewel-studded buckle that was worth a small fortune. A white scarf was wrapped around her graceful throat in the manner of a man's stock and was tucked into the low neck of her yellow silk dress. For greater comfort in traveling, her full skirt was looped up between her ankles by a black velvet sash secured at her waist, and Jeremy, staring at her ankles and legs, had to use all of his willpower to look away from her. He was wasting his emotion, and it would be far better for his peace of mind if he forgot that he wanted her.

Deliberately emptying his mind, he half dozed in the saddle and let his gelding do the work as the party moved down through the mountain passes to the coast. The path was narrow, but the coachmen were familiar with the road, so Jeremy dropped behind, telling himself that if the khana was out of sight he would not be inclined to think about her so constantly. Here and there he saw fragrant evergreens that reminded him of New York, and occasional cypress trees and yellow poplars made him homesick for North Carolina, too.

As he jogged along the road at a sedate pace, he could not help wishing that he were back in the United States, where he understood even the most illogical customs and unreasonable habits. It occurred to him that he was coming to hate royalty as vehemently as did the people of France, but he could not return to America until he completed his assignment. Alexander Hamilton would see to that, and he thought that, if possible, his loathing for the secretary of the treasury was even greater than his anti-pathy toward Tule Yasmin.

A woman's scream brought him back to the present. The carriages were momentarily out of sight around a bend in the road, and as he pushed forward he realized that they had pulled to a grinding halt. Alert to danger at last, Jeremy loosened his sword in its sheath, cocked his pistol, and advanced cautiously. When he arrived at the turn he halted for a moment, and the scene that was spread out before him was a nightmare that had been transformed into reality. Four armed brigands had halted the carriages and were in command of the situation.

All had dismounted, and two of them, holding cumber-some old-fashioned muskets, were training their weapons on the coachmen, who sat helplessly on their boxes, their hands raised high above their heads. A third ruffian was hauling a leather box from the top of the first carriage, and he handled it with ease, demonstrating that he was no novice at the art of highway robbery.

One of the elderly servingmaids was making all the noise, and she stood at the side of the road with the other servants, who huddled near the base of a large cedar. The old woman was wringing her hands and shrieking, scream-ing each time she exhaled. The brigands ignored her, and it apparently did not occur to her that she would serve a far more useful function if she attacked them instead of wasting her breath. But fear had rendered her helpless, and the other women seemed unable to move, too.

The khana was in real trouble, but her face showed no fear as she faced the man who, judging by the expensive cut of his clothes, was the leader of the band. He held her at bay with a pistol, and with his free hand was trying to wrench the gem-studded buckle from her belt. Tule Yasmin stood proudly, unmindful of the man's exertions or his rel-ish as he eyed her. At last the buckle came loose, and after he jammed it into his pocket he began to paw her crudely.

She remained calm and unflustered and did not move,

apparently realizing that if she raised her hand to strike him she would incense him and add to her woes. But she said something to him in a low voice, and her words had a far greater effect than a meaningless feminine slap. The highwayman snarled something at her, looking as though she had branded him with a hot iron, and Jeremy waited to see no more.

The brigands were unaware of his existence, so the initial advantage was his, and he used it to the utmost. Taking careful aim with his pistol, he fired it at the thief who was keeping the driver of the first coach covered with his musket. The ball landed in the rogue's shoulder, incapacitating him; he howled with pain, but he fired his own weapon before he dropped it, and his shot was lucky, for it struck the coachman in the leg. The brigand staggered and fell, and the driver bent over double, clutching at his leg.

The highwayman who was covering the other two coachmen could not turn from them, but the man who had been untying the box on the carriage roof immediately drew a brace of pistols and fired them at Jeremy. The target was almost impossible to hit, for Jeremy had spurred forward, and the bullets whistled harmlessly past him. He was only dimly aware of the activity around him, for he was concentrating on the rogue who was annoying the khana.

He charged down the road, not realizing that the third coachman, who was behind him, had taken a musket from beneath his box and had fired at the man on the roof. At this moment only the leader mattered to Jeremy, and he headed straight for the man. But the brigand promptly showed that he, too, could think and act quickly in a crisis. The path was too narrow for the gelding to pass the carriage, and the highwayman took shelter behind the end of the coach. Using it as a cover, he reached out coolly and fired his pistol at the American, who was thundering forward.

In spite of the short range even the best of marksmen would have had difficulty in hitting his target, for the carriage partly obstructed the brigand's aim, and the horse was moving at such speed that it was almost impossible to take accurate aim. These factors saved Jeremy's life, but they were his undoing, too, for the gelding, unaccustomed to being shot at, was frightened by the flash and roar. Whinnying in terror, the animal reared, and Jeremy was thrown to the ground. He rolled over several times, and too late he saw there was a steep precipice at the side of the road. Before he could check his momentum, he tumbled over the edge and began to slide down the steep incline that ended in a ravine some five hundred feet below.

The unexpected catastrophe momentarily unnerved him, and for an instant he thought his end was near. But he recovered almost at once and began to claw desperately at the ground in an effort to give himself a hold. He braced his feet against rocks as he fell, but they slid down ahead of him, and it appeared that nothing would halt his rapid descent. When he had dropped about one third of the distance down the slope, however, his luck suddenly changed; growing out of the rubble of loose stones was a thick, tangled bush, and he grasped it with both hands, unmindful of the sharp thorns that studded the branches.

Having halted himself, Jeremy took a deep breath and began to climb again, crawling on his hands and knees when he could, inching up on his stomach when there was no other way. At the top of the precipice, looking down at him, was the brigand, who was trying to reload his pistol. Jeremy could see, however, that he was having a difficulty of some sort; apparently the weapon had jammed, and that gave the American an extra minute or two in which to attempt his perilous ascent. He climbed as rapidly as he could, sending a shower of stones cascading down the slope behind him. His hands were sore, and he had sustained numerous small but painful cuts that annoyed him, but his sense of balance had always been good, and he rose to within a few yards of the top.

The rogue, a handsome, broad-shouldered man with trim mustaches, was working feverishly in an attempt to restore his pistol to working condition, but as Jeremy came closer and still closer to him, he lost his patience and hurled the weapon at the American. It struck Jeremy on the collarbone, and although it bruised him, it neither halted nor slowed him, and the brigand drew his sword. The peril was now even greater than before, and the man stabbed again and again at the prostrate figure crawling toward him.

A single mistake now would mean a catastrophe: Jeremy had to keep out of range of the murderous, probing blade; and at the same time he had to remain flattened against the steep incline, for one false move would send him plunging to his death. The situation appeared hopeless, and he saw no way out of his predicament. Then, without warning, he received help from an unexpected source. Tule Yasmin had been left unguarded, and she hurried forward, walking with difficulty in her high-heeled slippers on the broken ground at the side of the road. In her hands she carried a large stone, and as she approached the brigand she threw it at him.

It struck him a glancing blow on the side of the head, and the surprise of the attack stunned him as much as did the pain. He swayed for a moment, looked dazed, and rubbed his head. The respite was brief, but it was sufficient; Jeremy scrambled up over the edge of the precipice. He looked around wildly, saw his sword lying in the dust of the road, and raced to it. Then he turned, barely in time to meet the violent attack of the enraged brigand.

The highwayman slashed recklessly with his sword, apparently hoping that the very ferocity of his assault would overcome this opponent who refused to be killed. But Jeremy, who had been taught the art of dueling by a young French naval officer who had made a cruise with the Revenue Service, met his foe coolly, turned aside the other's strikes with no visible effort, and then calmly launched a counterattack.

It became immediately obvious to the highwayman that he was facing no ordinary swordsman, and he changed his tactics. Growing more cautious, he backed hastily toward the center of the road and then devoted himself to beating off Jeremy's insistent, probing blade. Jeremy was the better duelist, but the effort he had expended in his fall and torturous climb had tired him, so he and the brigand were fairly evenly matched.

A rhythm was quickly established, and the cadence of thrust and parry, feint and riposte would have become monotonous had not both men known that a single slip meant death. They circled each other slowly, searching for openings, waiting for the error in judgment or in timing that would enable one or the other to break through his opponent's guard. Jeremy had no idea how the coachmen were making out in their struggle with the other robbers, for he had to concentrate his full attention on the leader, and not once did his eyes waver from the point of the long sword that flicked toward him so deftly, then darted away again at the touch of his own blade.

Jeremy realized that his arm was beginning to ache and that his footwork was becoming unsteady; he guessed that his eye was probably not as sharp as it had been, either. He had to end the match quickly or be beaten, for the brigand was still fresh, an advantage that was sure to favor him if the duel was prolonged. In trying to achieve a rapid victory, Jeremy knew he would have to take his handicaps into consideration and make allowances for them, and this need made his problem all the more difficult.

At the edge of the road, only a few yards from the spot where he had fallen over the precipice, was a large, flat-topped rock that stood about four feet high, and when he caught a glimpse of it he recalled having seen it just before his horse had thrown him. A daring scheme occurred to him, and he weighed the thought for no more than an instant before putting it into effect. As he told himself, there was nothing to lose.

Calling on his fast-ebbing strength, he took the offensive and gradually forced his opponent closer and closer to the precipice. The man grinned, obviously thinking it was Jeremy's intention to prod him over the edge, but he made no attempt to halt, and his confident attitude seemed to imply that he believed two could play at the same game. The highwayman gave ground easily, making Jeremy's task momentarily easier.

When they neared the drop they stopped and fought parallel to it for a few seconds, then Jeremy deliberately allowed himself to be driven back, step by step, along the rim. This was the most dangerous part of his scheme, and he maneuvered slowly, taking care to avoid the step that would send him hurtling to his death. Then, when his heel scraped against the high rock, he knew that the climax of the duel had come. Shifting his position slightly so that he stood directly beside the rock, he vaulted suddenly onto it. If he slipped, if he lost his footing for one instant, the highwayman would surely skewer him, and he strained every muscle in an attempt to gain the top of the rock while simultaneously holding off his opponent. His jump was somewhat less than graceful, and for a terrible second he did not know whether he would succeed. Then, to his relief, he felt the heavy, smooth stone under his feet.

The height of the rock gave him an enormous advantage, and he utilized it to the utmost. Lunging forward with all of his might, he drove his blade straight at the throat of his foe. The point sank deep; the brigand screamed and then fell back, his hands flying high above his head. And the thin, high sound of his agonized shriek echoed through the mountains as he crashed to the bottom of the ravine five hundred feet below, with Jeremy's sword still in his body.

Jeremy was exhausted, but he turned to see how the coachmen were faring. To his dismay they were taking a beating from the other robbers. The man who had been on top of the first carriage was using the butt of a pistol as a club and was striking one of the coachmen repeatedly with it, while the other brigand continued to hold the remaining driver at bay with his musket. Jeremy blinked and tried to assimilate this latest development.

Before he could act, a new participant entered the fight.

The khana, kicking off her shoes and running in her stock-inged feet, picked up the sword the leader of the band had dropped before he had crashed to his death. Then, tugging at the loop that divided her skirt, she tightened the velvet band so the voluminous folds formed a pair of loose panta-loons. With her greater freedom assured, she sprinted to Jeremy's horse and leaped into the saddle with the lithe grace of a young boy.

The gelding was startled and showed his resentment by rearing and plunging forward, but Tule Yasmin quickly proved herself to be a superb horsewoman and brought the animal under control with what appeared to be a minimum of effort. The horse recognized the touch of one who had absolute mastery over him, and when the khana urged him forward, he responded at once, breaking into a canter after moving only a short distance. She undoubtedly resembled the cavalrymen who served her brother, Jeremy thought, as she sped forward, her velvet coat flying out behind her. She held the sword above her head and twirled it in an exhibition that was as exhilarating as it was frightening to her foes.

She was laughing joyously, and Jeremy was as amazed at her display of emotion as he was by her prowess. She continued to laugh as she approached the struggling men, and when the brigand who held the musket fired it at her, she did not bother to duck. The bullet passed close to her, but she seemed unaware that she had been in any danger, and she proceeded to ride down the highwayman, slashing him wickedly with the sword without slowing her pace.

He fell, making no sound, and she checked the gelding, turned him around with marvelous dexterity, and then started toward the man who was using his pistol as a club. He, wanting no more of the fight, tried to flee, but Tule Yasmin cut him off, then coldly ran him through. The bat-tle was over, and it was suddenly very quiet. The khana dismounted and spoke a few words to the coachman who had been wounded at the start of the fight and was now able to hobble to his box.

Then, retrieving her shoes and slipping into them, she approached Jeremy, still carrying the sword of the dead leader of the band. "You'll want this," she said, "to replace the blade you lost." She handed it to him, and before he could reply she ordered her women to their places and stepped into her carriage. Closing the door firmly behind her, she smoothed her hair and sat back against the cushions ready to resume her interrupted journey.

Jeremy and the battered coachmen stared at her and then took their seats, leaving the bodies of the two dead highwaymen on the road. The man whom Jeremy had wounded at the beginning of the battle was nowhere to be seen and had apparently made good his escape in spite of his injury. Jeremy had no intention of searching for him, and the drivers, tired after their exertions, were anxious to reach San Remo as soon as possible.

Jeremy felt faint during the remainder of the ride, but he could not resist looking into the carriage at Tule Yasmin every few minutes. Never, he told himself repeatedly, had he encountered a woman like her, and he knew he would never forget the remarkable contribution she had made at the climax of the fight.

The Inn of the Gray Eagle, which nestled in the hills above San Remo, was one of the most luxurious hostelries in northern Italy, and Jeremy felt no sense of loss when the khana retired to a suite of her own after handsomely rewarding the coachmen. As they were no longer in France, there was no need to maintain even the semblance of domesticity, and Jeremy was given a bedchamber of his own for the first time since they had left Paris.

He bathed slowly in tubs of hot water brought to him by members of the staff, and then he repaired to the taproom for a delicious meal. Food had never meant much to him, but he certainly knew good cooking from bad, and he had rarely tasted anything that could compare with the capon stuffed with olives, oysters, and chestnuts that was served to him, and a wine jelly made his cold veal pie a delight. He drank a carafe of delicious red wine with his meal, and he finished off the repast with a small beaker of excellent brandy. Feeling refreshed, he made his way to his room, humming softly. It occurred to him that he was in no way disturbed by the khana's failure to speak to him after the battle, for he had learned to expect nothing from her. They had disposed of a rather formidable enemy together, but she had subsequently behaved as though nothing out of the ordinary had taken place, and that fact did not surprise him.

Tomorrow, he told himself, he would devote further thought to her unusual personality, and he kept remembering her pleasure, bordering on ecstasy, when she had ridden down the highwaymen. He had been given a clue of some sort to her nature, and he would pursue the matter at his leisure; right now he was looking forward to a night of uninterrupted sleep in a soft bed.

Arriving at his room, he lifted the latch, stepped inside, and lighted a candle with a tinderbox of the latest design, a mechanism that required only a single, short motion to spark its flint. Then he closed the door, and as he turned back he heard a faint, scraping noise at the far side of the chamber, beyond the bed and several cushioned chairs. He instinctively reached for his sword but let his hand drop when he saw one of the servingwomen waiting for him. She was wearing a veil over her face, a practice he had forbidden while they were traveling in France, and he could not resist a smile when he realized that the women had reverted to their own customs at the first possible moment.

"Allah be with you," she said, and salaamed.

Jeremy yawned. "Allah be with you," he replied politely.

"Her Sublimity will receive you in audience now," the woman said.

"I beg your pardon?" He looked at her blankly.

"It is the command of Her Sublimity that you attend her at once," the woman declared, and without waiting for a reply, she stepped out into the corridor, waited for him to join her, and then started off down the hall.

The summons was so unusual that Jeremy did not know what to make of it, but he refused to speculate on its possibilities until he arrived at the khana's suite. As he entered, two of the servingwomen who had been puttering around in the drawing room quickly scurried out, leaving him alone. Jeremy selected the most comfortable chair and sat down in it, but a moment later the door to the bedchamber opened, and he stood, involuntarily, when Tule Yasmin walked into the room.

She was already dressed for the night in a white silk gown trimmed with pale blue silk ribbons at the wide neck, waist, and wrists. Over the nightdress she had thrown a voluminous, fringed white silk scarf, and she held it wrapped closely about her as she advanced to the center of the room.

"You fought well," she said, and there was an unusual warmth in her voice.

"So did you," he replied, and grinned.

The khana shrugged. "It has been the tradition of my family for many hundreds of years. But I have never before seen a Frank who comported himself so bravely. I am pleased with you."

He enjoyed the compliment, the first she had ever given him, but his mind was preoccupied with her reasons for receiving him so informally. The right behavior now might send him far toward his goal of winning the sultan's favor, but one misstep could ruin everything. "Thank you," he said, and waited for her to make the next move.

Tule Yasmin met his eyes boldly, and for a long moment they looked at each other in silence. Then slowly, and with a deliberation that could not be mistaken, she let the scarf drop from her shoulders and slide to the floor. They stepped toward each other at the same instant, and Jeremy, exulting, gathered Tule Yasmin into his arms and kissed her passionately on the mouth.

After a moment she pulled away and led him into the adjoining chamber. She swiftly removed her nightdress and lay on the bed, where, her eyes closed, she moved her body seductively, waiting for his lovemaking. Jeremy quickly shed his clothes, and as he climbed on top of her, ready to take her, she suddenly came to life like a wild animal. She pulled him down hard on top of her as she writhed beneath him and raked his back with her nails. He entered her, and she wrapped her long legs around him tightly and began to moan.

Jeremy had a hard time keeping up with her as she constantly cried out for more. Despite his great experience with women, he had never encountered any female so demanding, so aggressive, so domineering. He continued to thrust deeply into her, and he thought he would drop from exhaustion before Tule Yasmin reached her climax. But suddenly she let out a piercing cry, and he knew she had found fulfillment, just as he, too, felt his release.

Totally spent, breathing heavily, Jeremy rolled over to one side, then reached to take the woman beside him into his arms, so they could rest in each other's embrace. When she didn't respond, he looked over to where she lay to see what was wrong. Tule Yasmin was fast asleep.

The following day, when the journey through the Italian states to Venice was resumed, Jeremy felt satisfied with himself, for his doubts regarding the future of his mission had vanished. He was certain that when they arrived at Constantinople Tule Yasmin would present him to the sultan in a favorable light, and he spent the better part of the long day on the road composing the speech he intended to make to Selim on behalf of the United States. In spite of his feeling of well-being, however, he realized that he would need to watch his step at all times. His future depended on the khana's continued goodwill, and even though they had been intimate, she was not an easy person to fathom.

She had given herself to him with an ardor that was unique in his experience, yet behind her physical desire she had continued to maintain an impenetrable reserve. Her inner core was apparently something that no man could reach; she had made no attempt to wrap herself in a veil of mystery, yet even when Jeremy had been making love to her, she had somehow given him the impression that she, not he, had been in command of the situation at all times. This morning she had clarified her attitude, at least to an extent, when she had told him that although she had accepted him as a lover, he must treat her with the respect due her exalted rank, particularly in the presence of others. She had taken pains to inform him, too, that their marriage was only a temporary alliance, and that she did not truly think of him as her husband. That point of view matched his own, of course, but he had exercised restraint and had not told her that he felt precisely as she did.

As the day wore on, Jeremy became increasingly anxious to make love to Tule Yasmin again, and when they halted at a spacious inn shortly after sundown, he looked forward eagerly to the night. The khana had maintained her usual air of indifference to him on the road, speaking to him only when necessary, and although she had not indicated that she expected him to visit her again that evening, he nevertheless presented himself confidently at her suite after his meal in the taproom. Several of the servingwomen who were attending her departed hurriedly after first informing her of his presence, and he entered the drawing room.

The door leading to the bedchamber was closed, and Jeremy curbed his initial impulse to open it. As Tule Yasmin apparently enjoyed the feeling that she was in control of the situation, he told himself that he would lose nothing by catering to her whim. When a quarter of an hour passed, however, he thought that she was certainly taking her time, and he began to grow restless. At last he decided that he would wait only a few minutes more before walking in on her, but at that moment she opened the door and stood in the frame, attired in her nightdress and robe.

Jeremy stood and would have gone to her quickly, but something in her expression halted him. Her features were composed, but in her eyes was a look that made him feel she was faintly bewildered.

"I didn't send for you," she said.

Relieved, he laughed and strolled toward her. "There's certainly no need for us to pretend to a formality that doesn't exist anymore. Especially when we're alone."

The khana brightened and smiled. "I suppose you're right." She made no objection when he slid his arms around her, but she held him off when he leaned forward to kiss her. "I wonder," she said, with just a trace of hesitation, "if I could ask a favor of you."

"Of course."

"My women have gone for the night, and I very much dislike being seen in casual dress by the staff of an inn. Something I ate this evening seems to have made me thirsty, and there's nothing I'd enjoy more than a cup of dry wine. Would you get it for me?"

Only twenty-four hours previous, Jeremy thought, she would have ordered him to bring her the wine, and her manner would have been cold, peremptory, and abrupt. He could not ask for more conclusive evidence that his conquest of her had been complete, and he smiled at her expansively. "I'll return at once," he said, kissed her lightly, and left the suite.

The innkeeper was faintly surprised that a guest should come to him in person for wine, but after a short delay he gave Jeremy a bottle that had been cooling in a stream that ran behind the building. Taking two silver cups as well, Jeremy mounted the stairs quickly, humming to himself. But he broke off sharply when he saw one of the khana's veiled women standing before the entrance to the suite. He could see only the woman's eyes above her veil, and they were regarding him steadily, without surprise.

"What's this?" he asked, halting when she failed to step aside for him.

"Her Sublimity has retired for the night," the woman said flatly.

Jeremy stared at her, barely conquering an impulse to thrust her aside.

"The door," the servant told him, "is locked from the inside. Her Sublimity has retired."

"I'm afraid I don't understand," he replied stiffly.

"Her Sublimity commands, and we obey. It is not necessary that we understand," the woman declared, her tone gently chiding.

For a long moment Jeremy stood very still, trying to control the blind rage that surged up in him. Tule Yasmin had played the most elementary of tricks on him, and he had unsuspectingly walked into the trap she had set. It was obvious to him that she had chosen a crude and humiliating method of teaching him a lesson and that she intended to give herself to him only when it suited her fancy, not his. It was equally clear that their intimacy meant nothing to her and that his status was not changed in any way. In her mind he was still no more than a rather useful servant, but a servant nevertheless. He had not achieved any degree of real standing with her, and it was painfully evident that he exerted no influence over her.

Perhaps the most galling aspect of the immediate dilemma in which she had placed him was that she had reversed the usual roles of man and woman. Jeremy had always taken his prerogatives for granted and had conducted his love affairs accordingly. Whenever he had wanted a woman, he had paid court to her, and once he had conquered her, his subsequent treatment of her had depended upon his moods. If he wanted her again, he had taken her; if not, he had ignored her and forgotten her.

Now Tule Yasmin was behaving toward him as though their relationship depended entirely on her desires. She was calmly and deliberately abasing him, shaming him by trying to rob him of his masculinity. He realized, too, that unless he could win her real respect, she would do nothing to help his mission; she, not he, needed to be taught a lesson, for unless she learned to value his strength, she would cast him aside as soon as his immediate usefulness to her ended.

He needed time to think, but he knew he was too angry at the moment, so he thrust the wine and cups at the servingwoman. "Here," he said harshly, "give these to Her Sublimity with my compliments."

Jeremy stalked down the corridor to the small room that had been assigned to him, and there he spent the better part of the night pacing up and down its narrow confines. He knew he could not rest until he had evened the score, and not until then would he be able to perform the task that meant so much to his country. Shortly before dawn he finally evolved a plan that was logical and promised to be effective, too, and after refining it as best he could, he went to bed for a few short hours of sleep.

When he awoke he had no appetite, and after a small breakfast of cold beef, cheese, and red wine, he went out into the courtyard of the inn and waited for the khana and her entourage to appear. Tule Yasmin slept late, but Jeremy was not impatient now; he knew precisely what needed to be done, and he was no longer in a hurry. Sooner or later the khana herself would create the opportunity for him to put his scheme into effect.

The sun was high above the hills of Savoy when she stepped out into the courtyard, and Jeremy bowed to her, his face wooden. Tule Yasmin nodded to him impersonally, and there was nothing in her attitude that hinted at their relationship. The other guests at the inn, who watched her party depart, could not have guessed that Jeremy had been her lover and that she had repulsed him the preceding evening.

The day passed without incident, and that night Jeremy went straight to his own quarters after he finished his meal. He was beginning to understand the khana, and he felt certain she would emphasize the stand she had taken by keeping her distance from him. She did not disappoint him, and he enjoyed a much-needed night of rest. They were now a scant two days' journey from Venice, and Jeremy could only hope that she would give him the chance to demonstrate his reaction to her studied insult. The ride that day seemed long and dull, and when evening came the party stopped at an inn that was considerably smaller than any at which they had previously halted. There were no accommodations for the servingwoman in the main building, and Jeremy's room was a tiny, cramped closet.

However, he enjoyed his meal, and he lingered over it deliberately until the tavern keeper's wife, who was the establishment's only waitress, began to yawn. At last he pulled himself to his feet and slowly climbed the stairs; when he reached the landing he saw one of the khana's women standing in the shadows, and he could scarcely conceal his elation. He had gambled, and his guess had been right. He pretended not to see the servingmaid until she stepped in front of him.

"Her Sublimity commands that you come to her immediately."

Jeremy raised an eyebrow and smiled.

"Do not tarry," the woman said sharply. "Her Sublimity has been prepared for a long time to receive you."

Shrugging, he turned and walked down the hall to the khana's quarters, where another servingwoman stood guard at the entrance. She moved quickly to one side, and he tapped politely; a voice inside called out softly, and he opened the door. He was surprised to see that she was already in the bedchamber; obviously there were no suites at the inn, hence no drawing rooms were available even for royalty. He was pleased and thought that the arrangement was perfect for his purposes.

Then he saw Tule Yasmin standing on the far side of the chamber, and she looked so bewitching that he almost forgot his resolve. She had chosen her costume for the occasion with care, knowing what its effect on him would be, and her faith was fully justified. He stared hard at her and felt the blood pounding in his temples. She was attired in a nightdress of white finespun silk, with a wide neck and tiny scalloped sleeves; the close-fitting bodice was embroidered all over in provocative open cutwork of a leafy design, and the full skirt fell softy to the scalloped hem at her ankles. As a dressing gown, she wore a circular cape of pleated blue silk, and as Jeremy closed the door behind him she untied its ribbons.

"You were hungry tonight," she said.

"I was, now that you mention it," he replied in the same light tone.

"And you enjoyed your meal?"

"Very much."

"So I thought. You spent so long a time downstairs that I thought you would never be done." She removed the cape and tossed it carelessly onto a chair.

Jeremy took a deep breath and discovered that he was trembling slightly. This was going to be far more difficult than he had realized. "You've been thirsty, perhaps, and wanted me to get you some more wine?"

Tule Yasmin frowned. "There is no need to refer to that which is in the past. All those who wait upon me require instruction, naturally. I bear you no ill will, for like all the others who serve me, you had to be taught your proper place. Now you know how to please me, so there will be no need for either of us to mention that occasion again."

"Yes, Your Sublimity," he said flatly, with no trace of irony in his voice.

She moved closer to him. "There are times when conversation is desirable, and other times when talk is superfluous." Smiling, she swayed slightly and raised her arms. "Surely you need no instruction in what I want and expect now."

Jeremy took her into his arms, kissed her passionately, and caressed her. Her fiery ardor inflamed him, and he lifted her off her feet, still kissing her, and then lowered her onto the bed. He needed all of the strength he could summon to leave her there and stand upright while she gazed at him from beneath lowered lids. He regarded her in silence for a moment, and she stirred impatiently, waiting for him to join her.

He forced himself to laugh.

Tule Yasmin raised herself to one elbow, and her night-dress slipped off her shoulder.

"I feel an unquenchable thirst," Jeremy said distinctly. "Only a cup of wine will satisfy it."

He heard Tule Yasmin gasp as he turned away from her, but he ignored the sound and did not look back. There was a dead silence as he left the room and firmly closed the door behind him.

The following day the khana greeted Jeremy with her usual bland, cool smile, and he could not help admiring her courage. Not many women capable of administering a tart rebuke could accept the same stinging treatment in return with such imperturbable spirit. She did not betray her feelings, and Jeremy could only hope that she had learned a measure of respect for him.

It was possible that she was wildly angry with him, but nothing in her attitude gave him even a clue to her feelings. As she kept him at a distance during the last stage of the journey, it was useless to speculate, and he reconciled himself to the thought that before long, either in Venice or in Constantinople itself, he would find out whether his gamble had succeeded, or whether by jilting Tule Yasmin he had spoiled all chance for a treaty between the United States and the Ottoman Empire.

In the meantime the renewed tension in his relationship with the khana was curiously pleasant. From the first moment he had seen her she had challenged him, and he felt sure that she had reacted in an identical way to him. They had silently declared war on each other from the beginning, and sooner or later one or the other would emerge triumphant. Jeremy realized that Tule Yasmin was a princess who had never in all her life been thwarted, yet he felt an absolute confidence in his own ability to conquer her. The day would come when she would acknowledge him as her master, and he would not be satisfied until he subdued her.

She was enjoying the battle, too, he realized, and he

warned himself not to reveal to her how much he would be forced to depend on her in Constantinople. There were no rules in the strange war they were fighting, and he had no illusions about Tule Yasmin. An unscrupulous person himself, he recognized the same streak in her. But, in spite of his misgivings, he knew when the party arrived in Venice that the time was fast approaching when he would have no choice but to ask her to intercede for him with the sultan. She would agree, he thought, only if she now regarded him as a man rather than as a servant, and as the party entered Venice he knew that a crossroad had been reached, both literally and figuratively.

The English merchant ship slowly made its way through the Strait of Gibraltar, and when she entered the open waters of the Mediterranean, Mary Ellis was joined on deck by Rosalind and Robert Tate. The latter was pouting and looked worried about something, but the actress, who was busy memorizing lines from one of the speeches in *Antigone,* was unaware of her cousins' presence. She stood at the deck rail and recited:

> "Your edict, King, was strong,
> But all your strength is weakness itself against
> The immortal unrecorded laws of God.
> They are not merely now: they were, and shall be,
> Operative forever, beyond man utterly.
> I knew I must die, even without your decree:
> I am only mortal. And if I must die
> Now, before it is my time to die,
> Surely this is no hardship: can anyone
> Living as I live, with evil all about me,
> Think death less than a friend? This death of mine
> Is of no importance; but if I had left my brother
> Lying in death unburied, I should have suffered.
> Now I do not."

"Oh, Mary, that was wonderful!" Rosalind exclaimed. "I could listen to you recite all day."

"Well, that's all you're going to hear for today, Cousin," Mary said as she closed her manuscript and smiled from beneath her wide-brimmed straw hat trimmed with ostrich plumes. "The Mediterranean is so beautiful that I'm having trouble concentrating."

"See. You're just as romantic as I am," the younger girl said.

"Yes, but when we reach the Aegean and visit the Greek islands—which we should be approaching in just a few days' time—I'll really have to go to work, even if it's a battle to concentrate."

"I just hope there aren't any other battles," Rob said petulantly, leaning on the deck rail.

Mary looked quizzically at her cousin. "Rob, whatever do you mean?"

"I mean a battle with the Turks when we enter their waters," the young man said, frowning.

"Oh, Rob, don't be so sour," his sister chided him. "The Mediterranean is so beautiful, and none of the crew seems worried in the slightest degree."

"That's because they don't know what I know," Rob said mysteriously.

"And just what do you know, dear Cousin?" Mary asked, strolling past him and looking out at the sea.

"That we don't have a Royal Navy escort after all. Or at least if we do, it may be hundreds of miles away. The captain just told me this morning. He said he knew it ever since we left Blackwall."

"But Uncle John arranged for a navy escort!" Rosalind was becoming concerned.

"Yes," Rob said, "but as the captain just told me, the ship that was to escort us was late returning from another mission. So assuming the ship followed us at all, it may be hundreds of miles behind us—though the captain doesn't seem to be any more concerned about it than Mary."

"Oh, my," Rosalind couldn't help saying, and she brought her hand to her face.

Mary Ellis decided it was time to speak firmly. "Now

listen, you two, all this talk about battles and navy escorts is morbid. Rosalind, what happened to your spirit of adventure? Rob, what happened to your resolve to protect us? You two sound like my father, always fretting and expecting something dreadful to happen." She turned and looked out at the bright blue sea. "It's a beautiful day," she said rapturously, holding out her arms in a theatrical gesture. "We're almost at our destination, and I refuse to believe anything could possibly go wrong!"

V

Through the centuries Venice had become accustomed to many strange sights, for ships from every known part of the world had long anchored in the basin of San Marco. Trade had made the little republic rich, and her cosmopolitan air was unique in the Western world. The sight of the veiled servingwomen aroused only a mild curiosity as a guide led the party to the Ca' Molin Palace, where the Turkish envoy to Venice lived. The republic, Jeremy knew, had long enjoyed the distinction of being the only European state with whom the Ottomans had bothered to maintain diplomatic relations, but the present sultan, more liberal than his predecessors, had also exchanged ambassadors with France and Spain.

The outside of the twin-towered palace looked like many of the other great buildings of Venice, and although there were touches of the Orient in the architecture, there was nothing about the place that particularly suggested the Ottoman world. The interior, however, was an unusual blend of West and East. Luxurious rugs from remote Turkish possessions covered the floor, but the tables and chairs scattered in profusion through a series of anterooms were of French design, and most of them looked as though they had been made around the turn of the century, when the tastes of Louis XIV had dominated the Continent. The many servants who salaamed before the khana were dressed in livery, after the fashion of London and Paris, but Jeremy noticed that virtually all of them wore narrow, engraved silver bands around their left ankles, which meant they were slaves.

Tule Yasmin was escorted to an apartment that had been prepared for her, and a stammering majordomo told her that the ambassador would wait on her at her convenience. Jeremy was taken to a small but comfortably furnished room, and when he saw a thick mattress on the floor instead of a bed, knee-high tables, and a prayer rug, he knew he was in Selim's domain. A servant brought in a tub with gold handles, the bath water was faintly perfumed, and a small bowl of candied dates known as *gasa* was placed beside the tub, to revive the bather if the hot water exhausted him. It required little imagination for Jeremy to think himself already in Turkey, and he smiled in anticipation of the days to come.

When he returned to the United States, he would demand an enormous reward from Alexander Hamilton; the secretary believed himself to be infallible, but there was a weak spot in his armor, and Jeremy intended to exploit it. At no time would Hamilton want it known that he had deliberately concocted a scheme behind Secretary Jefferson's back, but he would be vulnerable to exposure after Jeremy was publicly recognized as the man responsible for the establishment of diplomatic relations with the Turks. Mr. Hamilton would pay a pretty penny for discretion, and Jeremy planned to get as much as he could in return for keeping silent.

The prospect made him lighthearted, and he whistled as he dried himself with a thick towel after his bath. He was still whistling when a manservant knocked on the door, entered, and bowed low. "It is the wish of Her Sublimity to sail for Turkey on the afternoon tide today," the man said. "His Excellency, Bjoram Tal, has urged her to remain here as his guest, but the ships which His Magnificence himself sent to transport her have been waiting for many days, and she is anxious to leave these Frankish lands behind her. So I have been instructed to inform you that you are to prepare for an immediate departure."

Jeremy nodded and glanced inquiringly at a neatly folded pile of clothing the man carried in his arms.

"It is the command of Her Sublimity that you attire yourself in these," the servant said, and placed the clothing on a table.

Annoyed, Jeremy made no reply. Tule Yasmin's high-handed, peremptory way of making her wishes known always irritated him.

The man looked at Jeremy's left ankle and then seemed confused. "You are not one of Her Sublimity's Frankish slaves?"

"No." He had no idea what explanation, if any, the khana had given the Turkish envoy to account for his presence in her entourage, and Jeremy had no desire to complicate matters when affairs were running smoothly. So it was better to say nothing.

The servant started to say something, thought better of it, and checked himself. Then, bowing again, he retired quickly from the room, leaving Jeremy to examine the clothing. In a short time he had dressed himself in loose white trousers, which he tucked into calf-high boots of soft white leather, an open-throated white silk shirt with voluminous sleeves, and an open vest of cloth-of-silver, and then he slipped a burnoose on his head. The burnoose, which seemed to be shapeless, caused him some difficulty until he realized that a thin silver cord that came with it was to be bound around his forehead, holding it in place.

He was amused to see that the khana had also provided him with a silver-hilted scimitar, and after sliding it under the sash, he slipped the bone-handled knife from Paris and his own pistol into his belt, too. Then he wrapped the sword he had won on the road into a length of cloth, and thought he would present it to Tule Yasmin as a souvenir of their fight with the highwaymen. The gesture, he reflected, would please her.

After a short time the servant returned and, after quickly packing Jeremy's Western clothing, led him out and down a long corridor. As they started to descend a broad staircase, Jeremy caught a quick glimpse of himself in a tall pier glass of exquisite Venetian glass that stood opposite the landing and could not help gaping at himself. No one who had ever known him would recognize him now, and he wondered what Alexander Hamilton would think of his appearance. The secretary could not possibly be more startled than Jeremy himself.

When they reached the ground floor the servant conducted him to a door that opened onto a canal at the rear of the palace. A gondola was waiting there, and Jeremy stepped into it. His belongings were tossed in after him, and a laconic Venetian gondolier immediately shoved off. He seemed to take his passenger through every canal in the city, but at last they arrived at the basin of San Marco, which was filled with merchant ships flying the colors of virtually every seagoing European nation.

The gondolier steered his craft past them, and Jeremy saw three galleys anchored at the far end of the harbor. They were narrow vessels, which sat high in the water, and from a distance they looked frail. But when the gondola drew closer to them he saw they were far sturdier than he had imagined, and they carried surprisingly heavy armaments. The largest of the flotilla, which was approximately the length of an American frigate, displayed a dozen eighteen-pounder cannon and half again as many twenty-four-pounders. And the upper decks of the smaller ships were studded with six-pounders and nine-pounders.

Long rows of oars could be seen on the lower decks at the level of the water, and Jeremy assumed that these were manned by galley slaves, wretches who were serving criminal sentences or prisoners captured in war. The presence of the slaves, Jeremy realized, explained why the galleys were isolated from the ships of the Christian nations and occupied an otherwise deserted part of the basin. But the Turks did not rely on manpower alone to propel their craft, and each vessel also carried three lateen sails. The triangles of canvas were painted a bright yellow, and they made a cheerful sight as they sparkled in the sunlight.

From the masthead of each galley a Turkish flag, scarlet with a gold border, waved in the gentle breeze, and when Jeremy was deposited at the largest of the ships, habit caused him to salute the ensign as he stepped aboard.

His gesture pleased a young Turkish officer, who smiled broadly as he conducted the guest to a raised deck at the stern. Two silken tents had been erected on it, and before the larger of them three veiled women were preparing a dish of lamb and rice in pots set out in the open in a cleverly constructed fire pit that was lined with thick stones to protect the wooden deck. A burly, broad-shouldered man whose clothing was embellished with gold braid stood on the deck, peering down and stroking his gray-flecked beard.

When Jeremy approached, the man touched his heart, lips, and forehead in the Islamic greeting, and when the stranger did the same a faint look of surprise showed in his penetrating eyes. "I am Mustafa el Kro, pasha of one horsetail, commander of this fleet, and personal custodian of the khana Tule Yasmin on behalf of His Magnificence. May Allah be with you."

"May Allah be with you." Jeremy introduced himself and thought that he was indeed traveling in exalted circles. During his visit to Constantinople he had seen pashas of horsetail rank riding through the streets there, but never before had he spoken to one.

Mustafa el Kro studied the American for a moment and then sighed unhappily. "You've caused me to lose an expensive wager," he said in his deep, booming voice.

"How so?" Jeremy asked innocently.

"The janissary pasha of infantry is better acquainted with Her Sublimity than I am, and I owe him fifty sheep, along with one of my favorite knives, because of his superior knowledge. He wagered that the khana would be certain to bring back a Frankish male concubine with her from her journey, but I was sure she wouldn't."

Jeremy flushed at the description and struggled to conquer an impulse to punch the Turk's thick-lidded, heavy face. He reminded himself that he was in an alien world now, where values and customs were vastly different from his own and where no one thought as he did.

"I must admit," Mustafa el Kro continued, "that I'm surprised. I thought the sister of the khagan Buyantu Yassan would show better sense than to become involved with a dog of an infidel. However, I suppose you know what you're doing." Again he inspected Jeremy carefully. "You look capable enough, to be sure. For your sake I hope you don't suffer the fate of the others."

Before the startled Jeremy could reply, the sound of a ram's horn blasted the quiet, and a long line of gondolas approached the galleys. Uniformed, scimitar-bearing Turks rode in most of them, and in a large boat in the center, attended by her women, was Tule Yasmin. She, too, had changed into Eastern garb, and as she stepped on board the flagship, Jeremy stared at her. She was the same person, of course, but the change in her appearance was astonishing.

Her hair was brushed back, and she wore gold earrings shaped like bird cages, with a tiny gold and enamel parrot in each. The upper part of her body was encased in a long-sleeved jacket that ended just below her breasts, leaving her midriff bare. The garment of red brocade was richly embroidered with emeralds and rubies that were dazzling in the afternoon sunlight. Trousers of heavy red silk, clasped to her ankles by bands of brocade, matched her jacket, and her high-heeled slippers of red satin, embroidered in gold thread, had long, curled-up toes. She looked lovelier than ever before to Jeremy, but the Eastern garb gave her an air of inscrutability.

The pasha hurried forward to meet her, with Jeremy at his side, and she walked slowly up the length of the main deck, accepting the deep salaams of the officers and crew as her due. Jeremy noticed that the galley slaves, naked except for brief loincloths, had prostrated themselves at the benches to which they were chained, too. Mustafa el Kro threw himself to the deck, facedown, and two young officers who had fallen in behind seemed to expect Jeremy to do the same before making their own obeisance. An American did not prostrate himself before anyone, and although Jeremy was willing to follow foreign customs to an extent and bow more deeply than he would to a woman at home, he could not tolerate the idea of humbling himself so completely.

But the two young Turks were glaring at him steadily, and he had the feeling they would run him through if he showed what to them would be a sign of disrespect to the khana. Unless he complied quickly he would become involved in what promised to be a vicious fight, and remembering the goal he was struggling to achieve, he swallowed his pride and lowered himself to the deck. No woman was worth such a gesture, he told himself, but by sacrificing his pride he might be helping to win incalculable benefits for the United States.

In spite of his arguments his self-esteem was not improved when Tule Yasmin walked quickly past him without pausing or bothering to glance in his direction. And his dignity suffered still more when, as she swept close to him, he was sure he heard her laugh softly to herself.

The galleys sailed promptly, according to schedule; they moved slowly and majestically through the Adriatic to the Mediterranean, and a new routine was established for Jeremy. He saw very little of Tule Yasmin, so his time was his own, and he spent it principally in the company of the janissary officers who commanded the guard of honor that had been assigned to escort the princess on this last stage of her journey.

As there was little to do for hour after endless hour, Jeremy questioned the officers closely regarding the organization, discipline, training, and tactics of the janissaries. The Turks took pride in their army and answered him politely, but he felt they were patronizing him. At first it seemed that their attitude was caused by the natural contempt of Moslems for non-believers, but finally the truth dawned on him. The janissaries, like Mustafa el Kro, looked down on him because they considered him no more than a male concubine.

It became increasingly difficult for him to accept their disdain, and he began to count the days until they would arrive in Constantinople and his ordeal would come to an end. He had given great thought to the timing of his appeal to the khana for help and had decided that he would request her intervention at the last possible moment, preferably the night before they landed. In that way, if he was able to persuade her to intercede for him with the sultan, she would have less opportunity to change her mind.

Two days before the flotilla was due to reach Turkey, the monotony of life at sea was broken by an incident that gave Jeremy an opportunity to observe the effectiveness of the Turks' naval gunnery. The waters of the eastern Mediterranean were under the absolute control of the sultan's subjects, and it was surprising to find the vessels of any but friendly nations in these parts. Occasionally a trading ship or a brig carrying pilgrims to the Holy Land braved the possible consequences of Moslem wrath, however, and shortly before noon the lookout stationed on top of the tallest of the stubby masts on the flagship shouted that he saw a foreign sail.

The galleys raced toward her, and when they drew closer Jeremy saw that she was an old-fashioned merchant ship of some four hundred tons, slowly making her way through the Aegean. She was flying the red, white, and blue flag of England, and Mustafa el Kro, bored and anxious for exercise, saw an excellent opportunity to demonstrate his prowess to the khana, at the expense of a nation the Turks disliked.

At his directions the smaller galleys pulled ahead, one to starboard and the other to port, while he headed straight for the English ship. Tule Yasmin sent word to Jeremy to join her on her private deck, and when he arrived there she stretched out on a small divan piled high with cushions, waiting to be amused. Mustafa el Kro did his best to entertain her and signaled the English ship to stop and cast anchor. Her captain chose instead to disregard the command, and the pasha ordered a shot fired across her bow.

One of the eighteen-pounders went into action at once, and the shot went wild, much to the chagrin of every Turkish officer. The merchantman tried valiantly to increase her speed, and the pasha, outraged and trying to make up for the inept handling of his gunners, commanded his men to sink her. Four or five of the larger cannon went into action, but no more than an occasional shot struck the target, and Jeremy winced. Tule Yasmin, who was watching him as he stood at her side, reached up and touched his arm.

"No doubt you can do better?" she asked. "If so, show me your skill."

Jeremy hated the English and had fired at them more times than he could remember, but that had been during the war, and there had been a reason for his actions then. He could not bring himself to fire on a helpless, badly outnumbered merchantman for the sake of sheer sport, just as he could never accept or approve the use of galley slaves. "No, thanks," he said. "I'm out of practice."

Tule Yasmin raised her shapely eyebrows, then turned back as the two smaller galleys joined in the attack. The English ship fought valiantly, and although she carried only a few small six-pounders, she gave better than she received for a time, and the starboard galley in particular was hit repeatedly. But the size and superior armaments of the Turkish flotilla determined the outcome of the unequal battle in advance, and in a quarter of an hour the English ship was in flames.

Mustafa el Kro sent his smaller ships in for the kill, boarding parties swarmed over her decks, and a small number of prisoners were removed and carried to the flagship in longboats. By this time the merchantman was burning furiously, but no one on board the big galley paid any attention to her. The prisoners were coming aboard now, and in addition to the eight or ten power-grimed men, one of the victims was a young woman.

Jeremy looked at her, realized that she was exceptionally pretty, and felt sorry for her. No matter what fate might be in store for her, it would certainly not be pleasant. However, he knew better than to intervene, at least at the moment. The khana would be sure to misinterpret his interest, and would decree an even more severe punishment.

The girl, no more than twenty or twenty-one, was tall, with an unusually slender and supple figure. She was too thin, Jeremy thought with relief, to attract Turkish bordello owners, for the Moslems liked their women heavier. Her red hair flowed freely beneath a wide-brimmed straw hat trimmed with ostrich plumes, and although there was obvious fright in her green eyes, Jeremy could see there was a depth of solid character in her gentle but firm mouth and strong chin.

Mustafa el Kro grinned at the prisoners and ordered them lined up before him. Some of the men were exhausted, but all showed spirit, and the girl, recovering her equilibrium, held herself proudly erect. The pasha, removing a jewel-hilted knife from his belt, moved slowly down the line. "This one and this," he said, touching the men with the point of his blade, "look young and strong. The janissaries can use them. Send the others to the galleys. Put the woman up for auction when we reach port. See that she's fed plenty of rice, and she'll bring a higher price. Whatever is received for her," he added gallantly, "will be given to Her Sublimity as a token of today's excursion." He looked at the khana, beaming and expecting to receive a sign of approval from her.

But Tule Yasmin frowned thoughtfully. "Bring the wench closer, and remove some of those trappings so we may examine her more carefully."

The girl was dragged forward, and the pasha, with simple brutality, cut away her dress of pale green satin with his knife and then hacked off her petticoat, too, so that she stood only in her shift. She shivered, in spite of the sun's warmth, and the khana smiled. "We have often wanted to own a Frankish serving girl," she said calmly. "They make excellent slaves, once their spirits have been broken. So we shall keep her."

"My God," Jeremy exclaimed involuntarily in English.

The girl stared at him in astonishment, but Tule Yasmin barely glanced at him. "Here is a chance for you to make yourself useful. Find out who she is, tell her what her kismet is to be, and warn her that her pretty little back will be scarred unless she learns to obey promptly."

Swallowing hard, Jeremy turned to the girl. "Who are you?" he asked hoarsely.

"Mary Ellis," she replied, and then added contemptuously, "there's no need to ask your identity. A renegade Englishman—with these scum!"

"I'm American, not English," he said rapidly, "and there's no time now to tell you how I happen to be here." He explained her plight, and then, somewhat to his own surprise, added, "I'll do what I can to help you."

Mary Ellis looked straight at him but made no reply. Only a few hours earlier she had been a supremely happy, self-confident woman—full of anticipation about playing the greatest role of her acting career. But now that her father's worst fears had come true and she was a captive of hostile barbarians, she didn't know whether she was more angry or afraid. All she could do was pray that her cousins—from whom she had been separated—had come to no harm.

There was a commotion down the deck, and Jeremy saw an officer approaching with two other prisoners, their hands tied behind their backs. One was a young man, the other a girl, and it was evident at a glance that they were twins. Apparently they had fought hard for their freedom, and the young man had sustained a cut on his forehead.

"These two were caught trying to escape in the ship's gig," the officer told Mustafa el Kro.

Tule Yasmin examined the pair with interest. "Let them be brought nearer," she said.

The officer motioned the pair forward, but neither moved. "We are British subjects," Robert Tate declared in a ring-ing voice. "And so is Mistress Ellis. I presume you realize you have abducted one of the most renowned—"

"Quiet, Robert!" Mary cried. "Don't make matters worse by identifying me!"

Tule Yasmin gestured impatiently. "I do not have all day to waste. Remove their clothes, too, so I may inspect them more carefully."

Knives flashed, and Rosalind Tate gasped as she was revealed in her skimpy shift. Although she was small, she had a full and athletic figure.

Robert Tate kicked and cursed as his clothes were cut away, and Jeremy knew what the young Englishman failed to realize, that he was helpless and that he was merely causing problems for himself. "Calm down, lad," he called in English, "or you'll pay a heavy price for insolence."

Robert stopped struggling and stared at him. So did Rosalind, and he realized that Mary Ellis, whoever she might be, was studying him, apparently wondering who he might be and whether he was sincere in his attempts to help the prisoners.

Rosalind and Robert were prodded by scimitars until they stood closer to the khana. Tule Yasmin seemed delighted. "I have never been served by twins," she said. "Perhaps I will have the young man gelded so he may live in the harem. I shall think about it."

Robert was so outraged over the treatment that his sister, Mary, and he himself were receiving from their captors that he ignored Jeremy's advice. Lashing out with a foot, he kicked Mustafa el Kro hard in the shin. The blow undoubtedly was painful, but Mustafa el Kro reacted with a phlegm that was typical of the Turkish ruling class. His face expressionless, he sucked in his breath and made no move.

Jeremy, deeply concerned for the safety of the young Englishman, started forward to halt Robert but realized he would be wise not to interfere. He couldn't allow sympathy to place his own mission in jeopardy, but the glitter in Mustafa el Kro's dark eyes made him uneasy.

"Please, Rob!" Mary called. "You'll make things worse for all of us!"

She was right, but the young man she had called Rob was so enraged that he no longer cared. He knew he had been stripped naked, and he disliked the smile on the face of the gaudily attired young woman who seemed to be in charge of these barbarians. It was too much for him when Tule Yasmin looked at his genitals and said, "Yes, I believe I shall require the sacrifice of his manhood for the pleasure of serving me."

Robert Tate did not understand the woman's words, but it was enough that he knew she was mocking him. Becoming so violently angry that he scarcely realized what he was doing, he spat in her face.

Tule Yasmin grew pale beneath the rouge on her cheeks, but stayed motionless, making no attempt to wipe the spittle from her face. "Mustafa el Kro," she said quietly.

"Yes, Your Sublimity." Even the pasha was shocked by the young Englishman's behavior.

"You know the penalty for defying and humiliating one in whose body flows the blood of the Ottomans."

"I do, Your Sublimity."

"Let this miserable infidel be punished accordingly, and let the women who were captured with him learn well the lesson they are about to witness." Tule Yasmin spoke in a toneless voice.

Mustafa el Kro hesitated, aware of the complications that might ensue; certainly he was conscious of the might of Britain's Royal Navy.

Tule Yasmin spoke more forcefully. "You may proceed," she said in a hard, dry voice.

The cousin of the sultan had spoken, and the pasha had no choice. He turned, gave an order, and a rope was tied under Robert's armpits. Within moments the young Englishman was hoisted to the yardarm, where he dangled helplessly.

"There's nothing you can do for him," Jeremy said to the two female captives, addressing them urgently in English. "Close your eyes and don't watch. He's insulted the cousin of Selim the Magnificent, so may the Lord have mercy on his soul."

Mary's long training as an actress stood her in good stead. She remained impassive, regally erect, seemingly impervious to the degrading scene she was being forced to watch. But Rosalind Tate was in no way able to control her feelings. She knew only that her beloved brother had been placed in jeopardy, and although she had no idea of the fate in store for him, she screamed loudly.

Jeremy approached her at once, drawing his scimitar before any Turk could intervene. "Be quiet, you little idiot," he told her, clapping a hand on her bare shoulder. "Keep on making a fuss, and the sultan's cousin will punish you, too."

"I don't care!" she sobbed.

He knew he had to restore her common sense, so he reached out and slapped her across the face twice. Tule Yasmin smiled faintly and made no attempt to halt the interplay.

A flicker of understanding registered in Mary Ellis's eyes. "Do as he tells you, Rosalind!" she said sharply. "He may be a renegade, but he's trying to help you."

With a great effort Rosalind controlled herself.

One of the Turks handed Mustafa el Kro a long whip of bull hide. It was a weapon used on the miserable galley slaves below deck, and Jeremy shuddered when he recognized it.

The pasha took careful aim, the whip cracked, and a long, ugly welt appeared on Robert Tate's naked body. Tule Yasmin's eyes gleamed, and Mary Ellis moistened her lips but otherwise showed no emotion. Rosalind moaned softly, unconsciously leaning against Jeremy. He supported her weight delicately, surreptitiously, without putting an arm around her.

Tule Yasmin spoke softly to an aide standing a few feet behind her. He hurried away to the lower part of the galley, returning a few moments later with a slave overseer, one of the men who drove the galley slaves to greater efforts with a long whip, which he wielded expertly.

The man knew what was expected of him. He took one look at the helpless Robert Tate, and his whip flicked expertly. He barely seemed to be exerting any effort whatsoever, but the long length of rawhide uncoiled, and the tip of it creased the side of Robert's face. As the whip fell away there was a blood streak on his face, made as expertly as it would have been by a knife.

All at once Jeremy understood what was in store for the helpless victim. It was the intention of Tule Yasmin literally to strip Robert Tate of all the skin on his body, little by little. The agony in store for the young man was indescribable, impossible to imagine. Why he had to go through such torture for the sake of satisfying the blood-lust of an insatiable woman was too much, more than Jeremy could tolerate.

He didn't stop to think. The time had come to act, and act fast. He reached into his belt and drew his pistol, a long-barreled, cumbersome instrument. He knew that he had to make it a highly effective shot. He would have, at best, the opportunity to fire only once.

He looked up at Robert Tate and caught the young man's eyes, and Robert understood what his deliverer had in store for him. He was going to be put out of his misery at once. He knew he had a clear choice: Either he would die instantly, or he would be killed little by little, in slow stages, making it necessary for him to exert the greatest of willpower. His alternative was all too clear. Either his life would be snuffed out instantly, or he would be obliged to suffer so slowly, to endure such pain that he would be sure to beg for deliverance. He had no desire to beg.

Mary Ellis saw the pistol in Jeremy's hand and divined his purpose. Shock and incredulity mingled in her eyes. Little by little she came to understand what he had in mind, and little by little she accepted the inevitability of the choice that he was making.

Afraid to say anything to Rosalind, she nevertheless

signaled to the younger girl with her eyes. Somehow Mary's message managed to get across, and Rosalind stiffened as though she had been struck a blow with the overseer's whip. But she resigned herself to the inevitable, knowing there was no real choice.

The overseer struck again, causing a long, ugly welt to appear on Robert's shoulder. By gritting his teeth, the victim managed to refrain from crying aloud, but the effort was all he could muster.

Tule Yasmin smiled and moistened her full lips. It was obvious to anyone watching her that she was enjoying the spectacle thoroughly, that the cruelty being inflicted on the helpless young Englishman gave her the greatest of pleasure.

No one was paying the slightest attention to Jeremy, and he took full advantage of the situation. Raising the pistol, he took careful aim; he would have only one opportunity to determine Robert's fate.

Jeremy steadied himself, squeezed the trigger slowly, steadily, the barrel unwavering as it pointed at Robert's head. Suddenly the entire group gathered on the deck was startled by the explosion of the pistol shot.

Too late it occurred to Tule Yasmin and to the high-ranking Turks who surrounded her what had happened. As they gaped at Robert Tate they saw that a bullet had entered the center of his forehead. The shot had killed him instantly, putting him out of his misery for all time. Now he was beyond the vengeance of Tule Yasmin.

Jeremy had killed a human being deliberately, in cold blood, but he did not feel like a murderer. He had had no real choice, and his conscience was clear.

Tule Yasmin stared at him, her eyes blazing, color rising in her cheeks as she realized he had deprived her of her quarry. But Mustafa el Kro looked with new respect at the man he had regarded as the concubine of the Mongolian princess. Jeremy's act of defiance had required great courage, and the Turkish pasha well knew it.

Mary Ellis also gazed with new respect at the man she

had regarded a few moments earlier as a renegade. She was aware that what he had done had required courage, and she was grateful to him for saving her unfortunate cousin from torment.

Rosalind was crushed. All she knew was that her beloved brother was no more. She was on the verge of fainting, but Jeremy grasped her arm and shook her roughly.

His work was not yet done. Ignoring Tule Yasmin, he struck an imperious pose and said sharply, "Cut down the body."

Several of the Turks hastened to do his bidding.

"Now," he said, "wrap his body in the English flag that you captured from the ship."

The Turks hesitated for a few moments, but there was no denying the authority in his tone. They hesitated briefly, then hurried off and returned with the Union Jack and wrapped the still body of Robert Tate in it.

One task remained for Jeremy, a very important task. He moved to the ship's rail, gestured to the men to carry the flag-draped body, and then, lowering his head, he spoke in a low but clear voice:

"The Lord is my shepherd; I shall not want.
He maketh me to lie down in green pastures:
He leadeth me beside the still waters.
He restoreth my soul: He leadeth me in the
    paths of righteousness for His name's sake.
Yea, though I walk through the valley of the
    shadow of death, I will fear no evil: For
    Thou art with me; Thy rod, and Thy staff they
    comfort me.
Thou preparest a table before me in the presence
    of mine enemies: Thou anointest my head with
    oil; my cup runneth over.
Surely goodness and mercy shall follow me all the
    days of my life: And I will dwell in the house
    of the Lord forever."

Jeremy gestured abruptly, and the Turks holding Robert's flag-draped body threw their burden into the sea. He stood silently at the rail, watching, not moving, his face registering no emotions. Only after the body sank from sight beneath the blue-green water did he turn away abruptly and stalk to his cabin, not deigning to look again in the direction of Tule Yasmin. His attitude made it clear that she might be related to the ruler of Islam, she might be a mighty power in her own right, but she had no control over the man who—for better or worse—had become her husband.

Mary Ellis, still suffering from a multitude of shocks, stared after him as he left and wondered whether she had made a mistake, whether she should revise her opinion of this extraordinary self-willed man, a man who apparently did what he believed right regardless of the consequences. She had no idea who he was and why he was here, but she prayed with all her heart that somehow he would help Rosalind and herself.

A still breeze from the west enabled the galleys to rely completely on their sails as they sped majestically across the Aegean toward Turkey. The night was warm, the sky was clear and bright with stars, and a half-moon seemed to be suspended above the horizon. Jeremy bided his time until the flagship began to grow quiet for the night, then he made his way to the deck reserved for the khana and her entourage. He was uncertain whether she would see him, and he was both surprised and pleased when one of the servingwomen led him to the larger of the silken tents. Tule Yasmin received him there, dressed as she had been earlier in the day. She was reclining on a pile of pillows spread out on the deck, and she propped herself on one elbow, smiling enigmatically as Jeremy entered.

Giving no indication that she was distressed at the events earlier in the day, she said smugly, "So you have realized that our journey is drawing to a close."

"I've thought of little else," he replied truthfully.

"And you wanted to visit me again." She was very sure of herself and obviously felt she was forcing him to declare his desire and need for her.

"There is nothing on earth I've wanted more," Jeremy declared, looking straight at her.

Tule Yasmin looked pleased with herself. "Then you admit you were in the wrong."

"Oh, I admit it freely." Mere words, Jeremy thought, cost him nothing, provided they helped him achieve his goal. The khana was not the first woman he had ever fooled with assurances of his devotion, nor would she be the last. "You hurt my pride, as you well know, so I had to retaliate. Naturally, I've been thinking of nothing except you. We'll soon go our separate ways, so I decided this was no time to stand on false conceit."

A lesser woman might have been taken in, but the khana was not one to accept a declaration at face value. She and Jeremy were so much alike that something in either his tone or his manner made her suspicious. Her eyes became hard, and she sat up, balancing herself by clasping her hands around one knee. "You have some reason for trying to win my favor," she said harshly, daring him to contradict her.

His mind raced as he tried to think of a suitable reply. A bald denial of her charge would be the easiest at the moment but would cause complications later, when he indeed asked her to use her influence to seek an interview for him with the sultan. On the other hand, if he admitted her claim, she would undoubtedly order him to leave her presence immediately. There was also the further complication of the English hostages, and he had no idea at the moment how he could help them.

Suddenly a ram's horn sounded and began to blare repeatedly. Jeremy was relieved, for at that instant the interruption seemed welcome as it spared him the need to answer Tule Yasmin. The horn startled her, and jumping to her feet, she hurried out to the open deck, with Jeremy at her heels. Men were racing in every direction, and Jeremy realized at once that they were moving to their battle stations. Before he could discover the reason for the alarm, however, Mustafa el Kro ran up the steps and approached the khana.

"Your Sublimity, go below!" he shouted, too perturbed to address her with the respect due her rank. "An English frigate has followed us and is going to open fire on us!" He pointed past the stern.

Jeremy saw a vessel of forty-two guns approaching rapidly, and he peered at her through the night. In spite of the hour she had run up her flag, and by the light of the moon he recognized the English ensign; it was a pennant that had signified the enemy for all the long years of the war, and he hated it still. The frigate's gun ports were open, and he saw dim, white-clad figures in position on her decks. Obviously she had seen the burning merchantman and had sailed after the Turks to obtain revenge and, perhaps, to rescue the prisoners. What Jeremy had no way of knowing, of course, was that this was the Royal Navy escort of the merchantman, finally arriving on the scene after the unexpected delay.

"We will watch you destroy the infidel from here, Pasha," Tule Yasmin said confidently, and she either had no fears for her own safety or else she believed the flotilla would quickly destroy the impudent Christian vessel that was so badly outnumbered.

If that was her opinion, Jeremy knew better. Mustafa el Kro prudently kept his views to himself, and seeing he could not induce the khana to change her mind, he hastily backed away and rejoined his men. Jeremy had formed a less-than-flattering opinion of the Turks' abilities during the action against the merchantman, and he was not surprised now to see men milling about on the main deck in undisciplined confusion. Officers countermanded each other's orders, men struggled to unlimber the cannon but were hampered in their efforts by other gun crews, and the two smaller galleys, instead of fanning out and taking up positions to port and starboard, made the fatal error of closing ranks with the flagship.

In the meantime the English vessel coldly and methodically made ready for battle. The seamanship of her captain and crew was beyond reproach, and she plainly knew precisely what she was doing. Tacking neatly, she presented her port side to the Turks, and no sooner was she in position than three of her guns fired trial rounds in quick succession at the small galley that stood between her and the flagship. The shots fell short, and in the pause that followed Jeremy knew exactly what was taking place on the frigate: The gunnery officer and his assistants were carefully adjusting their range.

The little galley made no attempt either to slip away or to close in on the Englishman, which would have been the better tactic. Instead she held her position and opened fire on the enemy with her nine-pounders. Jeremy winced involuntarily when he saw the shots going wild; the marksmanship of the Turks had been deplorable in daylight, but at night their efforts were ludicrous. He knew what would happen next, and he was not mistaken. The twenty-one port guns of the frigate fired a mighty salvo that made the whole sea seem to shake.

The small galley shuddered and appeared to leap out of the water as the broadside decimated her crew and made her a wreck in a matter of seconds. She tried to respond to the blow, and the other two Turkish vessels opened fire, too, but the frigate ignored them and unleashed a second salvo against her initial target. When the smoke cleared away, Jeremy saw that the galley was listing badly and that her prow was jutting crazily into the air. Men were leaping from her decks into the water and tried to swim away from her as she settled and began to sink.

Tule Yasmin was pale and angry, and Jeremy, glancing at her briefly, saw that she was astonished, unable to believe that her champions could be losing the battle. But he

spared her no more than a single look, for the Englishman
was now shifting his attack to the flagship, and a pair of
trial shots landed near the bow, shaking the graceful galley, sending splinters of wood flying in every direction,
and killing several of the helpless slaves, who were chained
to their benches.

Mustafa el Kro was shouting hoarsely, and his men
continued to fire at the frigate without effect. Jeremy knew
that he had to intervene or perish. Certainly if the British
ship overtook the Turkish galley, the prisoners would be
safe, but it would mean the end of Jeremy's mission and
maybe even of Jeremy himself. Drawing his scimitar, he
ran down to the main deck and, waving his blade menac-
ingly, forced several of the gesticulating officers to draw
back. In his rage he reached out, caught hold of the pasha
by the shoulder, and shook him vigorously. "Lower your
elevation!" he said, "and make allowances for the sea."

Mustafa el Kro could only stare at him, and Jeremy
turned impatiently to the gunners manning the three nearest eighteen-pounders. "Lower your elevation by five degrees," he snapped, and the startled men obeyed. "Now,
compensate for the roll by adjusting three points to starboard. All right, load and fire at will! Fire, I say, or may
the curse of Allah be on you!"

The Turks responded to the voice of command, and
to their amazement all three shots struck the frigate. One,
a lucky blow, snapped her mainmast, and a second crashed
into her quarterdeck. Her guns were firing steadily now
at the flagship, and the Turk was taking heavy punishment,
but Jeremy ignored the danger as he ran from gun to gun,
ordering changes and directing an accurate stream of
heavy iron balls at the Englishman. Soldiers, sailors, and
officers were dying on both sides of him, and whenever
there was a pause in the roar of the cannon he could hear
the screams of the wounded, but he shut out the sounds
and concentrated on his duel with the frigate.

The flagship was giving as good as she received now,

and Jeremy continued to roam up and down the line of eighteen-pounders, shouting an unending series of commands. He realized dimly that the remaining small galley was trying to help, but her fire was still hopelessly wild. Nevertheless she distracted the attention of the English from time to time, and Jeremy was grateful for her inadvertent assistance.

He had no idea how long the battle raged but knew only that both of the principal participants were still afloat and were exchanging blow for blow. The Turks were fighting bravely, heartened by the knowledge that their efforts were under the direction of an expert, but Jeremy was afraid that in the long run the Englishman would destroy the lighter, more fragile galley. But the damage he had inflicted on the frigate was apparently greater than he realized, for when he least expected it she suddenly ceased fire and began to move off to the west under forced sail.

The flagship's cannon could no longer reach her, and the Turks began to cheer madly. Mustafa el Kro appeared beside Jeremy and threw his arms enthusiastically around the powder-grimed American. *"Bismillah!"* the pasha cried. "Never have I seen such shooting! You may be the khana's concubine, but you're the best naval gunner in all Islam!"

"Follow that frigate!" Jeremy retorted impatiently. "We can destroy her now!"

Mustafa el Kro shook his head and waved an arm at the battered flagship. Two of her lateen sails were down, and there were numerous gaping holes in her deck. "We have suffered too badly ourselves," he said sadly. "We have no choice now but to make our way to Constantinople as best we can and pray that Allah will guide us there."

Jeremy saw that the damage to the galley had indeed been great and offered the pasha his further help. It was eagerly accepted, and as the flagship and her one remaining escort limped off to the east, they supervised the cleaning of the decks, put carpenters to work repairing and patching as best they could, and generally tried to make the battered vessel seaworthy. The surviving galley slaves rowed rhythmically, and the remaining sail was hoisted on a makeshift mast.

At one point, when Jeremy and the pasha were supervising the clearing of wreckage near the stern, they heard the sound of stifled but unmistakable feminine sobs coming from the direction of Tule Yasmin's small private deck, which had somehow miraculously escaped being damaged. Jeremy was startled and looked inquiringly at the burly Turk.

"Her Sublimity," Mustafa el Kro said, unable to conceal a note of irony in his voice, "was very disturbed and annoyed at the poor showing we made before you stepped in and saved us. For some reason it seems to bother her that it was you who prevented us from being destroyed, that it was you who drove off the frigate. So she has had her new English slave—the shorter of the two—brought to her, and the girl is being whipped to relieve Her Sublimity of a sense of frustration. The khana says it is to teach the wench obedience, which also happens to be true, of course. But I know royalty, and whenever they are unhappy they take out their anger on some poor wretch."

Jeremy started toward the upper deck, but Mustafa el Kro gripped his arm hard and halted him. "No," the pasha said emphatically. "You must not interfere!"

"But—"

"Heed my words!" Mustafa el Kro declared, his voice firm but sympathetic. "Islam is in your debt tonight, and your rewards will no doubt be great. But you cannot halt the beating of a mere slave. One may treat a slave as one chooses, and Her Sublimity may deal with every last one of us as she pleases, as if all of us were her slaves. If you try to halt the beating of the slave girl, I will have no choice, hero though you are in the eyes of men and of Allah Himself. If you take one more step toward that deck, I must order my men to run you through."

Jeremy knew there was nothing more he could do, and

his shoulders sagged. It might have been better, he thought bitterly, had he allowed the frigate to send the whole Turkish flotilla to the bottom. He knew now that, no matter what the cost to the United States or himself, he could never again make love to Tule Yasmin.

VI

~~~~~~~~~~~~~~~~

Thirty-six hours after the battle with the English frigate, the leaking, bruised flagship passed through the Dardanelles shortly before dawn, fought her way across the choppy Sea of Marmara, and at noon approached the harbor of Constantinople, the Golden Horn, on the Bosporus. Her escort continued to hover in close attendance, and a score of galleys came out to meet her, including several imperial barges, but Mustafa el Kro scorned all assistance and proudly, almost defiantly, brought his ship to her anchorage without help.

Jeremy saw the towering, familiar minarets of the great mosques on the seven hills of the city, and he was aware, too, of the vast pink sandstone complex of buildings that comprised the imperial palace, where the fate of his mission would be decided. At the moment, however, he could not look ahead. He had worked unceasingly and without rest at the side of the pasha ever since the battle with the English frigate, and together they had brought the galley safely home. Jeremy felt a great sense of accomplishment, and equally important, he believed he had made a friend in Mustafa el Kro. Their incessant labors had created a bond of kinship between them, and Jeremy knew there was now one person in the Ottoman Empire to whom he could turn in case of need.

Another advantage of his preoccupation during the past day and a half was that he had seen Tule Yasmin only in passing. Their abortive conversation had never been resumed, which Jeremy believed was just as well, both for his own peace of mind and the sake of his mission. Mustafa el Kro assured him again and again that he would be rewarded for his feats of leadership and bravery against the English frigate, and he had made up his mind to refuse all honors and to ask instead for the privilege of an audience with the sultan. His one fear was that the khana would have their marriage dissolved before the opportunity for a talk with Selim was created, and in that unhappy event he would be in the same impossible position in which other Westerners found themselves, outside the pale and forbidden by Moslem law to have any contact with members of the ruling class.

A stately, silk-draped barge bearing the star and crescent banner that was the personal emblem of the sultan pulled alongside the flagship, and a host of dignitaries came aboard the galley to escort the sister of the khagan Buyantu Yassan to the dwelling of her omnipotent cousin. When she appeared on the upper deck they prostrated themselves before her, then formed in a semicircle around her as she walked slowly to the barge. She did not look in Jeremy's direction, and he wondered if he would ever see her again.

The khana was followed by her women, and Jeremy counted ten in the entourage. Two of them, he thought, must be the British captives, but he could not tell them from the others, for all of the serving maids looked alike in heavy face veils and voluminous clothing. He felt a sharp stab of pity for the lovely English girls and thought how unfair it was that they had been condemned to a life of degradation and servitude. But he had to put them out of his mind for the moment, for he could not let himself forget that the time of supreme crisis in his own life had arrived.

The harbor master, a pasha of one horsetail, rode out to the galley in his own gig, and during the next half hour he cross-examined Mustafa el Kro on the events of the voyage, writing down the replies he received on a complicated form. Mustafa el Kro often turned to Jeremy for corroboration of various details, and the harbor master looked admiringly at the American when he learned the part that Jeremy had played in the battle and in the frantic struggle for survival that had followed. When the reports were completed, the harbor master gave his fellow pasha and Jeremy a ride to the shore in his gig, and there they found a battalion of smartly uniformed janissaries awaiting them.

Jeremy was given a spirited white Arabian stallion, and with the cavalrymen in a column on either side, he and Mustafa el Kro were taken on a rapid ride across the old city of Stamboul. The streets were narrow and crowded, but pedestrians scattered as the janissaries pushed forward recklessly. The sights and smells of Constantinople were familiar to Jeremy, and he recognized the entrance to the Grand Bazaar, where he had shopped and traded and had lost his good friend, Selim. They moved at a fast clip through the city, and when the escort first took the road to Pera, the newer section of the community where many of the great nobles made their homes, he thought that perhaps he was to be Mustafa el Kro's guest. Then the horsemen veered off onto a street so cramped that the second and third stories of houses and shops on either side almost touched. And before he quite realized where he was, he saw the high, forbidding walls of the imperial palace looming up ahead.

The businesslike guards at the entrance, who were armed with rifles as well as scimitars, passed the party through the gate, and Jeremy looked around him curiously. Dominating the compound, which covered many acres, was the huge, ornate building that was the home of the sultan. The original structure had been built by Constantine, and later emperors had added a maze of new wings to it. Elaborate flower gardens surrounded the subpalace of the grand vizier, the home of the deputy caliph, and the residences of many other officials. Off to the left were the office buildings where the principal business of the imperial government was conducted, and on the right were the barracks of the two divisions of janissaries who were always on duty here when the sultan was in the city.

Behind the palace was the old seraglio, which had once been the harem of the sultans, and near it were the exclusive slave quarters. An inner wall surrounded the seraglio, and the cavalrymen halted before it. A general of janissaries was waiting there, and after Mustafa el Kro and Jeremy dismounted, the officer said something in a low, urgent voice to the pasha, who departed immediately with him in the direction of the palace, after first telling Jeremy they would soon meet again.

Sultan Selim had abolished the harem of his predecessors, Jeremy knew, and as he had only two of the four wives permitted by the Koran, they lived with him in the palace itself. The American wondered what use was being made of the seraglio now, but the question had scarcely formed in his mind when it was partly answered. A janissary colonel took him in tow, led him through the inner gate and past a small garden filled with rare, exotic flowers, and then left him inside the entrance to a one-story building of pink sandstone.

Here a fat, cheerful eunuch took charge of the visitor and took him to a large chamber in the rear, where a tiled swimming pool was located. Jeremy needed only one invitation to divest himself of his clothes and to wash with a bowl of soft, perfumed soap that the eunuch gave him. When he emerged from the pool he discovered that a complete change of attire had been provided by a second eunuch, and as he dressed he marveled at the silken texture of his open-throated shirt and baggy trousers. His headgear was of soft silk, too, and his white belt and calf-high boots were made of the finest supple leather. He picked up his scimitar and pistol and then, in spite of his objections, the eunuchs sprayed scent on his head and shoulders. At last they were satisfied with Jeremy's appearance and took him back to the entrance, where another janissary officer was waiting for him. The Turk led him through the gardens and out of the seraglio gate, and they walked at a rapid pace past a company of riflemen being inspected by a pasha of three horsetails, the highest-ranking Turk Jeremy had ever seen.

"Where are we going?" he asked his silent companion.

The officer did not turn his head. "In the imperial compound of Selim the Magnificent, one asks no questions and trusts to his kismet," was the stern reply.

It was difficult for a Westerner to accept the idea that whatever happened to him was inevitable, but Jeremy said no more, and after a short walk his new-found patience was partly rewarded when they came to the palace itself and entered through a small side door. The officer, who obviously knew his way about the building, conducted the visitor through several rooms in which troops were standing guard; they mounted a flight of stairs, and after making their way down a maze of corridors, they passed through a huge chamber that Jeremy mistakenly assumed to be a reception room.

Then he saw that both walls were lined with cages, and he gaped at them. The bars were of silver, the floors were padded with thick silk, and the edges were trimmed with jewels that gleamed in the sunlight streaming in through high windows. One cage, somewhat larger than the rest, stood alone, and the American saw that its bars were fashioned of gold; attached to two of them was a plaque of diamonds in the shape of a crescent. The cages were unoccupied, but Jeremy realized at once that they were the infamous devices used in the past to protect the rulers of the empire from their ambitious heirs. The large cage obviously had been the prison of the prince who had stood closest to the throne, and the others had housed those who had been next in the line of succession. The room was deserted, but it was significant that the cages had not been removed. The present sultan was reputedly an enlightened man, but Jeremy realized at once that he kept the cages as a reminder to his sons and his brothers that the fate of their ancestors awaited them if they conspired against him.

In an adjoining anteroom a number of high-ranking dignitaries were gathered, and as Jeremy and the officer walked past they fell silent for a moment and stared at the newcomer. Jeremy knew at once that he was in the presence of some of the most powerful and influential men in the empire: A thin youth with a wisp of beard was wearing a gold turban that identified him as a prince of royal blood; two tall men were attired in the flowing robes of desert chieftains; and in a far corner several pashas of three horsetails were studying what appeared to be a map. The only person who was seated was a dark-skinned old man with a double cord of gold on his headdress, and apparently he was allowed this special privilege because he was crippled.

The janissary led Jeremy into still another room, where a platoon of soldiers stood at rigid attention. Plainly these were no ordinary guards, for all stood well over six feet in height, and each wore a heavy gold sash at his waist. A pasha of two horsetails sat at a small table inlaid with mother-of-pearl at the far side of the chamber, and after acknowledging the officer's salute with a curt gesture, he looked inquiringly at Jeremy. The janissary nodded significantly, and the pasha held out his right hand. "Your weapons!" he said sharply.

Jeremy stared at him blankly.

"Give me your scimitar and your firearms," the pasha declared impatiently.

The order was clear, and Jeremy obeyed without understanding why he was being forced to surrender his blade and pistol.

"Are you carrying any other weapons?" The pasha ran his hands over the visitor expertly. "Are you concealing any knives or other lethal weapons on your person? I warn you to answer truthfully, as the penalty is death for those who lie."

The reason for the elaborate precautions suddenly dawned on Jeremy, and his blood raced. After his many weeks of planning and scheming, the unexpected had happened, and he was inexplicably about to be admitted to the presence of the man he had come so far to see, Sultan Selim III.

When the guards were satisfied that Jeremy was concealing no weapons, they opened a padded door for him, and he entered the chamber. Following the instructions he had just been given, he prostrated himself on a floor inlaid with gold, silver, and semiprecious stones in mosaic pattern. Ordinarily he would have resented the custom that forced him to abase himself, but his mind was working furiously, and he was concentrating completely on the unusual opportunity that had been given to him. He had no idea why he had been summoned to appear before the sultan, but he had no intention of wasting his chance to present his plea for Turkish recognition of the United States.

He was allowed to remain with his face pressed against the floor for what seemed like a long time. Then he heard a familiar feminine voice say, "You may rise now."

He stood and saw Tule Yasmin sitting cross-legged on the third of a flight of steps at the far side of a surprisingly small audience chamber. To her left, on the floor level, stood Mustafa el Kro and, at the top of the stairs in front of a curtain of gold, was the sultan, also sitting cross-legged. Sitting beside him was the grand vizier and his trusted friend, Mahmoud ben Ibrahim.

At first glance the ruler of one of the mightiest empires on earth was an unprepossessing man. He was in his early forties, of medium height and somewhat overweight, and unlike his great nobles and generals, he was clean-shaven. His attire was less impressive than that of any member of his retinue, for today he was dressed in a shirt and trousers of plain red silk. On his head was a simple white turban, but Jeremy caught a glimpse of a huge blue-white diamond nestling in the folds of cloth directly above his forehead. The sultan's expression was mild as he studied the American, but his dark eyes were keen and penetrating, and the lines around his firm mouth gave a hint of his character.

Jeremy returned his gaze steadily, and for a moment no one spoke. Then Selim sat back on his cushion and turned to the pasha who stood below him. "It is as you have said, Mustafa el Kro. He appears quick and alert." Turning finally to Jeremy, he smiled. "We are in your debt. You saved the life of our cousin, who is—ah—dear to us." Only Mahmoud ben Ibrahim knew of the sultan's dismay over the sudden return of his cousin from her brief sojourn in France, and they both finally had to agree that it was Selim's kismet to be saddled with the imperious khana. "And," the sultan went on, "you prevented Islam from suffering disgrace at the hands of those Frankish dogs, the English."

No reply was expected, so Jeremy merely bowed his head. He knew the praise he was receiving was deserved, but he reasoned that a show of humility would be helpful.

"We are curious," the sultan continued. "Many Franks serve our cause, but they have always been reluctant to take up arms for us until they have abandoned Christianity and have accepted the teachings of the One True Faith. You are a Christian, are you not?"

"Yes, Your Magnificence," Jeremy said quietly, without apology.

"We are told that you are the subject of a new nation across the seas that shares with us a hatred for the English. Nevertheless it has been our experience that Franks always forget their feuds against each other to join in battle against Islam. What caused you to lead our galleys to victory against the English?"

Jeremy smiled up at the sultan. "It is better, Your Magnificence, to live than to die," he said blandly. "Had I not directed the fire of the cannon, the frigate would have either taken us captive or sent us all to the bottom of the sea."

"We enjoy your candor," Selim said, and laughed. "It is refreshing to hear someone tell us the truth. The sycophants who surround us would have embroidered many falsehoods for our pleasure, had they been in your place. They would have claimed that they acted out of love for our person and that the glory of the empire was ever in their minds. You will be well repaid for your honesty." He was smiling broadly, and so was the pasha, but Tule Yasmin's face was devoid of all expression.

Jeremy ignored her and spoke quickly and earnestly. "I seek no reward for myself, Your Magnificence, for I am not here on my own behalf. I have traveled many miles to see you, and I ask only that you hear me as a representative of the United States of America."

His words were totally unexpected, and Selim frowned. "You have been brought into our presence because it was our wish, and for no other reason," he said, and there was a note of disapproval in his voice.

A wise man, Jeremy knew, would accept the hint and remain silent, but he could not stop now. "It is the great desire of my country to establish diplomatic relations with Your Magnificence, for it is our belief that such a friendship would benefit both our lands."

"Enough!" the sultan said, and waved a jeweled hand. "We do not open our ears to every itinerant beggar who knocks at our gates. You will accept the reward that we have prepared for you, and in time, if you prove faithful to our trust, perhaps we will listen to your request. At the moment we see no reason why the great Ottoman Empire should hold out a hand to a new and struggling nation that can do little for us. We have decided to accept future services for the greater glory of Islam and to give you the rank of subpasha."

Jeremy was stunned and could think of no immediate reply.

"We have heard from our dear cousin and from Mustafa el Kro that you can direct naval cannon with marvelous accuracy. The empire is in need of such a one as you. We spend all of our time and all of our energies trying to spread the light of knowledge and the torch of wisdom.

Our people prefer the old ways, the easy ways, and they must be led to accept that which is new and beneficial. We have reformed our army, and there is now none better, anywhere. The time has come to reorganize our navy. There are no seamen sailing the waters of our earth who are more skilled or more courageous than our sailors. But their gunnery is deplorable. Their ancestors fought without naval cannon, so they would follow in the paths of ancient times if they were not forced into new roads. We have instructed Mustafa el Kro to modernize our navy, and you will help him by teaching our sailors the proper use of sea cannon."

The mind of even a comparatively tolerant and advanced Easterner worked in curious ways, Jeremy told himself in dismay. Selim obviously thought he was conferring a great honor on a foreigner by giving him a remarkably high rank and ordering him to act as an instructor in the imperial navy, but it apparently never occurred to him that he, not the recipient of his "favor," would benefit from his generosity. It was dangerous to argue with an absolute monarch, but Jeremy doggedly refused to be intimidated. "I'm an American citizen," he said flatly, "and I place the interests of my own country first."

Selim evidently knew the sort of man with whom he was dealing, and he turned quietly to the pasha, whose face reflected his shock. "Your new assistant will join you shortly, Mustafa el Kro."

The pasha prostrated himself, rose and backed rapidly from the chamber. Jeremy paid no attention to him, however, but continued to look straight at the sultan.

"You are endowed with great bravery," Selim said calmly. "We are pleased that our new subpasha is not unworthy of his rank. You realize, of course, that we could have you put to death for your temerity in questioning our word?"

"Your Magnificence," Jeremy replied boldly, "has acquired a reputation throughout the world as the man who has led Turkey out of barbarism into civilization. I'll freely

grant you that I'm no one of significance and that I
wouldn't be mourned if you had me executed. On the other
hand, I don't think you'd want that blemish on your record. For the first time in many hundreds of years this is
a responsible nation, ruled by a responsible man. I've heard
it said that the empress of Russia signed a peace treaty with
you after centuries of warfare because she was convinced
that Your Magnificence is a man of great personal integ-
rity. I'm powerless to prevent you from putting me to
death, but I'll only lose my life. Your Magnificence will
forfeit your good name."

The sultan glanced at Tule Yasmin, seated two steps
below him.

"Some members of our court," he murmured, "would
do well to take lessons in rhetoric from your husband."

The khana was not amused. "If you'll order the deputy
caliph to sign the necessary papers, the marriage will be
terminated."

Selim gave no indication that he heard her and again
devoted his attention to Jeremy. "Those who serve us
willingly serve us best."

Jeremy, thinking rapidly, believed he knew how to help
the United States and at the same time save his own neck.
"I'll gladly teach your navy the modern techniques of gunnery, Your Magnificence, if in return you'll give consideration to my request for diplomatic recognition."

"We are not a merchant who haggles over terms in the
bazaar," the sultan said loftily. "Do as we have commanded, and you will find us receptive to any reasonable
plea. In the meantime do not delude yourself into thinking
that you are merely an alien in our employ. You are our
subject, and your first duty at all times is to be loyal to
our person and our empire." He paused to let his words
sink in, then added gently, "After all, have you not become our cousin?"

Before a startled Jeremy could reply, Tule Yasmin reacted violently. "Your jest is not amusing, Cousin!"

The sultan smiled at her indulgently. "In the days of

our father and our grandfather," he said in a tone of mild reproof, "your tongue would have been torn from your head for such a violation of our majesty. Let us remind you, Cousin, that only in our own reign could a woman of even your exalted rank enjoy the freedom you find so precious. Don't try our patience and force us to return to the old ways."

The khana made an effort to control her temper. "Your Magnificence is most gracious to remind me of my faults."

Jeremy, looking from one to the other, was confused. All that really mattered to him was that he would need to spend several months training the gunners of the imperial navy, and his one hope was that if he succeeded, the sultan would indeed entertain the idea of recognizing the existence of the United States. He had no idea what Selim meant by calling him a Turkish subject, nor could he understand why Tule Yasmin was so upset.

The sultan saw that he was bewildered and waved in the direction of one of the lower steps. "As a member of our family, you have the right to sit in our presence."

Tule Yasmin gasped and dug her long fingernails into the palms of her hands. "You make it difficult for me to remain prudent, Cousin."

"And you, Tule Yasmin, are doing nothing to make the task of educating our backward people any easier. Do you think our proud janissaries-of-the-sea will accept instruction from a Frankish infidel? They would prefer a lingering death to such dishonor! But all of them, even our battle-scarred veterans and great captains, will leap to obey the slightest command given to them by a member of the imperial family. We are going to issue a public proclamation at once, recognizing your marriage, and we shall send a copy of it to your brother."

Jeremy developed a quick appreciation of the wily sultan's tactics. Individuals meant nothing to Selim, whose sole concern was the progress of his empire. Certainly the improvement of his navy was of far greater importance to him than the marital happiness of the khagan of Mongolia's sister. The implications of the decision were staggering to Jeremy, and he availed himself of the sultan's invitation by sinking onto a step.

Tule Yasmin plainly was not going to give up without a struggle. Jumping to her feet, she faced the sultan furiously. "I refuse to be sacrificed because it suits your policy! This man is a Frank, and there isn't a drop of royal blood in his veins. Nobles who are his peers are bought and sold in the slave markets every day."

"So they are," Selim agreed, smiling pleasantly at her. "However, they aren't experts in naval gunnery."

"Marriages between members of the royal family and commoners are forbidden!" Tule Yasmin cried.

"True, true." The sultan's smile broadened, and he shrugged. "But we are powerless to intervene."

The khana's eyes narrowed. "Powerless?" she repeated hoarsely. "You are the Caliph of the One True Faith. A single word to the deputy caliph would dissolve the marriage."

The sultan shook his head and sighed. "Neither our father nor our grandfather would have tolerated such disrespect from a mere woman. Say no more, dear Cousin, or you'll force us to order you chained to your bed and have the soles of your feet beaten daily to teach you true feminine humility."

She realized that he meant what he said, and she sat down again, pale and trembling. "My brother will be deeply disturbed," she said, making a final effort. "Your Magnificence has no more loyal a subject anywhere than the khagan but how do you suppose he'll feel when he learns that you've forced me to remain married to an infidel, a commoner?"

"We have no doubt that Buyantu Yassan will share our own dismay. But as he will know we have no power to intervene, he will certainly agree that his sister married impetuously and that she must therefore suffer the consequences of her rash act. You forget, dear Cousin, that in our capacity as caliph we have the authority to dissolve only Moslem marriages. By your own admission the ceremony that united you with this man was performed by a protestant Christian clergyman. Not even the caliph has the power to break such a bond."

Jeremy was appalled by the realization that his marriage to this ruthless, abandoned woman would be permanent. Yet at the same time he could not help laughing at the extraordinary cleverness of the sultan.

Tule Yasmin glared at him and turned back to her cousin. "There are ways of being rid of those who are unwanted. After he has finished training your gunners, Your Magnificence, you surely won't object to a small dose of poison, or—"

"Your sojourn in Frankish lands has failed to curb your primitive desires," Selim said regretfully. "We are forced to remind you, Cousin, that your husband is now entitled to full protection under the law that prescribes slow torture for anyone—anyone—who dares to harm a member of our family."

It was a relief to Jeremy to know that at least he would be able to sleep without fear of having his throat cut.

The khana was forced to accept at least temporary defeat, and she bowed her head to signify complete submission to the imperial will. Selim folded his arms to signify that the interview was at an end, and both Jeremy and Tule Yasmin prostrated themselves before him as he said, "Our new cousin will be known henceforth as Jumai Khan, a title befitting one who is married to a princess of our province of Mongolia. Go now, together and in peace. Jumai Khan, we will visit our fleet in four weeks' time so that we may see with our eyes that our janissaries-of-the-sea are making progress under your direction."

Jeremy, backing out of the room, reflected that he had received a subtle warning from the sultan to produce tangible results within a month. The door of the audience hall closed, and he stood face to face with Tule Yasmin in the anteroom. The pasha of two horsetails and Mustafa el Kro, who were conferring at the far side of the chamber, bowed to the khana, but she was so angry that she paid no attention to them.

"You needn't think," she said to Jeremy in a low, menacing voice, "that you're going to enjoy any special privileges in my household merely because it suits the sultan's purposes to have you act as an instructor to his sailors."

Never before had Jeremy seen her so completely disconcerted, and he took great pleasure in chuckling openly. "I've learned better than to expect anything from my wife." For an instant he thought Tule Yasmin would strike him, but she controlled herself in time and started to move away from him. He knew there would be gossip at the court if they created a scene, but it was essential that they come to a clear understanding at once, so he reached out, caught hold of her arm, and swung her toward him again. "The sultan told us to go together and in peace," he said coldly. "I have no more desire for your company than you have for mine, but he's given me a difficult task to perform. I intend to carry out my assignment so that I can serve my own country, and I refuse to let any outward sign of disunity between us make my work more difficult for me. I'll need the good opinion of the navy, and one way I'll get it is by having my wife show respect for me."

"Do you dare to give me commands?" Her eyes glittered.

"You're my wife, unfortunately. You've made your real opinion of me very clear, and I assure you that I feel the same toward you. Nevertheless you'll defer to me in public, as a Moslem wife always defers to her husband, or I swear to you that by Allah I'll take a rod to you."

They glared at each other in silence, and Jeremy thought that only their proximity to the sultan's private audience hall prevented Tule Yasmin from clawing his face. All the same he had meant every word he had said to her; he would permit nothing to interfere with the work that Selim had so unexpectedly given him. His instinct told him to challenge the khana to an immediate test, and he held out his arm to her. She made no move to take it, but instead of withdrawing, he continued to look at her, a fixed smile on his lips. He had created an impossible situation for her, and at last she was forced to admit defeat for the second time in a single day.

Sighing, she took his arm and they walked together to the officers at the far side of the room. There Jeremy released Tule Yasmin, and before she could leave he said to her with cheerful intimacy, "I'll see you this evening when my day's work is finished, dear."

She made no reply as she stalked off, her back rigid and her eyes stormy, but Jeremy did not care. He had achieved the effect he wanted, and in the eyes of the Turkish officers he had gained new stature because he was the happily married, openly acknowledged husband of the royal khana. When she disappeared from sight he was able to dismiss her from his mind temporarily and to ignore the potential problems their new relationship would inevitably create. Far more urgent matters required his immediate attention, and after he accompanied Mustafa el Kro to the small building on the palace grounds that served as the navy's headquarters, he began at once to plan the enormous undertaking on which so much depended.

In the weeks that followed, Jeremy worked day and night in an attempt to achieve the impossible. He quickly discovered that his task was formidable, for the men of the Turkish Navy, although not lacking in either spirit or courage, lived so much in the tradition-rooted past that they neither understood nor appreciated the techniques of modern warfare. The officers constituted the greatest stumbling block to progress, as they stubbornly adhered to the old-fashioned view that nothing was as important in a battle as individual valor. They could be depended on to storm an enemy ship, but they felt no sympathy for a concept of warfare in which they would be required to engage in long-range artillery duels with a foe whose ships they would try to sink rather than board and capture.

Mustafa el Kro, promoted to the rank of a pasha of two

horsetails in order to give him the authority he needed to discipline recalcitrant captains, struggled hard to adjust his own thinking to the revolutionary principles of sea fighting that Jeremy was trying to teach, but his long experience as a raider handicapped him, and he could not help reacting as did so many of his subordinates. Nevertheless he gave Jeremy a free hand, and the American struggled desperately to create a corps of naval gunners out of unresponsive raw material.

He discovered that he achieved his greatest success with young Turkish recruits who had never known the thrill of climbing aboard an enemy ship swinging a scimitar, and with former Christians from various European lands who had embraced the faith of Mohammed and had become janissaries-of-the-sea. Whenever Jeremy found a man who responded to his instruction, Mustafa el Kro promptly transferred the sailor to the new corps of gunners, and as there were few officers sufficiently competent to command the crews, Jeremy freely promoted promising students from the ranks.

His problems extended into realms other than those of personnel, and for a time some of them seemed insoluble. There was a shortage of cannon, and he learned that the only guns the navy possessed were those that had been captured. There was no opportunity to buy weapons from friendly nations, as France, the only country that manufactured guns in quantity, was too deeply immersed in her own troubles, and neither Spain nor Imperial Russia had cannon to spare.

As a consequence Jeremy was forced to seek an interview with the sultan, and after he explained his dilemma he received authorization to build his own foundries in the open country beyond Pera. Hundreds of slaves and free artisans were assigned to follow his directions, and when he was not laboring with the fleet in the Bosporus, he rode inland to supervise the construction of foundries and, subsequently, the making of guns and cannonballs.

Work seemed to occupy every moment of his waking

time, and he tried to console himself with the thought that it was just as well that he had no chance to relax, for Tule Yasmin saw to it that he had no personal life. One of the larger buildings in the old seraglio had been given to her, and there Jeremy lived in a small wing of his own. It appeared to the court as though he and the khana were dwelling together amicably, but Tule Yasmin actually kept her distance from him at all times, and even though they slept under the same roof, Jeremy caught only an occasional glimpse of her.

He returned to his quarters late each night. One of the khana's women brought his supper to him, and every morning after he rode down to the Golden Horn they cleaned his rooms and kept his clothes in good condition, so he could not complain that his creature comforts were being neglected. But Tule Yasmin, having been thwarted in her attempt to divorce him, seemed to feel that she was evening the score by neither seeing him nor speaking to him. Jeremy, deeply involved in his assignment from the sultan, was content not to disturb the routine she had established, and on the rare occasions when he had time to spare he made no effort to seek her company.

When Jeremy discovered that he was expected to take his pick of the serving maids to help look after his personal needs, he decided to take a bold step. Suiting action to thought, he sent a brief note to Tule Yasmin that was as curt as it was explicit. "Send me the taller of the English slave girls," he directed. "I need her to keep house for me."

He could imagine Tule Yasmin's rage but knew there was nothing she could do about it. She dared not flout his will directly; as a result Mary Ellis appeared in his chambers late one evening. At first, because she was enveloped in a voluminous yashmak and veil, he did not recognize her, but as soon as she raised her luminous eyes, he knew her.

"I asked for you specifically," Jeremy said with a slight

smile. "I hope you don't mind, but I needed assistance, and I figured you wouldn't mind being free of Tule Yasmin."

Mary sighed gently. "Any escape from that she-devil is welcome."

Her duties would be light, Jeremy explained: She would be required to serve his meals and make his bed, but otherwise her time would be her own.

The girl realized that he was trying to help her. She still didn't know who he was and what he was doing here, but being out of Tule Yasmin's clutches was better than nothing, and she entered into her new duties with spirit. As an actress, she knew little about being a serving maid, but she did her best, and he made no complaints, even when the food she served was cold.

Mary was often in the company of the other maids who worked in the household, and Jeremy noted that Mary, during her working hours, went about making it her business to become acquainted with these women and to learn their language. The servants were not particularly cooperative, looking down on her as a barbarian, but Mary was slowly learning a few words of Turkish. The thought occurred to Jeremy that in one way or another he would be able to help her terminate her captivity. Perhaps he could also help Rosalind Tate. At least, when he had time, he would be able to try to do something for the two girls who were so unjustly held in captivity.

Although the task he was expected to perform for the sultan was formidable, Jeremy found his thoughts often drifting toward Mary. Living in such close proximity with her undoubtedly was responsible for the complications that were growing in their relationship, but he was reluctant to terminate the arrangement, and certainly he had no intention of allowing her to go back to Tule Yasmin's control. He needed no one to tell him that she would be abused and mistreated, especially now that he had showed her favoritism.

One day Jeremy worked particularly long hours, starting early in the morning, shortly after daybreak, and not finishing until several hours after sundown that night. Mary was waiting for him when he returned to his quarters and served him a simple meal of soup, meat, and bread. For reasons he did not stop to analyze, Jeremy asked her to remain with him while he ate. She nodded obediently and sat at the table opposite him, folding her arms and lowering her head meekly.

Somewhat to his own surprise he found himself telling her a little about his own background, how he happened to be in Islam in the first place and why he was married to the Mongolian princess.

Mary asked no questions, but her eyes widened, and she listened intently to everything he said.

"I don't like to make promises that I can't keep," Jeremy told her, "but when I get a chance, as soon as my duties permit, I'm going to do all in my power to have you released from a very unfair bondage. The same goes for the other girl, too."

"That's very kind of you," Mary replied. "Are you sure you can do all this without causing harm to yourself?"

Jeremy did not reply in words but grinned at her, and his smile was answer enough.

His offer of help signaled a change in their relationship. Mary no longer held him at arm's length but relaxed often in his presence and found that she was confiding in him, too. Jeremy was astonished to learn she was an actress of considerable stature in her native England, and he was somewhat impressed, although the theater was so alien to him that her vocation failed to impress him as it otherwise might have done. He also learned that her father was a prominent statesman, and he wondered what he would do when he learned a British ship had been attacked, his daughter and niece had been taken hostage, and his nephew had been tortured and killed.

Of far greater significance to him than Mary Ellis's vocational standing and her family background was the fact that she was an attractive young woman. Gradually, as the days passed, Jeremy knew that he wanted her. But he recognized the desire within himself and was troubled by it. Was it because she spoke his own language and he was in a land far from America? Was it any number of factors related to her helplessness? He couldn't be sure, but he knew he didn't want to take advantage of her while they waited for an opportunity to end her captivity.

One evening, however, the proximity into which they were thrown worked its own magic and created its own problems. When in his private quarters, Mary was attired in only the breastband and abbreviated skirt of the slave girl and did not wear the full yashmak. Perhaps her costume was as responsible as anything else for the inevitable development.

Jeremy was at work at his desk making up a training schedule for the following week but was conscious of the girl's movements as she cleaned up the remains of the supper he had just consumed. Suddenly, without thinking, he reached for her, grasped her wrist, and roughly pulled her toward him. Mary made no resistance whatsoever, but something in her expression stopped him. "Do you find me distasteful to you?" he asked.

Mary shook her head but did not trust herself to reply in words.

Jeremy released her wrist and stood. Peering hard at her, his face only a few inches from hers, he muttered, "Dammit! Living like this is very difficult!"

"I know," Mary replied quietly.

"If you don't want me to make advances to you, just say the word, and I'll stop," Jeremy said, his voice becoming defensive.

Mary faced him and somehow managed to smile. "You place me in an untenable position," she said. "You seem to forget that I have no free will of my own in this matter. I am your slave as much as I am Tule Yasmin's slave. I must do your bidding, just as I must do her bidding."

Jeremy was stricken. "I would never force my attentions on you in that way," he said.

He observed her smile, and it occurred to him that she

had halted him, that she had tied his hands as effectively as if she had erected a stone wall between them. He shrugged, turned away, and sank onto the three-pronged stool that sat in front of his desk. "You win," he said curtly.

Mary contrived to look innocent.

"If you ever want me—really want me—you'll tell me," Jeremy muttered. "Or at the very least, you'll find some way to let me know." She turned her back to him, and as she gathered up the remaining supper dishes, she was glad he could not see that she was smiling again.

But Mary was less sure of herself than she appeared on the surface. She knew, deep within her, that she wanted Jeremy as much as he wanted her. What bothered her was the depth of her own desire. She didn't know why she felt as she did, and she had no way of finding out, but of one thing she was sure: Their relationship was due for further exploration, was due for further development of one kind or another. They were not fated to live apart, but she didn't know whether they would live together. Only time would tell, and the strains that she was under—the strains from which he suffered, too—were contributing to a volatile situation in which anything could eventuate. First she would have to be set free—and she was prepared to go to any lengths to defeat her captors and end her captivity—then she would see what happened.

Occasionally Jeremy wondered what was prompting him to cling to the determination to pursue his original mission. His position in the Ottoman Empire was higher than any he had ever achieved at home, and even if he succeeded in the assignment that Alexander Hamilton had given him, it was unlikely that he would ever enjoy the power and prestige that he now took for granted in Constantinople. It would be easy to settle here permanently, he thought, and even if his marriage to Tule Yasmin should never be terminated, there was nothing to prevent him from following the example of many high-ranking Turks and taking a number of concubines.

The temptation was great, but in spite of it he refused to abandon his original project. Perhaps, he reflected, prominence and accomplishment in Turkey meant less to him than did achievement for the United States. He had never believed himself to be particularly patriotic, yet at the same time he knew that America was dear to him and that, more than all else, he wanted the recognition and approval of his fellow citizens.

His hopes moved closer to realization on the day that he gave the demonstration of naval gunnery that the sultan had demanded. Selim and virtually all of the dignitaries of the court were rowed out into the Bosporus on a fleet of royal barges, and Jeremy did not disappoint them. In the short period of a month he had trained only two gun crews to his satisfaction, but these teams, operating from the deck of a large galley, fired round after round at a series of targets and never once missed. Jeremy saw that even Tule Yasmin, who watched the show attended by her women, applauded enthusiastically and basked in the reflected glory of his performance.

At the end of the demonstration the sultan summoned Jeremy to the imperial barge, and there, in the presence of the grand vizier and a score of prominent janissary officers, he promoted the American to the position of a pasha of one horsetail. Such a rank was unprecedented for a man who had not given up Christianity for the faith of Mohammed, but Jeremy understood why the wily Selim did not press him to embrace Islam. It was enough that he be known as Jumai Khan; if he renounced his own beliefs, Tule Yasmin would find it far easier to renew her demand for a divorce on the grounds that the ceremony had been performed in a rite that was now alien to both of them.

The pace of work increased after Jeremy received his promotion, and he had even less time to himself. At the order of the sultan the shipyards were turning out scores of new galleys, the iron foundries were casting cannon and ammunition at a furious rate, and hundreds of new naval recruits were assigned to the command of Jumai Khan and were trained in the art of gunnery.

Time had little meaning for Jeremy, and he thought Colonel Hamilton had undoubtedly concluded that he had either failed or had deserted his nation. Actually, however, he felt increasingly confident that the Turks would grant diplomatic recognition to the United States. In a few months, at the most, the gunners of the Ottoman fleet would be the equal of those in any other navy on earth, and then the sultan could not fail to show his gratitude. It was true that absolute monarchs were often capricious, but Selim was an intelligent man who would surely show his appreciation when his orders had been executed to perfection.

One morning, several weeks after the demonstration, while Jeremy was instructing some newly created officers in the art of loading a gun quickly, a messenger arrived from the palace with word that the sultan requested the immediate presence of Jumai Khan. Jeremy was rowed ashore in his own gig, and his personal escort of cavalrymen, to which his rank entitled him, awaited him. They rode to the palace at a fast clip, but Jeremy was unconcerned about the unusual summons until he entered Selim's private audience hall and, after prostrating himself, saw that Tule Yasmin was also present.

As Jeremy regained his feet he thought that the khana had never looked more attractive than she did at this moment in a sleeveless hip-length tunic of richly brocaded satin with curled-up shoulder pieces that matched the turned-up toes of her green satin slippers, and a full purple skirt that was gathered into a band at her ankles. A huge sunburst of gold, set with emeralds and pearls, closed her tunic at the waist, and she wore matching sunburst earrings.

Even more apparent than her beauty was the fact that she was wildly angry. Her eyes flashed, her brow was furrowed, and a thin, white line had formed around her mouth. In spite of her rage, however, she was sufficiently in control of herself to remain in the background and to let the sultan do the talking. Selim was holding a sheet of paper in his hand, and it looked as though it had been folded and crumpled and then smoothed out again.

"Jumai Khan," he said, "English was the language of your fathers. You alone at our court speak that tongue, so tell us if this document is written in English."

A single glance at the paper was sufficient. "It is, Your Magnificence."

"What is written on it?"

Jeremy studied the sheet briefly. "This is a list of naval vessels in our fleet, together with a record of how many guns each of our ships carries."

The khana clenched her fists. "It is precisely as I have said, Cousin."

Selim frowned at the interruption. "Is the information contained in the document accurate, Jumai Khan?"

Jeremy read the paper more carefully. "No, Your Magnificence. Not one fact listed here is correct. The number of ships, their sizes, and the armaments they carry are all inaccurately listed."

The sultan allowed himself the luxury of a faint, brooding smile. "Then Allah continues to favor us. This paper was taken from a janissary in our household guard who was once an Englishman and who was obviously a traitor to Islam even after he was converted to the One True Faith. He was caught in a silversmith's shop in the city while he was trying to pass the document to a man whom our secret police were watching because they suspected that he was an English agent. Both have now been executed."

Jeremy nodded but said nothing.

"Before he died," Selim continued, "the janissary confessed that the paper was prepared by Tule Yasmin's English slave girl and that she passed the document to him."

It was certainly not surprising that Mary should hate her captors and should seek revenge against them, but Jeremy was amazed by her courage. Surely she had known that she was taking great risks in trying to act the part of an espionage agent for England, but he could not believe that she had stopped to think of the penalty she would be forced to pay if her act should be exposed.

"Our cousin," the sultan said, "first thought that you might be involved in the plot." He glanced at the khana, smiled deprecatingly, and then looked back at Jeremy again. "We pointed out to her, however, that this was impossible."

"Quite true, Your Magnificence," Jeremy said firmly. "I have no need to persuade you that I hate England. I proved my feelings in the battle with the frigate, and you know enough of my background to understand that I would hardly cooperate with a nation against which I fought for many long years. What's more, I would have nothing to gain by such a transaction, not even money. The wages you pay me as a pasha are far greater than anything I could be expected to receive from the English."

"We have already made these points clear to our cousin," Selim declared.

"In addition," Jeremy went on, "the data contained in this paper is erroneous, although I have access to the complete and accurate information regarding the size and power of the fleet."

"There is no need to convince us of your innocence," Selim replied.

Tule Yasmin could remain silent no longer. "Nor is there a need to prolong this discussion," she said heatedly. "The wench is guilty and must be whipped to death."

Jeremy was startled by her vehemence, but he saw an opportunity to help Mary, and he intervened quickly. "Your Magnificence, the girl is innocent of wrongdoing of any sort. I can establish that fact to your complete satisfaction if you'll have her brought before you here and now."

Tule Yasmin tried to protest, but the sultan cut her off with a sharp gesture. "Very interesting," he murmured, and rang a tiny, ivory-handled gold bell.

The aide who appeared hurried out again to fetch the slave girl, and Jeremy, his mind racing, did his best to forget the khana, who was glaring at him malevolently. If his scheme succeeded she would hate him all the more, but the intensity of her feelings against him no longer bothered him. And it was just possible that he could save Mary's life. There was silence in the audience hall as they waited, and the sultan, aware of the tension between the couple below him, was obviously amused. The espionage plot had failed, so it was no longer a matter of concern to him, but the human drama that was being played for his benefit diverted him, and he was eagerly looking forward to the next act.

He did not have long to wait; within a few minutes two burly officers thrust Mary into the hall. They had snatched her from her duties in such haste that they had given her no chance to don her veil and voluminous robes, so she was dressed only in the breastband and short skirt that she wore at work in the khana's household. The officers shoved her into the hall so forcibly that she stumbled and fell forward, which was fortunate, as she probably had no idea that she was expected to prostrate herself before the sultan.

"You may lift your face," Selim told her, but her knowledge of Turkish was still so limited that she did not understand him, and at his request Jeremy translated the order into English.

Mary showed the effects of her training by rising to her knees, folding her hands over her breasts, and keeping her head lowered. It was plain that this was a position she had been forced to assume frequently while serving the khana. She was alert, however, in spite of her air of meekness, and when she saw the paper that Jeremy held in his hand she grew pale. But he saw that she gave no other indication that she was aware of the significance of the document, and he silently applauded her courage. There was a slim chance that she would be able to play the role he had in mind for her—more so because she was a renowned actress.

"Tell her," the sultan directed, "that if she fails to tell

us the truth, she will be put to death in the Torture of One Hundred Days."

Jeremy turned to the girl and addressed her in English. "Your spy plot has been discovered, and your life is in danger," he said quickly. "I'm trying to help you, and you'll have to trust me. When I tell you something, answer me by paraphrasing whatever I've said. But don't repeat my actual words, or they'll hear the similarity and will become suspicious. Now, nod your head."

She obeyed, and he felt a sense of relief. The sultan and Tule Yasmin were both looking at him expectantly, and he smiled broadly at Selim. "Your Magnificence," he said, "it is unquestionably true that the wench wrote this document." He held the paper out to Mary and said in English, "Admit that you are the author."

A flicker of suspicion came into her eyes, but she replied proudly, "I wrote it."

"She prepared it at my direction," Jeremy declared, and again addressed Mary. "Say that I instructed you to do it."

It was difficult to tell which of Jeremy's auditors was the most amazed. The sultan looked bemused, Tule Yasmin's face reflected complete incredulity, and Mary, perhaps thinking that he was about to sacrifice himself for her sake, wanted to protest. "Say it!" he declared firmly.

"You told me to write it," she repeated in a faltering voice.

"Say also that the contents were prepared at my direction."

"You told me what to write." There was a note of wonder in her voice, and she could not bring herself to look at Jeremy.

"Jumai Khan, you will need to explain yourself," the sultan said querulously.

"To be sure, Your Magnificence." Jeremy's manner was confident, and his voice was glib. "England is the enemy of your country and of mine. She would destroy Turkey if she could, just as she would destroy the United States. Knowing this, I deliberately conceived a plan to feed false information to the English spies who infest Constantinople. I knew they would believe any figures that came to them from the home of Jumai Khan, who is privy to all the secrets of Your Magnificence's Navy, so I persuaded this wench to help me. She is a heroine, not a traitor, and I am happy that Your Magnificence called me here before a miscarriage of justice could be perpetrated."

The hall was very quiet as Selim digested his words. Even Tule Yasmin could not refute them, and Jeremy felt pleased with himself. He had utilized the incident to his own advantage by emphasizing that Turkey and the United States had an enemy in common, and he was sure that the chances of obtaining diplomatic recognition of his country were vastly improved. What was more, he had saved the life of Mary Ellis; he knew it the moment the sultan smiled.

"Our thanks to you, Jumai Khan," the sultan said. "You have served us well, as you do in all things. Our felicitations to the wench, too. As a reward, she is to be spared all beatings from this time forward. Tell her that, Jumai Khan. And, Cousin, you have heard our decree? Under pain of our displeasure, the slave is not to be beaten in the future."

Jeremy translated the command quickly to the bewildered Mary, who, having understood none of his explanation, was unable to grasp what was happening. She knew only that in some miraculous way he had saved her life and, in addition, had improved her sorry lot. She stammered her thanks, but Jeremy cut her off and smiled blandly at the sultan.

"The wench is grateful to Your Magnificence," he said blandly.

The khana was unable to disprove anything Jeremy had said, but she was humiliated by the order not to have one of her own slaves whipped in the future, and she turned angrily to the man who was responsible. "You dared to involve one of my women in this scheme?"

Jeremy stared at her and then forced himself to laugh

loudly. "Dare, my dear wife? I acted as I did for the safety and welfare of the empire. What would a man not dare for the honor and glory of His Magnificence? And since when is it necessary for a husband to ask his wife's permission when he wants to use one of her servants? You seem to forget that my wife's property is mine, too."

Again he laughed, and Selim joined him, pleased to see his haughty cousin humbled; too often she was inclined to forget that even a princess was a member of a vastly inferior sex. The interview came to an end, and Tule Yasmin stalked back to her quarters in the old seraglio, curtly ordering Mary to follow her. Jeremy returned jubilantly to his duties in the harbor, congratulating himself on the quick thinking that had enabled him to win increased favor for the United States from the sultan. And as he rode back to the training ship in his gig, he kept remembering the expression of profound gratitude he had read in Mary's eyes before she had followed the khana. Not until much later did he realize that he should have concentrated on Tule Yasmin's look of sheer hatred, but at the time he was too proud of his own cleverness to realize that her hostility to him was now deadly.

VII

～～～～～～～～

Tule Yasmin remained in seclusion after Jeremy caused her to lose face, and whenever he spent even a brief time in his quarters at the seraglio, she kept herself behind bolted doors in her own suite. During the previous period she had avoided him, she had exercised some degree of subtlety in keeping her distance from him, but now she seemed to go out of her way to let him know she would have no more to do with him. One or another of her serving-women was stationed at the seraglio entrance at all times to report on his arrivals and departures, and he became accustomed to the sight of one of the slaves hurrying down a corridor to inform her mistress that Jumai Khan had just returned or that he was leaving. It amused him to hear heavy bolts being moved into place behind the closed door of Tule Yasmin's private rooms, and he was tempted to send word to her that her precautions were unnecessary and that he had no intention of seeking her company. But he refrained from indulging in a gesture that would serve no purpose other than to satisfy his vanity, for he knew that the less he saw her, the fewer complications she could create for him.

He was undisturbed, therefore, when she openly snubbed him on two occasions, in spite of his realization that some of his colleagues were undoubtedly whispering behind his back that he couldn't handle his wife. It was true that she should have stood at his side when he attended an imperial levee and a reception in honor of a holy man from Mecca. But he was content to go to such affairs alone and let the court gossip as much as it pleased. And it did not bother him that Tule Yasmin went out of her way to emphasize their estrangement by sending word to the grand vizier that her absence from the levee was caused by illness yet pointedly strolling through the gardens, so all could see she enjoyed good health the moment her husband left the palace and returned to work.

What did bother Jeremy was that he no longer caught even an occasional glimpse of Mary. She did not clean his quarters or bring food to him anymore, and the old women who were sent to wait on him told him nothing about her. He made several attempts to question them, but they were obviously under orders from the khana to remain silent in his presence, and they stared at him blankly when he asked them about Mary. It was good to be able to assure himself that, thanks to the sultan's order, she was suffering no physical abuse, but he was afraid that a woman as clever as Tule Yasmin could find innumerable hidden ways to punish a helpless slave girl who had been responsible for humiliating her before the sultan.

It would be easy enough, Jeremy frequently told himself, to demand that the khana send Mary to him, and no wife in the Ottoman Empire, not even a woman who was a princess of royal blood, would dare to refuse a direct command from her husband. But even though such an order would give him an opportunity to talk to Mary again, he was afraid that if he gave in to his desire he would be causing more trouble for her in the long run, as the gesture would be an open admission to the already infuriated Tule Yasmin that his interest in the English girl was increasing.

Certainly his time was fully occupied as he weighed the matter in his mind, and as the days became weeks he worked harder than ever before in his life. The captains of sea rovers that preyed on Christian merchantmen in the Mediterranean and sometimes dared to sail out into the Atlantic Ocean brought a stream of reports to Constantinople that the English were expending great efforts to enlarge their fleet rapidly. Mustafa el Kro and Jeremy felt certain the day would come when King George's ministers would decide to declare war against the only power on earth that challenged London's naval supremacy, and the Turks had to be ready to meet the test at any time. More immediate, Jeremy realized, was the likelihood that England would attack Constantinople if the men and women who were taken captive were not returned to her.

Indeed, as Jeremy soon learned, the sultan had already received a communication from Sir William Pitt, the English prime minister, condemning the Turks for their attacks on British ships and demanding the immediate release of the British prisoners. The sultan had no intention of giving in to British demands, and this put Jeremy in a delicate situation. If the British attacked Constantinople, he would be forced to help the Turks—that is, if he wanted his mission for the American government to succeed. This in itself didn't distress him, for he had no love for the British. What did cause a predicament, however, was Mary Ellis. It was a great irony that Jeremy's efforts to help the Turks meant that he would be fighting against the people who wanted to save her and the other prisoners. But there was no choice. He had to help the Turks, and he would find a way to help Mary Ellis, too. He just hoped she would eventually understand.

The training program of the janissaries-of-the-sea was increased, and recruiting parties scoured the seaports, offering bonuses to experienced sailors if they would join their country's service. Hundreds of new workers were hired by the shipyards, the forges of Jeremy's foundries glowed day and night as ironsmiths cast the barrels of cannon, and the inhabitants of the city became accustomed to the incessant roar of the guns that were tested on board ships in the harbor. The demands on Jeremy were unending, and when he was not supervising the training of gun crews, he was needed at the foundries or was summoned to conferences by Mustafa el Kro. His day usually started at dawn, when he rode down to his headquarters and outlined the day's schedule to his staff, and he rarely finished his labors before late at night, when he wearily returned to his quarters to snatch a few hours of sleep.

He was proud of his accomplishments, and he became increasingly convinced that his men would more than hold their own if and when the English attacked in force. He learned that the Turks had to be allowed to work at their own pace if he expected results, and by curbing his impatience, he slowly created a corps of naval artillery which, he believed, was second to none. He discovered that when he pressed the metalworkers to increase their output, they turned out guns with cracked barrels, so he wisely let them work at their own rate and built several additional foundries to get all the cannon he needed. Similarly he found that the gunners became bewildered if he tried to teach them too much too quickly. But by patiently rehearsing them again and again in the same operations, he achieved results, and although he could have instructed American gunners in a fraction of the time he spent with his janissaries-of-the-sea, his men never forgot anything they really learned.

The fleet's growing strength pleased the sultan, and the officers of the high command were satisfied that they were hammering an efficient force into shape, but one question remained to be answered. No one knew how the men of the navy would react under battle conditions, whether they would become panicky. Jeremy therefore suggested at a staff conference that a surprise alert should be sounded and that the call to arms should be followed by a week of practice maneuvers at sea, under conditions simulating those of actual war. Mustafa el Kro agreed enthusiastically, and plans for the test were prepared secretly by a few trusted staff officers.

On the day the alert was to be given, Jeremy returned to the palace at noon for the clothes and equipment he would need during a week at sea. He had deliberately left his gear behind when he had gone to headquarters as usual that morning, for fear that a sharp-witted seaman might

see his pack and guess what was in the wind. An orderly
accompanied Jeremy to carry his belongings, and as they
approached the entrance to the seraglio, Jeremy was
amused to see that for the first time in many days there
was no sign of one of Tule Yasmin's women hovering
nearby to warn of his approach. As he never spent time at
home during the day, his presence at this hour was completely unexpected.

It was possible he might see the khana, and as he made
his way to his own rooms, he noticed that the door at the
far end of the corridor that led to her suite was wide open.
So he thought that with any luck he might find Mary and
be able to explain to her what was in the wind without
creating undue complications for her. He hastily showed
the orderly what to pack and then walked quietly to Tule
Yasmin's quarters. The antechamber was deserted, as was
the principal sitting room, so he moved cautiously through
a series of smaller connecting rooms, all of which were
empty, too. It was likely that the khana had gone out
somewhere, which relieved him, and he was mildly surprised when he came upon one of the elderly servingwom-
en, who was sitting in a tiny room, sewing. She gasped,
dropped her work, and fled, but she ran off in the direction of the slaves' sleeping rooms in the rear. Thus he
reasoned she had not gone to tell her mistress of his presence, and therefore he continued his search.

No one was in Tule Yasmin's bedchamber, and Jeremy
walked through it quickly, noting in passing that she kept
an amazing number of jars and pots on her dressing table.
All women enjoyed using salves and unguents, but no one
else he had ever known owned so many. A faint sound on
a terrace beyond the bedroom attracted his attention, and
when he peered out through an open blind, he saw that
his hunt had come to an end. Mary, attired in her informal breastband and short skirt, was on her hands and
knees, scrubbing the tiles of the terrace floor.

Jeremy went to her at once, and when she became aware
of his presence, she looked up with a wan smile and

brushed her hair back from her damp forehead. "I've been looking for you," he said in English. "Where is the khana?"

"Her Sublimity," Mary replied bitterly, "has gone to the palace and has left me behind, as always, to do the hardest work."

"She's treating you badly, then?"

"I suppose I can't really complain. She doesn't beat me anymore, and the eunuchs aren't allowed to whip me, either. But until these past few weeks I never really knew what hard labor meant."

"I'm sorry I haven't been able to do more to help you." He reached down, caught hold of her hand, and raised her to her feet. She listened intently as he explained the current state of affairs, and her hopes were raised when she realized that the English government was aware of her plight. But she realized Jeremy's predicament, and she just prayed that he would be able to do something for her, Rosalind, and the other prisoners before it was too late. Although Rosalind was also forced to work as Tule Yasmin's serving-woman, the khana's staff was enormous, and Mary rarely saw her cousin. She hoped the young girl was holding up well, and she shuddered as she remembered the fate of her cousin's twin brother, Rob.

"I have several ideas, none of them very definite as yet," Jeremy went on, "but I simply wanted to tell you not to give up hope. Sooner or later I'll find a way to win your freedom for you. It's possible that if I carry out my assignment here to the sultan's satisfaction, he'll grant me an extra boon and let you go back to your own country."

Although Mary stood in the hot sunlight, she again shivered slightly and rubbed her bare arms. "You're being wonderfully kind to me," she said.

"I may be a renegade and a barbarian," Jeremy told her wryly, "but I do have something of a conscience."

"I'm sorry I called you those things." She looked down at the tiles for a moment, then raised her head again. "I never did apologize for having misjudged you. And I never really thanked you for saving my life."

"I want no thanks." It was absurd to feel gauche, but looking at the lovely girl who stood before him, Jeremy was suddenly tongue-tied.

Mary gazed up at him curiously, her green eyes puzzled. "I've learned something of your reasons for being in Turkey from what you told me. But I still can't say I understand you."

A man who had known many women should have accepted the remark as a provocative compliment, but Jeremy felt embarrassed. "I don't think there's anything difficult or complicated about me."

Her expression was quizzical as she shook back her red hair. "England and her former colonies aren't exactly on the best of terms," she retorted. "In fact, we're enemies, to be crude about it."

"That doesn't mean you and I must be enemies, and it certainly doesn't mean I've got to stand by silently when a girl who has done no harm to anyone has been unjustly enslaved. I'll grant you that I haven't led a perfect life. But even though an Englishwoman might not believe this, Americans do have decent instincts occasionally."

Mary ignored his sarcasm. "You say you're here to win recognition for the United States from the sultan. Why does the United States want help? To protect her against England, obviously."

"You're extremely well informed." Her unusual grasp of the relations between nations surprised him; few women ever showed an interest in politics.

"The information I tried to send to London," she continued relentlessly, "would have been useful to His Majesty's Navy and would have hurt the American cause. Yet you went out of your way and took great personal risks to save my life when my gamble failed."

"That's easy enough to explain." It was actually far from easy, but he tried hard. "The message had already been intercepted, so no harm could be done. And whether you realize it or not, the sultan's agents are keeping watch on you to see if any other spies try to get in touch with you, so you couldn't possibly repeat your effort." Jeremy took a deep breath and thought he had never seen anyone lovelier. Her brief costume was perhaps part of her attraction, he told himself, and it was possible, too, that her fair skin and red hair, which were unique in Constantinople, also drew him to her. "Anyway, I thought it would be criminal to waste the life of someone so beautiful, particularly when you were doing what any patriot would do. It didn't matter that you owe your allegiance to a country against which I've fought."

Color rose in Mary's face, and although something was lacking in his explanation, she seemed unwilling to probe more deeply. "I'm grateful to you—Jeremy," she murmured.

Even when she had spent time working in his chambers, she had not called him by name, and it sounded strange to hear himself addressed as something other than Jumai Khan.

"I have wanted to speak to you again for some time now, but Her Sublimity forbade me to see you."

"Her Sublimity," Jeremy said emphatically, "may go to the devil." He felt an overpowering urge to take Mary in his arms and kiss her, and moved forward unthinkingly.

For an instant he thought she would respond, but she suddenly took a single step backward and looked through the blind into the bedchamber. The servingwoman who had run away when she had seen Jeremy had returned and was observing them from the shadows inside the room. So he let his arms fall to his sides again; the fact that he and Mary had conversed would undoubtedly be reported to Tule Yasmin, who would take great pleasure in increasing her slave girl's work load. And her vindictiveness would be even greater if her servingwoman reported that there had been a physical demonstration of affection between the couple from the Western world.

A gong boomed dully in the distance, and Jeremy, glancing hastily at the sun overhead, knew he had to hurry to keep his rendezvous with the fleet. He would command the attacking force in the war games that would begin within the hour, and he had to leave at once for his flagship. So he looked hard at Mary for a long moment and then bowed deeply to her, as a gentleman did when taking leave of a lady.

"That means more to me than you can possibly know," she said, and although she tried to maintain a light tone, there were tears in her eyes. "I'd curtsy to you, but I'd look ridiculous in these frightful clothes."

He smiled, turned away abruptly, and started back to his own quarters to pick up his orderly. He could not resist the temptation to glance back over his shoulder, and he saw that Mary was standing very still, watching him. Then she dropped to her knees again, dipped a thick rag in the jar of water at her side, and resumed her task of scrubbing the terrace tiles. Her face was hidden from Jeremy, and as he turned into the seraglio he caught a final glimpse of the burnished crown of her head.

That last look remained in his memory during the grueling week that followed, and he discovered that his thoughts returned to Mary repeatedly during the naval exercises. He maneuvered the light, swift ships of his attacking fleet, he drilled his gunners mercilessly as they fired live ammunition at targets being towed by Mustafa el Kro's defending vessels, and he drove himself as hard as he drove his men, yet Mary's lovely face and gleaming hair kept distracting him from his work.

When he stood on the quarterdeck of his flagship, he remembered the day she had been captured and brought aboard a similar vessel; when he conferred with his sub-pashas and captains, her voice seemed to intrude and interrupt his talks; and when he stretched out beneath his silken canopy on the open deck for a few hours of sleep, he remained wide awake, unable to banish her from his thoughts. Her inability to understand why he had placed his life in jeopardy for her sake caused him to examine his motives carefully, and before the week at sea ended he reluctantly concluded that he was in love with her.

The knowledge did not make him happy, however, nor did it contribute to his peace of mind. A man who had always come and gone as he pleased could not enjoy the prospect of being tied to one woman for the rest of his life. A man who had made love to many girls and who knew that such relationships were transitory, without significance, was unable to escape the feeling that he would be trapped in a Western-style marriage. He had known some girls who were more seductive than Mary and others who were more flamboyant; he had passed innumerable hours in the company of women who were wiser and wittier. So he was annoyed with himself, irritated because his feeling was stronger than his reason, angry because he certainly knew better than to become involved in a romance that seemed likely to lead nowhere.

For one thing, he and Mary knew almost nothing about each other, and it was highly doubtful that she reciprocated his love; she appreciated his efforts on her behalf, but she had not shown even a hint of stronger emotion. Then, too, she had made it plain to him that she was loyal to England and felt contempt for the United States, so the chance was remote that she would ever consent to spend the rest of her life in a land whose people she viewed as her enemies. There were immediate, practical problems to be taken into consideration, too; Jeremy could not allow himself to lose sight of the fact that his situation in Islam was precarious and that he had no real future in America unless he produced the results that Alexander Hamilton had demanded of him. Nor could he let himself forget Tule Yasmin; he might feel nothing but loathing for her, but since she was his legal wife, he had no right to be contemplating a marriage to someone else. And he had to remember, as well, that Mary was the khana's personal slave, a miserable creature who could not wed anyone unless she were given her freedom. Tule Yasmin, he reflected, was incapable of showing such generosity to anyone, especially a rival.

All in all, then, the chance was remote that he and Mary

would spend their days as man and wife. Nevertheless he was eager to talk to her, to tell her of his feeling for her, and to work out a feasible plan of action with her; if they discussed the situation frankly, he thought, they might find a joint way to solve their difficulties, particularly if she were capable of returning his love. He was determined to force an immediate showdown with Tule Yasmin, and as the success of the war games had emphasized anew the importance of his contribution to the empire, he was willing to plead Mary's cause before the sultan.

By the time the week at sea ended, he was anxious to go ashore at once and could scarcely control his impatience when the sultan, accompanied by his grand vizier and his pashas of three horsetails, held a ceremony on board his barge in the harbor and, in a series of seemingly interminable speeches, offered his congratulations to all who had taken part in the exercises. The fleet anchored in the early afternoon, but it was dusk before the last junior officer had salaamed before Selim, and Jeremy, standing at rigid attention, wondered if the rites would ever end. Then the sultan suddenly conceived the idea of taking a cruise on Mustafa el Kro's flagship. The commander of the navy, who was tired, had to pretend to be elated, and his weary crew had no alternative but to erect huge canopies on the deck for Selim and his entourage, while supply officers hurried to the warehouses for food and linen.

The cruise was to last at least two days, possibly three, judging by the sultan's enthusiastic comments, and although Jeremy felt sorry for Mustafa el Kro, he wasted no time. He himself was free at last, and after granting a well-deserved forty-eight hours' leave to all the janissaries-of-the-sea except the unfortunate members of the commander in chief's crew, he set off at once for the palace. Selim had singled him out repeatedly during the ceremonies, heaping praise on him for all he had done to create an efficient naval fighting unit, and he felt confident of his ability to count on the sultan's help when Tule Yasmin opposed him. As a first step he intended to demand that Mary be set free, transferred from the khana's custody to his own—permanently—and he was tempted to become a Mussulman, if necessary, to achieve his purpose. The Koran permitted true believers to take four wives, and even though he was married to Tule Yasmin, there would be nothing to prevent him from making Mary his wife as well.

As Jeremy rode through the streets of Constantinople behind a squadron of cavalrymen who cleared the way for him, various obstacles to his scheme occurred to him. Chief among them was the fear that Mary might be very reluctant to embrace Islam and to become the number-two wife of a man whose future remained cloudy. On the other hand, such a status would be far preferable to slavery, and Jeremy was counting on her good sense to make her see the obvious advantages of accepting his immediate solution and trusting him to work out the rest of their dilemma, step by step.

When the sultan was away, fewer guards stood duty at the palace, and only a few sentries patrolled the grounds. Jeremy returned their salutes absently and dismissed his escort when they reached the entrance to the seraglio. Leaving his orderly to take his belongings to his quarters, he hurried straight to the khana's suite, and as he walked he was faintly disturbed to see that none of the servingwomen were loitering nearby, waiting to tell their princess that he had returned. It was possible, of course, that Tule Yasmin had not yet heard that the fleet had landed, but as she always made it her business to know what was happening, he doubted that she had not been told he was back.

Perhaps, he reflected, there had been another abrupt change in her attitude toward him while he had been absent. He could not exclude the chance that she might feel more warmly toward him now, and if this were the case his immediate task would be made far more complex, so he braced himself as he tapped at the closed door of the entrance to her chambers. No one answered his summons, so he knocked again more loudly but heard neither footsteps nor voices, and growing impatient, he raised the latch. The door creaked open, and he hurried through the empty antechamber into the drawing room. The major pieces of furniture were in place, but a score of satin-covered cushions that had been the khana's property were gone, and he felt misgivings as he headed straight toward her bedchamber.

The top of Tule Yasmin's dressing table was bare, and not a trace of her many cosmetics remained. Jeremy, his heart pounding, opened wardrobe drawers and discovered they were empty, too; he raised his voice in a shout, but even as he did he knew there would be no reply. Leaving the suite, he went at once to the outbuilding that was the home and office of the principal eunuch, who hurried out to greet him, bowing low. Jeremy glowered at him and cut short his flowery salutation.

"Where is Her Sublimity? And where are her servingwomen?"

The principal eunuch raised his pudgy hands in fluttering horror. "I thought, Your Excellency—that is, I assumed—"

"Never mind what you thought or what you assumed. Where is Tule Yasmin?"

"By this time she must be well on her way to the domain of her brother, the khagan Buyantu Yassan. She left the very day after Your Excellency went off to sea. I am grieved if Your Excellency knew nothing of her plans, for she told Selim the Magnificent himself that you had given your approval for her to visit her brother, whom she has not seen in years."

Jeremy knew, even before he asked his next question, that Tule Yasmin had outsmarted him. "She took her servingwomen with her?"

"All of them," the principal eunuch replied with relish, his eyes gleaming maliciously, "including the red-haired maiden Your Excellency covets." The eunuch laughed quietly as he watched the downcast Jeremy turn and leave. What the wily eunuch did not tell the American was that his mistress had taken not only the red-haired slave girl but also the Great Mongol Emerald as well. Once again, she had managed to seduce the court jeweler, had played on his sympathies for weeks, and had succeeded in getting him to secure the jewel for her by telling the sultan that the stone needed to be cleaned and polished. The principal eunuch had witnessed all this intrigue with great interest, and he was gleefully looking forward to even more excitement: the execution of the court jeweler when the sultan learned that the man had once again betrayed his trust by plotting with the khana Tule Yasmin.

Jeremy retreated slowly through the rooms of Tule Yasmin's dwelling as he made his way to his own quarters, and suddenly he became aware that someone was watching him. He looked around but saw no one; then he searched more carefully, and in the shadows he saw a slight movement. Moving closer and closer, he suddenly pounced and was astonished when he found that he had Rosalind Tate in his grasp.

Rosalind was frightened, but she had not lost her courage. "I was hoping I'd see you," she said. "We've got to act quickly."

"What does that mean?" Jeremy demanded.

"If you'll let me go and stop squeezing my arm half to death I'll be able to talk a little more freely," she said. He flushed as he released her, somewhat taken aback by the young woman's spirit.

"Tule Yasmin has gone off to Mongolia to see her brother, the khagan. For reasons that she didn't explain to anyone, she took Mary with her. I guess she would have taken me, too, but I hid. She was in such a hurry to leave that she left without me."

"Good Lord!" Jeremy muttered. "I'll have to go after them. I don't trust Tule Yasmin alone with Mary."

"Neither do I." Rosalind didn't say it, but she was relieved that he was going to intervene actively.

"I've got to figure out what to do next," he said.

"I beg only one favor of you," Rosalind said. "Tule Yasmin was responsible for the death of my brother and has ruined my life. Please, if you're going to go after them, take me with you. More than anything else in this world, I want the chance to get even with her. I won't rest until I've balanced the score!"

Jeremy paced up and down the sitting room of his suite for hours, trying to decide on the most effective course of action. It was obvious to him that the servingwoman who had watched him talking to Mary had been more perspicacious than he had realized, and that, after she had reported to the khana, Tule Yasmin had decided to remove herself and her attractive slave girl from the city before her husband could embarrass her with some scheme such as the very one he had in mind. It was clear to him, too, that she had started to prepare for her departure as soon as she had heard that Jumai Khan and her Frankish slave had talked at length and looked deeply into each other's eyes.

A party of women could not travel at a rapid rate, Jeremy thought, but nevertheless the khana undoubtedly had been given the best horse for her journey. And as she had left Constantinople almost a week ago, it was dubious that even the swiftest messenger could overtake her before they reached the land of Mongolia. Jeremy knew, too, that it would be useless to send word to her demanding that she return and bring Mary with her. Tule Yasmin could always pretend she had not received his command, and once she reached her brother's realm she could blithely ignore it.

Or if she chose to come back, it would be absurdly simple for her to leave Mary behind. The slave was her property, and despite the fact that her husband could claim that anything or anyone she owned belonged to him, there would be nothing to prevent her from selling Mary or giving the girl away. It was even possible, Jeremy knew, for the khana to have Mary put to death rather than lose face. And if the worst happened, he would never be able to prove a murder charge against Tule Yasmin. There were so many slaves in Islam and so few princesses of royal blood that the disappearance of a mere serving maid would have no significance and would not warrant even a cursory investigation.

Once Mary vanished into Mongolia, it was unlikely that she would ever leave that remote land; certainly Tule Yasmin, jealous of her, would not bring her back to Constantinople unless forced to do so by someone whose authority or will was greater than her own. Jeremy's analysis led to a single, inescapable conclusion: If he hoped to rescue Mary, he would not be able to depend on either emissaries or messengers but would have to go to the khagan's capital, Urga, himself.

His knowledge of Asian geography was vague, but he knew that the Mongol realm was at least a month's journey from Constantinople. By pursuing Tule Yasmin, he would be forced to absent himself from his post for many weeks and consequently would neglect both his obligation to the sultan and his all-important mission for the United States. A man who was not charged with responsibilities could afford to indulge in reckless acts, particularly when the girl he loved was involved, but an American who sought Turkish recognition of his country and who held the rank of pasha of one horsetail in the sultan's navy couldn't allow himself to act rashly.

But in a sense, Jeremy reflected, he had already carried out the orders that Selim had given him; the fleet exercises of the past week had proved that the naval gunners were now a trained, efficient force. They had not yet been put to the test in real war, of course, and he realized that the sultan would want him to remain and continue to train the janissaries-of-the-sea until the day when England openly challenged the growing Ottoman might. But there were others who could now follow the path he had charted, sub-pashas and captains who had learned enough to supervise the remainder of the training program he had laid out.

He consequently decided that, under the circumstances, he would not be harming either his own cause or that of the Turks if he made a long journey into the interior. He would prepare detailed instructions for his assistants, and the training program would continue smoothly until he returned. But he did not fool himself, and facing the situation honestly, he knew he was taking one great risk; if while he was gone England sent in the huge ships of the line and the sleek frigates of the navy to attack the Turks, the sultan would undoubtedly feel that his absence was inexcusable. In that case he would not only fail to win recognition for the United States but would be lucky if he stayed alive. He had no way of knowing what long-range plans London was making, of course. He had learned that the sultan had received—and ignored—another message from the English demanding the release of their prisoners, and he could only hope that, as no Turkish captains had as yet reported a major concentration of English vessels in the Mediterranean, the attack would not begin in the immediate future. And when he thought of Mary he realized he would not be able to live with himself unless he took the chance for her sake.

What complicated his problem was the absence of his senior from the city. Ordinarily he would have gone to Mustafa el Kro, and his friend would have granted him a leave of absence from his post. Or at the very worst he might have gone directly to the sultan. But Selim, Mustafa el Kro, and the pashas of three horsetails who made up the imperial council were all at sea, and if he waited several days until they returned, he might be too late to help Mary. Every hour was important, Jeremy felt, and he knew it would be useless to put out to sea in search of the flagship, as he had no idea where the imperial party was sailing and would waste precious time hunting for them.

He had to rely on his own authority, and the moment he realized it his doubts vanished. He would follow the khana and Mary. He wrote a letter of explanation to Mustafa el Kro and then worked feverishly through the rest of the night, drawing up training schedules for the janissaries-of-the-sea and orders for the foremen at the gun foundries. He did not finish until shortly after sunrise, but he was not tired, and after sending the various documents to headquarters, where they would be waiting for Mustafa el Kro when he returned, he hastily prepared for his own trip.

He had accumulated a considerable sum of money that had been paid to him in monthly wages. He opened his strongbox and poured all of the gold into a stout leather purse, which he wore inside his belt. He changed into fresh clothes, packed only the few items that would be essential on the road, and armed himself with a brace of pistols and the jewel-handled scimitar that was a symbol of his rank. Then, eating a breakfast of bread and cold meat as he walked, he went to the imperial stables and selected a white Arabian stallion, a strong, swift horse able to stand long hours on the road. He was tempted to take an escort of cavalrymen with him, which was his right as a pasha of one horsetail, but he resisted the impulse; his journey was personal, not official, and the presence of a squadron might hinder him.

The question of what to do with Rosalind bothered him, but he felt he had no choice. Granted he would travel far more rapidly if he traveled alone. But the girl's request was legitimate, and he could certainly understand how she felt. Perhaps he was being foolish, but he felt he owed her this chance to leave the palace and to assert herself. Her pride was also at stake, and he didn't want to be responsible for denying her the opportunity to help herself.

Obviously it would be far too difficult to travel with a female slave, especially an attractive one. Therefore he had male clothes brought to the house for her and brusquely ordered her to dress in them.

Rosalind's eyes glowed, and she made no comment as she hurried off to another chamber, reappearing in a few minutes in the guise of a young man.

"Can you use firearms or a sword?" Jeremy asked her.

She shrugged. "I don't know. I've never tried," she replied with a slight laugh.

"Well, you'll have to carry arms because you'll be too conspicuous without them," he said. "And we've got to get you the best mare available."

He gave rapid-fire instructions to one of his naval aides, and soon all was in readiness for the journey. Rosalind was obviously excited but kept her emotions well under control. Her disguise proved to be so effective that none of the men who were members of Jeremy's normal entourage suspected that she was a woman, disguised as a man.

By the time the sun rose over Constantinople, Jeremy and Rosalind were riding through the ancient gates of the city, heading toward the east, and when the capital was behind them they cantered down the open road at such a fast clip that farmers en route to the markets, beggars, and merchants all scurried out of their path. He felt better now that he had taken action, and his fears were lulled by the steady pounding of the horses' hooves on the dirt that had been packed hard by countless travelers who had used the road for centuries.

His military maps, which he had packed at the last minute before leaving the seraglio, proved to be of enormous benefit to him, and he charted the most direct route for himself and Rosalind. The first part of the trip was fairly simple, for they followed the road that stretched out along the southern shore of the Black Sea, through a region that was an integral part of the Ottoman Empire. They made overnight stops at sumptuously furnished inns that were prepared to cater to every traveler's desires, and at all of them he was greeted cordially and respectfully, and his "servant" was treated well, too. But neither the innkeepers nor their servants fawned on him, as these establishments were accustomed to waiting on the great and near-great; a pasha of one horsetail was a man of consequence, but others far more important had come this way before him.

Road conditions were less pleasant when Jeremy and Rosalind turned north and rode through the Caucasus Mountains to the old city of Astrakhan at the north end of the Caspian Sea. Not many travelers ventured into this area, the roads twisted through narrow valleys between the mountains, and there were only a few crude inns that offered food and shelter. Sometimes they rode for hours at a time without seeing another human being, occasionally they made their way through forests that reminded Jeremy of the American wilderness, and often they were forced to sleep in the open beside a running stream.

Jeremy was astonished by Rosalind's ability to keep up with him. No matter how swift his pace, she did not complain. No matter what rigors they encountered on the road, she was able to surmount them with good grace, and his opinion of her soared accordingly. When sumptuous meals were available she gladly ate them, successful in her pose as his servant, but when nothing but simple fare of lamb, onions, and coarse bread was served, she ate what was placed in front of her without complaint and remained cheerful. When it was necessary to sleep in the open, she did so gladly, just as she happily enjoyed a comfortable bed at the better inns, since Jeremy always insisted his "servant" be given quarters of his own. Certainly she gave him no reason to regret having brought her with him on his journey.

Rosalind also had the ability to become one with her surroundings. Although her knowledge of the Turkish language was limited, she had the good sense to remain silent in the presence of others and spoke only when directly addressed. Therefore she was able to maintain the pretense that she was a young male, and no one who encountered the pair on the road or on any of the stops they made was any the wiser.

So they encountered no difficulties, and Jeremy was surprised at the docile orderliness of the people. Generations of sultans had forced peace on even the inhabitants of remote sections; there were no bandits on the roads; and small companies of imperial soldiers, riding or walking, patrolled the countryside, punishing anyone who dared to disobey the law or create a disturbance. Jeremy's headgear and scimitar were the only passports he needed, and although he grew weary after riding from dawn until sundown for day after day, he could not complain about the treatment he received anywhere.

The military commandant of Astrakhan insisted that the pasha stay at his own house, and when he heard that Jeremy intended to ride east to Mongolia, he made all of the arrangements necessary for the next stage of the journey. The city of Samarkand, at the opposite end of Turkestan, was Jeremy's immediate goal, and the commandant said that no stranger could possibly make such a trip accompanied only by a servant, who from the looks of him was not very sturdy. The road crossed high mountains, cut across blazing stretches of the Kara Kum Desert, and travelers who did not know the area were in danger of wandering across the Kirghiz steppes into the territory of Imperial Russia. The border between the Ottoman domain and that of the Russians was ill-defined, and as the two great powers had been at peace with each other for only a short time after hundreds of years of warfare, the border patrols on both sides were suspicious and inclined to shoot all strangers without bothering to learn their identity. Furthermore, the commandant said, the Russians would become alarmed if they saw a pasha in their territory and would be sure he had come to spy on them in preparation for a new war. So it would be better for Jeremy to move more slowly than to end his days being hacked to pieces by the swords of Russian troops.

He was forced to remain in Astrakhan for four days and did his best to conceal his impatience as the governor of the city and the commandant arranged a series of banquets and entertainments for him. He suffered these occasions with the best grace he could muster, and he was grateful that Rosalind was not forced to live in the servants' quarters but was given a small room adjoining his own. But Jeremy was anxious to push on and was infinitely relieved when arrangements were made for him to join a caravan of merchants, pilgrims, and minor government officials traveling to Samarkand. A troop of the sultan's famed camel corpsmen escorted the party, and Jeremy was astonished at the ability of these resilient, dark-skinned warriors to make their stubborn, cumbersome mounts obey their commands.

The soldiers rode in formation at the front, sides, and rear of the caravan, and no traveler was permitted to stray from the group. Jeremy and Rosalind, riding in the van with the leader of the unit, were pleased that they had not ventured through this desolate land alone.

Only once was there a close call with Rosalind, who for the most part had succeeded in her disguise as Jeremy's young servant. The leader of the camel corps had his own serving boy, but the lad was sullen and uncooperative and, during the trip, constantly talked back to his master. Finally the soldier approached Jeremy and offered to buy Rosalind for a large sum.

"I couldn't possibly sell him to you," Jeremy quickly responded, hoping the troop leader didn't see his discomfiture. "I promised the lad's father I would look after him until he was old enough to serve in the sultan's army."

"Well, I can understand your reluctance to part with him," the officer said, patting Rosalind's shoulder. "He's a good lad, quiet and obedient—and good-looking, too. If you ever change your mind, let me know. I could use a lad like this."

"I certainly will," Jeremy said, thankful that the officer hadn't pressed the issue. He sighed inaudibly and exchanged a quick, profound glance with Rosalind.

Jeremy's "servingman" was completely forgotten as they continued on their journey. The mountains were wild and lonely, the passes were rough, and the roads were narrow, but the trip through the desert was by far the worst, as the sun beat down mercilessly by day, and the temperature dropped below freezing at night. The merchants grumbled, the government officials complained openly, and the pilgrims, some of whom were inadequately clad, suffered in silence. One of the latter, an elderly man who had sworn on his wife's grave to make the journey to the Golden Mosque at Samarkand, became ill, but the soldiers refused to slow their pace for him, and after several days his condition became so bad that he could not travel at all.

Jeremy felt sorry for the old man, and in spite of his

own desire to reach Mongolia as soon as he could, he assumed that the caravan would halt to give the invalid a chance to regain his health. The leader of the troop had other ideas, however; he said it would be impossible to wait, and if the sick man were left behind he would suffer a slow death. There was only one way to handle the situation, he declared, and that night, after the others had gone to sleep wrapped in their robes, he sent two of his men armed with scimitars to put the pilgrim out of his misery.

When the journey was resumed the following morning, no one but Jeremy was shocked, and no one else bothered to look back. He understood their seeming callousness when he did turn in his saddle, for swarms of black vultures had appeared from nowhere and were swooping down from the cloudless sky on the body of the unfortunate pilgrim. And in the days that followed, Jeremy gradually came to accept the wisdom of the troop leader's decision. An American, born and raised in an expanding land, normally thought in terms of great distances, it was true, for his nation extended from the border of English Canada in the north to Spanish Florida in the south, and every citizen of the United States knew that someday he or his children after him would claim sovereignty over the whole of the territory lying west of the Mississippi River. But the size of the Ottoman Empire staggered the imagination.

Turkestan alone covered an area many times larger than the entire Ohio Valley, and when the desert gave way to another range of mountains, Jeremy began to understand why the man who bore the title of sultan was revered by his subjects as the mightiest potentate on earth. Certainly no other ruler could claim dominion over so vast a realm, and the differences in climate and people were bewildering. The inhabitants of tiny desert towns slept under palm trees, ate dates, and eked out a miserable existence in subtropical heat, while one hundred miles to the east prosperous farmers grew wheat, raised sheep and cattle, and enjoyed weather as brisk as that of Boston or Fort Detroit.

A somewhat harsher version of the desert appeared again

on the last stretch of the journey to Samarkand, and in this primitive wilderness of coarse gray sand hills, no human being or animal could survive. A few stunted trees and an occasional patch of sickly yellow grass broke the monotony here and there, but even these token signs of vegetation served no useful purpose. No caravan could travel rapidly over such terrain, and by the time the towers and domes of Samarkand's mosques appeared on the horizon, Jeremy knew he had been badly mistaken in estimating the time it would take him to reach Urga. He had hoped to arrive in Mongolia within a month of his departure from Constantinople, but he had already spent almost two months on the road and was still far from his goal.

In Samarkand itself he was delayed again, and although the city was allegedly a great metropolis, Jeremy found it stultifying, dull, and depraved. It had enjoyed an era of unprecedented prosperity after Genghis Khan and his warriors had used it as a headquarters, and in the centuries that had followed it had attained a considerable reputation in the Moslem world. It was true that the Golden Mosque, a glittering edifice made of precious metals and filled with priceless gems carelessly set in the walls, was unique, but Samarkand lived in the past, content to bask in the glow of the glory it had once enjoyed. There had been a time when the sharif of Turkestan had been a great power in Asia, but the present ruler of the land, who paid a heavy annual tribute to his master in Constantinople, was a weakling who had no influence on his own people or at the council tables of the empire.

At the request of the sharif Jeremy had no choice but to accept lodging at the ornate palace that stood on a hill in the center of the city, but the experience became a nightmare. The officials of the court amused themselves with the women of the royal harem, and the sharif, an amiable fat man with liquid brown eyes, surrounded himself with delicately handsome youths who dressed in women's clothes and daubed their faces with cosmetics. The presence of a visitor was a sufficient excuse for a round of frantically gay, dissolute parties, and the sharif, who jealously wanted nothing to interfere with his pleasures, slyly put one obstacle after another in the way of Jeremy's departure.

Jeremy's stay in Samarkand was further complicated by his fear that the dissolute sharif of Turkestan would discover that Rosalind Tate was a woman wearing man's disguise. Certainly if her secret were revealed it would be far more difficult for the couple to leave Samarkand intact. Even as it was, Jeremy feared that any day Rosalind would be summoned to the sharif's court to join the youths who served him. Only Jeremy's insistence made it possible for Rosalind to stay with him in a chamber adjoining his own. Therefore, in spite of the many excuses the sharif made to keep his visitor in the city, Jeremy restlessly sought to escape from the overwhelming hospitality of his perverted host.

Not even a pasha of one horsetail was immune from the wrath of the vindictive monarch, and when Jeremy tried to demand that he be allowed to leave, he was taken on a tour of the dungeons and torture chambers beneath the palace as a warning to hold his tongue. So he had no choice but to endure the daily feasts, but whenever he saw the indignities to which the pretty slave girls of the harem were subjected, his fear for Rosalind and his determination to help Mary increased. It was sheer good luck that Rosalind had not been forced by the sharif to take part in lewd performances for him and his intimates, but for all Jeremy knew Mary had been subjected to an even worse fate, and he made careful plans for his escape from the palace.

Ten days after his arrival in Samarkand his opportunity came, as he had known it would. The sharif and his entourage spent an especially long afternoon and evening at their revels in the banquet hall, and in spite of the injunctions of the Koran against the consumption of intoxicating beverages, virtually the whole court was in a sodden state by midnight. Jeremy, who had carefully thrown the cups of wine he had been given into the bases of potted palms, waited until he was sure that his hosts were in no condition to stop him. Then he sneaked off to the room he had been assigned and found Rosalind waiting for him. He collected his few belongings and his weapons and bribed a slave to lead him to the stables by a flight of stairs in the servants' wing.

The grooms who were on duty were reluctant to release his stallion and Rosalind's mare, but they changed their minds when they found themselves staring into the muzzles of his cocked pistols, and without further protest they saddled the animals. Before one of them could report the irregular procedure to some official still sober enough to understand it, Jeremy and Rosalind were gone. They rode rapidly to the high walls of the city, and there they encountered no difficulty, as the troops on duty, who received their pay from the sultan rather than the sharif, promptly opened the gate for them. An icy wind off the desert cut through their thin woolen garments, but Jeremy welcomed the discomfort and inhaled the clean air gratefully. When he returned in this direction, he told himself, he would avoid the degenerate capital of the sharif at all costs.

By dawn they had put more than twenty miles between themselves and Samarkand, and after halting at a small oasis for a brief rest, Jeremy studied his maps once more before continuing the journey. Few roads led into Mongolia, it was true, but he was on his own now and could make far faster time than was possible when he had been forced to travel at the pace of portly merchants and feeble pilgrims. In another two days, three at the most, he estimated that he and Rosalind should reach the border, provided he followed the main caravan routes, and in another week, barring accidents, they would arrive in Urga.

Inevitably Jeremy's relationship with Rosalind grew more complicated. He had been so busy dealing with the hazards of the road, his mind was so filled with the knowledge that each passing day he was drawing nearer to Mary Ellis, that he paid scant heed to the attractive young woman who was accompanying him on his journey. This, how-

ever, was far from true for the girl. If the truth be known,
she had idealized him, and her ordeal had only served to
intensify the heroic mold in which she had cast him. In
her eyes he could do no wrong, and she was very much
in love with him, although she would have denied it had
she been accused of it. Certainly he had no idea of the
state of her feelings.

As they drew nearer to the wild, inhospitable land of
Urga, a vast country of wastelands that extended as far as
the eye could see, they were subjected to violent extremes
of weather. By day the temperature soared, the ground
became parched and dry, and animals and men alike suffered from the extreme heat of a blazing sun shining from
a cloudless sky on a terrain where there was no relief. At
night, however, the temperature plunged precipitously.
Drops of fifty to eighty degrees after the sun went down
were not unusual, and the winds that swept across the
vast, uninhabited plains were bone-chilling.

Jeremy accepted the extremes of weather as an ordinary
hazard of travel, but Rosalind was less fortunate and suffered from the swing from heat to cold to heat again. At
night Jeremy refrained from lighting a fire for fear of at-
tracting potential foes, so he slept wrapped in a blanket,
and the girl did the same.

One night, however, sleep would not come for her. At
last she sat up, her teeth chattering, and drawing her inadequate blanket around her shoulders, she rose and
walked the short distance to the spot where Jeremy lay.

"You may have ice water running in your veins," she
said, "but I don't. I'm half frozen!"

Jeremy hoisted himself onto his elbows and grinned up
at her. "It isn't that bad," he said.

"Speak for yourself!" she retorted. "I really can't stand
it."

He considered her problem and made an intelligent suggestion. "Combine your blanket with mine and sleep with
me," he said.

She hesitated briefly, realizing she had no sensible alternative and if she refused she would be condemning herself to a night of sheer misery. So much had happened that was unorthodox that she forgot—or cast aside—her strict upbringing, all that she had been taught. A smile touched her lips; then she dropped to the ground beside him and made room for him beneath her blanket.

They arranged the two blankets to cover them both, and the double layer, combined with their joint body warmth, was sufficient to ward off the extreme chill. For the first time in many nights, Rosalind was actually comfortable.

Tired after his long day, and lulled by the girl's proximity, Jeremy was soon drifting off to sleep again, but Rosalind remained wide awake. She was being enfolded in the arms of the man she loved, and the experience overwhelmed her. All at once she began to act in defiance of her lifelong training. She seemed to have no control over her hands as her fingers crept to Jeremy's shirt and unbuttoned it, then stroked his chest for a time. Then her hands slid lower and undid his belt buckle as well.

He was almost asleep when he realized that the girl was undressing him beneath their blankets. This created a totally unexpected dilemma for him. Certainly he did not love her, but at the same time he was not insensitive to her beauty. In spite of himself he reacted without thinking and began to treat her in kind.

His fingers became active, too. He fumbled with the buttons of her shirt, then cupped a breast in his hand. Rosalind responded instantly to his touch. She nestled still closer to him, her nipple hardening beneath his fingers.

By now they were both too far gone to turn back; without realizing it, they had cast the die. Unaware of anything and everything in the limitless wasteland except their mutual desire, they made love beneath the star-filled skies of Turkestan. All Jeremy knew was that he wanted this desirable creature.

As for Rosalind, she could scarcely believe her good

fortune. She had dreamed so often of Jeremy's lovemaking—and now all that she had imagined was coming to pass.

Both were aliens in a foreign land far from home, a primitive, savage land unlike any they had ever known. Certainly this feeling of isolation contributed to their mutual desire for each other, heightening their responses. Their lovemaking became more frantic, their ardor became wilder, less restrained, and at last they became one.

As Jeremy's balance was restored, he realized he faced an unprecedented predicament. The proprieties of the situation required him to say something appropriate to Rosalind, perhaps to tell her of his great love for her. But he could not lie to her. The truth of the matter was that he was in love with Mary Ellis. He knew that Mary and Rosalind were related, and indeed he wondered if that had something to do with his attraction to the younger woman. But whatever the case, he could not dissemble for the sake of saying something that would make the situation more tolerable for the girl.

Consequently he said nothing. It was best to remain silent, he decided, and he was willing to risk causing her temporary hurt rather than lie and create a serious long-range problem for her.

Their lovemaking removed all barriers between them, to be sure, and thereafter they slept together regularly. This proximity, this closeness made the journey into the wilderness of Urga more tolerable for both of them. Somehow they were comforted.

Certainly Jeremy was conscious of the fact that his long, arduous journey was coming to a close. Soon he would be compelled to face harsh realities, and his previous experiences with Tule Yasmin left him in no doubt that he would have no easy time awaiting him. Somehow he had to rescue Mary Ellis. Somehow he had to contend with Tule Yasmin's brother. He knew very little about the khagan, but he had to be prepared for the worst.

The knowledge that they had embarked on the last stage of their long journey made Jeremy increasingly conscious of the possible difficulties that awaited him in the principal city of the Mongols, and as they pushed on through the wastelands he indulged in numerous flights of fancy. In each of them he pitted himself against Tule Yasmin, and after imagining how she would react to something he would say or do, he then reexamined each potential situation and discussion carefully to see whether he had erred in his estimates of the khana's strengths and weaknesses. He realized, of course, that he was merely playing a game with himself, for he had no way of knowing what he would actually find at Urga. The most important of the intangibles was the khagan Buyantu Yassan, and Jeremy had no notion of whether the man was close to his sister and indulged her whims, whether he held the traditional orthodox Moslem views of women, and whether he was truly loyal to the sultan or merely paid lip service to his overlord in Constantinople.

It was safe to assume that the khagan was fiercely independent, Jeremy felt. In the first place, no ruler so far removed from the seat of government could be intimidated easily by the sultan. And if Tule Yasmin was a typical member of her family, her brother was probably headstrong, arrogant, and sly. It was hard, too, to picture the direct descendant of Genghis Khan and Kublai Khan as anything other than ruthless. Grizzled janissary officers in Constantinople had spoken with respect of the prowess of Mongol fighting men, so it was probable that their ruler was the strongest person in the principality.

By the time Jeremy and Rosalind had spent another day and a half on their ride out of Turkestan, the countryside began to change again, and he saw that they were approaching the foothills of a chain of mountains unlike any they had crossed previously. Snowcapped peaks towered in the distance, and the lesser slopes were covered with a red clay earth that for some reason was bare of all covering except a stubbly, prickly grass. There were no trees, no lakes, and no rivers, and whenever Jeremy looked out across the land from the top of one of the hills, he could see neither the huts of peasants nor any signs of animal life. He recalled vaguely that someone in Constantinople had once remarked that Mongolia was surrounded by an arid belt that kept strangers out and held her own people in, and he began to feel that he was entering a realm cut off from all the rest of the earth.

The sensation was an eerie one, and he wondered whether he was mad to make this journey in the hopes of helping a girl who might want nothing to do with him. His rank in the sultan's navy presumably would mean nothing to a remote people who had never seen the sea, and he might be lucky to escape from Mongolia with his life. It was some consolation, however, to reflect that the khagan's subjects were probably very much like other people, in spite of their isolation. And if Tule Yasmin was any indication, they were certainly earthy and passionate.

Jeremy couldn't help being fond of Rosalind Tate, who demanded nothing from him, who asked for nothing other than his lovemaking, so the startling development, the catastrophe that struck, was as devastating as it was unexpected.

One night they slept together as usual, with neither of them thinking of anything beyond the immediate present. Eventually, warmed by each other and by their blankets, they drifted off to sleep.

Jeremy had no idea how long he slept or what awakened him. To the best of his knowledge he heard or saw nothing. The first thing he realized was that Rosalind's position seemed rather strained. He propped himself on one elbow, peered at her, and was horrified to see that she was dead. An arrow had been shot with great strength and velocity and penetrated deep into her forehead, with the shaft still emerging. Whoever had killed her had taken careful aim, and the girl had never known what struck her.

Certainly he was accustomed to the silent approach of savages in the North American forest, but nothing prepared him for this kind of a reception in Urga. Badly shaken, the aroused Jeremy waited until dawn, then scoured the nearby countryside, but he saw no sign of any other human being. Whoever had killed Rosalind had vanished from the face of the earth, taking the girl's mare but carefully covering up the tracks.

He lacked the tools to dig her a proper grave, but he managed to place her body beneath a large boulder, which he rolled into place above her so that wild animals would not be able to reach her. Once he had completed the task he felt bereft, strangely alone. He was not a religious man, but he couldn't help feeling a sense of great loss for this young English girl who, like her brother, had lost her life so needlessly, so very far from home, so very far from those who were near and dear to her.

He tried to think of an appropriate prayer, but his mind refused to function. Eventually he spoke aloud. "Lord God," he said, "I commend this, your servant Rosalind, to your keeping and your care. She was loyal and true. She caused harm to no one. Had fate willed otherwise, she would have lived to become a wonderful wife and mother somewhere in her own world. So take pity on her, Lord, and keep watch over her in this desolate land."

Alone now, Jeremy resumed his journey, plunging deeper into the countryside of Urga. He tried to put the girl out of his mind; he realized that he was immersed in a strange, alien land in which death was no stranger and violence was a common way of life. It was useless to speculate on what might have been; he had to accept things for what they were.

The ground became rockier as Jeremy rode higher into the mountains, and the stallion had to travel at a slower pace. There were no roads across the passes that led from

Turkestan into Mongolia, but Jeremy constantly checked his bearings, using his maps as a guide, and as nearly as he could judge, he was taking the easiest and most direct route. His stallion climbed steadily higher, and huge, naked boulders loomed up on both sides of the tortuous passes. A wind blowing from the plains of Mongolia whistled through the mountains, and although it was cold, it was so dry that it burned Jeremy's face.

Again he thought this was the most lonely region he had ever seen, and a sense of depression stole over him, heightened by the absence of Rosalind. Then the stallion suddenly snorted and pawed the ground, and a moment later Jeremy realized the area was not as deserted as he had imagined. Three men appeared from behind boulders, one directly ahead of him, the others slightly to each side. All were mounted on small, shaggy ponies, and the first thing Jeremy noticed was that they were leading Rosalind's mare behind them. They were armed with long, double-edged swords reminiscent of the ancient Chinese weapons about which Marco Polo had written. They carried daggers with iron hilts in their belts, too, and their dark faces beneath high sheepskin hats were definitely menacing.

The trio blocked Jeremy's progress, and as he pulled his mount to a halt he let his other hand fall on the butt of one of his pistols. He did not draw it, however, and waited for the men to make the first move. Their high boots, leather breeches, and shapeless padded felt coats convinced him they were Mongolians, but he told himself they weren't necessarily bandits who intended to rob him. It was quite possible that they were members of a border patrol, and he remembered being told by the military commandant at Astrakhan that the khagan permitted no one to enter his realm, not even friends and fellow citizens of the empire, without first subjecting every visitor to a careful scrutiny. They obviously had been responsible for the death of Rosalind Tate, and Jeremy could only surmise that they had thought they killed him instead. But why they wanted to kill him was a mystery—unless someone had told them to do so.

They stared at him, their black eyes shining balefully, but he smiled in return, even as he shifted his position slightly in his saddle so he would be ready for action. "May Allah be with you," he said politely, hoping to disarm them with his calm manner.

There was no reply, and the rider on the left tugged at a long, drooping mustache. "Is this the one?" he asked his companions, and although he spoke a version of Turkish Jeremy had never heard, it was possible to make out the sense of what he was saying.

The others continued their careful inspection, and finally the man in the center, who seemed to be the leader by virtue of a faded gold tassel on the hilt of his sword, replied, "It could be no one else. See the horsetail that hangs from his hood?" Then the leader turned to his companion on the left. "You fool. I knew I shouldn't have trusted you to go after him last night. No doubt the one you shot with your arrow was his servant. I suspected that when you returned with only a mare."

"But it was dark, my chief, and I could not see that there was more than one person. I also did not see that there were two horses."

"You were too hasty, and that's why you erred," the leader said. "I would have you horsewhipped except that we have found the one we want after all."

Jeremy realized that the time to act had come, and his fingers tightened around the pistol butt. At that instant the man to his right, who had remained motionless and had not spoken, charged forward, raising his sword. By the time Jeremy drew his pistol and cocked it, the Mongol was almost upon him, but he took careful aim and fired straight into his adversary's face. The attacker dropped to the ground, but his pony continued to gallop toward the stallion, and through sheer good luck momentarily blocked the approach of the other two men.

The riderless animal thus gave Jeremy time to draw his remaining pistol; the Mongol on his left threw a dagger at him, but it missed him by inches because the stallion, his dignity outraged by the antics of the pony, lunged forward, his teeth bared. Jeremy knew he would have no chance to reload, so his second shot would therefore either equalize the odds or would leave the attackers with a two to one advantage. He squeezed the trigger steadily and gently, but the violent motion of his enraged horse spoiled his aim, and the shot went far wide of the mark. The Mongol laughed, and Jeremy, reacting instinctively as he always did in a time of mortal danger, quickly whipped his scimitar from the loop that held it at his waist.

He raised the blade just in time to deflect a vicious thrust of his foe's long sword, and a stinging shock in his wrist surprised him. The power behind the Mongol's blow had been unexpectedly great, and had he struck home Jeremy would have been decapitated. The scimitar and the long sword clashed a second time, then a third, and meanwhile the leader started to manuever into a position on Jeremy's flank. The stallion was Jeremy's greatest asset in a duel with two men mounted on small ponies, and he felt sure the leader would try to cut down his mount and thus render him helpless.

In a protracted fight, Jeremy realized, he would beat the man with whom he was crossing swords, but he could not devote his full attention to a single opponent, and he knew he had to resort to unorthodox tactics to save his life. So he dug his heels into the stallion's sides, twirled the scimitar over his head, and for specific reasons he was never able to understand, shouted the fierce war cry of the Mohawk Indians at the top of his voice. His mount responded by rearing and then plunging forward again, his hooves flashing, and although the Mongol tried to get out of the path of the infuriated beast, there was no escape from the stallion's vengeance.

Pony and rider were sent sprawling together, and the

horse, his eyes wild and his mouth foaming, stomped indiscriminately on the man and the animal, crushing the life out of them. Jeremy quickly discovered he had set forces in motion that he could not halt, and although he knew his stallion well after the many long weeks they had spent together, he could not calm the beast. He had to devote all his skill and energy to keeping his seat, and while his mount screamed and continued to buck, the surviving Mongol prepared to deliver the blow that would end the conflict. Jeremy watched him draw his dagger and make several practice sweeps with his arm, but he was unable to divert the stallion's attention from the victims underfoot and realized he was helpless.

The one factor in his favor was the unpredictability of his angry horse, for neither he nor the restless animal made a good target. Nevertheless the Mongol was apparently experienced in this kind of fighting, and showing neither sadness over the death of his companions nor pleasure at the prospect of avenging them, he sat quietly on his motionless pony, awaiting the best moment to strike. The stallion suddenly stopped screaming, whinnied, and looked down at the ground with puzzled eyes, as though wondering what had come over him, and Jeremy knew that now was the moment the dagger would speed toward him.

He made a desperate effort to rouse his mount again, but before the stallion could respond he saw a dark blur shoot through the air, and at almost the same instant he felt a stab of pain in his arm, near the shoulder. He was stunned, and not until the horse began to pick his way daintily across the bodies on the ground did it occur to him that he had suffered only a superficial wound. The thick shoulder folds on his burnoose, which he had thrown back so he would not be hindered in his movements, had absorbed the greater part of the dagger's force, and after sticking in the heavy wool for a moment, the knife fell and clattered onto a rock.

The cloak had saved Jeremy from serious injury, and

he felt the tension that had gripped him dissipate. At last he and the leader of the Mongols could fight on equal terms; each possessed only one weapon now, his sword, and the battle would be decided by skill, not trickery or the preponderance of numbers. As Jeremy turned the stallion to meet the Mongol, who was advancing cautiously, he suddenly thought that if either of them had gained the advantage, he was in the better position. The pony, although tough and spirited, could hardly compete with a huge beast almost half again its size, and it certainly lacked the enormous vitality and strength of the horse.

The Mongol headed straight for Jeremy, his long sword extended rigidly like a lance; then, just before he came within reach of the scimitar's sharp edge, his pony, responding to some unseen signal, suddenly swerved to one side. The Mongol came in under Jeremy's guard, and only a frantic flick of the scimitar stopped the sword's lunge in midair and prevented the heavy blade from cutting a deep gash in the stallion's neck. Jeremy was forced to revise his estimate and reflected bitterly that the man who rode the smaller mount might hold the upper hand after all.

For the next quarter of an hour the two opponents maneuvered unceasingly over the rough, uneven ground, and Jeremy had to admit to himself that he had never encountered a better rider than the Mongol. At times the pony and its master seemed to be one; they understood each other perfectly, they acted in unison, and Jeremy had no choice but to remain on the defensive at all times. His enemy darted in and out almost at will, appearing first on his left, then on his right, and twice almost taking him from behind.

The most discouraging aspect of the situation was that Jeremy knew himself to be the better swordsman, and although it was obvious from the respect his foe showed his blade that the Mongol knew it, too, the man was not deterred and pressed his attack vigorously. His pony showed no fear, either, and managed again and again to sidestep nimbly when the stallion kicked at him with hooves whose power could break bones. Eventually, Jeremy thought, the Mongol would be sure to land a blow unless he changed the pattern of the duel; he was fortunate to have escaped so far with only the minor dagger cut on his arm, but his luck would not hold indefinitely.

As Jeremy had long ago learned, and as he had preached constantly to the janissaries-of-the-sea at Constantinople, a man's worst enemy in battle was his own sense of recklessness. But there was a difference between disregard for danger that was caused by blind, unreasoning anger, and a calculated recklessness, a willingness to take unexpected risks in order to confuse the enemy. So Jeremy decided to chance the outcome on a single, bold stroke.

His spurs raked the stallion's sides, and he drove his mount at the Mongol, feinting wickedly with his scimitar. As he had hoped, his abrupt change in tactics alarmed the man, and he tried to back away, but before he could escape Jeremy drove the point of the scimitar into his throat, and the duel was over. The Mongol sat bolt upright for an instant, a look of astonishment on his face, then he toppled to the ground and lay very still. The pony, apparently realizing that his master was dead, cantered away madly, and Rosalind's mare followed, the sound of their hoofbeats echoing through the canyons.

Jeremy felt bone-weary as he surveyed the carnage, and now that the fight was over, a feeling of rage overcame him. The attack, he knew, had been deliberate, and the band had probably been instructed to kill him. It was peculiar that men who had not acted like robbers had attempted to kill a lone traveler, and it was even stranger that subjects of the khagan had attacked a pasha of one horsetail whose regalia identified him as an officer of the staff of the sultan, who was the overlord of every man and woman in the Ottoman Empire. Jeremy therefore concluded that Tule Yasmin had inspired the undertaking that had almost cost him his life and had taken the life of

Rosalind Tate. Either she had surmised that he would follow her and try to rescue Mary, or else she had learned that he had pursued her, but in either case the results were the same: She had declared herself his enemy, and from this time forward his life was in constant jeopardy.

VIII

~~~~~~~~~~~~~~~~~

When Jeremy descended from the mountain heights into the heart of Mongolia, he was surprised and pleased to see that he had ridden into a fertile grassland watered by numerous small streams fed by the snow at the peaks of the great range. His maps, which were sadly incomplete, gave him far less information than he needed, but he was able to make out the approximate location of Urga, and he doggedly continued his journey toward the city. Occasionally he saw a small mud hut, surrounded by vegetable gardens, but after his experience near the border he was suspicious of the inhabitants and carefully avoided them. When his food supplies ran low he stole oats and rye from a semicultivated field for his stallion, and he was fortunate, shortly before dusk on his first night in the foothills of Mongolia, to kill a young mountain lion with a pistol shot. The meat was tough, but he discovered that if he boiled it long enough it became edible, and he subsisted on it for a day and a half.

On the second day of his trip through the khagan's realm he noted that the farms were becoming more scattered, that the soil was again sparse and dry, and he guessed that he was nearing the approaches to the great Gobi Desert, which occupied almost all of the central portion of the vast country. A little before sundown he came across a waterhole fed by an underground spring, and when he discovered that the water was sweet, he decided to halt for the night, even though he might have continued on his journey for an hour or two longer. It was unlikely that he would find another source of potable water, and common sense told him not to push his luck too far.

He fed his stallion the last of the oats, and after drinking thirstily himself, he led the horse to the waterhole. Then he settled down to consume what was left of the boiled lion meat, and while he ate, night fell with dramatic suddenness. One moment it was broad daylight, and then it was dark; dusk in Mongolia, it seemed, was a transition period of extraordinary brevity. As he was finishing his unappetizing repast, he heard the sound of rapidly approaching hoofbeats, and jumping to his feet, he hurried to his stallion, who was now nibbling the grass that grew in a circle around the mouth of the waterhole. Before Jeremy could mount, however, a large party of horsemen swooped down on him and surrounded him.

There were at least forty men in the group, all of them dressed like the trio he had killed in the mountains, and all of them mounted on long-haired ponies. At first he thought they had tracked him here, and was grimly prepared to force them to pay dearly in return for his life, but as nearly as he could judge in the gloom, their faces showed surprise when they saw him. So he revised his estimate and guessed that they had not been searching for him but instead had merely come to the well. Several carried ancient muskets, which they pointed at him, but he assumed their action was precautionary, for they displayed no real hostility and moved aside quietly to permit a young man in a silk tunic to push to the front.

"Who are you?" the leader demanded abruptly but without rancor in his voice.

"Jumai Khan," Jeremy replied firmly, "second in command of the imperial navies of His Magnificence, Selim III. And," he added, "may Allah be with you."

The young man dismounted, stared at the stranger intently in the dark, and after satisfying himself that the insignia on the hood and the jewels on the hilt of the scimitar were genuine, he drew himself up stiffly and held his long sword before his face. "May Allah protect Your

Excellency," he declared in the harsh dialect that Jeremy
learned was the Kalmuck offshoot of Turkish. "Duglai
Effendi and his troop of fifty are at your service."

"What is your purpose in these parts, Effendi?" Jeremy
asked, and contrived to make the question sound perfunc-
tory.

"We keep the peace in the name of His Sublimity,
Buyantu Yassan." The young officer drew a deep breath;
he had no desire to offend a senior, yet it was his duty to
interrogate all strangers, regardless of their rank or position. "Your Excellency has just arrived in Mongolia across
the roof-of-the-world?" He gestured with his sword toward the dim outlines of the mountains in the distance.

"I have." Jeremy smiled with simulated good nature.

"Your destination is Urga, I presume?"

"It is."

"And your purpose there, if the pasha will forgive my
temerity in making inquiry?"

"I intend to see His Sublimity on a matter of the greatest importance." It would be folly, Jeremy decided, to
reveal that he was the khagan's brother-in-law and the
husband of Tule Yasmin. For all he knew she had alerted
the whole army to his possible arrival and had invented
some false charge against him, so it was possible that if
he identified himself too closely, the cavalrymen would
unhesitatingly slit his throat.

"Your Excellency travels without an escort?" Duglai
Effendi could not conceal his surprise.

"Yes." Jeremy offered no explanation.

"Then it will be a privilege for my troop of fifty, the
finest in the land, to offer Your Excellency guidance and
protection, and to see you safely to Urga."

"That won't be necessary, Effendi," Jeremy replied, pro-
testing lightly. "I have no desire to take you and your men
from your duties."

"*Bismillah!* I would fail in my duty if I did not accord
the proper honors to Your Excellency, and Allah would
never forgive me if I allowed you to go on alone and some

harm befell you. Buyantu Yassan would not forgive me, either, and would cut off my nose."

That settled the matter. The young officer's suspicions would certainly be aroused if there were any further objections, so Jeremy accepted with good grace, nodding and smiling politely. At a command from the effendi, the troop pitched camp, and a number of tents of padded felt were unrolled, the sections were pieced together, and a small village sprang into being around the well. The men cooked a stew of oxtails and lamb, heavily seasoned with garlic and strange spices, but Jeremy, who was served first, discovered that anything tasted good after his diet of boiled lion. With the stew the soldiers ate a flat bread with a unique flavor, and they drank an alcoholic beverage, very similar in taste to the bread, which they poured from skins. Jeremy questioned the effendi and discovered that the two were indeed alike, for both were made of fermented mare's milk.

After the ponies were fed and the stallion was given a liberal ration of grain, too, the men settled down for the night, and the officer hesitatingly asked if Jumai Khan would mind sharing his tent. Jeremy was delighted and discovered that the interior was exceptionally comfortable, for the felt kept out the icy, dry winds of the desert. In spite of the fact that he was more comfortable than he had been in many nights he slept lightly, for after his initial reception in Mongolia he did not know whether another attempt would be made on his life. But his fears proved groundless. The troop awakened at dawn and ate a breakfast of stew and bread; then they broke camp, and the ride to Urga began.

The stallion needed his great strength to keep up with the tireless ponies, and Jeremy discovered the riders were as inexhaustible as their mounts, remaining cheerfully in the saddle for long hours at a time without bothering to rest or eat. And what impressed him most was that they were traveling at what they considered a slow pace out of consideration for him. As he learned from several anecdotes that Duglai Effendi told him, virtually every man in the country had been raised in the saddle and by the age of fifteen or sixteen had learned to cover incredible distances.

The reason for such teaching became readily apparent on the six-day ride to Urga, for Mongolia proved to be a sprawling, sparsely populated land. The better part of the principality was a plateau high above sea level, and although some portions of it consisted of low, rolling hills, the chief characteristic of the terrain was its flatness. The soil was poor and the climate so dry that few vegetables could be grown, so most of the people raised sheep. The effendi explained to Jeremy that over the centuries various Hindu influences had infiltrated into the Mongolian culture, so there were virtually no cattle in the country, as the cow was considered sacred and the Mongols could not afford to keep animals whose meat, hides, and milk they could not use.

What astonished Jeremy was the almost complete absence of organized communities, and in the six days of the ride he saw only two or three tiny villages clustered around small springs. But several times each day he and his companions encountered what he could only describe to himself as traveling towns. Large groups of men, women, and children, numbering anywhere from five hundred to more than one thousand, each under its own khan, were constantly on the move from one end of the land to the other, searching for suitable grazing areas. These units never settled in any one place for more than a few days at a time, but they still managed to enjoy various benefits that were ordinarily denied to nomads.

Displaying a remarkable ingenuity, the Mongolians literally carried their houses with them, and when they stopped to set up a new camp, they placed their tents in rigidly defined patterns, so that each family always lived next to the same neighbors. Their homes were large, circular structures of padded felt, which could be dismantled and put together again in sections, and each had its own wooden floor, which could also be taken apart. Families carried their belongings in long, heavy ox carts, in which the women and younger children rode, but Jeremy noted that the wives, concubines, and daughters of the khans and other leaders always traveled by camel. The men, of course, used only their ponies, and the boys were taken from their mothers at the age of five to begin their rigorous training.

As nearly as Jeremy could make out, the sheep of each group were owned in common, and the people shared food and clothing on an equal basis; only the khan, by virtue of his responsibility for the welfare of all, was given a larger portion than anyone else. But even he put on no airs, and aside from wearing a tunic of silk instead of wool and a black hat of lamb's hide instead of white, he was indistinguishable from his subjects.

The nomads, in spite of their poverty, were hospitable people, and each night the troop was invited to share the lamb and oxtail stew of one or another group. The great delicacy of the nation was a flat, hard cake made of fermented mare's milk, and Jeremy, who was being honored because he was a foreign visitor, was offered so many cakes that by the fourth night he blanched at the sight of one. But he accepted the sweets as though he enjoyed them, for the Mongols were quick to take offense, and every khan he met told him stories of recent duels and fights in the tribe.

Jeremy was treated with respect by the effendi and the soldiers of the troop, yet he could not rid himself of the feeling that he was being watched closely, and he was uncertain whether he was a guest or a prisoner. At no time was he left to his own devices; a guard invariably stood sentry duty outside the tent he shared with the officer at night, and when the party was on the road, Jeremy was always surrounded by several of the men, who took turns escorting him. Yet not one hostile word was spoken to him, and not one member of the troop made an unpleasant or threatening gesture toward him.

Early in the afternoon of the sixth day the party arrived

at Urga, and by this time Jeremy was sufficiently accustomed to Mongolia that the unique appearance of the city did not surprise him. Most of the houses were somewhat larger versions of the felt tents used by the nomads, and only a few of the wealthier and more influential citizens, most of them members of the nobility and high-ranking army officers, lived in more substantial two-story buildings. These structures were almost identical: Their lower portions were made of fieldstone, held together with a rough cement, and the upper parts were of wood, topped by pagodalike roofs painted in bright colors. The bazaar, or marketplace, in the center of the city consisted of long rows of ramshackle, open stalls, behind which stood small huts of stone and clay.

Jeremy and his escort rode past four mosques, all of them unpretentious, with minarets topped by peaked and swooping roofs in the pagoda style. The mandarins of China, who had once ruled the land, obviously had left their mark on it before being driven out. The palace of the khagan, which stood only a short distance from the bazaar, was no larger than the houses of the nobility, but there were five or six smaller buildings behind it; these, the effendi said, housed the wives and slaves of the ruler, but their unpretentiousness was startling, and no soldiers were on guard outside the shabby front door of weathered wood. The grounds surrounding the palace were not cultivated, the grass was unkempt, and the only trees on the property were a few stunted, shabby evergreens. The absence of a formal garden was surprising, as virtually every man of substance in Islam followed the example of Mohammed and created a garden for himself as a reminder of the joys he would know after death, in paradise.

A heavy door knocker of silver, made in the shape of a dragon's head, was the only indication that someone of stature lived in this house. The servant who responded to the effendi's summons was plainly dressed in clothes of padded felt, and the rooms through which he conducted

Jeremy and the officer were quietly furnished with solid, unobtrusive chairs and tables. At the end of a long corridor was an office in which a short middle-aged man wearing the twisted silver and black cord of a subpasha across the front of his lamb's hide hat was writing at a desk. The effendi left Jeremy in his charge and departed hastily, obviously relieved to be rid of a burden.

The subpasha respectfully asked Jeremy to wait, disappeared briefly, and when he returned conducted the visitor to the threshold of a large, sparsely furnished chamber. Inexpensive cotton drapes with a dragon design on them hung at the sides of high windows overlooking the buildings in the rear, the wooden floor was clean but bare, and there were no decorations on the walls. A huge, rectangular pine table stood in the center of the room, with a number of stools scattered around it, and at the far end was a high-backed chair with a dragon's head burned into the wood.

The room was unoccupied, and the subpasha, after waving Jeremy into it, left and closed the door behind him. But the American's wait was short, and after a few moments a door at the opposite side of the chamber opened. A tall, husky man in his late forties walked in and, seemingly unaware of the presence of anyone else, headed toward the table. For an instant Jeremy was deceived and thought that some minor official had been sent to greet him, as the man was simply dressed in high boots, dark wool breeches, and a simple padded tunic. He was hatless, and his hair, which was cut short, was liberally sprinkled with gray. But he carried himself with an air of authority, and a single glance at his face was sufficient to identify him as Tule Yasmin's brother. The family resemblance was marked, but the khagan's features were ruggedly masculine; his chin was clean-shaven, his thin, drooping mustache was a reminder of the mandarins who had once ruled Mongolia from this palace, and his eyes beneath shaggy brows were alert.

Probably the only man in the world who had any influence with Tule Yasmin, the khagan had nevertheless been sorely vexed when his sister had run off to Constantinople with the Great Mongol Emerald. No sooner had she returned to Urga than he had ordered the return of the ring, and she had acceded to his demands at once, afraid to incur her brother's ire.

Now wearing the emerald ring on his left hand, he seated himself in the chair, stared at the ceiling, and tapped with the index finger on the tabletop. Jeremy, waiting for him to speak, saw that he wore a large emerald ring on the finger, but knowing nothing about the legendary properties of the coveted ring, he assumed it was probably the khagan's official badge of rank. Suddenly Buyantu Yassan stopped tapping, and when he looked at his guest there was a spark of humor in his black eyes. "Welcome to Urga, Brother-in-law," he said in a deep voice, speaking the dialect of the Constantinople court.

"Your Sublimity." Jeremy bowed but did not salaam.

"Your journey has been long."

"Very long," Jeremy agreed politely, and felt the black eyes studying him.

"And rather arduous. Someday you must tell me the story of how you disposed of three veteran warriors."

Jeremy's eyes narrowed, but he controlled himself. "The men who attacked me and killed my servant were your soldiers?"

"All troops in Mongolia are mine. But I don't order assaults made on unwary travelers, any more than I would attack a personal enemy while he sleeps." The khagan sat erect, and although his face was impassive, his voice became rough. "I don't plunge my knife into a man's back." Reaching into the top of his boot, he drew out a long dagger with a silver hilt and, flipping it into the air, let it fall point first into the table, where it remained, quivering.

"Your soldiers' knives barely missed my throat," Jeremy

replied flatly. If he was any judge of character, he could speak bluntly to this man, without subterfuge or subtlety.

Buyantu Yassan looked at him in admiration, then threw back his head and laughed. "I have wondered about you for a long time, Jumai Khan. And I have been grateful to you. I knew you had courage when I first heard that you had married that she-wolf."

Jeremy could not resist grinning but said nothing.

"Even when I learned the circumstances of your marriage I applauded you, and the reports I received on your progress at the court of His Magnificence confirmed the opinion I had formed of you. But I should have known Tule Yasmin would grow tired of you. And when she came home only seven days ago, I confess I was disappointed, as I had hoped you would keep her in Constantinople permanently. Perhaps that is why I was not thinking clearly. I should have known you would follow and that she would prepare an ambush for you."

"It was Tule Yasmin who tried to have me killed, then."

"I must apologize to you. I am ashamed that one who enjoys the confidence of His Sublimity should have been received so inhospitably in my land. But by the time I learned what my sister had planned as a reception for you, it was too late to stop her. The best I could do was to send Duglai Effendi for you in the hopes that if Allah was good to you and spared your life, I could then offer you protection for the last stage of your journey."

It was difficult for Jeremy to believe what he had just heard, but the khagan appeared to be sincere. If his bluff outward manner was any indication, he was not the sort who would deign to dissemble. "Has my wife told you why she wanted to have me murdered?"

"Repeatedly." Buyantu Yassan smiled wearily and tugged at his mustaches. "I have divorced myself from one or another of my wives on occasion, and I saw no reason why you couldn't end your marriage to her in the same way. But she insists that, as you were married in a Frankish ceremony, she is tied to you until one or the other of you dies. It's a very gloomy prospect, and I must admit that I don't envy you. Life here is always much simpler when she is elsewhere."

Jeremy warmed to the khagan's sympathy and wondered how far he could trust the Mongol. "Did Tule Yasmin arrive here with a large entourage?" he asked carefully.

Again Buyantu Yassan laughed, and before he replied he waved Jeremy to a stool, clapped his hands together twice, and told the servant who came to the door to bring them two cups of *ilya,* the fermented mare's milk. When the door closed he turned back to the visitor. "The Frankish slave girl is in her company," he said, "and from the first moment that my sister began urging me to take her into my harem, I suspected that you coveted the wench. I see by your face that I was right, so I'm happy that I resisted the temptation, at least until I found out whether my guess was correct. It's no wonder my sister hates you, Jumai Khan. The thought that the beauty of any other woman might be equal to her own is intolerable to her."

The servant reentered with large cups of chilled *ilya,* and the brief pause gave Jeremy a chance to collect his thoughts. He was alarmed at the khagan's offhand reference to the possibility that he might take Mary into his harem, but it was a relief to know she was alive and well and that, so far at least, no harm had befallen her. Obviously nothing could be taken for granted under the roof of a man who was a law unto himself and whose civilized veneer was thin. Buyantu Yassan might be too forthright a person to resort to sly chicanery, but perhaps he was direct in his dealings for the very reason that he was in a position to take what he wanted. However, the situation was far from hopeless; the khagan patently despised his sister, and Jeremy made a mental note to exploit that hatred.

They raised their cups in a silent toast to each other, and although Jeremy could take no more than a small sip of the strong potion, Buyantu Yassan drained his cup and crashed it on the top of the table. "How long do you expect to remain in Mongolia, Jumai Khan?"

"My duties to His Magnificence won't permit me to absent myself too long from Constantinople," Jeremy replied vaguely.

"When you go back, I hope you'll take your wife with you. Years ago I gave up the hope that any man could really subdue her, but perhaps I was wrong. Someone who has killed three brave fighting men in the Pass of the Little Snows must have unusual talents."

A feminine voice sounded from the doorway. "No man is my master."

Turning, Jeremy and the khagan saw Tule Yasmin, and the change in her appearance was remarkable. In Europe and Turkey she had always taken pains to wear seductive clothes that reflected the latest fashions, but here she dressed in boots, breeches, and a padded tunic that were a replica of her brother's attire and that concealed her figure. Had it not been for her hair, hanging in lose waves over her shoulders, it would have been difficult to identify her as a woman. She barely bothered to glance at Jeremy as she sauntered into the room, fingering the dragon-ornamented knife hilt in her belt, and she directed her full attention to her brother.

"Genghis Khan looks down on you from the heights of the afterworld and is displeased," she said.

"Then he will tell me about it himself when I join him there," her brother replied tartly.

"The khans who bow their heads to you would be unhappy, too, if they knew that you accept the companionship of one who has not passed the Test of the Koni."

Buyantu Yassan frowned, while Jeremy looked on in bewilderment. "One who was badly outnumbered but killed his foes," the khagan declared, "has proved his valor."

Tule Yasmin shrugged and showed no embarrassment at the mention of the murder attempt she had arranged. "We know the warriors are dead, but we have no proof Jumai Khan killed them."

"I killed them," Jeremy told her dryly.

She stared at him, and her eyes were cold. "I should have had poison dropped into your wine at Samarkand, as I first intended. But when the sharif assured me he could keep you there indefinitely, I foolishly believed him. Yet I knew better in my heart, or I wouldn't have arranged for the soldiers to stop you in case you broke away and continued to follow." She seemed to lose interest in Jeremy again and faced her brother, her hands on her hips. "The khans would not be pleased to know that you offer hospitality to a man who has not proved himself in the Test of the Koni," she insisted.

Buyantu Yassan stood and, towering above her, glowered at her. "I take no commands from a woman."

Tule Yasmin met his gaze coolly. "The blood of the great Genghis flows in my veins as freely as in yours," she said. "And if you forget my position, let me remind you that I am different from other women. I am entitled to my place at the table of the khans, and I have a right to make my voice heard. If you fail to do your duty, I shall insist that the khans of the realm be summoned. I shall present the facts to them, and then we shall see whether the test will be held." Unflinching and defiant, she did not move when her brother took a single, threatening step toward her.

The khagan halted, then threw himself back into his chair with such force that the wood creaked in protest. "There are times I can't believe my noble parents brought this devil into the world," he said, as much to himself as to Jeremy. "Jumai Khan, even I am restricted by tradition, and as I have twice been forced to compel rebellious khans to obey me within the past year, I can't afford to give them a fresh opportunity to take up arms against me. If the sultan had been content merely to appoint you a pasha, there would have been no problem. But he made you a khan as well, and in this land everyone who holds such rank must prove his ability to be called by that name."

Jeremy was confused but knew from Tule Yasmin's gloating expression that no good was in store for him. However, he would not let her see how he felt. "I am at Your Sublimity's service," he said to the khagan.

"You are willing, then, to take the Test of the Koni?"

"Of course." Jeremy realized his pride was robbing him of caution, but under no circumstances could he admit ignorance.

The khana looked out the nearest window and smiled softly. "The day is not yet too far advanced. The test can be held at once."

Her brother shook his head sourly. "You don't believe in taking chances."

"I don't." Tule Yasmin started toward the door, then paused and glanced back at Jeremy, her smile broadening. "The rites of the Koni will accomplish what the blades of my soldiers could not," she said, and was gone.

Large crowds hurried out of Urga to a bare, flat field located north of the city. Most of those in the throng were men, but a sprinkling of women and children were present, too, taking their places inconspicuously behind the heads of their families. A small tent of felt had been erected at one side of the field, and when Jeremy arrived, escorted by Duglai Effendi and his troop, he was taken there. Four elderly women waited for him inside, all of them veiled, and after the effendi left him they requested him to remove his clothes. He was somewhat startled but was faintly amused, too, and complied. They rubbed an evil-smelling oil over him and poured some of it into his hair, too, in spite of his objections. This, they told him, was the ancient requirement for the Test of the Koni, and no departure from tradition was permitted. Then they gave him a pair of short, loose-fitting trousers, and after he had donned them they indicated that he was to step outside.

The sun had lost much of its intensity, but it was still bright, and Jeremy blinked as he looked around. At least four or five thousand people had gathered, and at the far end of the field was the khagan, mounted on a pony and surrounded by a score of his officers. Tule Yasmin, still hatless, was conspicuous as the only woman in the party; indeed, she was the only woman present who was not heavily veiled. Jeremy met her eyes for a moment, and her mocking laughter angered him. He had no idea what he would be called upon to do, but her scorn hardened his resolve, and he promised himself he would not fail.

Buyantu Yassan cantered forward, halted before Jeremy, and addressed himself to the people, speaking in their own dialect.

"One who is called a khan but has not been born a son of a khan," he said, "has come to Mongolia. Perhaps the stranger is worthy of the title that the great Genghis has made famous throughout the world. Perhaps he is a coward and a weakling, and in that case he deserves to die. The Test of the Koni will determine his fate!"

The crowd cheered, the khagan looked down at the man standing before him, and Jeremy was amazed at the change that had come over Buyantu Yassan. Whatever compassion he had felt earlier had been caused by his opposition to his sister, and his eyes now glowed with excitement. He was about to witness a spectacle he would enjoy, and nothing else seemed to matter to him.

Leaving the field abruptly, he returned to his place at the head of his entourage, and Jeremy was left alone in the center of the field. Gradually the throng became quiet, and even the vendors who were selling roasted sheep hearts and pomegranates soaked in wine fell silent. The hush that followed seemed to last for an eternity, and then four soldiers guided a brown and white pony onto the field. One of the men led the animal, which had not been saddled, by a rope tied around its neck, and the others prodded it with long sticks but kept a respectful distance from its flailing hind hooves. They halted before Jeremy, gave him the rope, and after indicating in pantomime that he was to mount the beast, hastily withdrew.

Although no one had told Jeremy that the animal had not been broken, he knew it at once from the wild look in the pony's eye and from the way the creature kept turning in an attempt to kick him. He sidestepped each time the animal moved, giving it no opportunity to direct its hind hooves at him, and after awaiting his chance, he suddenly leaped onto the pony's back. He had often ridden horses that were at best half tame, and certainly the stallion that had carried him here from Constantinople had been anything but gentle, yet he had never before encountered such a violent, ill-tempered mount.

The pony shook its mane, twisted its neck, and tried to bite the rider. Failing, it reared and pawed the air frantically with its front hooves, then plunged forward suddenly, attempting to get rid of the unwelcome burden by hurling the man over its head. But Jeremy hung on grimly, gripping the animal's sides with his legs and clutching the long mane. The little stallion grew angrier, danced sideways, and then churned the air with its hind hooves; still unsuccessful, it galloped and bucked wildly, hurling itself in a frenzied abandon from one side of the field to the other. The spectators, watching the performance impassively, scattered whenever it threatened to break through their ranks, and each time several men waved large white cloths to frighten it and send it back into the arena.

Jeremy, painfully aware of his limitations, knew he was not a sufficiently accomplished horseman to break the pony, but he had no choice. If the animal threw him, he realized, he would surely be trampled under those hard, dainty hooves. His technique was awkward, and he was undoubtedly making one mistake after another, but the details were unimportant to him. All that mattered was that he stay on the little stallion's back, and the harder the beast fought, the more determined he became to keep his seat.

His legs ached, his head throbbed, and he was gasping for breath by the time the pony finally halted and stood quivering, seemingly admitting defeat. But instinct warned Jeremy that this was a trick, so he didn't allow himself to give in to the desire to relax and instead remained alert. He did not have long to wait, as the pony suddenly started to buck again, and in a final, desperate effort to be rid of its rider it behaved like a maddened creature. Jeremy thought every tooth in his head was being shaken loose and that the bones in his back were cracking, but he held himself low, trying to anticipate the pony's moves and to brace himself accordingly. The mount plunged and reared for what seemed like an eternity, hurling itself around the field, but finally either despair or exhaustion overcame it. Slowly, almost imperceptibly at first, its antics became less violent, and this time when it halted everyone present knew it had been mastered.

A quiet murmur of approval ran through the crowd, but Jeremy wasted no time catering either to the people or his own feelings. Urging the pony toward the khagan, he halted, raised his left hand palm forward in salute, and grinned wearily. "My pony needs a reward," he said. "Do you have something sweet for me to give it?"

Buyantu Yassan and several of his aides exchanged significant glances; apparently Jumai Khan knew more about horses than they had realized. An officer rode forward and gave Jeremy a handful of pitted, candied dates, which he fed to the pony one at a time. The little stallion whinnied softly, and the khagan nodded in approval. "You have done well," he called. "May Allah continue to show you his favor in what is yet to come."

Jeremy felt Tule Yasmin looking at him, and when their eyes met it was difficult for him to believe that she was a woman with whom he had been intimate. She made no effort to conceal her disappointment over his success, and then she brightened venomously when she saw some activity at the far end of the field. Jeremy, following her glance, watched the approach of four soldiers, each armed with a long, double-edged sword, with coiled rawhide whips hanging from their saddles. The congratulatory smile faded from Buyantu Yassan's face, and he gazed at Jeremy sternly.

"Jumai Khan," he said solemnly, "the time of your greatest trial has come. Those horsemen will try to force you from your mount. Be warned that they will use their swords, although they are not permitted to kill you with their blades. Once you have been made to dismount, they must put their swords aside and will make sport with their whips. If they should beat you to death, then all will know it is the will of Allah and that you are not a true khan."

Jeremy was still perspiring from his exertions, but he suddenly felt cold. "What weapons will I use to protect myself?" he demanded, patting the pony's neck.

The khagan, his eyes gleaming in anticipation of the trial, laughed harshly. "Your only weapons," he said, enjoying his own humor, "are the toughness of your skin and the nimbleness of your wits. Let the Test of the Koni go on."

The four soldiers had halted near the center of the field, where they awaited their victim with drawn swords. Jeremy turned to face them, and as he did he weighed his chances of survival: At best they were abysmally thin. The quartet could maneuver him at will, and without even a scimitar to protect himself he would be helpless against them. Their mounts were fresh, too, while his was tired after the bad-tempered exhibition it had given. The odds were great that he would be thrown and then whipped to death.

The primitive brutality of the Mongolians angered him, and the callous indifference to human life and suffering he had encountered throughout Islam enraged him. There was no more reason for him to be tortured now than there had been justice in the enslavement of Mary, and when he thought of Tule Yasmin calmly waiting to see him humiliated and killed, he was tempted to turn on her and choke her with his bare hands. But he knew his fury would only render him more vulnerable, so he deliberately emptied his mind of everything but the grave, immediate problem that faced him.

His one chance of remaining alive was to surprise the four riders with a bold act that would put them off balance, and he watched them with a tight smile as they started to spread out across the field. He would need to act quickly, while his pony still retained some of its strength, before he himself was forced to dodge the blows of the double-edged swords. His rage gave him renewed energy and courage, and after hastily improvising a plan, he put it into effect before a sense of caution caused him to change his mind.

Digging his bare heels into the pony's sides, he sent the little stallion hurtling forward, and he marveled at the animal's sensitive response to his will. He had no reins, but the beast seemed to know what was required and headed straight for the nearest of the soldiers. The man was startled at the unexpected attack, as any sensible person who was forced to undergo the Test of the Koni always waited until he was approached and then tried to avoid being struck by the swords. But Jeremy continued to bear down on him relentlessly, and the soldier's pony became skittish. The rider made a frantic effort to turn away in order to avoid a head-on collision and raised his sword in front of his face to protect himself.

At the last possible instant Jeremy swerved slightly to the side to avoid crashing into the soldier, but they brushed against each other as they passed. And that brief contact was all Jeremy needed to snatch the man's whip from its saddle loop. He was armed now, and he shouted loudly in English, cursing all followers of Mohammed as he turned his pony back toward the quartet. Uncoiling the whip, he cracked it experimentally and then started forward again. He had learned to use a length of rawhide one spring years ago, when he had taken work driving a herd of cattle from North Carolina into the Cumberland, and the knowledge that he was no longer defenseless intoxicated him.

He took careful aim, and the whip sang out and cut deep into the flank of the nearest soldier's pony. The animal bolted, throwing its rider, and the crowd roared in dismay and excitement. They had come to watch bloodshed in the Test of the Koni, and they thought they were being cheated. But Jeremy did not disappoint them. Continuing to advance rapidly, he struck out twice more in quick succession. His first blow cut open the face of one of the men, and then he carefully wrapped the whip around the neck and shoulders of another. Turning his mount aside, Jeremy jerked the rawhide expertly, and the rider tumbled to the ground.

By now the spectators began to cheer their new hero, but Jeremy was impervious to the applause, and after freeing the whip by first slackening and then tugging it, he started after the remaining soldier. But the man had seen what had happened to his comrades and had no desire to do battle; spurring his pony, he fled ignominiously, while the crowd, parting to let him through, jeered derisively. The Test of the Koni had come to a sudden and unexpected end.

But Jeremy felt unsatisfied, and without thinking, he moved relentlessly toward the royal party at the end of the field. Tule Yasmin was the first to sense what was in his mind and shouted in alarm. The members of her brother's entourage, thinking that the khagan would be attacked, moved in front of their ruler and raised their muskets. The sight of the firearms restored Jeremy to his senses, but he continued to ride forward, then halted and raised the whip in an ironic salute. "It was Allah's will that I triumph, Your Sublimity," he said.

Buyantu Yassan shoved his retainers aside with the flat of his sword and rode forward. "His Magnificence, the mighty Selim, showed the wisdom of Mohammed himself when he gave the Frank called Jumai the rank of khan," he said in a voice that carried to the far reaches of the crowd. "Since the time my grandfather first sat in the Dragon Chair, only one other man has ever passed the Test of the Koni." Looking at Jeremy, he lowered his voice. "Obtain your release from the service of Selim, and join me here. I will give you command of my armies and your choice of concubines to keep you warm until you grow old. You will be second to none except me in all the realm."

The offer was tempting, but Jeremy could not consider it, although it was true that he was far from the United States, and if he failed to return home, Alexander Hamilton could not punish him. He had a mission to accomplish, and he did not hesitate for an instant before replying, "Your Sublimity's confidence is gratifying, but I must return to Constantinople."

The khagan had expected no other answer and accepted it with the fatalism that was instilled in every Moslem male from earliest childhood. "So be it, then. Accept as a gift the pony you have broken, and may all men in the land of the great Genghis pay homage to Jumai Khan."

Buyantu Yassan spurred his mount, and with his entourage at his heels he cantered off toward the city. As the party left, Jeremy saw Tule Yasmin looking back over her shoulder at him, and she made it plain that she had revised her tactics. His achievement had won him the praise of the khagan and the admiration of the people, so she was responding accordingly, but knowing her as he did, he paid no attention to the provocative smile on her lips and concentrated instead on the shrewd, calculating expression in her eyes. He knew what had to be done, and he would let nothing, not even her enormous physical appeal, deter him.

The troops of Duglai Effendi escorted Jeremy back to

the head of a procession in which everyone who had watched the trial joined, but Jeremy, busily making plans for Mary's future and his own, was unable to enjoy the celebration. When he and the soldiers reached the palace, he found that one of the outbuildings, a single-story structure of wood, had been assigned to him as a dwelling. There several of the khagan's own eunuchs awaited him with tubs of perfumed water to bathe him, and after his ablutions were completed he dressed again in his own clothes. He ordered the eunuchs to bring Tule Yasmin to him at once, and they hastened to obey, but when she failed to appear, he wandered out into the little courtyard of his house, the whip he had won under his arm, and sent one of the house servants for her. The woman scurried off after taking one frightened look at the ugly rawhide, and Jeremy leaned against the wall to await his wife's arrival.

She might take her time, but she would not dare to refuse his direct command, even though she was one of the most prominent women in Islam. She was still only a woman in a world ruled by men, and her attitude as she left the field where the Test of the Koni had been held had shown clearly that she intended to repair her relations with her husband. Jeremy coiled and uncoiled the whip absently, and when he heard someone enter the courtyard through the arch at the far side, he was not surprised to see that Tule Yasmin had taken care to change her clothes before presenting herself before him. She wore a tight-fitting tunic of gold-covered, heavy white silk and a skirt of the same material, slit high on one side, and Jeremy realized that she walked with the seductive grace that had marked every movement she had made in the days when he had first known her.

The khana saw his cynical smile and halted abruptly. "There was no need to demand my presence," she said, trying not to show her hostility. "It would have been enough to send word asking that I come to you."

Jeremy had decided to employ bold, brusque tactics, which he hoped would achieve the results he desired, provided he acted quickly. "A man does not beg his wife for favors," he said. "It is enough that you appear when you're summoned."

"You forget who I am," she retorted, bridling.

"Not for a moment, but it's time you learned who I am." He looked at her coldly but told himself he could not afford to dawdle. The scent she wore went to his head and brought back unwanted memories.

Tule Yasmin had no wish to quibble. "It's enough for me that you're here."

She would have slid her arms around his neck, but Jeremy held her off. "One moment," he said in a hard voice. "There was only one reason I sent for you. As the English slave girl is your property, no one else has the right to give commands to her. So I had to see you in person to tell you I wish her brought to me at once."

His request was not entirely unexpected, but the khana still bridled. Then, suddenly, she laughed. "Jumai Khan is clever but not as clever as he thinks." Clenching her fists, she looked up at him angrily. "When I learned you were following us from Constantinople, I knew it was because you wanted her. I tried to have you put out of the way, but I didn't succeed. I don't grieve over my failure, because I like a man to be strong. But you must be taught that I am far more clever than you."

"Send her to me, now." Jeremy spoke firmly and hid his misgivings.

"I was sure from your expression after my brother praised you that you thought you had won." Tule Yasmin had regained control of herself, and she spoke mockingly. "So on our ride back to the city I had a talk with him. He's never owned a fair-skinned concubine, and he's been interested in the girl since we first arrived here. While you were being bathed he examined her, and he has agreed to take her into his harem."

"But she has not yet been delivered to him." Jeremy's heart pounded, but his voice was still calm. "I want her immediately."

The khana looked at him in real astonishment and shook her head. "You're still a Frank and therefore a fool. Forget the stupid wench, and together you and I can become the most powerful couple in the empire. Don't you realize one of the reasons my brother is attracted to her is because she's a maiden? If you take her first, he won't forgive you. I know him far better than you do, so I warn you. He admires you, for the moment, because you showed courage today. But if you take the girl first and then hand used property to him, his vengeance will be terrible."

Jeremy had no intention of allowing even a hint of his plan to slip out, and he smiled faintly. "You'll order her brought to me."

Tule Yasmin stared up at him in the growing dusk. "I refuse," she declared flatly. "You're far too valuable to me." Turning, she walked toward the arch with her head high, then paused and called over her shoulder, "I'll return to you tomorrow, when your ardor for her has been cooled by your intelligence. You'll be better able to appreciate me then, as well."

Jeremy took careful aim with the whip, and in spite of the gathering darkness his aim was true. The rawhide sang through the air and wrapped itself around Tule Yasmin, binding her arms closely to her sides; Jeremy tugged at the handle, drawing her to him, and although she struggled violently, she could neither resist nor escape. When she was directly before him they glared at each other, and he continued to hold the line taut. His life had been in jeopardy twice in the past week thanks to her, yet she arrogantly expected to resume a relationship with him, and he could not keep his temper in check any longer.

"You've always had everything you've wanted," he said slowly, "but for once in your life you're beaten." Reaching out with his free hand, he slapped her across the face, and when she would have screamed he struck her again.

An elderly servingwoman appeared in the archway, took one startled look at the khana and her husband, and would have darted away again, but Jeremy called out to her. "Send the Frankish slave girl to us," he directed, and when the woman hesitated he added, "Her Sublimity commands it."

The old woman left at once, and Jeremy half dragged, half pushed the helpless Tule Yasmin into the house. Before she quite realized what was happening to her, he stuffed a heavy table cover, a cloth of wool, into her mouth to gag her, and then, stripping the bed in the adjoining chamber, he tore a silken sheet into long pieces and bound her wrists and ankles with them. When she was completely trussed he picked her up and threw her onto the bed, where she lay very still, watching him like a cat.

At that moment he heard someone tapping at the front entrance, so he hurried to it, carefully closing the bed-chamber door behind him. Mary stood in the frame, dressed in a breastband of blue cotton and full trousers gathered close to her ankles. She had been crying, her face was pale, and Jeremy felt an almost overwhelming urge to take her into his arms. But every minute was precious. "Come in quickly," he said in English, wasting no time on unnecessary greetings.

Mary obeyed unthinkingly, too agitated to wonder why he was being so curt. "When I heard that you had arrived here today, I thought my prayers had been answered," she said in a voice that shook. "And when the khana began to scold me even more than usual, I was sure you had come for me. Then, just a little while ago, I was taken before the khagan." She shuddered and rubbed her bare arms. "They had all been celebrating and drinking and they made me take off my clothes. The khagan walked around and around me, looking at me as though I were an animal he was buying. It was horrible. And they say I'm to become one of his concubines tomorrow. But I—"

Jeremy interrupted her excited story by opening the bedroom door and pointing to the trussed figure. When Mary saw the khana she gasped, and Jeremy closed the door again. There would be time for explanations later, but right now every moment was important. "Do you have access to her clothes?" he asked.

"Yes, one of my duties has been to keep them in order." Mary's green eyes were round, and she was obviously frightened, but she spoke crisply, responding to the urgency of Jeremy's tone.

"Does she own anything similar to what she's wearing right now?"

"She has one or two things that are something like it, although they aren't precisely the same."

"Are you able to bring a complete change of clothes here, to this house, without arousing the interest or suspicion of any of her servingwomen?"

"I—I think so."

"Don't just think so," Jeremy said dryly. "Be sure. Your life may depend on it. Get something as close to what she's now wearing as you can. Be sure to bring shoes, jewelry, everything. And include a veil, a turban, and a warm cloak. They're important."

Mary started toward the door, hesitated, and looked up at Jeremy questioningly.

It would be best not to tell her too much until she returned, he thought, or she might become too self-conscious and give away his scheme. "Hurry," he said. "And trust me."

Tears came into her eyes, but she wiped them away and left the little house quickly.

The khana's servingwomen had already retired, since they realized their services would not be required that evening, and Mary was able to take what she needed from the khana's chambers without hindrance. She quickly guessed that Jeremy was planning an escape and was going to take her with him, and she came up with a plan that was as audacious as it was daring: to abscond with the

Great Mongol Emerald. She knew that the khana had taken the emerald with her when she had left Constantinople, and she also knew how the sultan coveted it; the khana's servingwomen talked about little else. Some second sense told Mary that if she could somehow obtain the jewel, she and Jeremy would come to no harm. She didn't believe for a moment about the legendary jewel's protective properties, but she felt that somehow the jewel could be used to obtain freedom for her and Jeremy.

All that afternoon there had been reveling and carousing in the palace. The khagan and his entourage had drunk cup after cup of the potent *ilya*, and Mary had seen, before she received Jeremy's summons, the members of the court staggering through the halls of the palace. She had witnessed enough of these palace orgies to know that the khagan and his entourage would by now be sprawling drunkenly over the beds and divans in the khagan's chambers, rendered senseless and helpless by the strong drink. It was only a matter of sneaking down the passageway that connected Tule Yasmin's chambers with her brother's, entering the khagan's rooms, and snatching the emerald off his finger without being detected.

Mary put her plan into effect at once. She had been to the khagan's chambers earlier in the day when she had been subjected to the degrading examination, so she knew just where to go. She crept along the empty corridor and came to the padded double door leading to the khagan's suite of rooms. She held her breath for an instant, then opened it and entered.

The half-naked bodies of men and women were sprawled everywhere, and even the guards were asleep, having done some carousing of their own after their masters had become too drunk to notice or care. She did not see the khagan, and she suspected he was in the connecting bedchamber. She stepped over the bodies of the khagan's advisers and soldiers, and even when she inadvertently nudged one with her foot, the man simply groaned and rolled over.

The khagan was sprawled on his bed in his large sleeping chamber, his arms flung carelessly over the inert bodies of two of his concubines. Mary immediately saw the emerald ring on the hand that dangled over the side of the bed, and without hesitating she stepped to the bed and snatched the ring off the khagan's finger. Then she hurried back to the khana's rooms to get the bundle she had put together and to return to Jeremy.

But before she left Tule Yasmin's chambers she had one more thing to do. Taking a bottle of the khana's nail lacquer, she covered the emerald with the polish until the ring was completely transformed. Now it looked like a dull, insignificant garnet, and no one who saw it would suspect that it was really the Great Mongol Emerald.

While Mary was gone, Jeremy was busy, too. He went to a bell rope that hung from a wall in the living room and tugged it. A servant came to the front door immediately and salaamed. "Light a lamp," Jeremy directed, and stood in front of the bedroom door while the man obeyed. "Now bring us some supper," he said. "Some bread and cheese will be enough tonight, as we're hungry and don't want to wait. Oh, and bring us a jug of wine, too. *Ilya* is too strong a drink for a reunion."

The servant nodded, hiding a grin, and as he started toward the door, Jeremy promptly confirmed the conclusions he had drawn. "You may tell the staff that Her Sublimity and I don't wish to be disturbed this evening. We've been separated for a long time. And after you've brought our supper, have my stallion and my new pony saddled." The man halted at the entrance, perplexed by the strange request, but Jeremy continued glibly. "We frequently enjoy riding by ourselves into the open countryside and may want to indulge the whim later tonight."

The servant shrugged and shook his head as he left; the ways of the nobility were strange, and he had long ago stopped trying to understand them. As soon as he was gone Jeremy carefully drew cotton drapes over the windows to prevent anyone from peering in and placed the lamp, which burned a perfumed oil, on a table far from the windows. Anyone who might pass the building and who knew that Jumai Khan and his wife were together again after a long separation would see only a dim glow from within. The servant returned with the food and wine, and a moment after he left again, Mary slipped back into the house, a neat bundle under her arm.

"I saw the majordomo," she said breathlessly, "so I hid in the shadows until he left."

"Good. Did you have any trouble?"

"No, the khana's women are sure she'll spend the night here, so they've gone off to their own quarters. If I know them they're celebrating because they have a free evening." She did not mention that she had visited the khagan's quarters and that she had acquired the precious jewel. She refused to implicate Jeremy in such an audacious scheme.

Jeremy pointed at the things wrapped in a woolen cloak. "You have everything? You're going to impersonate the khana tonight."

"I thought so." Mary opened the bundle and pointed at a little pile of cosmetics jars. "So I'm really prepared."

He smiled approvingly. "You're quick-witted, and that's helpful. We'll need all the intelligence we can muster if we hope to escape. Now you'd better change."

A shadow crossed Mary's face for an instant. But she well understood this was not a time for false modesty, and she straightened and started to remove her breastband.

Jeremy turned away from her and tried to spare her as much embarrassment as he could by going into the bedchamber for his weapons. He closed the door behind him so the khana would not see Mary, and after taking up his pistols, scimitar, and burnoose, he looked down at Tule Yasmin. She had made desperate efforts to loosen her bonds, but they were still holding firm, and Jeremy was satisfied that she would not be able to free herself or call for help. It would be sometime the following day before a servant would dare to enter the bedroom, and by that time, with any luck, he and Mary would be miles away.

He was tempted to say something to Tule Yasmin before he left her, but anything he might say would be a useless expenditure of effort. They had never understood each other and never could; their ideas, their thoughts, the ways they lived were as different as the worlds from which they came. So he left her without a word, and as he returned to the living room, he hoped fervently that he would not see her again. But, knowing her, he was afraid she would not rest until she found him and obtained revenge for the indignities he was heaping on her.

Since Mary was still dressing, Jeremy cleaned and loaded his pistols, then carefully packed the bread and cheese in a large square of linen. But he took care to scatter crumbs on the platter that sat on the table, so the servants would think a meal had been consumed. There would be no need to hide the wine, Jeremy decided; he would carry it openly, and members of the palace staff who saw it would think it natural that two lovers who were going out for a ride in the moonlight would take some wine with them. He was just finishing wrapping the food parcel when Mary giggled and called out softly to him.

"How do I look?"

Jeremy turned and was amazed at the transformation she had wrought with clothes, a few jars of cosmetics, and a tiny mirror that she had shown the foresight to bring with her. Her long red hair was completely concealed beneath a high turban held together with a ruby pin in the center of the front, and enormous triangles of overlapping gold discs hung from her ears and further drew attention away from her hair. She had rouged her lips heavily, dusted her face with a dark powder, and oiled her eyelids, and with the aid of some black cream she had slanted her brows in a shape resembling the khana's.

Certainly she looked as seductive and regal as Tule Yasmin in a sleeveless, hip-length tunic of heavy white silk, which was covered with small gold discs, sewn close together. A border of similar discs weighted the hem of her calf-length skirt, which was deeply slit up one side so she could walk and ride. But her shoes were inappropriate for travel, and Jeremy was dismayed when he looked at them. No one could spend long hours in the saddle wearing backless, gold brocade sandals mounted on thick soles, lacquered black, with high heels.

Mary saw Jeremy's expression, smiled, and pointed to the cloak and veil resting on the table. A pair of soft calf-high boots stood there, and she could change into them later. Plainly she knew the khana and realized that Tule Yasmin would never deign to wear sensible boots with a beautiful gown and thus ruin the effect of her costume. Mary had been forced to spend so much time helping her mistress dress that every detail of her appearance was accurate.

"You're perfect," Jeremy said.

The disguise was put to an immediate test, for before he could say more there was a tap at the front door. Mary looked alarmed, but Jeremy hastily waved her into the shadows and hid his weapons and the food package under some cushions. She turned her back to the lamp, and then Jeremy called out, "You may enter."

The majordomo stood in the frame and took in the scene as he salaamed. "The animals Your Excellency requested have been saddled and await your pleasure in the courtyard," he said. "But if you have changed your minds, I'll take them back to the stables."

"You may leave them in the courtyard," Jeremy told him in a bored voice. "And as long as you're here, remove the remains of the food." He said nothing more until the man picked up the platter, then added, "We shall go out for no more than a short ride, and when we return we'll probably take the mounts back to the stables ourselves. So under no circumstances are we to be disturbed here until we call for our slaves tomorrow."

"Yes, Your Excellency." The majordomo started to back toward the door but halted. Obviously all servants at the palace were accustomed to receiving peremptory orders from the khana, and he looked at the girl in the shadows apprehensively. "Am I permitted to wait on Your Serenity before I go?" he asked humbly.

Mary replied before Jeremy could interrupt on her behalf. "When we want something, we make our wishes known," she said imperiously, and her imitation of Tule Yasmin's voice was so exact that Jeremy barely controlled a gasp.

After the servant bowed himself out, Mary laughed shakily. "If I ever get back to London, I must ask Mr. Sheridan to write me a special role as sister of the khagan. With my experience with the lady, it's sure to be one of my best parts." Then without saying anything more, she entered the bedroom where the khana lay helpless. She looked down at the prostrate figure of Tule Yasmin and smiled suddenly.

Her expression was very odd, Jeremy thought as he followed her. He had never seen that particular look on her face before, and it occurred to him that this girl was a stranger to him, that she had many facets to her character with which he was totally unfamiliar.

The eyes of the princess blazed, and if looks could have killed, Mary would have been dead on the spot. But the young English actress had been long awaiting such an occasion, and she paid no attention to the woman who had tormented her for so long. Staring down at Tule Yasmin's hands, she reached out, and the princess gasped through her gag.

But Mary paid no attention, even when Tule Yasmin began to writhe and struggle with her bonds. She wrenched the rings from several of the princess's fingers and donned them herself. Now the lacquered Great Mongol Emerald looked even more nondescript, surrounded by rings set with rubies and diamonds.

Jeremy surmised that Mary was not only attempting to complete her disguise but also to heap one more insult on the already debased princess, and he congratulated her. Then he went to the windows and peered out from behind the drapes at the retreating figure of the majordomo until the man disappeared into the night. Presumably the servant had returned to his own room, and as the moon was rising, it was best to leave at once before it became too bright. Mary donned the face veil, holding it in place with her earrings, and then Jeremy helped her into the cloak, beneath which she carried her boots. His hands gripped her shoulders for an instant, and when she felt his touch she turned slowly and faced him.

"I have no idea how we'll make out," he said. "I can't estimate our chances. I can only promise you I'll do my very best for you."

Emotion choked her, and she could not reply.

Jeremy threw the food parcel into his saddlebag, along with his spare clothes and Mary's slave costume. She winced at the sight of it, but he decided it might be useful at some stage of the journey; there was no way of knowing when it might be convenient to have her assume the role of a slave girl again as they made their way across Asia to Constantinople. He concealed the bulky bag under his burnoose and started toward the door, not bothering to look back at the bedroom. Mary followed him, and catching sight of her out of the corner of his eye, he realized she was copying Tule Yasmin's loose-hipped walk.

He smiled as they emerged into the little courtyard, and his grin broadened when he saw that the majordomo had followed his instructions to the letter and that no one stood guard over the two waiting animals. Jeremy helped Mary onto the pony's back, mounted his stallion, and started off through the archway. Mary joined him, and they rode side by side on the path that led to the street in front of the palace. The grounds seemed to be deserted, but as they neared the gate beside Buyantu Yassan's residence, a soldier stepped out of the shadows of the building. He stiffened and held his musket before his face; Jeremy returned the salute casually, and Mary, still playing the role of the khana magnificently, pretended the man was beneath her notice.

As Jeremy was almost completely unfamiliar with the city, he followed the one route he knew and headed past the bazaar toward the gate through which he had entered Urga early that same day. The stalls of the marketplace were empty now, no horsemen were abroad, and only a few pedestrians wandered through the streets. When they saw the pasha and the woman who appeared to be the khagan's sister, these wretches immediately scurried out of sight. They didn't know why the khana wasn't at home, but having had experience with her in the past, they had no desire to find out.

At last the walls of the city loomed up ahead, and Jeremy, after casting a warning look at Mary, slowed to a walk. A yawning sentry appeared, grumbling under his breath, but when he recognized the riders, or thought he did, he forgot how unusual it was for anyone to disturb him after dark and called the *authentik*, the junior officer in command of the guard. As the youth appeared from a small wooden hut beside the gate, hastily buckling on his sword belt, Mary deliberately unfastened the loop at her throat and let her cloak fly free so the officer could see her rich tunic and skirt. Only one woman in Urga could afford such lavish attire, and to the best of people's knowledge, only one woman in the land boasted a figure worthy of such magnificent clothes. As Mary raised her hand Jeremy noticed Tule Yasmin's rings, and for an instant he was alarmed. It suddenly occurred to him that if they were captured, Mary could be accused of theft, in addition to numerous other crimes. But, he told himself, one more charge wouldn't matter, as they would both be put to death, in all probability, if they were caught before leaving Mongolia.

In any event the open cloak was sufficient to fool the *authentik*, who merely glanced at the gold discs that shone in the moonlight and then drew his scimitar so quickly that he appeared to be in danger of cutting himself. "Go back to your rest," Jeremy told him sympathetically. "We won't disturb you again tonight; when we return we'll come by another gate."

The *authentik* remained standing at rigid attention, and two sentries opened the gate. Jeremy, still smiling amiably, let Mary precede him and then caught up with her again as they rode together over the barren wasteland toward the goal of freedom, thousands of miles distant.

~~~~~~~~~~~~~

IX

The fugitives maintained a steady pace through the night and all of the following day, pausing in their flight only to feed their mounts with hay that they obtained early in the morning from a small party of nomads. That single encounter with other people proved to be enormously helpful to them, for the khan of the group, suspecting nothing, drew a crude but accurate map for them, and by following it, Jeremy was able to pause at two water holes. He insisted on continuing across the open steppes, however, rather than halt for the night at the second, which they reached an hour before dusk, for he had learned a lesson when the cavalry of Duglai Effendi had found him. Pursuers would look first at water holes but would have a far more difficult time locating their prey in the trackless countryside.

As nearly as Jeremy could estimate, he and Mary had a start of at least a day and possibly a day and a half on the troops who would inevitably come after them. Certainly no one had dared to enter the house presumably being occupied by the khana and her husband until morning at the very earliest, and he was reasonably sure that Tule Yasmin had not been able to escape from her bonds during the night. What he could not know was how much of the day had passed before some members of the palace staff had finally summoned the nerve to go into the house. But each hour of grace carried him and his companion that much farther from danger.

They had little opportunity for conversation as they

pressed forward. Frequently Jeremy glanced at Mary to see how she was faring, and he was rewarded with her beaming smile. At these moments he would have liked to take her in his arms and declare his love for her, but he forced himself not to think of such things and to keep his mind on their safe escape from Urga.

When they stopped for a moment to rest their mounts, Jeremy told Mary about the death of Rosalind Tate. The young woman lowered her eyes and said nothing for a long while.

"I wonder if that will be my fate, too," she finally murmured.

"No!" Jeremy was vehement. "There has been enough tragedy already. I will allow nothing to happen to you."

She looked up into his eyes and saw his fierce determination. Once again she realized he was a remarkable man, and she knew he would somehow help her to safety.

He continued on for several hours after night had fallen, until Mary, gray with fatigue, was ready to drop. Then necessity forced him to call a halt beside a small clump of evergreens, the only vegetation visible for miles in the moonlight, and after tethering the mounts, he fed them. By the time he joined Mary under the trees she was already asleep, and he made himself comfortable near her, first placing his scimitar on the ground beside him, ready for instant use should they be attacked. The night was bitterly cold, and Jeremy wrapped himself in his burnoose before dropping off to sleep. His rest was disturbed by vague dreams that he could not recall the following day, but he certainly wasn't dreaming when he awakened shortly before dawn and discovered that Mary was in his arms. Apparently the cold had caused them to cling together, and her warmth was very real.

She stirred slightly, opened her eyes, and when she realized where she was she drew back in alarm. Jeremy, who had been about to kiss her, reluctantly allowed her to slide out of his grasp, and jumping to his feet, he began to prepare for the resumption of the journey. There would

be ample opportunity to discuss the future when and if they
were successful in their attempt to escape from Mongolia,
and in the meantime he knew he would be wise to permit
nothing to distract her from their immediate goal. So he
refrained from mentioning anything about the circumstances in which they had found themselves on awakening,
and Mary avoided the subject, too.

They resumed their ride just as the first streaks of daylight appeared in the sky, and again they traveled all day,
not halting for the night until several hours after sundown,
when they once more camped in the open. Mary took care
to keep a distance between herself and Jeremy when she
slept, and he curbed his growing desire to make love to her.
Although he wanted her, he learned that for the first time
in his life he had encountered a woman with whom a long-
term relationship was of far greater importance.

The next morning they exhausted their food supplies,
both for themselves and their mounts, but luck was with
them, and at noon they arrived at a large nomad village.
The khan, who was unfamiliar with recent developments
in Urga, insisted on entertaining them, and Jeremy, who
had introduced Mary to the nobleman as his wife, was
forced to waste precious hours at a simple but hearty
banquet. It was midafternoon before he and Mary could
break away from the natives and resume their journey,
but when they left they carried enough bread, cheese, and
cold meat to carry them past the border, and the khan had
given them enough grain for the horses to see them all the
way to Samarkand. So the delay had helped rather than
hindered them, and as they and their mounts were thoroughly rested, Jeremy made up for lost time by pushing
on that evening until after midnight.

On the fifth day they saw the mountains in the distance,
and when they reached the fertile foothills water was no
longer a problem. Out of habit they kept the wine jug filled,
but they and their animals were able to drink freely at
many little rivers. Their pace was necessarily slower as they
climbed steadily onto higher ground, but fortune continued

to smile on them; for an hour or two after nightfall, when the wind was cutting through their clothes, they came across a large, high-ceilinged cave with a stream running through it. Here was real protection from the elements, a perfect hiding place for the night, and for the first time since they had left Urga they would sleep with a roof over their heads.

Jeremy was able to relax, and Mary was in high spirits as they ate, too. He kept looking at her and marveling at her courage; not once had she complained of hardships, not once had she expressed fear of being captured. She did not know it, he told himself, but she was as strong and brave as the American women who accompanied their husbands on long treks through the wilderness from the thirteen seaboard states to set up new homes in the west. After a time Mary, who was sitting near the first fire they had dared to build, became aware of his admiring scrutiny and flushed; he had gazed at her frequently, of course, during the time they had been together, but the enforced intimacy of the cave created a different atmosphere.

"If everything continues to go well," Jeremy told her, "we'll be across the Mongolian border by this time tomorrow."

"You don't think they'll follow us until they catch us?"

"Once we're out of the khagan's realm, his men wouldn't dare touch us. You see, the ruler of each principality is responsible for maintaining order in his own country, but he's still responsible to the sultan. And as I'm a member of Selim's personal staff, the chief of one principality would consider any violence against me by another as an unfriendly act. The sultans have established and maintained their power by dealing very severely with such breaches of the peace, and Selim would send his own troops to cut off the hands of anyone who dared to harm me. My rank is our greatest protection."

Mary shuddered and stared into the fire. "I didn't know what brutality meant until I was captured and taken to Islam. I've prayed constantly for deliverance." Suddenly she raised her head. "And thanks to you, it looks as though my prayers are going to be answered."

Jeremy hesitated for a long time before replying; he had always found it easy to lie to a woman, but something inside him compelled him to be truthful with Mary. "The best I can do is take you to the gate of freedom. If you like, and if nothing happens to us in the meantime, I'll escort you to the border of Russia. I can give you enough money to see you safely on your way, and as Russia is a Christian country, you'll no doubt be able to get back to England from there."

She looked at him in astonishment. "But you wouldn't come with me? You're little better than a slave in Islam yourself."

"I must go back to Constantinople," he said stubbornly. "My mission there isn't finished."

"And you interrupted it because of me." Mary paused for an instant, then blurted, "Don't you want to go back to America?"

"I can't, until I've completed the work I was sent to do in Turkey." Jeremy had not intended to reveal to her the events that had led to his being in Turkey, but he found himself telling her his whole story, and somewhat to his own surprise he made no attempt either to excuse or to gild his past.

Mary listened attentively and said nothing until he was through speaking. "Have you damaged your own cause by spending so much time away from your work helping me?" she asked at last.

"I doubt it."

"But you aren't sure?" she persisted.

"Nothing in this world is certain," he told her casually. "But don't worry about me. I've been looking after myself for a long time."

"Nothing in this world is certain," Mary repeated slowly. "That's very true. I don't know much about Imperial Russia, but I've been told it's a wild country."

Jeremy rose and stood over her. "That isn't my first alternative."

"What is?"

"If you will, I'd like you to come back to Constantinople with me. In the eyes of the law Tule Yasmin's slaves are mine, so all that's needed to set you free is for me to take you before the bey of the High Court and declare my intentions. But it's only fair to warn you that in Islam even a free woman is under certain restrictions. You wouldn't be allowed to leave Turkey an unmarried girl."

"That isn't very encouraging." She laughed bitterly. "What would possibly become of me?"

Jeremy took a deep breath and discovered he was trembling. "I'd like you to marry me."

"But you already have a wife!" Mary exclaimed indignantly.

"A true believer is allowed to marry four wives, so I'd pretend to embrace Mohammedanism. Then I could take you with me when my mission is done and I leave Turkey."

Mary shivered and held her hands before the fire. "You married the khana in a Christian ceremony. Her serving-women told me about it again and again. They seemed to delight in describing every detail to me."

Jeremy realized instantly that the servingwomen knew, then, what he had not dared let himself see, that Mary cared for him. Reaching out, he caught hold of her wrists and raised her to her feet. "You know why I married her. It had nothing to do with my feelings. She was a complete stranger to me then, and she doesn't mean anything to me now." He grasped her elbow, then put his hands around her waist.

Mary struggled to break away from him. "But she's your wife, your real wife! The servingwomen told me how you looked at her, how you made love to her!"

Suddenly Jeremy lost his temper and started to shake her; she was not being logical, and her blindness infuriated him. "Can't you understand what I'm saying to you?" he shouted. "I love you, do you hear me? I love you!"

To his horror she burst into tears, and he released her so abruptly that she staggered as she fled to the far side of the cave. It was a moment or two before he could galvanize himself into action, and when he reached Mary's side she was sobbing. "Please," she begged, turning her tear-streaked face toward him, "don't come near me now." So much had happened, and for the first time in her life she was a very confused, shaken young woman. Her cousins were both dead, and she was thousands of miles away from home in a strange land. She had no idea if her father could do anything about her plight, and even if she did attempt to leave Turkey by way of Russia, there was still the matter of her growing interest in the young man who now stood beside her, watching over her protectively. She had never felt this way about anyone, but what would the future be with such a man? He was tied to a country—and to a woman—that were unfamiliar and hostile to her, and she didn't know what to do. As she gained control of herself, she looked up at Jeremy and said softly, "I need some time to think."

Jeremy had always been self-centered and indifferent with women, but he could not treat Mary callously, and he knew her happiness and peace of mind were more important to him than his own. Wondering at the remarkable change that had taken place in him, he let his hands fall to his sides. "I give you my word that I won't ask you again what you want to do, and I won't touch you," he said, "until you come to me."

That night, although it was warm and comparatively comfortable in the cave, neither of them slept well; each was too conscious of the proximity of the other. And the following morning, when they had eaten a hasty predawn breakfast and started off again, a new sense of constraint came between them and separated them. Conversation was difficult, and whenever they glanced at each other they hastily looked away again; both of them knew the tension would continue as long as the problem remained unresolved, and Jeremy, suffering an inner torment unlike any he had ever before known, could only hope that Mary would reach a decision soon.

By noon they were nearing the timberline, high in the mountains, and Jeremy broke the silence by remarking that in another hour or two they would leave Mongolia. No sooner had he spoken, however, than two shepherds suddenly appeared in front of them. The men, roughly dressed, were on foot, and both carried cocked muskets. Jeremy weighed the idea of riding them down but rejected it; Mary could be hurt, and such violent tactics seemed unnecessary, as the pair didn't appear to be unfriendly.

"Praise Allah," one of them said, and smiled.

Jeremy was relieved. "Allah be praised," he replied.

"The noble sir and lady are crossing the roof-of-the-world?" the second shepherd asked.

"We are." The men looked anything but menacing, yet Jeremy could not help wondering why they were separated from their flocks and why they were carrying muskets.

"It is a cruel journey. Before you go, we offer you the shelter of our mean home and beg that you accept a bowl of soup to help you ward off the chill and speed you on your way."

It would be rude not to accept, Jeremy knew, but he wanted no delay when they were so close to the border. He would refuse but would need to handle the matter delicately, and he searched for words that would not offend the shepherds. Suddenly Mary screamed, and the sound echoed through the canyons; Jeremy reached for his pistols, but it was too late, and his hands dropped. Mounted horsemen appeared from rocks on both sides of the pass, others blocked a possible retreat, and then Tule Yasmin, accompanied by an effendi, rode out into the open and joined the "shepherds."

Jeremy and Mary were trapped and realized that in all probability they had been under observation for some time. The khana had been playing with them and had deliberately waited until the last possible moment to seize them. She sat arrogantly in her saddle, a pair of daggers protruding from her man's belt, and Jeremy wondered how he had ever thought of her as feminine. "Arrest them!" she ordered the effendi, and her voice was harsh.

"One moment," Jeremy commanded as the officer started to move forward. "Since when is it possible for a man to be placed under arrest simply because his wife wishes it?"

The effendi and his soldiers glanced at each other a trifle uncertainly, but the officer did not dare hesitate. "Her Sublimity has told me what I am to do." He motioned his men forward.

But Jeremy, who had felt the uncertainty of the Mongolians, grasped boldly at a straw. "Her Sublimity happens to be my wife," he said, and laughed.

"I know that, Your Excellency," the effendi replied miserably.

Jeremy waved away the soldiers who crowded in on him and Mary. "By whose authority do you make this arrest?" he demanded. "I am Jumai Khan, second in command of the Imperial Navy of His Magnificence, Selim III, and I refuse to submit to anyone except the khagan himself." He saw a frown appear between the officer's eyes and pushed his advantage. "Show me the tablet on which Buyantu Yassan has written that you have the right to arrest one who is a pasha and a khan."

"I have no such tablet, Your Excellency," the confused effendi said. "The khagan was—ah—indisposed when we left, and we were in a great hurry."

Mary felt enormous relief to learn that Tule Yasmin and the soldiers had left the palace before the khagan became sober and realized his emerald ring was missing. If he knew it was gone, he would have suspected it was taken by the fugitives, and he probably would have gone after them himself. As it was, they still had to get across the border before Buyantu Yassan's soldiers came after them.

"Unless you have written authority from the khagan," Jeremy said gravely, "the sultan himself will pronounce sentence on you when you are punished."

Tule Yasmin had been listening in amusement, but she

saw the growing doubt in the faces of the cavalrymen and lost patience. "I've heard enough," she declared savagely. "Jumai Khan may be a pasha, but he had no right to tie me like an animal being led to slaughter and to run away with my slave girl. Take them at once!"

"No right?" Jeremy asked loudly. "Since when has a man not been permitted to treat his wife as he pleases?" His voice was haughty, and he barely bothered to glance in the khana's direction as he added, "You're lucky I didn't beat you."

Tule Yasmin was as unpopular with her brother's army as she was with the people of Mongolia, and the soldiers, delighted at seeing her humiliated, grinned broadly. No one had ever dared to cross her will, and they made no effort to seize either Jeremy or Mary. This incident would be a principal topic of conversation for months to come, and they were savoring every moment of it.

Jeremy hoped his hood hid the perspiration dripping from his forehead. He had gambled on a technicality, and because the khagan had not bothered to sign a formal arrest order, there was a chance he could beat Tule Yasmin at her own game. Pretending complete unconcern, he pointed at Mary. "The wench," he said, ignoring her flush, "was indeed one of my wife's slaves. But that which belongs to a woman is the property of her husband. So Mohammed himself wrote, and none here can deny." He paused to let his words sink in, then continued forcefully, "Nor can anyone deny that she is a juicy morsel. It is a man's privilege, when his wife grows old and plain, to find his joys where he wishes. I have taken the girl as my concubine, as is my right under the sacred law of Islam." The khana was neither old nor ugly, of course, but in her man's attire she looked dowdy compared to Mary.

The soldiers ogled the fair-skinned English girl, lusting for her. Clearly Jumai Khan's choice made complete sense to them, but their attitude was too much for Tule Yasmin, who lost her temper. "The clothes she wears are mine!"

she screamed. "Rip them from her back! The rings on her fingers are mine! Cut off her hand and give it to me!"

Jeremy, acting a part with a desperation that made every move seem convincing, laughed as though he had never before heard anything so humorous. "I hope," he said, ostensibly to the effendi but actually for the benefit of all the men, "that you never become wealthy, my friend. Once I thought that when I became a pasha my troubles would end, but actually they had just begun. Riches are the cause of all evil. And may you never have so much gold that you can afford a wife and a concubine at the same time, for they'll never give you an hour's peace. Night and day they shriek at each other, arguing over which of them owns this bracelet or that trinket. There are times when I think no woman is worth the noise."

The men roared, and Tule Yasmin could tolerate no more. Taking one of the daggers from her belt, she hurled it at Mary, but her rage spoiled her aim, and the knife went wide and landed harmlessly some distance away. Before she could draw the other blade, Jeremy rode up to her, plucked it from her, and slapped her so hard across the face with the back of his hand that she was momentarily stunned.

"Here," he said, flipping the dagger to the effendi, "you'd better take charge of this before she hurts either herself or someone else with it."

As he well knew, the critical moment had arrived, but he unhesitatingly beckoned to Mary and, without waiting for her to join him, spurred forward, past the effendi and Tule Yasmin. Mary came up to him, and they cantered in the direction of the border; after they had ridden a hundred yards, Jeremy glanced back surreptitiously and saw that the effendi, still undecided, continued to sit with the dagger in his hand, while his men had not yet stopped laughing at the khana, who was weeping in frustration.

The ride through the passes seemed endless, and Jeremy could not quite believe he had won until long after the border had been crossed and he and Mary began to descend into Turkestan. He half expected to hear pounding hoofbeats behind them, but as night approached he became increasingly confident that his bold front had succeeded.

"We're safe," he said.

Mary's shoulders shook, but her face was averted, and he couldn't tell whether she was laughing or crying.

The fugitives were not molested as they rode down through the mountains of Turkestan, but when they saw the minarets of the Golden Mosque of Samarkand in the distance, a new problem confronted Jeremy, who remembered with uncomfortable clarity that the dissolute sharif had made a deliberate attempt to detain him in the city when he had been traveling in the opposite direction. Tule Yasmin had made no attempt to conceal the fact that her influence had been responsible, and as she had far greater cause to create mischief now, she might try to make trouble a second time. Jeremy's rank and berth on the imperial staff afforded him a measure of protection, of course, but Mary was in an exceptionally vulnerable position, and recalling the sad lot of the young women in the sharif's household, he knew he had to guard her at all costs.

Had it been possible to avoid a stop in Samarkand, he would have gladly made a wide detour around the city, but he realized that he and Mary would be taking grave risks if they tried to cross the trackless desert wastes without the help of an experienced guide. So he decided they would have to ride into Samarkand, no matter how much he disliked the idea. He explained the predicament to Mary and then asked her to change into her slave-girl costume; he could not pretend she was his wife, for the sharif might demand proof of their marriage, and when they failed to produce it he could seize Mary and condemn her to a life in his own degenerate harem. But no man, not even the powerful ruler of a large province, could steal another's property. And so, paradoxically, Mary's safety depended on her willingness to assume the role of a slave again.

At first she was reluctant, but when she understood

Jeremy's reasoning, she changed into her hated breastband
and trousers and rode behind Jeremy rather than at his
side as they approached the gates of the city. Some of the
sharif's own troops were on duty there, and had Jeremy
followed the usual customs of Islam, he would have allowed
a squad of soldiers to take him to the palace. However,
as he wanted to see as little of the sharif as possible, he
decided to try an unexpected maneuver and demanded that
the young officer in command of the sentries take him to
the subpasha in charge of the independent brigade of imperial janissaries stationed in Samarkand. He knew the subpasha and his staff did not make their headquarters at the
palace, and he reasoned that even the sharif would be reluctant to invade a compound that housed the \personal
representatives of the omnipotent sultan.

The commander of the guard was puzzled by the strange
request and thought the pasha of one horsetail was showing
a shocking lack of manners by not paying his respects to
the sharif immediately. But unable to argue with a senior
officer, he had no choice in the matter and sent eight of
his men to take Jeremy to the barracks where the imperial
brigade lived. The compound was located within a quarter
of a mile of the palace, and Jeremy felt his tension increase
but turned to smile reassuringly at Mary as they approached
the high-walled enclosure from which the sultan's own flag
was flying. The step he was taking was completely unorthodox, he knew, and might arouse the sharif's wrath even if
Tule Yasmin did not come to Samarkand to create new
complications, but he had to take the risk.

The inside of the compound bore no resemblance to any
other part of Samarkand, and as Jeremy looked at the
disciplined, smartly uniformed men who patrolled the
grounds, he felt certain he had made the right move by
coming here. A noncommissioned officer took charge of his
horses, and an orderly led him into the headquarters building, while Mary, playing the part of the docile slave to perfection, trailed after him and pretended not to notice the
stares of the soldiers. Someone had told the brigade com-

mander of his superior's arrival, and he hurried out of his office to greet the newcomer. The subpasha was a short middle-aged man who had spent many years in the service of the sultan, and his experience stood him in good stead when he saw Mary standing behind Jeremy. His eyes widened in surprise, but he quickly concealed his reaction, and smiling blandly, he saluted and then extended both hands in greeting.

"Your Excellency does me great honor," he said. "I hadn't expected your kismet to bring you back to Samarkand so soon."

Jeremy had been trying for the past quarter of an hour to recall the man's name, and suddenly he remembered it. "Mohammed ben Ral," he replied, "it is good to receive your welcome. And," he added pointedly, "it is good to stand once more on imperial soil."

The subpasha, instantly aware that this was no ordinary visit, waved away the junior officers who were clustered behind him and conducted the visitor to his own large but severely furnished office. He would have closed the door on Mary, leaving her outside, but hesitated when Jeremy gestured to her, and she entered the room, too. Under ordinary circumstances Jeremy would have exchanged amenities with his host at length before mentioning the reason for his visit, but his insistence on bringing Mary into the brigade commander's sanctum required an immediate explanation, and having learned something of the temperament of the Turks, he decided to proceed accordingly.

"Mohammed ben Ral," he said, "look at the girl."

"I'm looking at her, Your Excellency." The subpasha moistened his lips.

"What is your opinion of her?" Jeremy continued, ignoring Mary's blushes.

"No fairer flower has ever blossomed in the desert." The pasha's words were polite, but his tone was enthusiastic.

"In your view, what would be the reaction of the sharif should he see her?"

"He would covet her, of course," Mohammed ben Ral

replied without hesitation. "Is it Your Excellency's plan to make a gift of her to the sharif?"

"Just the opposite," Jeremy said dryly. "Under no circumstances do I want her to fall into the sharif's hands. You've attended many of his entertainments in the time you've been stationed here, of course."

"Too many."

Jeremy saw that the subpasha was disgusted and was relieved that he had judged his man correctly; no forthright soldier could feel anything but revulsion over the spectacles presented at the palace. "The girl belongs to me."

"Your Excellency is very fortunate."

"I think so, and I intend to protect my good fortune," Jeremy declared. "I'm taking her back to Constantinople with me. And as you can imagine, I have been afraid of what might happen if I should accept the sharif's hospitality."

"I can tell you her kismet," Mohammed ben Ral said with a thin smile. "He would try to buy her from you, and failing in that, he would threaten you. Having observed him for the past three years—and I thank Allah that I will be transferred to another post next year—I have had ample opportunity to observe his threats. They can be very unpleasant."

"Then you can understand why I require your assistance, Mohammed ben Ral."

The subpasha stiffened to attention. "It is Your Excellency's place to command, and mine to obey."

"I don't take advantage of my rank to command in a situation of this sort."

"You are very gracious, Jumai Khan."

"Gracious? No. But I am grateful to my friends." Jeremy paused for a moment, and smiled. "I can understand your anxiety to be relieved of your post here. And I think I can assure you that when I have returned to Constantinople I can arrange for your transfer to imperial headquarters there."

The bargain was sealed, even before Mohammed ben

Ral knew precisely what his visitor wanted. "I have tried for the past six years to obtain a place in Constantinople."

"You may consider yourself as good as there." Jeremy extended his hand, and the subpasha grasped it warmly. "You can provide living quarters here in your compound for my wench and me?"

"It is no problem, Your Excellency!"

"And," Jeremy continued firmly, "you can provide me with an escort of your camel corpsmen to take me across the desert to Astrakhan?"

"I'll select every member of the caravan myself." Suddenly Mohammed ben Ral frowned. "It will be advisable, of course, to leave as soon as possible. Even if Your Excellency has planned to rest here for a time, I urge you to leave soon. I can have the caravan ready in two days, and I advise you to leave then. The sharif wouldn't dare send his men into the compound. At least, I'd like to see him try. But he's devious, very devious, and if you tarry here he might find some way to trick you and steal the girl from you. The arrival of anyone important is always reported to him at once, so Your Excellency may be sure he has already learned you're here and that you are traveling with a beautiful slave."

"I'm prepared to leave whenever the caravan is ready." Jeremy realized that Mary was exhausted after the trip from Urga, and he wished she could remain in Samarkand long enough to recuperate, but the subpasha's advice was sound. And the sooner they reached Constantinople the more difficult it would be for Tule Yasmin to stir up difficulties for them, too.

That seemed to settle the matter, but Mohammed ben Ral was not yet satisfied. "Forgive my presumption, Your Excellency, but I wonder if you've taken one other aspect into consideration. It's likely that the sharif will send a complaint to His Magnificence if you snub him."

Jeremy laughed, and his tension was gone. If he and Mary reached Constantinople safely, he could not worry about a petulant letter that the provincial ruler of Turkestan might send to the sultan.

A suite of rooms was provided for the guest and his slave girl, and Mohammed ben Ral, after inviting Jumai Khan to dine with him, made the necessary arrangements for the organization of the caravan. Fruit, bread, and cold meat were brought to Mary's room, sentries were posted at all entrances and windows of the suite, and orders were given to the guards at the compound entrance that none of the sharif's troops were to be admitted on any pretext. Mary, who felt more secure than she had at any time since she had first been taken captive in the Mediterranean, ate heartily and then retired, while Jeremy went off to share an elaborate meal with his host.

Before the evening ended a courier arrived from the palace with a written invitation from the sharif, blandly asking Jumai Khan to call on him. Jeremy, who had more or less expected such a message, sent back an equally courteous reply, in which he declined on the grounds that he was ill. So on the surface, at least, there was no friction, but Jeremy carefully refrained from mentioning the incident to Mary the following day, as he saw no need to upset her.

The subpasha, eager to demonstrate his efficiency to a superior who had promised to transfer him to the capital of the empire, supervised every detail of the preparations for the journey, and in two days the caravan was ready to depart. Jeremy swore he would keep his word to the man who had done so much to help him, and a squadron of thirty troopers, ten of them mounted on horses and the rest on camels, gathered in front of the headquarters building. Mary, still wearing her slave costume but heavily veiled, took her place beside Jeremy in the center of the group, and the party rode out into the streets of Samarkand.

Jeremy was uncertain whether an attempt would be made to take Mary from him by force, but he quickly discovered that his fears were groundless. Foot soldiers

and cavalrymen in the uniforms of Turkestan were everywhere and by sheer weight of numbers alone could have
overwhelmed the little imperial escort, but the sharif was
too cowardly to seek revenge openly, and the group was
unmolested. Jeremy could not allow himself to relax, however, and in the days that followed he insisted the unit
maintain a military formation at all times. Each night he
posted sentries around the encampment and took special
care to insure that two men were on duty outside Mary's
small tent, which was always raised next to his own large
one.

They encountered several other caravans on the long
journey, but no one molested the party and no one threatened it. Jeremy was still uneasy, for he had felt certain
the sharif would try to retaliate, and he could not imagine
that Tule Yasmin would admit final defeat so meekly, but
nothing marred the calm of the dull, grueling ride across
the desert, and at last he began to feel that perhaps his
audacious gamble would succeed.

Mary needed all her strength for the long daily journey
across the hot wasteland, and she conversed but little with
Jeremy; as she wore her veil at all times, due to the presence of the soldiers, he could not see her face clearly and
was unable to guess what she was thinking. However, he
frequently felt her watching him, particularly when he was
chatting with one of the janissaries and presumably was
unaware of her scrutiny. Again and again he was tempted
to go to her at night, but he respected the pledge he had
made to her in the cave near the Mongolian border; he
would not ask her again what she wanted to do and would
not touch her until she came to him of her own free will.
It was strange, he thought, that a couple who were spending weeks in each other's company should pass so little
time alone with each other, but the officers of the troop,
who were devout Moslems, took it for granted that Jumai
Khan would eat his meals with them rather than with the
woman. And they could not know that Jeremy never raised
the canvas partition that separated his tent from Mary's,

or that when camp was made each night she was so tired that she went to sleep immediately after eating her supper.

The days became weeks, and the party at last arrived at Astrakhan, but Jeremy still did not know whether Mary would choose to leave him and try to reach England via Russia, or whether she would accompany him to Constantinople. She needed a brief rest before she reached her final decision, and honoring his pledge, he made no attempt to force her to reach a conclusion. Most of the women he had known in his life could be bullied, but Mary was different, and he was determined to give her every opportunity to make up her own mind.

The escort brought them to the military commandant of Astrakhan, who greeted Jeremy like an old friend, set aside quarters in his own harem for Mary, and liberally rewarded every man in the squadron for loyalty and devotion to Jumai Khan. The governor of the city, an elderly sheik, gave Jeremy the news at dinner that evening by telling him that an English fleet had not yet attacked Constantinople and that, although tension was still mounting and even merchants in the bazaars of small towns were now discussing the inevitability of hostilities between Turkey and England, a technical state of peace was still being maintained. Jeremy knew that even if the English did attack, there was little chance that Mary or the other hostages would be turned over to their countrymen. Indeed their lives would be in even greater danger, and Jeremy said nothing of all this to Mary, who was having enough trouble deciding what she was going to do.

So, Jeremy reasoned, his departure from the capital had done no harm, and the sultan had no cause to be annoyed with him for his prolonged absence. He could not remember a time in his life when everything he had done had worked out so favorably, and he was in high spirits, the fatigue of the journey across the desert forgotten, when he and the military commandant returned home from their dinner at the governor's palace.

When they entered the house they saw that one of the

commandant's eunuchs was waiting for them, and Jeremy, assuming that the creature wanted to speak to his own master, was about to turn away. But the eunuch, much to his surprise, salaamed before him and said, "Have I His Excellency's permission to address Jumai Khan?"

"You have."

"The woman of Jumai Khan has sent me to him with word that she wishes to see him. I told her that she has forgotten the proper respect a woman must show her lord. I told her that she must wait patiently until Jumai Khan sends word to her that he will come to her. But she threatened to have me beaten unless I obeyed her and brought her message to him." The eunuch looked anxiously at Jeremy, then at his own master, who laughed.

"It would seem," the commandant said lightly, "that this is a woman who is worth a journey across half of the world."

"Yes," Jeremy said, "she's worth it." Excusing himself, he took leave of his host and followed the eunuch into the latticed corridors of the harem.

He heard whispers and giggles behind the grills that faced the hall, and he was sure that the commandant's women were peering at him, although he could not see them in return. The night was warm, and a scent that he finally identified as that of burning incense hung in the air; off to the right, through another wooden latticework, stood a garden, and he could hear water splashing in fountains. The atmosphere was unreal to him, and he had to shake his head to assure himself he wasn't dreaming.

At last the eunuch paused before a door at the far end of a corridor, opened it, and salaamed again. Jeremy stepped inside, the door closed behind him, and he blinked to acclimate himself to the light being cast by several small, slender candles attached to wall holders. He seemed to be in a small sitting room, in which a divan and several rugs were the principal objects of furniture. There was a table, on which a silver bowl piled high with candied fruits was placed, but to his surprise Mary was not present.

Then he heard faint sounds in an adjoining chamber, and he realized that she had been given a suite of her own and that she was on the opposite side of still another latticed door.

An oil lamp was burning somewhere at the far side of the other room, and its faint but rosy glow was visible through the latticework. Jeremy, ill at ease in the exotic surroundings, stood still for a moment, then called out tentatively, "Mary?"

"I'll be with you in a moment." Her familiar voice, at least, was real.

He waited for what seemed like a very long time; this might be the last time he would ever see Mary, but he rejected the thought as quickly as it occurred to him. He could not remain in Astrakhan while she traveled alone into Russia. If necessary, should she want to try to make her way to England, he would escort her as far as the Russian border, and in that way he could spend a few more days with her. The suspense was too great for him, and he moved closer to the inner door. "You've reached a decision?"

"Yes," she answered briefly, and again there was silence.

Then, suddenly, the door opened, and she came into the sitting room. Jeremy, gaping at her, thought she had never looked lovelier, but he was totally unprepared for what he saw. Her body was encased in a close-fitting gown of gleaming silver cloth, with a deep neckline and a single strap over one bare shoulder, and although the costume was Turkish in every respect, she nevertheless moved with the easy grace of a Westerner. Huge silver coins were mounted on the straps of her high-heeled red sandals, similar coins were clipped to her ears, and several more were linked in a bracelet on her upper left arm. A large silver comb, worn at an angle at the back of her head, swept her red hair in loose waves to one side, and as she halted she brushed her hair back.

"I don't think," she said with a self-conscious laugh, "that I ever wore a costume like this, even on the stage."

Jeremy continued to stare at her. "I'm not sure I would have known you."

"I browbeat the eunuchs into letting me use these things. I couldn't stand the sight of those slave-girl clothes anymore, and I loathe that dress of the khana's." Her silver comb picked up the gleam of the candles.

He nodded and, unable to take his eyes from her, watched her as she crossed the room. Apparently she didn't realize she was treating him cruelly, but it was almost more than he could tolerate to see her looking more desirable than ever when she was about to tell him that she had decided to leave him. He could not blame her for wanting to return to England, of course; she had been forcibly brought to the Ottoman Empire, she had been mistreated ever since she had been in the sultan's realm, and she had no real reason to remain. But she needn't have made this occasion doubly difficult for him by appearing in such provocative attire.

Mary seemed to know what was going through his mind, and smiled. "If it had been possible," she said, "I would have worn something that would be appropriate in London, or even in New York and Boston. I'm afraid I had to take what was available, though."

"I'll never forget the way you look," Jeremy protested.

The compliment pleased her, and her smile broadened, but as she looked at him she sobered. "You've been very patient with me. I can't imagine that any other man I've ever known would wait as you've waited, to hear what I want to do." She waved toward the divan, inviting him to sit.

But Jeremy shook his head; it would be easier to accept the bad news on his feet.

"I've known for some time what I intend," Mary said, betraying nervousness by touching first her earrings, then her bracelet. "I couldn't talk to you about it when we were surrounded by soldiers every day and every night, but now the time has come when I can't delay any longer."

"I'll make all the arrangements," Jeremy said curtly. "Our host will give me a fresh escort, but I don't want you to travel alone with his troops, so I'll take you to the border myself. I'll need a little time, though, to find some maps of Russia and to work out a route you can follow after you cross the border. Perhaps a day or two will be enough."

"You'll release me willingly?" She moved closer to him and stood directly in front of him, her eyes clear as she met his gaze.

"I'll release you, but not willingly," he replied roughly. "I offered you two alternatives, and I'm prepared to keep my word. I don't give it lightly."

"Why will you do all this for me?" she asked, and Jeremy could detect no mockery in her tone.

"Your memory," he said, losing his temper, "seems to be conveniently short. You may or may not recall that I told you I love you."

Mary sighed happily. "You don't know quite as much about women as you like to believe. I'll tell you a secret about us. We're dreadfully perverse. I just wanted to hear you say it again, that's all."

"All right. Now you've heard it, so I hope you're satisfied." He would have stalked out, but the table stood behind him, so he couldn't turn in that direction, and Mary continued to block his path.

"There's something else you told me." Mary's voice fell, and she spoke in a whisper. "You swore you wouldn't touch me until I came to you of my own accord."

Jeremy was startled, uncertain whether he understood her correctly, and he felt the blood pounding at his temples. He looked hard at her, but Mary averted her face and stared down at the floor.

"You seem to have assumed that I want to go to England," she murmured.

He reached for her, but she held him off.

"Let me finish what I've started to say," she continued. "It isn't easy for me. You've risked your life for me, first in Constantinople, then again when you followed me to Urga. You've undergone great hardships for my sake, and you've jeopardized the mission you were sent to perform for your country." She paused and forced herself to raise her eyes to his. "I know that you love me. You've proved it to me again and again, as few men have ever proved it to a woman. So it seems to me that the least I can do is to return that love."

He was afraid he was dreaming and that if he tried to touch her she would vanish. But he drew her into his arms and discovered she was alive and warm.

"I'll marry you in a Moslem ceremony, as you suggested," she whispered. "And when you leave Turkey, I'll come with you."

Jeremy should have been satisfied, but honesty compelled him to raise the issue that might remain as a permanent blot on their happiness. "I have no idea," he warned her, "how I'll go about getting a divorce from Tule Yasmin after you and I go back to the Christian world. I'm not even sure it will be possible to obtain a divorce from her."

"If there is a way," Mary said confidently, "I know you'll find it. Besides, after all that you've risked for me, it's my turn to take a chance. That's one of the privileges of loving someone."

Jeremy kissed her then, and Mary returned his embrace fervently. Exulting, he picked her up, and they continued to kiss as he carried her into the bedchamber.

Their lovemaking was unlike any Jeremy had ever known. He placed Mary on the bed and slowly disrobed her, feasting his eyes on her lovely nakedness. He kissed her on her mouth, on her breasts, on her thighs, and she ran her fingers through his hair, murmuring his name.

Now Jeremy removed his clothes, too, and lay beside her, exploring her body with his hands, as Mary stroked his neck, his back, his arms. He slid on top of her, and as she looked into his eyes with love and longing, he slowly entered her and they became one. His movements were gentle as he returned her gaze, then lowered his mouth to her lips.

Their lovemaking became more urgent as Mary moved her body with Jeremy's and they held each other tightly. He was inside her, and she was all around him; they were each the entire world of the other. As their passion grew, they called out each other's names, and suddenly they felt an explosion as they reached their climax together.

Then they lay quietly in each other's arms, both totally at peace. They had at last found fulfillment to the love that had been building for such a long time, and their happiness was as complete as it was unexpected.

Sir William Pitt, called "the Younger Pitt" to distinguish him from his famous father, was already becoming recognized as one of the greatest statesmen in English history for his parliamentary reforms and for his commercial treaties with other European nations. But at the moment, deliberating with some of his key advisers—among them Sir John Ellis—the prime minister felt anything but great.

"The Turks are causing chaos," Sir William said as he sat at his desk in his spacious office in Whitehall. "Their attacks on English shipping vessels—which they claim are illegally sailing in Turkish waters—are unpardonable, but this latest development is intolerable. It is an act of war for the Ottomans to take as prisoners English citizens— among them Sir John's daughter and his niece and nephew."

"They control so much territory that they feel they can act with impunity," an elderly, white-haired lord quietly suggested.

"They're barbarians, as I've been saying for some time now," Sir John Ellis now put in. Ever since he had learned of the abduction of his daughter, niece, and nephew he had become morose and bitter, and he vowed he would stop at nothing until his family was restored to him.

"Be that as it may," the prime minister said, "we still have to work through diplomatic channels. As you all know, I have already sent Selim III a number of very strongly worded messages demanding the release of our British subjects."

"And if he doesn't we should destroy the brutes," Sir John said.

"I'm afraid that's not so easy," Sir William went on. "We have just concluded a very costly war with the United States, and we now face a grave problem with France. Louis XVI and Marie Antoinette have been beheaded, and the French are hungering for a war with Great Britain." The prime minister shook his head, and his face showed the stress of a man in power. "Still, we will not allow the Turks to intimidate us. If we must, we will send our ships to their ports and destroy Constantinople!"

X

Jeremy and Mary remained in Astrakhan for a week, and it was a period of serene contentment. Every moment they spent with each other was precious, and they were reluctant to leave, but so much remained to be settled in Constantinople that they finally resumed their journey. The military commandant provided them with a small escort on the ride south through the Caucasus Mountains, and the soldiers left them only when they reached the heavily populated district on the coast of the Black Sea in Turkey. Mary, wearing the silver gown and jewelry that the commandant had insisted on presenting to her as a gift, traveled as Jeremy's wife, and they almost forgot the tribulations of the past as they rode at a leisurely pace, pausing each night at one of the luxurious inns on the coast road.

When they reached Constantinople, Jeremy told her, they would go immediately to the palace and, after reporting to the sultan, would immediately appear before the bey and make the necessary change in Mary's status from slave to free woman. Then they would be married, and there would be nothing Tule Yasmin could do to stop them. Jeremy, buoyed by the love he and Mary felt for each other, was certain his plans would materialize as he envisioned them, and Mary, who had unlimited faith in him, reflected his confidence. He was sorry he had not declared his love for her long ago, before she had been taken off to Mongolia, but his regrets were fleeting. All that really counted was that he had found the girl with whom he would spend the rest of his life, and nothing else really mattered. Even the problem of securing a divorce from Tule Yasmin was secondary, and he was convinced that he would find some way out of the dilemma.

Traffic on the road to Constantinople was heavy, but travelers were careful to clear out of the way of the young pasha of one horsetail and his resplendently attired, heavily veiled companion, so Jeremy and Mary arrived at the capital early in the afternoon of their ninth day on the coast road. If there were no complications, and they expected none, Mary would be free and would enjoy the protection of a Moslem marriage before the day ended, and they both smiled as they looked at the minarets of the mosques and spires of the capital's many palaces in the distance. It was the first time either of them had ever enjoyed the prospect of a sojourn in the city.

A large group of merchants and visitors was gathered at the iron gate, patiently waiting for admission to Constantinople while the guards painstakingly checked the credentials of each new arrival. The appearance of the pasha created a stir, the travelers were herded to one side, and Jeremy, with Mary close at his side, was ceremoniously received by a junior officer, who in turn summoned the effendi in charge of the troops at the gate. Two soldiers led Mary's pony to the shade of the wall, and when the effendi arrived he offered Mary the rare courtesy of a bow after he saluted Jeremy.

"Welcome, Your Excellency, in the name of Allah. We have been expecting you," he said.

A cavalry escort was quickly organized, and with the effendi leading the party himself, the last stage of the arduous journey was begun. The horsemen rode at such a breakneck speed through the streets of the city that Mary had difficulty in keeping her seat, and Jeremy was so concerned about her safety that he failed to evaluate the significance of the officer's greeting. But the thought did vaguely occur to him that it was strange he should be expected, as he had sent no advance word either to the sultan or to Mustafa el Kro that he was returning from his travels.

After a brief but hectic ride the familiar buildings of the imperial palace loomed up ahead: The sentries stood at attention and held their scimitars before their faces, and Jeremy had the strange feeling that he had come home. He had asked the effendi to take him to the main entrance of the palace itself, but the officer seemed to have forgotten the request and headed instead for the entrance of the seraglio. Pulling to a halt, he dismounted, and before Jeremy could protest he helped Mary to the ground. For a moment Jeremy was irritated, but he decided it might be preferable, after all, to remove the dust of the road from their clothes before he and Mary presented themselves before Selim the Magnificent.

So he jumped to the ground, too, and started forward toward the entrance on foot. Then, before he quite realized what was happening, janissaries of the imperial guard appeared on either side of him and seized him. He reacted instinctively and tried to break away, but four or five of the men had laid their hands on him, and they knew their business. He was powerless in their grasp, and the effendi, who had been watching the incident with a cool smile, stepped forward and relieved Jeremy of his scimitar and pistols. Meanwhile two other men had caught hold of Mary and laughed at her futile efforts to free herself.

Jeremy was stunned. Before he could demand an explanation, the heavy iron gate of the seraglio swung open, and as a familiar figure appeared he realized, even before he learned the details of what was taking place, that he had lost the latest round in his battle of wits with the khana. Tule Yasmin, her face masklike, strolled up to the captives and examined them calmly. Obviously she had been forced to travel at great speed in order to reach Constantinople first, but she looked as though she had never left the city. Certainly the soldiers felt the ultrafeminine impact of her presence; her diamond and jet earrings were so long they brushed her bare shoulders, her high-necked black silk jacket was cut up in a point at her waist, and her full, soft trousers were cut down in a point in front, leaving a diamond-shaped expanse of her midriff bare. But as always she seemed unaware of the effect she created, and she strolled up to Mary, then reached out and snatched away the veil that hid the English girl's face.

"As I thought," she said with venomous satisfaction, "this is my property." Tule Yasmin stepped closer, slapped Mary hard across the face, and taking a knife from one of the soldiers, deliberately slashed the silver gown. "That," she declared, "is only a taste of what's in store for you."

Jeremy struggled violently and almost broke away from the men who were holding him. "Release me at once!" he shouted. "I demand to know the meaning of this outrageous treatment."

Tule Yasmin pretended not to hear him, but the effendi, still respectful, stepped up to him again. "If Your Excellency will be patient, you will be told everything. Word of your arrival has already been sent to the palace, and I see that your questions are about to be answered."

Jeremy followed the direction of his glance and watched the approach of a pasha of two horsetails who wore the broad white ribbon of the imperial staff across his chest. He was flanked by two aides, and he walked so rapidly that his juniors had difficulty in keeping up with him. An elderly man with a thick gray beard, he took in the scene quickly, and his face became stern. "How dare you put your hands on the person of an officer who holds the rank of pasha?" he asked the effendi, who stood at rigid attention.

The men holding Jeremy released him immediately, and he saluted his superior. "Allah be with Your Excellency," he said.

"May Allah protect you, Jumai Khan," the pasha replied. "I bid you welcome."

"The welcome I have received is somewhat less than encouraging," Jeremy declared, forcing himself to remain calm in spite of the fact that Mary was still in the grip of the two soldiers who had seized her. It was difficult, too, to ignore the khana, who stood only a few feet away. "I have been grossly abused, and so has the woman who is about to become my wife."

A flicker of amusement appeared in the pasha's eyes. "I think you will soon agree, Jumai Khan, that one wife is more than sufficient. The wife you already have," he added ominously, "has caused you enough trouble to last for the rest of your short life."

Jeremy looked for an instant at Tule Yasmin, who smiled at him imperturbably. "Perhaps," he suggested politely, "Your Excellency will be good enough to tell me the meaning of that riddle."

"Of course," the pasha replied courteously. "It grieves me to tell you, Jumai Khan, that you are charged with the crime of desertion from the Imperial Navy and from the personal staff of His Magnificence."

"That's absurd," Jeremy said forcefully. "When I left the city several months ago, I wrote a letter to my immediate superior, Mustafa el Kro, and I left a detailed training schedule for my men to follow during my absence."

"That may be." The pasha shrugged and made it plain that the defense Jeremy offered was of no interest to him. "The fact remains, Jumai Khan, that you are charged with the crime. What's more, the accusation against you has been made by a member of the imperial family, the cousin of His Magnificence, the sister of the lord Buyantu Yassan, khagan of Mongolia. In short, your own wife."

Tule Yasmin laughed, but Jeremy tried to pay no attention to her. He knew that if she could she would have him executed; he had caused her to lose face, for which she could never forgive him, and it would suit her convenience, too, if he was put to death. There was no other way to terminate their marriage, and the khana, now as always, was seeking a practical solution to a problem that vexed her. But Jeremy refused to be intimidated.

"I'm sure," he said, "that Mustafa el Kro will gladly verify my account of what has happened. And I'm virtually positive that the gunners of the fleet have followed my training program, just as the foundries have surely continued to produce cannon according to the specifications I drew up before I left. So I have not deserted, and I request an opportunity to present my case before His Magnificence."

"As one who served on the imperial staff, Jumai Khan, you should know that Selim the Magnificent makes his own decisions in all things. If he wishes to hear your story, he will send for you. If he does not, that is his imperial privilege. In the meantime I have been instructed to relieve you of the rank of pasha of one horsetail. You may touch him now."

Someone snatched the insignia from Jeremy's hood, and the soldiers, who had been hovering close to him, seized him again. "I demand to be heard," Jeremy shouted.

The pasha raised his eyebrows. "Demand, Jumai Khan? Deserters have no right to demand anything. You may remove him!"

The soldiers started to drag Jeremy away, but he fought them, even though he knew that resistance was futile. They struck him again and again, and the blows made him groggy, but he continued to struggle, and when he could not use his arms he tried to kick and butt them. As they hauled him off, half dragging, half pushing him, he caught a final glimpse of Mary that caused him to lose all control of himself; Tule Yasmin had taken a riding crop from one of the cavalrymen and was systematically whipping Mary with it. Jeremy's frenzy gave him added strength, and he tore himself from the grasp of his captors.

Before they could catch hold of him again, he lashed out at a tall janissary; his fist caught the soldier on the cheekbone, and the man staggered. Meantime the others formed a circle and closed in on their prisoner, beating at him with the butts of their muskets and the broad flats of their scimitars. Jeremy lunged at a second janissary and managed to knock the man down, but the odds against him were overwhelming, and blows rained mercilessly on his head and shoulders. It was mad not to give up, but his rage deprived him of his reason, and he fought on furiously, indifferent to the terrible punishment he was absorbing. Only one conclusion to the unequal battle was possible, and at last one of the janissaries behind Jeremy tripped him with the long barrel of a musket. At the same moment something crashed against the back of his head, knocking him flat. Bright lights seemed to flash before his eyes, and he could no longer see his opponents. He tried to rise, but the effort was too great for him, and he realized dimly that his strength had deserted him. He clawed the ground in a final attempt to haul himself to his feet, and then, very suddenly, darkness enveloped him.

When Jeremy regained consciousness it was some time before he remembered what had happened to him, for at first he knew only that his head ached miserably and that it was agony to move. He raised his right arm, shifted the position of his legs, and heard the rattle of chains, but the significance of the sound did not dawn on him, and he drifted off to sleep again. When he awoke, his fever had subsided, and although he felt battered and sore, the ache that had gnawed at him was gone. His mind was clear now, and when his eyes became accustomed to the gloom of his surroundings he realized that heavy iron bands had been soldered to his right wrist and ankle, and that he was chained to a wall, unable to move more than a few feet in any direction.

The air was cold but stale, and the wall, which Jeremy was finally able to see in the darkness, provided him with the clue that enabled him to guess where he was being imprisoned. Smooth, heavy gray stones rose toward a high ceiling and were damp to the touch, a characteristic of the dungeons carved out of the rocks beneath the imperial palace. At one time or another every Turk who served the sultan was afraid he would be confined in what was known as the wet cave, and Jeremy was certain he had been brought to this dreaded prison.

He discovered that he was stretched out on a few wisps of straw strewn on the floor and that beside him was a loaf of heavy, stale bread. He was starved, and he started to eat ravenously although the bread was virtually tasteless. Then he saw a small jug and discovered it contained a bitter, faintly rancid wine. He had just lifted it to his lips when a voice spoke up in the darkness and startled him. "So, Jumai Khan, you're awake."

Jeremy remembered the voice but could not place it, and peering through the darkness, he made out the dim outlines of someone chained to the wall on the far side of the cell.

"When you told me you would bring me to Constantinople," the man declared bitterly, "I had no idea your influence would be responsible for such rapid results. *Bismillah!* I arrived here even before you did, and the great sorrow of my life is that it was my kismet to know you and to believe I was doing my duty to the sultan by serving you. I spent thirty years in the corps of janissaries, and until I met you there was never a blemish on my record."

Jeremy at last identified the speaker as the subpasha in command of the bridge of imperial troops at Samarkand. "Mohammed ben Ral," he said.

"Yes, Mohammed ben Ral, who dreamed of ending a distinguished military career as a pasha of one horsetail but who now provides sport for the rats and soon will be the host at a feast for the vultures that feed on the bodies of those whom Allah has damned."

"What happened to you?" Jeremy forgot the stale bread and sour wine.

"On the very evening of the day you left Samarkand," the Turk said, "the sharif invited me to attend a banquet at his palace, and his messenger told me again and again that his master knew I had merely done my duty when I had protected you and the girl and that he bore me no ill will. I should have realized that the whole story was a pack of lies. After all, I had been acquainted with the sharif for a long time. I should have refused the invitation. But it was my kismet to accept."

The repeated references to fate were annoying, but Jeremy controlled his impatience. "So you went to the sharif's palace?"

"I did. And when I arrived there, I was taken before that bride of the devil, the khana Tule Yasmin, who had just come to the city from Mongolia. She told me I was guilty of treason because I had befriended you. I was stripped and dressed in the clothes of a beggar, and the sharif's men smuggled me out of the city. *Bismillah!* How those rags smelled. And do you know, Jumai Khan, to this very moment I doubt if my troops have learned that I was secretly taken from Samarkand and transported across the desert in a caravan of Turkestanis disguised as pilgrims." Mohammed ben Ral laughed unhappily. "Even the khana hid herself beneath the robes of a pilgrim. Never have I seen such a determined woman. She was never fatigued, never needed food or rest."

"And she brought you here. Have you been given a trial so you can prove the charge of treason against you is ridiculous?"

"Don't interrupt me, Jumai Khan!" the subpasha commanded petulantly. "We'll both stay here until we hear each other's death rattles and we rot, so there's no hurry. I have very few joys left in this life, and I refuse to have the pleasure of telling my sad story to someone else spoiled, even if that person is you. How stupid and dull-witted you are, Jumai Khan! And how mistaken you were to become the enemy of the khana of Mongolia! The scouts who rode ahead of her caravan never lost sight of you, all the way across the desert."

Jeremy felt ill and blamed himself for everything that had happened. The scorn of his fellow prisoner was justified, and he knew he had given insufficient weight to the probability that Tule Yasmin would strike at him again. He was paying the penalty for his carelessness, and even

more important, so was Mary. She loved him, and so she
had trusted him; he should have insisted that she leave the
Ottoman domain and try to make her way to England
across Russia. But he had been selfish, and although he
had no idea what had become of her now, he was certain
she was suffering. Perhaps she was still in Tule Yasmin's
household, in which case she was certainly being cruelly
mistreated.

Another possibility occurred to him, too, but he could
not allow himself to dwell on it. It was conceivable that
Tule Yasmin, motivated by spite, would sell her slave,
and the thought that Mary would be forced to become a
concubine in the household of some wealthy, depraved
Turk was too much for him. She could never escape from
slavery and degradation without his help, and there was
nothing he could do for her. Thanks to him, her situation
was both desperate and hopeless, and there was virtually
no chance that she would ever be delivered from bondage.

"Jumai Khan, you aren't listening to me!" Mohammed
ben Ral hoisted himself to one elbow and rattled his chains
indignantly.

"My abject apologies. You were saying, I believe, that
the khana followed us across the desert to Astrakhan."

"She certainly did. And you can believe me when I
tell you her resources and ingenuity are unlimited. She
bribed one of the eunuchs in the house of the subpasha
who directs the military at Astrakhan, the man who was
your host. She learned your plans, and once she knew
when you were leaving for Constantinople, she hurried on
here ahead of you."

"I see."

"Do you? Then you see too late. In no time at all after
we arrived, she was received in audience by her cousin,
the sultan. There I was, bound hand and foot in her quarters in the seraglio, trying to ease my discomfort after being carried halfway around the face of the earth on the
back of a camel. *Bismillah!* And the next thing I knew, I
was brought here to the wet cave. Oh, the infamy of it. To

think that Mohammed ben Ral, the son of a sheik, should end his days as a traitor."

"Don't give up hope," Jeremy said. "There's still a chance that I'll be allowed to tell His Magnificence my story, and if men who were my colleagues, like Mustafa el Kro, will substantiate what I say, we'll both be released."

Either the subpasha did not hear him, or he chose to disregard the optimistic outlook. "At least I can rejoice in one thing," he said mournfully. "I have devoted my life to the janissaries and have never taken any wives. So I have no heirs, no legitimate children, at least, who will be forced to share my disgrace." He sighed lugubriously and turned his face to the nearest wall.

Jeremy became silent, too, and as he finished his unappetizing meal he concluded that Mohammed ben Ral was probably right. Most prisoners who were brought to these dungeons were never seen again, so the future was bleak. It was bad enough, Jeremy reflected, to know that he would probably die, but it was even worse to realize that his mission on behalf of the United States was ending in dismal failure and that he had ruined the life of the girl he loved.

Mary was brought to the khana's chambers, and there the whippings and beatings continued. The young Englishwoman had to fight hard for self-control, but she vowed she would not let her captors defeat her. There was too much at stake, especially now that she had met and fallen in love with Jeremy, and there was also a glimmer of hope, too. She still had the Great Mongol Emerald—disguised with nail lacquer, to be sure—and if she could just keep her wits about her, she might be able to do something for herself and for Jeremy.

Suddenly Tule Yasmin ordered the servants to cease whipping the young woman, and she stepped forward and slapped Mary hard across the face. "Now, slave," the khana said, "you have been punished for your impertinence, and I will take back what you have stolen from me." She began at once to wrench the diamond and ruby rings from Mary's hand, and when she came to the undistinguished red-colored ring, she said, "Now, what is this? You did not take this from me, nor do I remember seeing it on your finger before."

Mary was almost too weak to speak, but she summoned all her strength as she prepared to play the greatest role of her acting career.

"That," she said, her voice becoming stronger as she spoke, "is a garnet ring that belonged to my grandmother. I've always worn it, though you never took much notice of it."

Tule Yasmin scarcely heeded Mary's words as she studied the ring. "Such a gaudy stone," she said, her eyes inquisitive. "It is probably worthless, but I will take it anyway and have the court jeweler examine it."

Mary had anticipated that Tule Yasmin would want the ring, no matter what its apparent worth, and she tried the ruse that she had planned on her long journey from Urga.

"Yes, yes, please take it!" she exclaimed passionately, raising her hands, which were bound in front of her. Even on the stage she had never poured so much of her heart into a role, and she hoped Tule Yasmin would swallow the bait. "You are so greedy that even a worthless ring belonging to my grandmother would appeal to you. So take it and put it with your hoard of priceless jewels!" Mary's tied, outstretched hands were almost in Tule Yasmin's face.

The khana glanced quickly at the ring again, then her eyes focused on Mary. A look of disdain came across her face, and she shrugged. "What would I want with such an ugly ring? It would be demeaning." She turned away and commanded her servants. "Take the wench away and lock her up until I decide what to do with her. Perhaps she will bring a good price at the auction block."

The servants did as they were bid, and as Mary was brought to the slave quarters she breathed a sigh of relief.

Her ruse had worked, and no matter what else happened, she still had the Great Mongol Emerald.

Time was almost meaningless in the dreary gloom of the dungeon, and only the appearance of a deaf and dumb jailer once in each twenty-four hours enabled Jeremy to keep track of the days. The man, who brought each prisoner a loaf of bread and a little of the nearly undrinkable wine, was the only contact the inmates had with the outside world, and by the end of Jeremy's first week in the so-called wet cave, he found himself succumbing to the state of despair from which Mohammed ben Ral never emerged. Jeremy knew that inadequate food and lack of exercise were sapping his strength, and the few tentative hopes of escape that he had entertained vanished. In another week or two he would be too feeble to stand, much less run away. Besides, he often told himself, even if an opportunity to escape presented itself, he could not go off without Mary. So he was trapped and knew it; nothing seemed to matter anymore, and like his cell mate, he rarely bothered to speak.

On what was the ninth day of Jeremy's incarceration, as nearly as he could judge, there was a sudden break in the dreary monotony of prison existence. The heavy iron door of the cell swung open, and a smartly uniformed janissary entered, an oil lamp in his hand. Jeremy and Mohammed ben Ral sat up, and while they were trying to acclimate to the unaccustomed glare, a bulky figure in flowing robes appeared in the entrance and sniffed loudly.

"The stench in here," Mustafa el Kro said in a loud voice reminiscent of the quarterdeck, "is as bad as the odor on the slave benches of a galley."

Jeremy was surprised he could still laugh. "It's worse, Your Excellency," he replied, hope suddenly surging in him at the sight of his friend. "Galley slaves, at least, can breathe fresh sea air."

The naval chief tugged at his beard and stared down at Jeremy intently. "Are you in good condition?"

"Fairly good, I think. Living here isn't what I'd call ideal, but I'm not in such bad shape that a chance to stretch my legs and a good meal or two wouldn't cure me."

Mohammed ben Ral entered the conversation for the first time. "And a soft, dry bed. Don't forget that."

Mustafa el Kro looked at the prisoners sympathetically. "The Prophet was right when he ordained that women are to be treated as inferior beings. No woman should ever be given power, and if I could I'd wring the neck of the khana."

The subpasha from Samarkand suddenly became articulate and described in infinite, loving detail how he would treat Tule Yasmin if she ever fell into his hands.

But Jeremy said nothing, and Mustafa el Kro, waiting with ill-concealed impatience until the other prisoner finished speaking, looked at him in concern. "And you, Jumai Khan, wouldn't you beat her until her skin was stripped from her body?"

"I'm not interested in her, and I don't care what becomes of her," Jeremy said flatly.

Both of the Turks thought his attitude was oddly lacking in feeling, and Mustafa el Kro fingered the gold twin horsetails on the front of his hood. "Have you been subjected to torture, Jumai Khan? I was told the imperial executioners haven't touched you and that you should be reasonably sane."

"I'm sane," Jeremy replied dryly, "only because I don't allow myself to think about Tule Yasmin."

"Good." The naval officer, accustomed to the freedom of his quarterdeck, began to pace up and down the narrow confines of the cramped cell, and his heavy boots barely missed the prisoners. "You'll need all the wits you can muster if you agree to the offer I bring you."

"An offer?"

"You needn't look so pleased. If you accept it, you may lose your head before sundown. I've had a terrible time trying to arrange an appointment with the sultan on your behalf. I need you, and the janissaries-of-the-sea need you, but the khana has blocked me at every turn, so only this morning, after I finally sent a message to His Magnificence saying the security of the empire is at stake, did he give me five minutes of his time."

"What's the offer?" Jeremy could think of nothing else.

Mustafa el Kro hooked his thumbs in his broad belt and smiled grimly. "I reminded Selim that under the policy established by his grandfather, senior officers accused of crimes against the throne are entitled to a hearing. And I also hinted that Selim is reputedly far more generous than his ancestors. So he agreed. But then he reminded me that he's the sole judge, and that your plea will have to be extraordinary if he's to rule against a member of his own family who has accused you. And then he said he'd have to follow his grandfather's custom."

Mohammed ben Ral raised his free hand and massaged his throat gingerly.

"I don't understand," Jeremy said.

"The old sultan granted hearings to his senior officers when they were arrested. But his generosity was limited. When he found them guilty—and he usually did—their heads were cut off the same day. So you have a choice. You don't have to accept the hearing if you don't want it, even though I'll testify for you and will certainly do my best for you."

"What's my alternative?"

Mustafa el Kro shrugged. "No man knows the will of Allah."

"I accept," Jeremy said promptly.

Mohammed ben Ral cleared his throat. "My kismet," he declared sententiously, "is bound up with that of Jumai Khan. I deplore the situation, but there's nothing I can do about it. And as I've lived by the scimitar, I'm prepared to die by it, too."

The naval chief nodded. "I was sure you'd feel that way. So I spoke a word to His Magnificence for you, too. Don't think that I'm becoming soft, but I have a need for a new commandant of my naval marines. I've looked into your record, and I like it; if the sultan sets you free, I can use you." He turned to the janissary who held the lamp. "Have them made presentable for an audience with His Magnificence," he said, and stalked out.

Other soldiers appeared and cut the prisoners' bonds with thick steel files. Jeremy and Mohammed ben Ral were taken up a long, steep flight of stairs and, after catching their first glimpse of daylight in more than a week, were allowed to bathe and shave. Bowls of lamb stew, the regular fare of the prison guards, were handed to them, and after they had eaten they were given their own clothes, from which all insignia of rank had been removed. A strong escort of one hundred men, all heavily armed, formed outside the entrance under the command of a subpasha of infantry, and the mere fact that an officer of such high rank had been given charge of the guard detail indicated the importance that the case had assumed.

Then Jeremy and Mohammed ben Ral were led into the open, the janissaries surrounded them, and they were marched off across the palace ground to the residence of the sultan. Many military and civilian employees of the government had gathered to catch a glimpse of the celebrated prisoners and were loitering near the entrance, as though mere chance had brought them there. Mohammed ben Ral seemed to enjoy the notoriety and beamed appreciatively at the crowd, but Jeremy looked neither to the right nor the left as he was led into the familiar building. The janissaries headed straight for the great audience chamber on the first floor that had been built during the reign of Suleiman the Wise and had been used ever since as a throne room, so Jeremy realized that the hearing would be public.

He and Mohammed ben Ral halted at the threshold, and when the officer in charge of the guard whispered to them that the sultan was already present, they prostrated themselves on the mosaic-tiled floor and remained motionless until they heard Selim's voice granting them permission to rise. Then they advanced slowly into the hall, and Jeremy was surprised to see that the whole court had convened. The grand vizier and the pashas of three horse-tails who were the sultan's principal advisers stood in a row to the right of the carpeted steps leading to the throne. The treasurer of the royal household was on the left, and grouped around him were the beys and sheiks who headed the various civilian branches of the government. Crowded along the wall on both sides were other high officials, and Jeremy saw so many pashas of one and two horsetails that he was sure every military and naval leader in the city was in attendance.

The sultan, the only person who was seated, reclined on the throne of thrones, the large golden, jewel-encrusted throne of his ancestors, which he had moved into the audience chamber for the occasion. He was dressed in crimson robes, and around his neck hung the fabulous Collar of a Thousand Rubies, a necklace so heavy and uncomfortable that he donned it only on occasions of state. And across his lap, resting on the arms of his throne, was the Great Scimitar, the symbol of his office, a weapon fashioned of pure gold. The sultan looked weary, and for good reason. After what seemed like an eternity, Tule Yasmin had finally left with her servingwomen to return to the land of her brother, but no sooner had she gone than the sultan learned the court jeweler had given her the Great Mongol Emerald. Having put the man to death, the sultan despaired of ever seeing the jewel again, all the more so after the khana had the audacity to return to Constantinople and to say that the jewel was now in her brother's possession. There was nothing the sultan could do to get the jewel back, short of starting a war with Khagan Buyantu Yassan, and now the treacherous khana was starting more trouble by demanding the death of her husband, Jumai Khan.

Only one woman was present, Tule Yasmin, and Jeremy's heart sank when he saw that she stood in a place of special favor, on the stairs, two steps below the sultan and to his right. Her cunning had never been more evident, and she had dressed with care for the hearing, so that every man in the throne room would sympathize with her and think her desirable. Her gown was of white silk, which made her appear unexpectedly demure, but it was cut to emphasize every line of her supple body, and Jeremy saw that many of the pashas were staring at her surreptitiously. A deep border of gold cloth set with square-cut emeralds and pearls edged the wide neck of her dress and provided a touch of dazzling elegance. A similar band bordered the hem, which was fashioned in such a way that it was cleverly provocative as well as awe-inspiring, for it was knee-length on one side and fell to a point that swept the floor on the other.

Only a princess of extraordinary wealth and power could afford such rich attire, but the khana, intent on impressing every member of the court, had added a final, overwhelming touch. At her waist, drawing the silk into soft folds, was a huge gold buckle, thickly studded with emeralds and pearls. No one in the throne room except the sultan himself owned such priceless jewelry, and by wearing it Tule Yasmin was constantly reminding everyone, including her imperial cousin, that she was no ordinary person and no ordinary witness.

Her instinct for swaying men was perfect, as always, and although she was one of the few ladies of high station who rarely bothered to conceal her face, she chose today to observe the traditions of Islam. Her veil, which was held taut across the bridge of her nose, leaving only her eyes revealed, was actually no more than a thin piece of gauzelike silk, however, and merely created the illusion of concealing the lower portion of her face. So she was able to appeal to the masculine conservatism of the sultan and his advisers, yet at the same time she was taking pains to insure that they could really see her and enjoy her seductive beauty.

Her eyes blazed as she looked down at Jeremy, and he thought he had never seen an expression of such sheer, concentrated hatred in the face of another human being. But he reminded himself that in the eyes of everyone present she was his legal wife, so he forced himself to grin casually at her. His impudence had the desired effect, for the members of the court murmured to each other, and even the sultan could not resist a smile. Only a brave man would dare indulge himself in such an informal gesture on this solemn occasion when his life was in danger, and the Turks, who always responded to demonstrations of courage, began to view the prisoner more favorably.

"Jumai," the sultan said, omitting the title of khan, "you have been accused by one of our own blood of having deserted from our navy because you wished to gain possession of a slave girl who pleased you. Are you guilty of this charge?"

Jeremy stood erect and spoke with greater confidence than he felt. "No, Your Magnificence, I am not guilty."

"Mohammed," Selim continued, turning to the sub-pasha, "you have been accused by one of our blood of having given great aid to one whom you knew to be a deserter. If this is true, you have committed an act of treason against our person. Are you guilty of this crime?"

"No, Your Magnificence, I am not guilty," Mohammed ben Ral replied in a booming parade-ground voice.

Selim glanced down at his own reflection in the gleaming gold of the Great Scimitar, and for a moment he seemed lost in thought. Jeremy, watching him closely, thought he detected a hint of distaste on the sultan's part for the whole affair, and was encouraged. Certainly no intelligent man—and Selim had a clear mind—could fail to realize that Tule Yasmin was a conniving, vicious wench whose charges were motivated by blatantly obvious feminine spite. But when Selim spoke, his words were far from heartening.

"We will listen now," he said, "to our beloved cousin, in whose veins flows the sacred imperial blood of our ancestors."

The khana bowed her head to the sultan with such humility that Jeremy was astonished. He, more than anyone else present, was familiar with her arrogance, and her

ability to simulate respect for her cousin was disconcerting;
he had not known she was such an accomplished actress.
When she started to speak, her voice was soft, almost
tender, and her tone was one of infinite sadness, too. Patently she had prepared herself for this role with great care
and had studied every intonation and gesture to make
certain of their effect on her auditors.

The substance of her complaint was even more remarkable, however, and she twisted facts brilliantly, shading and
warping the truth to suit her convenience. She had first
met the man called Jumai, she declared, when she had
engaged him as a bodyguard to escort her out of the Frankish lands she had so foolishly visited. He had proved himself to be a man of valor, and although she had known
from the start that he was a commoner as well as a Christian, she had fallen in love with him. At this point she
paused and looked first at the sultan, then at the men in
the throne room, and her piteous expression seemed to be
begging their forgiveness for her feminine weakness.

She had married Jumai, she said, in spite of her misgivings, and for a time he had seemed to live up to the
high promise she had seen in him. Thanks to his position
as her husband, he had won the confidence of His Magnificence and had been given a post of trust. For a time, she
continued, he had justified the sultan's faith in him, and as
everyone connected with the Imperial Navy well knew, he
had achieved brilliant results. Naturally, she added, her
own happiness had been complete; she had been proud of
her husband, proud of the title of khan and rank of pasha
of one horsetail that His Magnificence had seen fit to
bestow on him. At that point in his career, she intimated,
he had deserved all the honors that had been heaped on
him.

Suddenly Tule Yasmin paused, her eyes became round,
and she weaved slightly from side to side, as though in
sorrow. But Jeremy, watching her in cynical admiration,
realized that her movements were deliberately undulating,
and that her audience was enjoying her performance. Jumai,

she said sorrowfully, had unexpectedly conceived a passion
for one of her servingwomen, a drab girl who had one
quality with which she could not compete; like her husband, the slave was a Frank. Her attitude indicated that
she thought any man who preferred another woman was
out of his mind, and her audience, nodding vigorously,
made it plain that they agreed with her.

But male tastes, the khana continued, were unpredictable
and beyond understanding, and as a man was entitled to
enjoy the favors of more than one woman, her love for
her husband had prompted her to make him a gift of the
girl. The mighty rulers of Islam were agreeably surprised
by this declaration, and remembering the jealous squabbles
in their own harems, they started to cheer. They became
quiet again only when the sultan silenced them with a wave
of his hand.

Then, Tule Yasmin said, Jumai had grown tired of the
slave, so she had taken the girl into her own employ once
more. But apparently he didn't know what he really wanted,
for no sooner had she gone on a visit to her own province
than her husband had deserted his post and followed, in-
tending to resume his relationship with the Frankish wench.
Warming to the climax of her story, Tule Yasmin related
how Jumai and the girl had humiliated her, the sister of
the khagan, who was one of the sultan's most loyal sup-
porters, by tying her hand and foot, and then escaping.
Before they had fled from Urga, however, they had discussed their plans in her hearing, she concluded triumphantly, and had boasted of their cleverness. They had
planned to return to Constantinople, take advantage of
Jumai's official position, and steal a ship, and they had intended to flee in it to one of the lands of Frankistan. But
she had spoiled their scheme by racing across Asia ahead
of them and, having reached the capital first, had come
straight to His Magnificence with the whole sordid story.

The girl, who was of no real importance, was once again
in her custody and was being severely punished; once she
became tractable, Tule Yasmin said lightly, she would give

the slave to any man in the assemblage who wanted her. But Jumai, the husband she had loved so much, had been unworthy of the sultan's trust, and as her patriotism meant more to her than her personal feelings, she said she felt compelled to ask that he be put to death, even though the request broke her heart.

She faced the sultan and bowed to him humbly as the men watched her in fascination, paying her the highest of all possible tributes by maintaining a silence so absolute that it was almost eerie. After a long moment the quiet was broken by Mustafa el Kro, who left the ranks of his colleagues, advanced to the base of the steps, and salaamed. Standing again, he spoke slowly, almost hesitantly as he tried to walk a narrow and treacherous path. He had no intention of trying to deny or contradict any of the obvious truths spoken by one who was a member of the family of the most powerful, fair, and enlightened of all rulers. And, he declared emphatically, he was certainly not suggesting that one word the lovely khana had said was a lie. However, there were certain facts in the case of which she seemed to be ignorant, through no fault of her own, and he believed it was his duty to bring these matters to the attention of His Magnificence.

Speaking more rapidly now, he told the sultan about the letter Jumai had written before going off to Mongolia, and asked permission to produce the document. Selim nodded, and Mustafa el Kro mounted the steps and placed the parchment on the Great Scimitar, taking care not to touch the person of the sultan, an offense that was punishable by instant death. Then he backed down the stairs again, and Selim read the letter while Tule Yasmin, giving vent to her true feelings, frowned and tapped her foot imperiously.

But Jeremy was scarcely conscious of her anger. He had learned at the end of her twisted recital that Mary was still in her possession, and he could think of nothing else. It was all too clear that the khana had treated her badly during the past nine days, but it was a relief to know that

Mary was still alive. He was disturbed, of course, by Tule Yasmin's calm offer to give her slave to any man who wanted her; nevertheless it was some consolation to tell himself that the worst had not yet happened, so he could still hope, however faintly, that Mary would not be forced to become an inmate of a harem.

The letter, as nearly as Jeremy could judge from the sultan's expression, did not seem to impress Selim, and he was afraid this inanimate scrap of evidence would have little effect on the verdict, as the opposite side of the scale was weighted down by Tule Yasmin's dramatic appeal. In a few moments he would learn whether he would live or die, and he braced himself for the sultan's decision. Then, suddenly, he heard a commotion at the rear of the throne room. Court protocol strictly prohibited any interruption of a formal imperial audience, and necks craned in the direction of the entrance. Selim, irritated, glanced up from Jeremy's letter and gestured sharply, but the noise, instead of dying down, became louder.

Several men, one of them a senior pasha of two horse-tails, were engaging in excited conversation, and at last the pasha hurried up the length of the hall and whispered anxiously in the ear of the grand vizier. Clearly something of momentous importance was happening, and the officials looked at each other questioningly. Then the grand vizier, the only man in the chamber who dared to risk an imperial rebuke, stepped to the foot of the stairs.

"Your Magnificence," he said, "I crave your indulgence."

"One thing at a time, Ibrahim!" The sultan looked annoyed.

"I kiss the ground beneath your feet, but this will not wait, Your Magnificence," the grand vizier replied firmly, and turned to the entrance. "Let the bearer of tidings be brought forward."

A grizzled sea captain hurried toward the throne, and so great was his agitation that he almost forgot to salaam. Remembering in time, he went through the prescribed ritual quickly, then scrambled to his feet again. "Your Magnificence," he cried, "the English have attacked!"

Everyone started to talk at once, and it was some moments before the man could continue. "My ship was one of a squadron of four that has been operating off the coast of Greece, capturing Frankish merchantmen. Two days ago a great English fleet suddenly fell on us, and the rest of the squadron was destroyed. I was crippled, but I managed to escape ahead of the enemy and sailed here as fast as I could."

"How far are they from our coast?" the sultan asked.

"They sailed close behind me," the sea captain said. "By sundown tonight the Golden Horn will be filled with English ships of war."

Mustafa el Kro, still standing at the base of the throne, managed to keep calm. "How many ships are they sending against us?"

"Scores of them, Your Excellency! Ships of the line as tall as mountains, armed with seventy or eighty guns. Frigates as fast as our swiftest galleys. There are bomb ketches and armed trawlers, every type of warship I've ever seen."

The throne room was in an uproar, and everyone was talking simultaneously. The senior officers in particular were excited and discussed quick mobilization plans with the grand vizier, while the heads of the nonmilitary departments gathered in small groups and whispered to each other earnestly. Jeremy's hearing was almost forgotten, but Mustafa el Kro did not lose his head. Shouting to make himself heard, he cupped his hands and looked up at the sultan.

"Your Magnificence, I need Jumai Khan more than ever now. We'll need every cannon we have to drive off the enemy, and there isn't a man in this room or anywhere else in the empire as competent as Jumai Khan to direct the operations of our naval artillery. And," he added, "I have an important task for Mohammed ben Ral, too."

Habit and discipline caused the members of the court to fall silent, even in this moment of emergency, and although every man present was anxious to hurry off to attend to his own duties, no one could leave until the sultan disbanded the gathering. Selim, obviously trying to make up his mind, frowned indecisively and tapped the jeweled forefinger of his right hand on the hilt of the Great Scimitar. As he hesitated, Tule Yasmin moved up the two steps to his side and spoke to him at some length in an undertone. He seemed to fear that her interruption might be interpreted as a sign of weakness, and he tried to wave her away, but she continued to talk, and at last he smiled and nodded.

"Let the girl be brought in," he said.

Ordinarily the officials would have enjoyed the scene, but far more important matters were on their minds, and they shifted about restlessly, waiting with unconcealed impatience to be dismissed. Jeremy, however, could think only that he was about to see Mary again, and he was surprised when two janissaries brought her into the throne room almost immediately; obviously Tule Yasmin had intended to use her at some point in the proceedings and had confined her in one of the nearby anterooms.

Mary's appearance was shocking, and she shuffled forward, barely able to sustain the weight of heavy iron chains on her wrists and ankles. She was dressed in the hated slave breastband and trousers, and her back and shoulders, heavily discolored, gave mute testimony of the beatings she had received. Her hair was matted, her face was dirty, and there were deep circles beneath her eyes. Jeremy, conscious only of the fact that she had been suffering, would have hurried to her at once had not Mustafa el Kro gripped his arm. He and Mary had to be content to look at each other, but he thought fiercely that there was nothing on earth that could keep them apart permanently.

"Hear our decision," the sultan said, as a blow from one of the janissaries sent Mary sprawling. "The needs and requirements of our realm take first precedence in this hour of crisis. So we restore Jumai Khan and Mohammed ben Ral to their former places of eminence. They will hold these positions only temporarily, however. We do not trust either of them, particularly Jumai Khan. But our beloved cousin has suggested a way to force him to work for our victory. The slave whom he loves is English, so he might pretend to labor for our cause while secretly trying to betray us to the enemy."

Jeremy wanted to shout that the notion was absurd and that he loathed the English as much as anyone present, but Mustafa el Kro's hold on his arm tightened, and he remained silent.

"We therefore decree," the sultan continued, "that the slave girl will take Jumai Khan's place in the dungeons. If he works diligently and well for us, no harm will come to her. But if he fails, the girl will die."

XI

~~~~~~~~~~~~

Ram's horns sounded in every quarter of Constantinople, summoning the men of the Imperial Army and Navy to duty, and the muezzins, who would be calling the faithful to prayer at sunset, alerted the civilian population to the imminence of the English invasion by beating incessantly on drums that they carried to the minarets of the mosques. The city had not been attacked in more than fifty years, and even though a British attack had been expected, the people became panicky and poured into the streets by the tens of thousands. Traffic became congested, troop movements were impeded, and merchants, afraid the crowds would get out of control, boarded up their shops and appealed to the authorities for protection. But the constabulary, which was incorporated into the corps of janissaries in times of emergency, was too busy to respond to the plea, and the citizens were left to their own devices.

Officers of the highest rank had to force their way through the milling, frightened throngs, and Jeremy, hurrying to the naval base with a group of his colleagues, had to use the flat of the scimitar that had just been restored to him in order to clear a path for himself. The fleet had not waited for a formal mobilization order, and more than fifty warships of various sizes had already sailed out into the calm water of the Golden Horn by the time the men who would direct the operations of the navy arrived at the wharves.

Mustafa el Kro went on board his flagship, the *Suleiman,* immediately, accompanied by members of his personal staff and Mohammed ben Ral, who was assigned the task of supervising the marines. Hundreds of janissaries-of-the-sea who had been enjoying leaves of absence in the city were rejoining their ships; crew chiefs armed with knotted lengths of rope were rounding up their subordinates; and officers were holding impromptu conferences on the docks, directing the loading of ammunition on barges that were supplying the vessels in the harbor and trying to find the location of their own flotillas. A young *yada*, whose rank corresponded roughly with that of an American lieutenant, gave Jeremy a list of the ships in the fleet, and after studying it briefly he decided to make his own headquarters on board the *Crescent*, one of the larger galleys, which mounted twenty cannon.

He sent word of his destination to Mustafa el Kro, then requisitioned a boat and had himself rowed out to the warship; he was accompanied by the signalman who had worked with him prior to his departure for Mongolia and by an officer of the rank of *ris*, a senior captain who would serve as his immediate assistant. The oarsmen sent the gig gliding across the water, and Jeremy, sitting alone in the stern, made a supreme effort to concentrate on the job that awaited him. He was worried about Mary, but he could not allow himself the luxury of thinking about her, nor could he permit his concern for her to interfere with his work. It was enough to be ever conscious of the fact that she had been imprisoned in the dungeons beneath the sultan's palace and that if he failed in his efforts she would die.

The captain of the *Crescent*, pleased that his galley would serve as the flagship for the bombardment force, welcomed Jeremy effusively and turned over the larger portion of the quarterdeck to him. The signalman immediately sent messages to the rest of the fleet requesting that all other ships carrying six or more cannon join the *Crescent* at once. The commanders of thirty ships responded quickly and moved toward the flagship, while the captains of others sent word they would join Jumai Khan as soon as their crews and extra ammunition arrived.

The *ris,* exchanging messages with the other galleys, began to draw up a precise list of the vessels that comprised the force, together with the strength of their armaments, and Jeremy, leaning on the rail of the quarterdeck, was free to survey the overall scene. The basic defense strategy of the Turks was extremely simple but would require an unusual degree of coordination if it was to be effective. The fleet was comprised of approximately two hundred ships, but as Jeremy had long ago learned, the number was not as impressive as it seemed. Most of these craft were very light and frail, suitable chiefly for raiding merchantmen but useless against a sturdy, heavily armed enemy.

The smaller ships would fan out to lead the order of battle, and Mustafa el Kro had instructed their captains to head straight for the smaller English vessels; by utilizing their speed, the Turks might be able to avoid too heavy a punishment from the English guns, and their captains might be able to ram the lesser enemy ships and board them, a technique at which all janissaries-of-the-sea excelled.

Jeremy's unit would sail in the wake of these screening vessels, and he had no false illusions regarding the difficulty of his assignment. It would be his task to exchange fire with the larger enemy ships, and he knew that his success or failure would depend in part on the size of the English fleet. His galleys were roughly comparable in size to the smaller English frigates, which they could outmaneuver because of their superior speed. But they were not in a class with the larger frigates, which mounted thirty or forty guns, and the great enemy ships of the line, some of which reputedly carried as many as eighty cannon, were powerful enough to blow the galleys out of the water. So if there were only a few giants in the enemy fleet, the two sides would be fairly evenly matched. But if the British Admiralty had mustered its full strength in an effort to administer a lasting defeat, the Turks would be in for an

extraordinarily difficult time, and Jeremy's unit in particular could expect to be a principal target.

Assuming that the forces of the sultan could hold their
own, the third echelon of galleys, bringing up the rear with
the high command, would then become a factor in deciding
the battle. Many of the larger galleys had not been armed
with cannon, and in the event that Jeremy's naval artillery
was effective, Mustafa el Kro planned to swoop down on
any English ship that was disabled. He hoped to board
and take possession of as many enemy vessels as possible,
and Jeremy's argument that booty was secondary to victory
had fallen on deaf ears; without exception the naval pashas
were looking for prizes of war, and even Mustafa el Kro
himself had boasted that he intended to transfer his flag
to a ship of the line before the battle ended.

This lust for plunder, which every man in the fleet
shared, was sure to weaken the defenders, who would be
fighting against a disciplined, organized force. But Jeremy
realized that his attitude would not influence the Turks; for
centuries their sea rovers had been robbers, so he would
have to accept their piratical habits and hope their greed
would not overcome their common sense. Tradition and a
lack of experience in modern naval warfare, Jeremy
thought, were the worst handicaps his colleagues would
need to overcome if they were to defeat the enemy.

Certainly Mustafa el Kro was already taking risks that
were placing his fleet in jeopardy, and instead of sailing at
once to meet the English before the mighty frigates and
ships of the line entered the straits, he wasted the better part
of the afternoon painstakingly mobilizing. Twice Jeremy
sent a message to him, urging that they weigh anchor immediately, and twice word came back informing him that
some of the crews had not yet reported. So it was only
two hours before sundown when the sailing order was finally given and the small raiders, traveling in packs of five to
ten each, started to move north through the Bay of Bosporus.

Thousands of citizens lined the shore on the European

side of the straits and cheered the departing seamen, but
the optimistic holiday atmosphere had no effect on Jeremy.
The Turks' speed was their greatest asset, but it would
avail them nothing if the British had already entered the
bay, which was only four miles long, and in that event
Mustafa el Kro would have deliberately sacrificed his best
offensive weapon because of his stubborn insistence that all
of his ships had to be fully manned. Jeremy told himself
that, had the supreme command been vested in him, he
would have made every effort to reach the open sea, even
had it been necessary to leave some ships behind.

But it was useless to speculate, he knew, and when the
artillery-laden galleys swung into line and sailed north behind the lighter shells, he became too busy to think in terms
of strategy. His unit was comprised of forty-two ships, and
he placed himself in the center of the flotilla, with the more
heavily armed galleys on either side of him and the
more feeble vessels on his outer flanks. Glancing back, he
saw the *Suleiman,* shepherding a covey of the larger vultures of the sea, bringing up the rear, and as he watched
the janissaries respond to the shouts of the people on shore
by waving their scimitars, he shook his head and smiled.
The Turks' understanding of the science of sea warfare
might be deficient, but they were not lacking in courage.

At Jeremy's command, each of his galleys unlimbered
its cannon, and gun crews were ordered to take their posts,
ready for instant action. If the report of the captain who
had first brought word of the approach of the English was
at all accurate, the enemy should have sailed into the
straits some hours earlier, Jeremy thought, and his worst
fears were quickly corroborated. No more than a quarter of
an hour after the *Crescent* moved into her battle position
he heard the dull booming of cannon in the distance, and
he and his *ris* exchanged a significant look. Obviously the
enemy had already passed through the straits and soon
would be close enough to Constantinople to shell the city
itself.

A courier boat disguised as a fishing smack was sailing

south under full sail, and Jeremy sent a message to it, asking for information, but the captain of the little craft was in too much of a hurry to reply and headed straight for the *Suleiman* to deliver a report to the pasha in command. The sound of cannonading increased, and although the day was hazy, Jeremy saw puffs of smoke drifting up into the sky in the distance. The battle had begun.

He signaled to his captains, ordering them to hold their formation at all costs, and then, figuring that enough time had elapsed for the courier to have given the flagship all the data it needed, he instructed his signalman to send a question to Mustafa el Kro. "How large is the enemy fleet?"

A confident reply came back at once. "Less than half our size."

But Jeremy was not satisfied and pressed his inquiry. "How many are ships of the line?"

There was a pause, and the roar of the British guns became deafening. At almost the same moment the high mainmasts of the enemy's larger vessels became visible in the distance, but Jeremy, awaiting Mustafa el Kro's reply, concentrated on the flags being run up on the *Suleiman*. "Twelve men-of-war," he read.

The *ris*, who was a competent gunnery officer and therefore understood what was at stake, cursed under his breath. Jeremy, his face grim, was sure they had not yet heard the worst and sent still another message to the commander. "How many are frigates?"

The reply was so discouraging that the *ris* groaned aloud. "Twenty-nine," Mustafa el Kro said.

Never had a fleet entered a battle against such odds, and Jeremy was in despair. The frigates and supporting ships alone would have been strong enough to crush a fleet whose largest galleys carried only twenty guns, and the English admiral, with twelve ships of the line at his disposal as well, had almost no problems. The only possible course of action now was to fall back and form a tight defensive ring around the city, thus forcing the enemy to batter its way through the Golden Horn in order to reach Constantinople. Jeremy, wording his message carefully, suggested the maneuver, but Mustafa el Kro did not bother to consider it.

"We will attack!" he signaled proudly.

There was no alternative but to sail ahead, and as the fleet drew closer to the foe, the disposition of the English ships became clearer. The admiral had divided his force into six squadrons, with two ships of the line as the nucleus of each, while three frigates provided cover for each group. The remainder of the frigates, operating independently, bore down on the little Turkish galleys that were providing cover. Their guns were blazing, and when Jeremy saw the quality of English marksmanship, he shuddered: Iron balls were crashing onto the decks of the raiders, and five of them, according to the *ris,* were already disabled.

One Turkish ship was burning, and several others hovered near it, waiting to pick up survivors, but Jeremy shut his mind to the disaster. Singling out one of the smaller frigates, which he estimated carried no more than thirty guns, he ordered the captain of the *Crescent* to open fire on it and sent a message to a sister galley, the *Scimitar,* to do the same. The cannon of the two vessels spoke simultaneously, and the commander of the frigate, who had carelessly assumed that the Turks were notoriously poor shots, paid for his ignorance. The starboard guns of both the galleys raked him twice, and before he quite realized what had happened to him he was listing badly to port.

The thunder of the guns drowned the cheers of the janissaries on board the lightly armed galleys, but the men on the artillery ships were too busy to shout. Jeremy ordered his entire flotilla to present its starboard side to the enemy and to fire at will. The first salvo caused considerable damage, and the second disabled another frigate. However, by this time the English admiral had recovered from his initial surprise and sent his frigates forward again. Tacking gracefully, the swift ships replied to the Turkish fire, and the *ris,* his voice anguished, announced that four of the galleys in the flotilla had been mortally hit.

The duel continued for thirty minutes, and the smaller Turkish raiders, which were contributing nothing to the battle, scurried to the rear when Jeremy, not bothering to check first with Mustafa el Kro, peremptorily ordered them to stop cluttering up the bay between his galleys and their targets. The long months of training that the janissary gun crews had undergone made themselves felt as the Turks exchanged round after round with their foes, but the power and seamanship of the English were still superior, and when dusk fell it was painfully evident that the fleet of Mustafa el Kro had taken a severe beating.

Ten of the artillery galleys had been sunk, and as no more than half of their crew members had been rescued, Jeremy estimated that he had lost at least one thousand trained men so far. Eight other ships carrying cannon had been crippled and would not be able to reenter the fight, so the strength of Jeremy's flotilla had been cut in half. And although the arsenals in Constantinople were filled with new cannon, there was no time to mount them on the few galleys that were still unarmed and heavy enough to sustain their weight. Even worse, it was impossible to guess how many of the light screening vessels had been sunk or put out of commission; the *ris,* whose score was admittedly incomplete, said that in his opinion no more than one third to one half of the original force remained.

Meanwhile only three English frigates had been sunk, along with half a dozen smaller ships, while four other frigates had sustained damages. It was only a minor consolation to know that no other nation had ever hurt the English navy so badly, for the striking power of the enemy fleet was still great. And Jeremy was keenly aware of the fact that the great ships of the line had not yet taken an active part in the battle. The frigates alone had carried the fight to the Turks, and not a single gun on the huge men-of-war had yet been fired. Obviously the British admiral had not felt it necessary to use his giants and presumably was saving their power for the climactic phase of the fight. Although the Englishman had learned to respect Turkish gunnery this afternoon, he could entertain no doubts regarding the final outcome of the fight, and he showed his contempt for the defenders by breaking off the engagement at nightfall and retiring to the northern end of the Bay of Bosporus.

Jeremy watched the enemy draw away, and in the darkness the huge ships of the line reminded him of chickens shepherding their infants. He lacked the power to pursue the English, so with a heavy heart he ordered the remnants of his flotilla to retreat. Certain defeat awaited the Turks when the battle was resumed in the morning, and all that had prevented the complete demolition of Mustafa el Kro's fleet today had been the coming of night. The Turks had fought honorably and courageously, and the naval gunners had more than proved their worth, but by noon, perhaps by midmorning, Constantinople would be at the mercy of the enemy. The cannon of the ships of the line would be trained on the mosques and homes and shops of the city, and the sultan would face the alternative of surrendering the prisoners or watching his capital burn to the ground.

The defeat could mean the end of the Ottoman Empire as a major power, and the English admiral would be hailed in the Christian world as a great hero. Jeremy, lost in thought as he paced up and down the quarterdeck of the *Crescent,* felt a deep respect for the enemy commander and had to admit that the admiral would deserve all the honors that would be heaped on him when he returned to London. But the mission of an American, whose country was depending on him, would end in abject failure and death, and an English girl who was being held as a prisoner in Selim's dungeons would die, too. Regardless of the odds that favored the British, Jeremy told himself, he could not meekly resign himself to the seemingly inevitable and would have to make one final attempt to drive off the enemy.

The Turkish fleet limped back to Constantinople, and

Mustafa el Kro regrouped his battered forces in the harbor for the night. No cheering crowds stood on the wharves now, the lights of the city were dim, and a fisherman, who was fleeing with his family and his few belongings through the straits, shouted up to the quarterdeck of the *Crescent* that thousands of citizens were leaving the capital, which they believed was doomed. The pessimistic outlook did not surprise Jeremy, and as he peered off through the gloom at the dark, silent city, he could well imagine the terror of the people. Suddenly he straightened and turned to the captain of the galley.

"Lower your gig for me," he said, and five minutes later he and the *ris,* not waiting to be summoned by Mustafa el Kro, were being rowed across the harbor to the commander's flagship.

The janissaries on board the *Suleiman* seemed to have given up all hope, and when Jeremy and the *ris* arrived at the quarterdeck, Mustafa el Kro and his staff were glumly eating a meal of *seksu,* which consisted of grain made into a mush and seasoned with peppers. The pasha of two horsetails dipped his right hand into the bowl of food and beckoned to Jeremy with his left. "Join us," he said heavily, "for what may be our last meal. You fought well, Jumai Khan, but the ships and guns of the English are too strong for us."

Mohammed ben Ral, who was eating heartily in spite of his despondency, nodded in agreement. "It is our kismet to be defeated by the Franks."

Jeremy looked at the faces of the men sitting in a circle on the deck and lost his temper. "Are you women?" he demanded, pointing an accusing finger first at Mustafa el Kro, then at a pasha of one horsetail. "Are you cowards who weep and bare your throats to an enemy when he frightens you?"

Several of the officers leaped to their feet and reached for their scimitars, but Mustafa el Kro restrained them. "The words of Jumai Khan are as fiery as this dish of *seksu,*" he said. "But a cup of water takes away the taste of *seksu*. What does Jumai Khan offer that will make his words strong enough to silence the English?"

"We have hundreds of cannon in our arsenals," Jeremy said. "And we have more than enough ammunition for them."

A pasha of one horsetail laughed hollowly. "Are you suggesting that we build a new fleet between now and morning? You seem to forget, Jumai Khan, that only Allah performs miracles. We had hoped to build ships for those guns, but there isn't time."

"We don't need those unbuilt ships," Jeremy replied quietly, and saw that he had the attention of his audience. "We have two ships the English can't sink, and I propose that we use them."

Mustafa el Kro stared at him. "Either you speak in riddles or the losses we suffered this afternoon have robbed you of your senses."

The Turks always responded to a dramatic gesture, so Jeremy laughed heartily. "Listen," he said, "and then judge for yourselves whether I have gone mad. The ships of the line can sink all of our galleys. But they can't make the land disappear into the sea. I suggest that we use ground on the two sides of the straits as our own men-of-war. I suggest that we take every cannon we possess out of the arsenals, that we mount half of them on the European side of the straits and the other half on the Asian side."

Mustafa el Kro lost his air of gloom, and his eyes grew bright. "Go on," he said.

"Then," Jeremy continued, "I propose that we lure the English into the narrow part of the straits. They're sure to follow us, as they'll think they can concentrate all their fire on us in an area where we'll have no room to maneuver, much less escape. If we're clever enough in leading them to the narrows, if they think we're confused, they'll be convinced that a quick victory is in sight for them. They'll be ready to finish us off and turn their guns on the city. In the meantime our batteries will be waiting for them, and when they sail within range we'll catch them in a cross fire from both banks."

The Turks considered the idea thoughtfully, and the pasha of one horsetail who felt he had been insulted was the first to speak. "It's probable, is it not, that we'll lose many of our fine galleys in such an operation?"

"Correct."

"I'm reluctant to see our ships sunk," the officer declared stubbornly.

"We'll lose them all if we sail out to meet the English in open battle again," Jeremy replied calmly. "It's far better to let a few decoys be sunk and hope their skeleton crews can swim to safety than to see Constantinople razed to the ground."

Mustafa el Kro, on whom the final decision depended, rose to his feet and frowned uncertainly. "Your scheme can succeed, Jumai Khan, only if the cannon in the arsenals are moved into position before daybreak. Can we accomplish such an enormous task in so short a time?"

"We'll need to use every man, every ship, and every barge in the navy," Jeremy said crisply, "and we'll have to call on the army for help, too. As to whether or not we can finish in time, I can only say that if we don't, all of us will die, and the empire of Selim III will perish with us."

The pasha of one horsetail was not yet ready to accept the suggestion of an insolent foreigner. "A radical plan like this must be submitted to higher authorities."

Mustafa el Kro glared at his subordinate. "With all due respect to His Magnificence, he and his advisers would waste the whole night arguing. I have been charged with the defense of the city from the English fleet, so I have all the authority I need. Jumai Khan, I accept your idea."

The fleet came to life again in the next few minutes, and not one man remained idle. The seamen from the unarmed galleys were sent off to the arsenals for cannon and ammunition, junior officers went ashore to round up all available barges, and the gun crews started to transfer their own artillery to the European side of the straits. Mustafa el Kro realized that if he reported to the palace in person, he could be ordered to call off the whole venture, so he sent a pasha of one horsetail instead to tell the sultan and grand vizier what was in store.

Meanwhile another subpasha went to the army to ask for the services of all janissaries who were available, and Mohammed ben Ral organized his marines into shore patrols to tour the dock area and make sure that no English spies infiltrated the zone. Galleys that were still sound after the battle and that were not being used for other purposes were made ready to assist the barges in carrying guns to the Asian shore, and several smaller craft were sent off to patrol the water between the harbor and the English fleet to make sure that no enemy vessel sailed close enough during the night to learn what was in the wind.

Jeremy was one of the first to go ashore, and when the cannon from the arsenals began to arrive, he directed their emplacement and assigned crews to them. But the work was going far too slowly to satisfy him, and he was afraid that although his plan was sound, it could not be executed in time to be effective. He sent message after message to Mustafa el Kro, who remained aboard the *Suleiman,* asking for more men to assist in the operation, but the frustrated commander had already exhausted his reserves. Progress was maddeningly slow, but the janissaries-of-the-sea, tired after their battle, could not be driven too hard. And Jeremy favored his gun crews, assigned them the lighter tasks, and refused to allow them to haul cannon. If the guns were put into place before morning, the rest would be up to the artillerymen, whose performance would be inferior if they were exhausted.

Shortly before midnight the army made its appearance and in size alone compensated for its tardiness. Five divisions of infantry, made up of ten regiments, arrived at the docks under the command of a pasha of two horsetails, and a few minutes later three independent brigades of cavalry followed them. A number of the higher-ranking army officers who were jealous of the navy wanted to withdraw when they learned what was expected of their men, and the cavalry leaders objected to the very idea of permitting their magnificent mounts to drag heavy guns to the shore. But the pasha of two horsetails was a sensible man, and after Jeremy had outlined the scheme to him briefly, he ordered his subordinates to lend the venture their complete support.

The tempo of the work picked up immediately, the guns, iron balls, and bags of powder began to arrive from the nearby arsenals at an increased rate, and soon the first barge loads were ready to be transferred to the Asian side. Jeremy had himself rowed across the straits in a gig and was waiting in the shabby residential district at the waterfront when the first barges and galleys arrived. Mustafa el Kro followed him a few minutes later, and together they decided where the cannon were to be emplaced.

Mustafa el Kro remained to supervise this part of the preparations, and Jeremy returned to the European side of the city to encourage the army and to make certain that the cannon on that shore were being located in the most advantageous positions. As he crossed the water in the gig, with the salt spray in his face, he looked out at the teeming harbor, and for the first time since he had learned of the size of the English fleet, he felt encouraged. The entire operation was being performed under cover of darkness, but the activity he saw dimly on every side heartened him. Barges and galleys carried the guns his foundries had forged; smaller boats laden with gunpowder struggled across the straits; and the army, determined not to be left out of the actual fighting, was sending several hundred of its own artillery men to the Asian banks of the Bosporus to man some of the cannon and to share the glory with the navy.

While preparations for the morning's surprise attack continued at a furious pace, Mary remained in her isolated cell, fighting hard to think clearly. First and foremost she realized that the attack by Great Britain against the Ottoman Empire had probably been caused by a fuss that her father had made over her capture. The man she loved and was going to marry was forced to fight against her country, and the defeat of either would be devastating.

Now she knew what needed to be done, and as she had taken measures in Urga to avert a possible catastrophe, she was determined to waste no time in seeing those measures put into effect. She walked to the bars and rattled them loudly. "Attendant!" she shouted. "Come here instantly!"

After a brief pause a pantaloon-clad man of middle years with a sad, drooping mustache ambled slowly down the stone corridor. "See here," he complained, "prisoners aren't supposed to make a commotion."

Mary's manner remained imperious. "If you know what's good for you," she said, "you'll do as I tell you and you'll be quick about it."

The man was totally unaccustomed to such talk from a captive and could only stare at her.

"Bring me some paper, a quill pen, and a stick of sealing wax." Her tone admitted no interference with her will.

The jailer stared at her, shrugged, and then moved off slowly. He knew she had been present in the sultan's chambers, and he was sufficiently accustomed to the doings of the high and mighty of the realm to take no chances. Those who were out of favor one day rose very swiftly in it the next, so it was best to do as he was bidden. It would do him no harm, certainly, to accede to her simple request.

While serving as Tule Yasmin's maid, Mary had managed to learn to write a few Turkish words, and now, provided with the materials she had demanded, she scribbled a line with great haste. Then she made certain that the document was securely sealed, holding the wax over a small flame until several blobs of it fell onto the letter and secured it.

"Be sure this is delivered in person to the sultan at once," she said.

The jailer stared at her. "The sultan?" he asked. "You don't ask for much, do you?"

"Do precisely as I say and you'll be rewarded," Mary told him. "Deviate from it in the slightest degree and you'll suffer excruciating pains."

The man knew better than to take unnecessary risks. Obviously this young woman knew her mind, and he would have to do as she had bidden him. He carried the letter upstairs from the dungeons and gave it at last to a captain of the imperial household guard, with instructions that he repeated carefully.

The officer smiled indulgently as he took the letter, but when he was alone again he, too, felt less sure of himself. Perhaps he would deliver the letter after all; the worst that would happen to him would be that the sultan might become slightly annoyed. This would be better than to arouse the enmity of the beautiful woman whose relationship to the sultan was unclear in the officer's mind.

Selim the Magnificent was seated cross-legged on a stool in his private chamber, reading the battle reports that had been pouring in throughout the day. He looked up in annoyance at the captain who thrust the letter at him.

Rather than say anything, he was intrigued by the many seals on it and tore it open. Color drained from the imperial face, and the imperial voice shook as the sultan said, "Fetch the female prisoner and have her brought to my presence immediately!"

To the surprise of everyone but Mary herself, she was soon admitted to the sultan's sanctum.

"Well?" the sultan demanded, his voice strident.

Mary was remarkably calm. "If it pleases Your Magnificence," she said, "I would like to borrow a small knife or dagger from you for a few moments."

The sultan looked at her uncertainly. "If you intend to attack me you know it means instant death."

"I would hardly be so stupid," she said.

The sultan shrugged, took a small poniard from his jeweled belt, and threw it onto the table in front of him.

To his astonishment Mary picked it up and began to chip away with the short, sharp blade at a ring she was wearing on a finger of her left hand. The ring was drab, apparently of no consequence, and her jailers had not gone to the trouble to remove it.

To the sultan's astonishment chips of what looked like paint or nail polish were removed from the ring, and a deep green stone began to be revealed. Something stirred within him, and he stared at it incredulously.

Mary concentrated on her task, paying no attention whatsoever to the most powerful man in Islam, who was stunned as he watched her.

At last she finished her labors, and her sense of the theater asserted itself. She made a deep obeisance before the sultan, then extended both hands to him. "Your Magnificence," she said, "I offer you the Great Mongol Emerald. It is intact, none the worse for wear."

The sultan's hand trembled as he snatched the precious bauble from her. He looked at it, and it was indeed the most valuable emerald in the world, a gem that he had despaired of ever seeing again.

"How did this ever come into your possession?" he demanded hoarsely.

"I knew Tule Yasmin had stolen it from you," she said. "Before I left Urga I regained possession of it and disguised it with nail lacquer. In all this time no one has guessed its identity or its real worth."

The sultan slipped the ring onto his finger and regarded it for a long time; then he picked up a silver-handled bell and shook it vigorously until a colonel of household troops stood at rigid attention in the doorway.

"This lady is to be released from bondage instantly," the sultan ordered. "She is to be treated as an honored guest, and anyone who fails to pay proper homage to her will be punished accordingly."

"I would also ask one more thing of Your Magnificence," Mary said, her eyes unwavering.

"Ask, and it shall be yours."

"I would ask that whatever the outcome of the battle with the English, you release the British subjects you are holding captive."

The sultan pondered for a moment. From the reports he had received, the battle was going poorly, and it was possible the English would even take Constantinople. Perhaps, then, it would be wise to free the prisoners. In the event the Turkish navy was defeated, the sultan's concession to the British demands for the release of their citizens might mean Constantinople would be spared. And even if the Turks were victorious, the release of the prisoners would have cost nothing and would please the red-haired maiden who had restored the precious emerald to him. Finally the sultan said, "You shall have your request. The captives will be allowed to go free." He smiled at Mary, then dropped something into her hand.

She lowered herself to the floor before taking her leave and waited until she was in the outer corridor before she peered at what was in her hand. Then she gasped aloud. The sultan had given her a magnificent ruby ring, the size of a bird's egg. It was by far the loveliest and largest gem she had ever seen, and she realized this was his way of thanking her for returning the Great Mongol Emerald to him. He was not forgetting that the wearer of the Great Mongol Emerald enjoyed good fortune all of his days, and Mary, suddenly free, realized that the emerald had something to do with her own good luck, too.

Now, however, she faced a curious situation. So much of her future depended upon Jeremy. The gunners he had trained even now were locked in combat with the most powerful flotilla on earth, a Royal Navy fleet for whose presence in Turkish waters she could claim at least partial responsibility. What made her situation unique was that instead of wishing for the success of the British, she hoped with all her heart that Jeremy's men would be successful in driving off the enemy. Only then would Jeremy's mission for his country succeed, only then would the man she loved be able to leave Islam with dignity and respect.

By the time the first streaks of dawn appeared in the eastern sky, more than one thousand cannon were in position, ready to greet the enemy. The guns located in exposed places were camouflaged with tree branches and strips of cloth, and old sacks covered the piles of ammunition beside them. When the English sailed into the narrows, even the sharpest eyes on the quarterdecks of their ships would not be aware of the trap that had been set for them. Quantities of bread had been given to the janissaries-of-the-sea and the army artillerymen who would man the cannon, and the gunners sat on the ground beside their weapons, talking quietly and awaiting the forthcoming battle with a calm that only Moslems could achieve.

In a final conference only an hour previous it had been decided that Jeremy would command the batteries on the Asian shore, as the enemy would have to sail closer to those banks, due to the tides and sandbars, so his experience would be used to its best advantage. Mustafa el Kro, who would be in charge on the European shore, allowed him to select his staff; he took most of the officers who had worked with him in the past, and as Mohammed ben Ral now had nothing to do, he asked that the subpasha be assigned to him, too.

They stood together on a small hill beside a hastily evacuated workers' settlement, and as it began to grow light they watched the Turkish fleet, manned by the fewest possible number of sailors necessary, move in formation toward the enemy. A few cannon bristled on the decks of the larger vessels, and the men who had been assigned to them had received instructions to substitute noise for accuracy. It did not matter whether they struck any of the English ships; all that counted was that the foe be fooled into thinking that the galleys carried their full complement of guns.

The enemy was astir, too, and Jeremy, looking out at

the English fleet through his spyglass, was impressed anew
with the power and majesty of this force that was the un-
disputed ruler of the seas. He saw the admiral's pennant
flying from one of the ships of the line and made out the
name of the vessel in letters of gold on her prow. She was
the *Renown*, which he knew was a capital ship of seventy-
four guns, and he was not surprised to see that two of her
twins, the *Revenge* and the *Repulse*, were in the fleet, too.
Clearly the sea lords in London had decided to send their
best and heaviest men-of-war against the Turks in order
to teach the sultan a lesson for all time.

The light galleys that led the decoys darted toward the
enemy, and when the frigates broke the early morning
silence by opening fire on them, they darted first to starboard, then tacked to port to elude punishment. The guns
on the larger galleys opened fire, and Mohammed ben Ral,
who was stolidly eating a small loaf of bread, laughed as
his compatriots hurled their ammunition across the water
indiscriminately; the courageous janissaries-of-the-sea on
board the doomed galleys were following their instructions
to the letter and, not bothering to take careful aim, scattered their shots recklessly.

The English responded methodically and continued to
sweep forward until the Turks, understandably apprehensive, turned and fled. It was unnecessary to simulate confusion, for the accurate English fire, which sent heavy iron
balls crashing into the hulls and through the decks of the
light Turkish craft, was sufficient to make any but the
most extraordinary seaman lose his head. The withdrawal
became a rout, and for the first time the mammoth ships
of the line entered the battle. The admiral obviously
wanted the honor of leading the final phase of the attack
in person, and the ground beneath Jeremy's feet trembled
as the port guns of the *Renown* roared in unison. Two of
the galleys staggered under the impact of the blows and
began to sink within a few minutes, almost as though a
giant hand beneath the water were hauling them under the

surface. The English had demonstrated their full power at last, and their strength was frightening.

Seamen on the two stricken galleys were jumping into the Bosporus, and their comrades on other vessels threw lines to them while the English, in an unusual display of gallantry, silenced their guns for a few minutes. Then they resumed their relentless attack against the helpless Turks, and the janissaries on the shore, who were now standing beside their guns, looked anxiously at Jeremy, hoping he would give them the order to open fire. He understood their eagerness, for he shared it, but he controlled his impatience and continued to wait. He wanted to achieve the maximum effect with his opening salvo, and the enemy had not yet sailed close enough to be caught in a cross fire from the opposite sides of the narrows.

Mustafa el Kro had given Jeremy the authority to fire first and had promised that the cannon on the European shore would remain quiet until Jumai Khan decided the appropriate moment for the counterattack had arrived. But the tension was almost unbearable, and Jeremy was uncertain how much longer his impulsive colleagues across the straits could hold off. The English fleet seemed to be inching forward now at a maddeningly slow pace, under reduced sail, and for a moment Jeremy was afraid that the enemy had sensed the trap and was preparing to pull out. Then he realized that the English were maneuvering into a new position; the frigates and several of the smaller ships, which were in the lead, were chasing the retreating Turks, and the men-of-war were taking up positions in a single line, their gun ports open and their cannon gleaming in the morning sunlight. Apparently the admiral, confident that the remnants of the Turkish fleet could inflict no damage on him, was preparing to bombard Constantinople and was contemptuously sailing as close to the city as he could.

His tactics suited Jeremy perfectly, and he concluded that the English could not know of the greeting that awaited them. The *Renown* was the first of the men-of-war to sail into the narrows, and it moved through the passage until it reached a point approximately a quarter of a mile from the Asian shore and less than a mile from the European banks. There it swung around gracefully, presented its starboard side to the city, and dropped anchor. One by one the other giants did the same and were so confident of their power that those already in position waited for the others before opening the bombardment.

Jeremy drew his scimitar, and his artillerymen smiled expectantly. Gun crews took their battle positions, and word was passed up and down the line of cannon that Jumai Khan was about to give the order to strike. It was a temptation to wait until the last two men-of-war came into position, but Jeremy decided not to be too greedy; it was possible that the admiral might commence his operations at any time, and it would be far better if the Turks opened their attack first. So he raised his scimitar high over his head, and subpashas, stationed at intervals on either side of him, did the same. He gave all of the janissaries time to set themselves for the barrage and then brought his blade down in a sharp, sweeping gesture.

"Fire at will!" he shouted.

The cannon roared, and clouds of smoke rose into the air, momentarily concealing the English. A few seconds later the guns on the European bank took up the battle cry, and the echo of their thunder rolled across the Bosporous. Then the smoke cleared, and Jeremy saw that only one of the ships of the line had been hit. Her mainmast was down and there was a gaping hole in her hull near her stern, but the rest of the giants were intact. Jeremy ordered his staff to increase the range, and as they hurried off he ran to the nearest of the guns to test the elevation himself.

He helped the crew raise the barrel, assisted in the breech reloading of the weapon, and himself touched off the powder. A puff of wind carried the smoke away quickly, and he had the satisfaction of seeing the shot smash into the side of the *Repulse*. Then he moved to the next cannon and repeated his performance amid a deafening uproar that seemed to shatter his eardrums. His subordinate commanders were working crisply and efficiently, too, and one by one the cannon corrected their range and began to train their shots directly on their targets. It was impossible to determine whether or not the units on the European shore were equally effective, but so far, at least, Jeremy had every reason to feel encouraged.

Meanwhile the English were not taking their punishment meekly. The first of the ships of the line to recover from the initial shock was the *Glorious*, and her artillerymen quickly proved that the British reputation for efficiency and courage was well deserved. The guns of the *Glorious* spoke up furiously, and shortly after they had fired their first salvo Mohammed ben Ral reported to Jeremy that five of the Turkish positions had been wiped out, four by direct hits and one by a strike on a pile of powder bags.

Gradually the other men-of-war took up the gage of battle, too, and exchanged round for round with the janissaries. The two sides were more or less evenly matched, and those frigates whose guns could reach the shore positions came to the aid of the ships of the line. Stamina as well as skill would be a determining factor in the outcome of the fight, and Jeremy moved incessantly up and down the long row of cannon, encouraging his men, shifting crews from disabled guns to other cannon, and showing by his own fearless refusal to take cover that he could not be intimidated. Casualties were heavy and increased rapidly as the English guns found their targets with greater accuracy; the dead were everywhere, and whenever there was a lull in the firing, the screams of the wounded pierced the air.

But Jeremy, his face and uniform powder-blackened, was everywhere, cheering his janissaries; the men knew him and trusted him and, heartened by his example, held grimly to their positions in spite of the toll the enemy was taking. Eventually, Jeremy told himself, the British would be forced to withdraw, provided the Turks did not panic first, for the ships would inevitably take a more severe beating than would forces stationed on dry land.

Two of the English frigates, ignoring the pounding they were receiving, crept toward the Asian shore, their guns blazing, and before some of the Turks' cannon could be retrained on them, they wrought considerable havoc. Their maneuver was a bold one, as surprising as it was audacious, and Jeremy took personal charge of the counteroffensive against them. Accompanied by Mohammed ben Ral, he dashed to a score of guns located on his right flank and frantically redirected their fire, shortening his range and sending his shots at the superstructures of the ships that were taking his positions.

Mohammed ben Ral, whose knowledge of artillery was limited, was nevertheless an experienced soldier, and after seeing what Jeremy was doing, he started to direct the aiming of other guns at the frigates. Suddenly there was a deafening crash, and Jeremy, who was just moving from one cannon to the next, was thrown to the ground. The air around him was curiously still for an instant, and when he sat up he felt dazed. Feeling himself gingerly, he realized that although he had been knocked down by the nearby impact of an enemy shot, he had escaped injury. So he shook himself and stood groggily, surveying the damage.

A senior officer was lying on the ground some ten feet away, and when Jeremy's eyes began to focus again, he recognized Mohammed ben Ral. Forgetting his own condition, he ran to his friend and dropped to one knee beside him. The Turk, he saw at once, had been severely injured and was bleeding from a deep wound in his side. It was no novelty to Jeremy to see a comrade hurt, but he and the subpasha had suffered so much together that he felt closer to Mohammed ben Ral than he had to most of his friends who had been injured in past battles. He was dismayed, but he hid his feelings and smiled down at the Turk.

"I'll have you moved to a safer place," he said with feigned cheerfulness, "and you'll soon be all right again."

Mohammed ben Ral was in great pain but managed to grin weakly and shake his head. "Don't bother," he replied hoarsely. "I have met my final kismet in this world." He tried to say something more but could not; then his head fell back, and he stared vacantly at the sky.

His death infuriated Jeremy, who returned to the battle with renewed vigor. The frigates had to be destroyed at all costs, and he devoted his full attention to the problem, changing the range of his cannon as rapidly as he could move from one to the next. He was concentrating so intensely that he remained unaware of anything other than his immediate targets until he heard the janissaries off to his left cheering wildly. He straightened, glanced out into the narrows, and was amazed to see that the ships of the line, executing turns with the greatest of difficulty, were withdrawing under forced sail. The significance of the frigates' slashing attack immediately became apparent to him, and he knew they were sacrificing themselves in order to provide cover for the rest of the fleet.

He ordered his men to forget the smaller ships and to strike again at the giants as long as they were still within range. The janissaries obeyed, but the enemy accomplished his disengaging action brilliantly, and very little additional injury was inflicted on him. The smaller English vessels, hovering in the wake of the men-of-war, fired a few parting rounds at the Turks, and at last the two frigates that had been assigned to draw the janissaries' fire sailed away, too. It would have been comparatively easy to put these rear guards out of action, but by this time the Turks on both sides of the straits had ceased fire and were singing, cavorting, and dancing around their smoking cannon.

The quiet seemed strange after the artillery duel, and Jeremy, looking up at the sky, suddenly realized it was late afternoon and that the battle had lasted most of the day. The abrupt end of the fight stunned him, and it was some time before his mind began to function clearly again. Then, counting the ships in the departing English fleet and assessing the wrecks in the narrows with his spyglass, he finally realized the magnitude of the victory he had won. Four proud ships of the line had been sunk, another had been transformed into a battered hulk, and the seven men-of-war that had been able to leave the scene under their own sail had sustained heavy damages, as had many of the escort ships. Jeremy watched the fleet that had been without an equal on the seven seas limp out toward the Mediterranean, and it was difficult for him to recognize the fact that he, more than any other man, deserved credit for the unprecedented victory.

The defeat of the English had been achieved at a great price, however, and a tour of the lines revealed that the janissaries' casualties had been exceptionally high. At least one member of virtually every gun crew had been wounded or killed, and many units had been wiped out. As nearly as Jeremy could estimate, he had lost more than forty percent of his fighting force. With the aid of the surviving officers of the rank of subpasha and *ris* he arranged for the evacuation of the wounded to the hospitals across the straits, and then, leaving volunteers to guard the cannon that had not been destroyed, he and the others who had not been injured sailed across the narrows in a motley collection of barges and small boats.

Not until he sat in the stern of the last gig to leave the Asian banks did Jeremy realize that he was bone-tired, and when he arrived at the other side, he hauled himself to his feet with an effort. As he stepped ashore an effendi wearing the sash of the imperial staff stepped up to him, saluted, and told him his presence was requested at the palace. He shook off his exhaustion, and escorted by a troop of cavalry that pushed its way through wildly celebrating crowds, he rode through the streets of Constantinople.

Many senior officers, some of whom Jeremy did not know, gathered around him in the corridors of the palace and insisted on shaking his hand. So his progress toward the throne room was slow, and when he arrived at its entrance, Mustafa el Kro, who had been inside, hurried to him and embraced him. The naval commander was filthy, his clothes were tattered, and his beard had been burned, and although no one ever dared to appear in such a disreputable state before the sultan under ordinary conditions, today was far from ordinary. As Mustafa el Kro proudly led the grimy Jeremy into the hall, Selim, who had been seated on his throne, broke all precedent by coming down to the floor, his right hand extended.

"Jumai Khan," he said warmly, "you have saved our capital, our empire, and our life. No prize within our power to bestow is too great for you."

Jeremy shook the sultan's hand and smiled wearily. "I want no prize, Your Magnificence. All I ask is diplomatic recognition for the United States—"

"Granted."

"—and freedom for the Frankish slave girl and myself to leave. I would also ask that she be released from the dungeons at once."

"She has already been released," the sultan replied, "and is waiting for you in the seraglio." He went on to explain how Mary had brought to him the prize jewel that he had coveted for so long, and Jeremy was amazed anew at the ingenuity and fortitude of the young woman he loved.

After a pause the sultan said wistfully, "If we could we would try to persuade you to remain in Islam and would gladly promote you to the rank of pasha of two horsetails as an inducement. But we know your heart and your kismet are in the West, so we ask Allah to watch over you, wherever you may go."

When Jeremy and Mary met in a small house in the seraglio a quarter of an hour later, they clung to each other in silence for a moment, and Mary wept. There was so much they wanted to say to each other that they could not find the words to express their thoughts. The following morning the grand vizier himself came to the house, carrying a parchment that he handed ceremoniously to Jeremy.

The document officially recognized the existence of the new nation called the United States of America and agreed in principle to an exchange of ministers between the two countries. Thus the mission that Secretary of the Treasury Alexander Hamilton had called upon Jeremy to perform had been brought to a completely successful conclusion.

Later in the morning the two Westerners were summoned to appear before the sultan in his private audience chamber, and they went to the palace at once, feeling somewhat abashed that they owned no clothes other than the dirty garments they had worn for so long. At breakfast they had wondered what had become of Tule Yasmin, and they more or less expected to see her at the palace, but when Selim received them in his private audience chamber, she was not there. They forgot her for the moment as the sultan handed Jeremy a heavy bag of gold as a parting gift and gave Mary a huge leather chest, which, he said, was filled with Frankish clothes that had come into the possession of some of his sea rovers at one time or another. He informed them that he was making one of the few large galleys that was still seaworthy available to them for their voyage, and when they tried to thank him, he brushed aside their expressions of gratitude and dismissed them.

The galley was waiting at the harbor, and after exchanging farewells with Mustafa el Kro and a number of other naval and military leaders in an anteroom, Jeremy, with Mary on his arm, started toward the main entrance of the palace, where the last cavalry escort he would ever need in Constantinople was assembled. Suddenly Mary's grip on his arm tightened, she gasped, and following the direction of her gaze, Jeremy saw Tule Yasmin standing in the doorway to one of the private chambers on the first floor where, obviously, she had been watching for them.

The khana, insolently beautiful and immaculately dressed in a gown of emerald green studded with long rows of matched topazes, laughed as she let her glance flicker over Mary's ragged slave-girl attire. Then she turned to Jeremy and, still smiling cynically, took a single step toward him. "Do you think you are rid of me, Jumai?" she asked. "You are wrong. I make no effort to hold you here, for I know you will return to me."

It was Jeremy's turn to laugh.

"You will return to me," Tule Yasmin repeated calmly. "I learned much of the ways of the Franks when I traveled in the West. So I know that you and this wench will eventually quarrel and grow tired of each other, because you cannot marry. In time you will part. And then, Jumai, you will return to Islam and to me. You will never be able to forget that I, and I alone, am your legal Christian wife." Her expression unchanging, she disappeared into the room from which she had emerged and closed the door.

Tule Yasmin's prediction marred what otherwise would have been a peaceful and untroubled voyage through the Mediterranean. It was plain to Jeremy that Mary had taken the khana's words to heart, and he himself knew there was a grain of truth in what she had said. It would be unfair to Mary to expect her to spend the rest of her life with him as his mistress rather than as his wife, yet Tule Yasmin had made it plain that she had no intention of releasing him.

On the last day of the trip, when the great harbor of Venice was already in sight, Jeremy stood on the deck of the galley, dressed for the first time in many long months in a conservative suit of Western cut, and gazed moodily at the skyline of the city that was the gateway to Christian civilization. The dilemma seemed to be insoluble, and in a world where standards of morality were important, Mary would be shunned by decent people if she remained with him. As he pondered the problem she raised the flap of the silken tent that had been erected on the deck and came toward him. From the gifts the sultan had given her she had selected a pink dress with a full, hooped skirt and a broad-rimmed straw hat, with a velvet ribbon tied around her throat, and Jeremy, seeing how radiantly lovely she looked in familiar Western clothes, was afraid he lacked the strength to give her up.

Certainly, he told himself, he could not part with her voluntarily. He tried to grin at her reassuringly, and she responded with a tremulous smile, but behind it he sensed her insecurity. And although the day was warm and the breeze mild, Mary was shivering slightly as she gave Jeremy her hand and walked with him to the rail. They said nothing as they looked out at the harbor of Venice, but the same thoughts were in their minds. Suddenly one of the Turkish officers on the quarterdeck shouted and pointed to two ships anchored on the far side of the harbor undergoing repairs. They were English warships, part of the defeated fleet; obviously they had been unable to reach Gibraltar and had been forced to put into a neutral port for temporary repairs. One, a frigate, was badly battered, and the other, a squat bomb ketch, was listing sharply to starboard.

But the presence of some of his recent enemies meant little to Jeremy when he and Mary went to an inn after first passing the inspection of the Venetian immigration officials. They carefully engaged separate rooms and, after arranging to meet for dinner, parted company for the first time since they had been reunited in the seraglio. Jeremy unpacked his few belongings quickly, and then, as he stood at the window of his room looking down at the canal that ran beside the inn, he wondered whether a trip to Sweden would serve any useful purpose before he returned to the United States. The minister who had performed the wedding ceremony uniting him with Tule Yasmin had come from Stockholm, and if he could find the cleric, the man might be able to tell him how the bond could be broken.

There was a knock at the door, and when Jeremy answered it, he saw a gray-haired man standing in the frame. "Mr. Morgan? I'm Harvey Clarke, the American agent to the government of Venice," the stranger said in a Bostonian accent.

Jeremy was overjoyed to see a compatriot and ushered his visitor into the room. "I've been expecting you for the past six months," Clarke said, "ever since I had a letter from Mr. Jefferson asking me to watch for you."

"Secretary Jefferson?" Jeremy was confused.

The American agent smiled broadly. "Someone in the State Department learned about your mission, and I'm told that Colonel Hamilton revealed the whole plan at a rather stormy cabinet meeting. Ever since then the whole country has been hoping for your success, but until yesterday no one knew for certain whether you were alive or dead. Then," he continued dryly, "when those two English warships arrived, and their officers came ashore with stories of an American artillery expert who was responsible for the Turks' victory, I deduced that you were very much alive. How did you make out in Constantinople?"

Jeremy handed him the official document of recognition bearing the sultan's seal, and the diplomat nodded in delight. Then as he gave the parchment back to Jeremy he sobered. "It would seem you were extraordinarily busy in the Ottoman Empire, Mr. Morgan. I noted on the Venetian immigration manifest that a young lady arrived here with you, and that she's English. We in the diplomatic corps have known for months that an English theatrical star and other British subjects were captured and enslaved by the Turks. Could the young woman who accompanied you be the famous actress Mary Ellis?"

"She is. The sultan set Mistress Ellis and the others free."

"You may think this is none of my business, but what do you and this lady mean to each other?"

"If I could, I'd marry her," Jeremy said.

"Splendid. I saw on the manifest that you were coming to the same inn, so if I could I'd like nothing better than to meet her," the American agent declared. "Now," he added firmly, when Jeremy hesitated.

Jeremy was somewhat bewildered by the unusual request but nevertheless complied and hurried off to Mary's room. When he returned with her he performed the necessary introductions, and Clarke bent over her hand. "You'll be pleased to hear, ma'am," he said, "that your husband-to-be is going to be hailed as quite a hero at home. Congress will probably give him a citation."

"That's wonderful," Mary said, and then turned in embarrassment to Jeremy. "I'm afraid he doesn't understand about us."

"We can't be married, Mr. Clarke. I have a legal wife. It's quite a long story—"

"You mean the Mongolian khana, of course," the American agent interrupted calmly, and chuckled when the young couple stared at him. "Mr. Morgan, you have a friend, a very valuable friend, in General Lafayette. What with the revolution in France, I reckon he's one of the busiest men in Paris, but he's found time to send you a message in care of every United States diplomat in Europe in the hope of reaching you." He paused for a long moment and looked significantly at Jeremy, then at Mary. "Mr. Morgan, your marriage to the khana isn't binding. The Reverend Mr. Arneldson, who performed the ceremony, had no right to marry you to her. He had been defrocked before he went from Stockholm to Paris. General Lafayette knew this all along, but he thought it would be wiser if he kept it to himself. Until now, of course."

Jeremy could only stare at him, and Mary was speechless, too.

Clarke picked up his hat and walked quickly to the door. "I'll make all the necessary arrangements for your wedding," he said. "And I hope you'll let Mrs. Clarke and me give you a supper afterward."

It was very quiet in the room after he had gone. Finally Mary broke the silence. "Tule Yasmin," she said, "still believes she's your wife. She'll never learn the truth."

"So she can't marry again." Jeremy smiled quietly. "She wants power, but the only way she could have achieved it would have been through a new marriage. She won't know a day of satisfaction as long as she lives, and I can't think of a more suitable punishment for her." He looked at Mary, and suddenly he forgot Tule Yasmin as he realized that the hopes he had nurtured for so long were all within his grasp now. He would be recognized in America as a hero, and he would be able to afford the grand house and fine clothes he had coveted for so long.

But he was startled to realize that he no longer wanted any of those things. All his former ambition for renown and great wealth had somehow dissipated, and he realized that his amazing experiences of the last few years had changed him for all time. He had what he wanted—Mary Ellis—and he would now be content to live a quiet, simple life—if that was what *she* wanted.

As the two happy lovers discussed their future, Jeremy told Mary what was on his mind. "I thought we'd take that money the sultan gave me and cultivate that property I own in the Ohio Valley. There's more than enough to give us a wonderful start there."

Mary listened intently and without comment as he told her about the farm they would create for themselves in the wilderness. This was not the moment to insist they would do nothing of the kind. Jeremy was a romantic dreamer, and she knew he had to be allowed to talk himself out. Her own plans, she decided, were far more mature. As Mr. Clarke had said, Jeremy had won considerable glory for himself; he would have no difficulty winning a government appointment, where his knowledge and experience would do the most good for the United States, for him, and for his family. They would use part of the sultan's gift to buy a house in New York, and the rest would be put aside for the education of their children.

She decided she would write to her father at once and let him know what she intended to do. By now, no doubt, word had already been sent to England that although the English fleet had been repulsed, the prisoners were free. Sir John Ellis would be ecstatic to know his daughter was safe, although he would be distressed to learn that his niece and nephew had died. What his reaction would be to his daughter's news that she was going to marry an American and settle in the United States, Mary did not know. But he had always trusted her judgment, and perhaps even someday he would come to the United States to visit his daughter and son-in-law.

Certainly Mary had no intention of abandoning her career in the theater. She well knew that an infant theatrical industry was flourishing in New York, where three playhouses were filled regularly to capacity. She had been told that the productions there were the equal of those in London, and now the American stage would be graced by the presence of a star from London, a star whose talents would add to the glory of the American theater.

However, she had no intention of telling all this to Jeremy just yet. She knew him well enough to realize that he needed to feel that he was making all decisions in all things, and that was all to the good. In due time he would learn about her own plans, and he would happily accede to them. Of that she felt very sure.

Mary continued to listen as Jeremy explained in detail the life he imagined they were going to lead on the frontier, but what she pictured was far different. She saw him sitting in his armchair in front of the fireplace, smoking a fine cigar and reading his book. Their children would come into the room to say good night before going to bed, and he would clasp each of them in his arms and give them each a kiss. Then she and Jeremy would be left alone again in the parlor, and as she sat at his feet in front of the roaring fire, his hand would caress her hair.

Mary now looked at the earnest expression on Jeremy's face and felt her love grow to overflowing. He continued to talk about all the land he would own and the cattle and crops he would raise, and she nodded and smiled tenderly. "Yes, dear," she said softly.

VOLUME I IN THE EPIC NEW SERIES

The Morland Dynasty

The FOUNDING

by Cynthia Harrod-Eagles

THE FOUNDING, a panoramic saga rich with passion and excitement, launches Dell's most ambitious series to date—THE MORLAND DYNASTY.

From the Wars of the Roses and Tudor England to World War II, THE MORLAND DYNASTY traces the lives, loves and fortunes of a great English family.

A DELL BOOK $3.50   #12677-0